T0208901

I, Jonathan Blue

a novel based on a life

JAMES HAYDOCK

authorHOUSE®

AuthorHouse™
1663 Liberty Drive
Bloomington, IN 47403
www.authorhouse.com
Phone: 1 (800) 839-8640

Published by AuthorHouse 04/22/2019

ISBN: 978-1-7283-0826-5 (sc)
ISBN: 978-1-7283-0825-8 (e)

Print information available on the last page.

This book is printed on acid-free paper.

Because of the dynamic nature of the Internet, any web addresses or links contained in this book may have changed since publication and may no longer be valid. The views expressed in this work are solely those of the author and do not necessarily reflect the views of the publisher, and the publisher hereby disclaims any responsibility for them.

By James Haydock

Portraits in Charcoal: George Gissing's Women

Stormbirds

Victorian Sages

On a Darkling Plain: Victorian Poetry and Thought

Beacon's River

Against the Grain

Mose in Bondage

Searching in Shadow: Victorian Prose and Thought

A Tinker in Blue Anchor

The Woman Question and George Gissing

Of Time and Tide: the Windhover Saga

But Not Without Hope

I, Jonathan Blue

As the river surges onward in frost and sun,
so flows the stream of a thousand lives.
This is the story of one life.

CONTENTS

CHAPTER ONE

Thomas Blue in Transition

Daybreak came raw and bleak with an icy wind. Dark clouds hovered low in the eastern sky. A damp and piercing chill promised snow. In the narrow street carts and wagons were grinding the pavement. On the busy street the shop of Thomas Blue, an apothecary and dealer in pharmaceutical products, stood silent. Its window displayed the tools of his trade, an over-sized mortar and pestle. Near these, artfully arranged, were gallipots holding medicinal drugs and pretty bottles holding colored liquid. Above the shop, closed for three weeks, lay Thomas Blue near death. At another time customers in the shop could hear the romp and laughter of children. Now in the gloom of a winter morning all was quiet. A woman came into the cluttered room of a boy of thirteen and drew back the drapes. She glanced mechanically at the street below, misty with patches of snow. Clearing her throat as a signal, she went softly and quickly to her sleeping son.

"Wake up, Jonathan," she said almost in a whisper. "Your brothers and sisters are already up, and I'm fearing this will be the day."

I opened my sleep-heavy eyes and rubbed them with my fists. My brothers were out of their rumpled bed and gone. In the chamber below my father was propped on pillows. The room smelled of an antiseptic unlike any I had known in papa's shop. I tried to associate the scent with something I knew and strangely thought of lemons in a bowl of onions. Both windows were closed tight and shaded by heavy drapes. A small gas lamp struggled to light up the room. Two boys and two girls younger than me were standing stiffly against the wall. Father reached out to

1

grasp my hand. His fingers, bony and cold, sent a chill that increased my agitation. Half delirious, he mumbled softly but clearly familiar words that seemed curiously inappropriate.

"Break, break, break on thy cold grey stones, O sea . . . ."

He paused as if puzzled by what he was saying and left the quotation unfinished. His pale eyes were riveted on mine.

"Look after them, my son. They will need you in years to come." His words seemed to come from a great distance.

"I will do that, Papa. I promise."

I looked into the dying man's haggard face, saw a glimmer of understanding, and stepped away from the bed. From that moment I viewed myself as mentor and guardian of my brothers and sisters.

Dr. Flint, the family physician, had hurried in cold and darkness from his cozy home and was standing near the bed. He had brought all five of us into the world and was now watching Father leave it. Tall and thin and unassuming, he sounded a hesitant note whenever he spoke, and seldom did he give a direct answer to any question. Many years of medical practice had taught him never to offer false hope to loved ones. He was a kind man and wanted to speak good and positive words in a bleak situation, but found it safer to be blunt. He lifted his patient's wrist and checked his pulse. It was melting and draining away like the trodden snow on the pavement outside.

"It won't be long now," he said to Mother. "Mr. Blue is very tired."

The dying man on the bed opened his mouth to speak but found no voice. A gush of tears, glistening in the gaslight, rolled down the gaunt cheeks and wet his beard. He knew he was dying, and to die years before his time was hideous. The physician bent down to examine his patient's face. It was drawn and spent but calm. The gray-blue eyes were wide-open but unseeing. Dr. Flint closed the eyelids with the tips of his fingers and placed his hand on the fevered brow. With awkward self-consciousness he glanced around the room and fastened his gaze on the children. He sought his patient's pulse once more and found nothing. Though Thomas Blue had clung tenaciously to life, cleaving dearly to the good earth, he lay dead at fifty-one.

"I don't think there's anything else I can do," said Flint, glancing at Mother. "I understand your clergyman was here for last rites. I'll have him come back and talk to you. I'll call again if you need me."

He picked up his bag, hustled smartly to the door, and looked again at the children silent against the wall.

"I'm sorry," he said, speaking to no person in particular. "I want you to know I did all I could. I'm sorry."

"I'll show you out, sir," Mama quietly offered.

They made their way downstairs in silence. The woman's eyes were dry and her face calm. I could sense intense feelings of loss churning within her. In her youth she had been a beautiful woman. Now a widow with five children and weighted by grief, she was matronly but tall and stately. At the doorway the two paused for a moment. Sitting alone on the stairs I could hear every word.

"Will you continue the business?" Flint asked.

"No, sir, I don't see how I can. But don't worry, we'll manage."

"If you need anything, Mrs. Blue, just let me know. Parson Weeks will be here shortly."

"Thank you, sir. Have a pleasant holiday, you and your family."

The doctor nodded and buttoned his coat. He lifted the collar to shield his face, opened the door, and walked heavily into the wind. It was December and cold, and the year was 1870.

2

Two weeks passed slowly, and we returned to our daily routine. After supper in the room I shared with my brothers, I looked at some of the many books Papa had left behind. He had been a man of active mind, a chemist with an interest in botany, politics, music, and poetry. Once he had traveled from Yorkshire to London and had seen Queen Victoria as she passed by in her carriage. A loyal subject of the royal family, he brought home a portrait of the Queen, massed produced in those days, and put it on display in the parlor. We owned a piano, and to amuse us in the evening hours, he coaxed music-hall tunes from it. We listened with delight and learned to love music and books. Seven years before his untimely death he published a little book on the ferns of the locality. He was a botanist as well as a chemist and a lover of poetry. Once he persuaded me to memorize some of Tennyson's lyrics and recite them with theatrical flourish before the family. Now in distress I was able to complete the line he had mumbled: *"And I would that my tongue could utter the thoughts that arise in me."*

In another book I found the drawings of Albrecht Dürer, a painter, printmaker, and scholar of the German Renaissance. I remembered how much Papa liked those marvelous drawings. Putting the volume aside to examine later, I gathered up several novels by Dickens and placed them on a shelf near my bed. I had read them at least once but planned to read them again. A large, vellum-bound folio of Hogarth's etchings held my attention for half an hour, and eagerly I examined Lemprière's *Classical Dictionary*. Flipping through its pages with gentle care, I breathed satisfaction. It was mine now and precious. At thirteen I was already developing an interest in the classical past.

The door opened and Will, who seemed always out of breath, entered the room. He was a freckled youth, two years younger than me, with round shoulders, large hands, a round head with a tuft of reddish-brown hair, and a lumbering gait. A jolly, easy-going boy not as shy as his older brother, he was talkative and cheeky.

"I'm here for my medicine, Jon," he said with a shrug. "You know I must take it in cold weather to keep the coughing and wheezing down. Didn't want to bother you looking at Papa's stuff."

"Just a trip down memory lane," I retorted. "Nostalgic remembrance, Will, nothing serious. You're no bother."

"I can tell Mama is worried about us. Worried about us and the future and Christmas so soon after Papa died."

"Of course she's worried, but she doesn't want us to worry. She said to follow a normal routine, go on doing the things we like. Well, I like to read and write and study the purple past. You like building things with your hands. Any more work on your boat model?"

Will's eyes brightened and a smile swept over his plump and freckled face. "Did a little yesterday and hope to do some more today! Can't wait to see her finished!"

"Have you chosen a name for the boat?"

"Not yet. I must give it more thought. I want a catchy name."

"And what about that steam engine you started building? Have you made any progress on it? Looked like a real piece of work."

"I put it aside to finish the boat. I wanna launch her come spring. She's big enough to put a mouse on her to do the steering!"

"Well I dunno if Mum would like that," I laughed. "You know how she can be with small animals. Remember last summer? She demanded we throw our fish back into the river. Of course it didn't matter. They were too small and too bony to eat."

"Yeah, scrawny little fish," agreed Will with a chuckle.

He selected two bottles from the medicine chest and turned to go. "I'm gonna get back to my boat, and maybe Quentin will help. I sure hope the girls will leave us alone and not interfere. They're too bossy, and they bother me sometimes."

"Yep, bossy. But they love you, Will, and you want to be tolerant with them. More so now that Papa's gone. You can do it."

When our father died, Maggie was seven and Emma was five. Maggie was reserved but assertive. Little Emma was loud and talkative, eager for attention. Her mind was quick and she learned fast. She was probably the brightest of us all and knew exactly how to get her way. Yet by the time I was ten or twelve, Mama insisted I was showing a surge of insight and intelligence. It made her think I was destined for something beyond the ordinary. With her prompting I resolved to work hard and never dawdle to reach unreachable goals.

After dinner, as my brothers pitched in to wash the dishes and set the table for the next meal, I asked Mama a private question.

"How are we gonna live, now that Papa's gone?"

"Don't worry," she firmly replied. "Your father left us enough to live on for a year or two, and I can rent the shop for extra income. Also, if I have to, I can become a milliner or dressmaker and take in sewing. I hope it won't come to that and doubt it will."

"Papa said women of our class should never work outside the home, should never be seamstresses. He liked what Tennyson said about wives and women and their place in the home."

"That's perhaps the ideal," Mama smiled, "but you should know the lives of women in England today are far from ideal."

As we talked out of the hearing of the younger children, I realized I was no longer a carefree child to be guided by a loving father. With the loss of my father I had become the head of a large family that could soon be facing hard times. I didn't know until later that Father had left a trust fund in the name of his wife with me, the eldest son, the beneficiary. It provided a small income based on the market. Aided by the woman's native frugality, it would keep the wolf from the door.

3

Another week of raw Yorkshire weather came and went. The holiday season was in full swing, and people in a festive mood thronged the streets and shops of Harrogate. Mother was able to rent the shop for a reasonable fee, and the tenant agreed to buy its chemicals and equipment. She signed an agreement with Peter Finch, a pharmaceutical person, who said he would run the business with his wife in much the same way as Papa. He was a lean and rangy man of more than average height with thinning gray hair and pale, tired eyes. He had the look of a man who could benefit from walking in the open air but spent most of his time indoors. His manner was mild and casual, and he readily agreed to pay Mrs. Nora Blue a month's rent in advance.

The windfall allowed Mama to prepare a memorable Christmas even as she struggled with loss. But it troubled her when Finch informed her that he would have to occupy the quarters above the shop to be close to his customers. It was more than a convenience, he said, because people would be coming to him in the middle of the night seeking medication. Thomas Blue had been in the same predicament. Mama dreaded having to move but knew it was necessary. Reluctantly she agreed to look for another residence after the New Year.

Christmas fell on a Sunday in 1870, and the entire family went to church. Before and after the sermon we prayed for peace and happiness and good will toward men. We prayed for the heavenly welfare of the husband and father who had been called away when we needed him most. With simple Puritan sincerity, and sensing no irony whatever, we thanked a loving God for all he had done for us. Sitting side by side in the family pew, we dutifully bowed our heads and closed our eyes. I looked furtively around the large room to see what others were doing. I saw only bowed heads and moving lips and the face of my brother Quentin, who quickly closed his eyes.

The little girls and Will were praying fervently, and so was our mother. Quentin and I lacked the religious turn of mind that governed our mother's daily life, and so we let our curiosity get the better of us. Eventually we would lose faith in the religion our parents dutifully maintained but not the morality it preached. After the church service the family chatted for half an hour with the women of the congregation and with Parson Weeks. In the afternoon we went home to open our modest presents and eat a good dinner. I was selected to say grace.

I was tempted to say, "Good bread, good meat, good God let's eat!" but dared not offend Mama. Already I had become impatient with the custom of thanking a mysterious Almighty Being for a meal so obviously earned by the hard work of mortals. I was beginning to question the passionate Protestant beliefs passed on to us by a man who struggled with belief. However, habit and hard instruction required me to mumble a few traditional words of thanks for the bestowal of blessings, and that I did. For a moment there was silence at the table, and then all the children began to talk at once. Emma was the loudest. She was a chubby and cheeky child, squarely built with bright eyes and flaxen hair.

"I want some jam on my bread!" she cried, "I want some butter on my bread. I want some pudding and pie! Where's Mummy?"

"Shhhh," scolded her sister Maggie. "Your mum is in the kitchen, you little pest. Now stop the noise and be patient!"

"I don' wanna be patient! I wanna eat and open presents and sing Christmas carols and have fun!"

Little Emma keenly enjoyed the commotion she was causing and wanted to make the most of it. We boys, chattering among ourselves, stopped to listen and laugh. Our merriment was infectious, and the room exploded with giggling and horseplay at the table. That was a forbidden activity, especially on this most holy of Sundays.

Mama entered the room with a platter of lamb chops. She had once been slender and delicate of frame but was now a matron with ample breasts and a thick waistline. She had an open and honest face, a clear complexion, and a pleasant voice. Father always said in the bloom of youth she was the best-looking girl in any town. Around her neck she wore a tiny, gem-encrusted cross on a golden chain, a gift from her loving husband. On this Sunday of Sundays she wanted warm and quiet decorum, but the children were raising a ruckus. She had to speak louder than usual to be heard, and that bothered her.

"Settle down, children, settle down! This is the Lord's Day and a very holy day, and we must be dignified. Each of you will have a sweet and juicy lamb chop and a slice of roast beef, but only if you behave!"

"We will, Mummy, we promise!" chirped Emma.

"We have potatoes au gratin and Yorkshire pudding. Let's remember last year when your father was here to celebrate with us. Let's remember without bitterness the Lord giveth and the Lord taketh away."

"The Lord *giveth* and the Lord *taketh*," repeated Quentin under his breath, emphasizing the old forms and not able to suppress a snicker.

"No lamb chop for you, young man!" Mama announced, pretending to remove the succulent chop from his plate.

"Awww, Ma," the jokester in the family protested, "I didn't mean to be mean. Can't we have a little fun on Christmas Day?"

Mama was a good dissenting Protestant and often stern when she had to be, but now after tragedy had struck her family she was permissive to a fault. Her children were more important to her than anything else in her life, and that included religious rules and the promise of an afterlife. So when she didn't reply to Quentin's question, in high spirits we celebrated just being alive. Each of us ate with a hearty appetite as we joked and laughed. After dinner we sang carols.

"In spite of the tragic loss of a superlative husband and father," I wrote to Mama years later, *"your brood under your wing that year enjoyed a jolly Christmas Day. Let's remember it fondly."*

I wasn't surprised when she replied: *"I often wonder if I was a good mother to all my children. I should have been sterner."*

CHAPTER TWO

Education Beckons

When the New Year began there was talk of finding a smaller house and sending the boys off to boarding school. In the cold and shifting light of a January afternoon, Mama sat by the window and discussed the matter with me, excluding Will and Quentin. Her eldest son in a time of crisis had become the nominal head of the family. She wanted thoughtful replies from me, though only thirteen, and she knew I would listen carefully. Decisions had to be made and quiet talk was the way to do it.

"Your father didn't leave us much," she began. "From now on I must look at every penny I spend. We have little more than his life insurance, and what we can get from the lease of the house and shop."

"Does that mean we're poor, Mother? Papa always warned us about the workhouse. He urged us to study hard and prepare for good jobs so we wouldn't end up in the workhouse."

"Well, it's never been as bad as that, Jonathan. Your father was joking, but I have to be serious. I'm not good at managing money, and so I worry. I do know we shall have to move to a smaller house. What we get from letting the property here should keep us afloat. Mr. Finch and his wife Sara want to move in next month."

"So that means looking for another place soon. Then what?"

"The girls will stay with me, of course. But you and your brothers will go away to a boarding school. It's going to be touch and go with money for a while, but we'll manage."

I heard what she said with no surprise. The family was soundly rooted in the Yorkshire middle class but had struggled to make ends meet for as long as I could remember. On the table, spread in a half circle, were several recent bills. Printed on blue, white, and pink paper, they caught my eye. I began to finger them with concern.

"We must pay all the bills you see there as promptly as we can," Mama was saying. "I don't like being in debt."

I picked one up and looked it over. It was from the local florist who had delivered flowers to adorn Papa's casket. His fee seemed enormous, and it left me astonished.

"Did Mr. Worthington really charge all that much for the flowers?" I asked in disbelief. "Maybe there's some mistake here."

"No mistake, Jonathan. I ordered too many. I shouldn't have. Flowers are expensive in the middle of winter."

I picked up another bill. It was from the funeral parlor and detailed the costs of the funeral and burial. The amount seemed outrageous.

"I never knew it was so expensive to die, Mama. Is it just as expensive to be born? Seems from cradle to grave we have to pay and pay just to breathe what people call free air."

"The bill is high but not unreasonable, dear. Those people perform a very necessary service, and they have to live too."

"Well, it seems to me their fees allow them to live like royalty."

"Now, son, you can be sarcastic maybe, but don't be irreverent."

"Sorry, Mum. We'll pay the bills and go on living. The wolf may be at the door, but we don't have to let him in."

"That's my boy," was her response. "The bills will certainly get paid and the wolf will keep his distance. No fear, none at all. Now let's talk about that boarding school in Cheshire."

"We're eager to go there but what about the cost?"

"The cost isn't exorbitant. It'll tax my budget probably, but it's not really exorbitant. I've heard it's a very good school. You'll learn all kinds of good things that will benefit you later. Don't worry about the cost, at least for now. I'm fairly certain the rental money from Mr. Finch will cover most of the school expenses. And with three mouths to feed instead of six, our food bill here will be cut in half."

"Or less than half," I laughed. "Will alone eats as much as you and the girls. Did you see what he ate for dinner? A huge helping of roast beef and a lamb chop plus vegetables, bread, and dessert!"

She nodded and chuckled but continued in a somber mood. "You and Will and Quentin must do well in school. All three of you must remember to make your father proud, and your mother too. The girls and I will get along just fine here in Harrogate, and of course you boys will spend your summers with us here at home."

2

March came with cloud and drizzle. A lively west wind brought warmer weather and a hint of spring. Three boys who had never been away from home were packing to leave. Our sisters stood by and watched as item after item went into valises and a large wooden box. Breckenbow was a Quaker school in the village of Wilmslow in Cheshire. It catered to boys of the middle class and was well known for its strict, no-nonsense discipline and efficiency. The school's brochure featured high praise from former students. It named with pride notable public figures, some of Quaker persuasion, who had studied there.

The county was famous for its cheese and for Lewis Carroll's Cheshire Cat, grinning and fading until only its grin remained. Also for many years its famous wild white cattle had roamed unmolested on the moors but were now becoming domesticated for their milk. Cheshire was a small county compared to Yorkshire. Its industrial centers were of little interest to us at our age, but we were delighted to hear of castles, ancient villages, and haunted houses. The county also boasted picturesque farms and rivers swiftly flowing to the sea. William wanted to know if ships were harbored in the Mercy. I wanted to learn about the Quakers.

In the parlor overlooking the street below we gathered to receive our going-away presents. Mama had decided on the gifts but allowed the girls to present them. Maggie, thin and straight as a stick, conducted the ceremony in her best schoolmarm manner. She made a little speech for each present and then allowed Emma, keeper of pretty things, to give them to us. Will received the first present.

Wheezing softly because of the change in weather, he stood in front of Emma and held out his hands with his eyes closed. His chubby fingers touched a rectangular package that seemed sturdy and heavy. Quickly he tore off the wrapper and smiled broadly. It was the toolbox owned by his father. Inside were the tools he had coveted for a long time.

"Thanks so much!" he said with feeling. "I'll take good care of Papa's tools and pass them on to my son! Before that happens, though, I'll be using them to build lots of things."

Maggie made another speech and Quentin came forward. Emma placed in his hands a present smaller than Will's. He opened it to find the pocketknife he had often borrowed from Papa. He was delighted.

"Last but not least is Jonathan! Come forward, big brother!"

At thirteen I was socially awkward even among members of my own family. I had Papa's good looks but Mama's reticence and reserve, and so I moved cautiously to the center of the room. Emma gave me a present even smaller than the one Quentin had received. I slowly unwrapped it. A round object all shiny and ticking nestled in the little box.

"It's Papa's watch! Thank you! I'll keep it and pass it on to my son!"

"I gave it to you," Mama explained, "because your father wanted you to have it. At school it will help you make good use of your time."

An hour later the transit cab rattled to a stop and we ran into the street shouting and hooting, eager to experience an adventure in our lives. We stuffed our luggage and storage box in the vehicle, kissed our loved ones on the cheek, and waved goodbye. Mama and the girls stood in the street waving white scarves. She drew them close to her.

3

April came with showers that made the grass a brilliant green. Something was happening in the ground, and winter was surrendering to spring. Nora Blue found a house she liked and planned to move there with her daughters at the end of the month. It was smaller and less imposing than the dwelling in Market Square but large enough. Maggie and Emma would share a room, and a couple of bedrooms would be reserved for their brothers when home from school on holiday. The house with its two stories and attic was old but in good condition. It was located in a neighborhood with a good school. Peter Finch would move into his new quarters, leased for five years, and the new address would become our permanent home. The rental income would help pay for the new residence with some left over for the boarding school. I was relieved to learn that while Mother and the girls would have to live frugally, they would not suffer want.

From Breckenbow in Cheshire I sent a long letter, hoping they would find the new house comfortable. *"I do hope it will be to your liking, but I'm afraid you will never like it as much as the old house. Father lived with us there, and that made the difference."*

I wrote that letter with nostalgic remembrance of better times. Near the end I asked about Emma and said Maggie could look at my books any time she liked, but only if she took good care of them. I wanted both girls to develop a passion for reading. In another letter I spoke of visiting *"a very old town seven miles away."* I had walked there with friends on a chilly May Day to witness the traditional ceremony of people gathered around the May Pole. As the shadows lengthened, we hiked the seven miles back and sat for examinations from seven to ten.

In most of my letters I spoke of taking numerous examinations. They would help me obtain a scholarship to a reputable college that might open the door to Oxford. I was behaving like a person destined to do well in the world. Unlike most of my classmates, I was ambitious. One year I won so many prizes, pompous little statuettes and worthless books on bad paper, that I had to take them home in a hansom. A boy we called Dawson was standing nearby and hooted with derisive laughter but with unrestrained envy.

"Didn't leave much for the rest of us, did you?" he yelled.

I didn't like Dawson. The boy tried to get by doing as little as possible. He was lazy and too familiar with everyone he met and too big for his age. He was cocky at times and something of a bully. I replied with banter, hoping to avoid a scene.

"Some of the books will come in handy," I joked. "I can always use a few as a sturdy door stop."

"Oh, don't you dare!" Dawson scolded, admiring their appearance. "They're beautifully bound in tooled leather and carefully stitched. Oh my, they're handsome! My father would like them so very much."

Later I heard that Dawson's father had inherited the family's bookbinding business and was making it profitable. As I got to know Dawson better I found that his braggadocio was mainly a show to mask his loneliness. All the time I knew him he had no friends.

My brothers and I eased into the life of the school without difficulty and began to breathe its social and academic ambience. William and Quentin reached out to make friends and worked at their studies with just enough diligence to please the masters. I, on the other hand, worked around the clock. To do well in all my courses and to prepare for examinations that could win me a scholarship, I allowed myself only five and a half hours sleep in a narrow bed that was never comfortable. I plunged into my studies with abandon, admitting that I had a compulsion to do my best as a student. In my leisure time, precious because of the regimen I had set for myself, I composed plays in blank verse and wrote what my teachers called passable poetry. In the spring of 1872 I was cramming for my great exam, the Oxford.

I passed the exam with a high score and won free tuition for three years at Thatcher College in Manchester. That was good news, for at times I was having difficulty warding off depression. Also, even though my brothers were at the same school, I felt lonely and isolated. But in the fall of 1872, leaving for industrial Manchester, I was feeling much better. The city was very different from Harrogate or the Breckenbow location. The difference in fact was astounding. A small-town boy had to adjust to living in a big city worlds away from past experience. Yet because I liked a good challenge I found the prospect exciting. I entered into the life of the city and student activity at Thatcher with no obstacles to overcome or stand in my way. My dream was to become a Renaissance man embracing all that higher education could offer.

CHAPTER THREE

College in Manchester

As soon as I got to the bustling city I wanted to explore it. Instead, because time was precious, I made my way to Thatcher College. There in single-minded application I lost myself in academic labor. In time I began to win prizes as I had done earlier at Breckenbow. My penchant for study was due in part to love of learning, but in a practical sense I competed for scholarships as a way to advance academically. With thin financial backing, I had to work harder than other students. Thatcher was a new college founded in 1852 to educate young men of uncertain future. Those enrolled were the sons of businessmen and small professionals. As with me, they hoped to earn a college degree to advance in Great Britain. The college was primarily a scientific institution, but to my great satisfaction I was able to specialize in the humanities.

During my first year I won the poetry prize for a long poem on the capital of Italy. In twenty-one dignified and technically correct Spenserian stanzas, I displayed my love of England's romantic past and Italy's convoluted antiquity. In the next year I won prizes in classical studies and gradually accumulated one academic distinction after another. By 1876 everyone who knew me was certain I was ready to enter Oxford or Cambridge to pursue a scholarly career. My dream was to publish definitive books in my field and become a distinguished classical scholar. I wanted to be held in high esteem by academicians of the first rank. I assured myself I wouldn't settle for anything less.

At eighteen in 1875 as Christmas was coming, I was living alone in a shabby rooming house in sprawling Manchester. The dreary weather of fall and winter and many hours of solitary study had produced a loneliness that grew more intense during the holiday season. I went home to Harrogate to spend Christmas with my family but remained there only a few days. Before the New Year came I was back in Manchester deep in study and feeling very much alone. I had made a few friends at the college, but they were away and I saw no one. Living in a cold, impersonal rooming house inhabited by workingmen was very different from the warm family atmosphere of Harrogate or the sheltered life at Breckenbow. At school I was lonely at times and fighting depression but had my brothers for company. Also I had formed a friendship with a boy named Emeritus Gifford and was on friendly terms with the headmaster.

In Manchester my awkwardness in a social setting and my compulsion for hard study left me largely alone. But one day I met a student named Dylan Crenshaw. We had lunch together and decided to stroll through city streets to view sights new to us. We were different in personality but shared similar interests and liked each other immediately. Crenshaw was a tall and healthy fellow with a mane of reddish-brown hair, fair skin with freckles, and blue eyes. His nose was large, his mouth ample, and his voice loud. He took things as they came and enjoyed life as he found it. With high spirits and easy laughter and no small degree of swagger, he was one of those fortunate students whom everybody liked. The one quality that endeared him to others was a vitality which seemed to give vigor and gusto to anyone he met. A life force within him affected all who knew him. He was hamstrung by a lack of money but somehow managed to be indulgent, extravagant, and cheerful.

By nature an adventurer, he wanted to travel the world, record what he had seen, and publish books to defray expenses. He readily confessed one day he would become a well-known author. This time in college, he explained with a tired metaphor, was the necessary tilling of the field before reaping the harvest. I read some of his writing.

"What do you think?" he asked impatiently. "Is it good? Be honest for God's sake and tell me. Is it good?"

"Well," I lied. "It's good, old boy, but I believe you can do better."

I didn't have the heart to tell him his stuff was lamentable. His syntax was deplorable; he couldn't spell simple words; he couldn't punctuate a compound sentence; and he didn't know how to end a paragraph and begin another. Any point he wished to make was lost in a jumble of ill-formed sentences in the lamest of paragraphs.

"You can do better," I repeated, suppressing a sigh.

"Oh I'm sure I can do better. It takes time to write well, y' know. You have to find your subject and work on the style that best reflects you. '*Le style est l'homme,*' that fellow in France said, and that's what I want to keep in mind. Let the reader know *me* as well as what I'm saying."

Crenshaw truly had everything to make a good writer, everything but talent. Almost as poor as me, even though his father was a well-paid civil servant and sent him pocket money, his fond ambition was to become rich and famous. Even though everyone who knew him could feel an undeniable drive and energy, he never became rich and famous. He did travel the world and he did publish many books, but for reasons he couldn't understand they were never popular. Undaunted and without humility, he labored prodigiously as a man of letters writing on a multitude of subjects. If he had chosen to write exclusively about his travels as a world adventurer, as many intrepid travelers were doing, he might have won the fame he sought. Instead, when one subject didn't please his audience, or when a single critic complained, he shifted to another. In time, after producing an amazing number of mediocre books, he confessed he wasn't cut out to be an author. By then, however, it was too late to pursue something more fitting.

2

Another young man who became my friend was Bobby Bobeck, the son of a banker in Liverpool and better off financially than Crenshaw. Of medium height and thin of build, his eyes were dark and restive beneath a sallow brow. His sharp nose resembled that of a ferret or the beak of a predatory bird. He had a lop-sided smile and his lips were thin and dry.

From time to time he flicked his tongue to wet them, and he seemed always to have a cold. It was Bobeck who came to my rooms one evening to smoke and chat. He was a year or two short of legally becoming a man, but the big cigar made him feel older and sophisticated. He puffed on it and exhaled smoke rings that expanded and brought laughter but made the room smell. His air was sociable but somehow nervous, and his laughter a bit forced and too loud. He was looking for excitement, he said more than once, looking for something that would take him away from the dull routine of academic drudgery.

"Surely," he was saying, "you don't expect to coop yourself up in this . . . these two rooms . . . and never have an ounce of fun."

He glanced around my shabby quarters. I had only the small sitting room, a larger bedroom, and a tiny nook with no window where I could make a pot of tea or a scanty breakfast. The sitting room had a window that allowed one to see the street below where pedestrians came and went in a steady flow regardless of the weather.

"Maybe we should be down there," he announced. "Mingling with the people, going somewhere, doing something."

"What do you propose?" I asked. "I like to walk. At school in Cheshire I made a walking tour in April of northern Wales. Walked scores of miles and had a wonderful time. Seems like yesterday but it was three years ago. Beautiful countryside, glorious!"

"Walking in the city can be glorious too and more exciting than any country scene, especially if you're looking for quail."

Sexually alive and not altogether naive, I caught the drift of what Bobeck was saying but pretended not to understand.

"Looking for quail?" I asked.

"Yes, of course, friend. Birds, the human kind! Quail . . . tail . . . whatever. It's a manly sport!"

"You want to look for lively girls that might provide easy, flirtatious banter or something more?"

"Well, maybe. Looking to see what we can scare up. You never did any hunting? The quail is a marvelous game bird. Its brown plumage blends in with its surroundings. You don't see it till you're right on it."

"Well, let's go! I'm not a hunter but could use a little excitement."

It was drizzling rain when we went into the street, but we walked close to the wall to keep dry. We scuttled along as foxes in the field, excited and wary and half afraid. We stood in dark shadows and watched pedestrians in the gaslit street. We went to a well-known square and thrilled to the sight of two slender women in long skirts walking up and down. They were prostitutes, Bobeck declared. Of that he was certain.

We were now pals with a mission, and we roamed the night streets of Manchester whenever we could. Energized and curious, we prowled locales where prostitutes were known to gather. We peered into dark doorways and stared lustfully at shadowy figures under the gaslamps. Neither I nor my friend seemed to know what we were doing. It was a game we were playing, exciting but nothing more. Though guileless and lacking experience, in several places we found what we were looking for, a gathering of quail. Our senses told us our search was over. Near theaters and music halls and places of entertainment, in the streets and squares and even the parks, were prostitutes of every description. Most were tawdry and painted but young enough to attract a college man with the proverbial itch. Some were old and raddled before their time: tired, unkempt, unwashed, and perhaps sick.

Raised in the midst of Puritanism and retaining many of its values, I couldn't put down a negative attitude toward those women even while feeling sorry for them. I shuddered at the thought of touching such a woman. No longer religious but with a moral sense highly developed, to have sex with a prostitute was in my opinion the ultimate act of human depravity. Bobeck with a different orientation eventually found a girl he liked. She was a blousy, big-boned, freckled, blue-eyed young woman from the country. Her face was round and chubby, her nose red and pimply, and her frizzy yellow hair tightly curled. She laughed with a chirping sound and chattered like a jackdaw. They quickly became lovers, but within a month the affair Bobby Bobeck thought would last forever was over. She stole his heart and money and skipped away laughing. In a panic he asked his father to send more money –*"books are expensive"* – and he used it to find another girl.

Although I remained aloof while looking over the women we stumbled upon, my growing interest in the way they lived their lives kindled a fervor amounting almost to recklessness. Sheltered for most of my life and deeply immersed in middle-class mores, I believed they were different from any female I had ever known. It seemed to me they came from another planet, a world I wanted to explore. Before long I made up my mind to learn about those ladies of the night, as their customers called them. That meant talking to one I would carefully select and getting to know her. In my notebook I jotted down questions I would ask. I hoped she would be articulate, open, and talkative.

3

One night early in March of the New Year it happened. As Bobeck and I were leaving a cheap eating-house, we brushed against a slender girl with dark hair and flashing eyes. Tall and thin, she looked frail and vulnerable as though easily damaged. The encounter threw her against the wall, and she struggled to regain her balance. Instinctively I reached out to grasp her arm to steady her. In its long sleeve the slender arm was soft and yielding to my touch. I quickly released her and drew back. She stood unflinching and carefully looked me over. Her eyes were large, intense, sharp, and sullen. Her oval face with a hint of rouge on the cheeks was very white. In the glare of the gaslamp she gave me a soulful glance that expressed in seconds what seemed to me a deep and abiding sadness. In all my life I had seen that expression only once on a woman's face, my mother's the moment she knew her husband was dead. It caused me to catch my breath in anguished remembrance, but somehow I managed to stammer an apology.

"I'm awfully sorry," I said with feeling. "I do hope we didn't hurt you in any way, didn't cause you injury."

I expected Bobeck to apologize also, but my companion remained silent. More experienced than Jonathan Blue, he knew in an instant the girl was a prostitute down on her luck. It didn't occur to him to apologize to so lowly a person or even be civil. He was simply amused.

"If you would like to stay here and talk to this young lady," he chortled theatrically, "you may chat as long as you wish. If you decide to join me later, dear friend, you'll find me at a greasy table inside. The place is crowded with unwashed humanity, and the air is heavy with an earthy scent, but there I belong. I am one with the universe."

Bobeck was laughing sardonically as he turned and went back inside. While I caught the cadence of his little speech, the young woman seemed oblivious to it. She continued to look with concern into my face and assured me that she was jostled but unharmed.

"I don't usually stay out this late," she explained, "but it's getting on toward spring, y' know. The night air ain't so cold any more, and I really like to walk evenings. I was on my way to my aunt's flat."

"I'll be glad to escort you there," said I quickly. "This district of Manchester isn't very safe, I've heard."

"Well, I'm not sure that's a good idea. My aunt frowns on me having gentleman friends. She can be so unreasonable at times, thinks I should be an old maid for the rest of my life. She makes me so mad at times I just don't know what to do."

"I won't come inside. I'll walk with you to see you safely home and we can chat as we go. Perhaps we can meet again some other day. My name is Jonathan Blue. I'm at the college, a student there."

We were walking already, and I was eying the girl as best I could. I could see in the half-light that she was very young and seemed respectable. She was looking at the pavement, her face half concealed by the gloom, her dark hair aglow under the street lamps. The reply that came from her was gentle but cynical and sad.

"A college man, are you? Well, you wouldn't be interested in the likes o' me. I'm a work girl and I have to make a livin' as best I can. Right now I'm between jobs. I used to be a waitress, but the hours were too long. Would you believe six days a week from early mornin' till well after dark? I was always on my feet and they ached somethin' awful. My back hurt awful at night and I couldn't sleep. It didn't matter. I had to be up early every mornin' to start all over again. The job was makin' me sick and I had to quit. I'm lookin' to get a position in the Women's Apparel Department at Welterheim's. I'm on their list but it's a long one, and shop girls work many hours too. Not sure my health can take it."

"Have you thought of finding a job where maybe you can sit and work?" I managed to ask. "I will help you if you will let me."

The girl made no reply and we strolled along in silence. For ten minutes we walked without a word between us. At last it occurred to me that this pretty girl was surely a prostitute. In my nightly ramblings with Bobby Bobeck I had seen girls of similar description. With the bloom of youth still on them, they looked like shop girls or milliners or even librarians. Perhaps forced into prostitution by destitution and surely in need of help, they were despised by the moralistic middle class and labeled "fallen women." I found it hard to believe this girl could be that kind of woman. And yet it seemed clear to me from all she said, and the way she said it, that she was in desperate straits. Was she really looking for a job? If so, wouldn't she seize upon an offer to help her find one? I wanted to ask her bluntly if she were a prostitute, an unwitting victim perhaps, and have an end of it. But what if the question should offend her? What if she answered with an emphatic and angry No? I couldn't summon the nerve to be so daring. I would try to know her better to see how life in careless, indifferent Manchester was treating her.

"I told you my name," I mumbled as she stopped walking and stood before me. "Now will you tell me yours?"

"Oh don't be so forward," she answered. "I'll tell you that and a lot more the next time we meet. I must hurry now. My aunt will be cross. I walk in the afternoon between two and three in Humboldt Park."

We were standing in front of a flight of concrete steps with a metal rod for a banister. The steps led upward to another street on which old houses of stone and brick stood in deep shadow. Even in the dark I could see the neighborhood catered only to poor people.

"My room's up there," she said, pointing to a tall structure looming against the sky, "but don't visit me there. Don't even try, please, 'cause my aunt would object. She's a bitter woman, you must know, and I can't

23

afford to get on her bad side. Can you be in the park on Sunday?"

"Yes, I think so. I'll make a concerted effort to be there. I'll see you in the park between two and three as your friend and admirer. I wish you now a very good night."

"Good night to you, funny boy!" she called as she ascended the steps and melted into shadow.

I could hear her nasal twang in the damp air long after we parted. I thought I heard a murmur of muted laughter at the top of the steps but couldn't be sure. The exciting, all-too-brief encounter was done with, and she was gone. I wanted to see her again but couldn't be certain I ever would. I remember thinking our chance encounter might be nothing more than ships passing in the night.

CHAPTER FOUR

A Girl in My Life

It was Friday and late. I would have to wait two nights and half a day before I could see her again. Although she had hinted at distress, she had told me nothing, not even her name. Walking in the dark with her made me feel sympathetic, but surely it was only pity for one less fortunate. As I made my way back to my cluttered rooms, I couldn't be certain how this stranger of the night impressed me. I slept soundly but woke up feeling tired. I got through Saturday by pushing the girl out of my mind to concentrate on my studies. Prudence told me to forget her, but even as the thought crossed my mind I knew I would look for her in the park.

Saturday night I slept fitfully, dropping off to sleep more than once to wake up with a start. I didn't dream of the girl but found myself thinking of her while trying to sleep. I got up before eight feeling dizzy and fixed a breakfast of bread, butter, and hot cocoa. Most of the time I ate my meals at the college, but breakfast was my own affair. Later I relaxed with a book beside the window. Drowsy from lack of sleep, I lay down for a nap and didn't awaken till after the noon hour. I felt hungry and went out to have a blueberry muffin with tea at a nearby restaurant. It was a shabby place and noisy, but the muffin was cheap and filling and I could linger there while eating. A man and woman nearby were at sixes and sevens, wrangling fiercely but in undertones. An odor of fried food wafted in from the kitchen, a greasy mix of fish and beef and pork. It struck my nostrils as pungent but not unpleasant. A waitress asked if I wanted another muffin. I drank the last of my tea and began walking toward Humboldt Park.

The weather had slightly improved from the day before but the air was frosty, and I was glad to be wearing my warmest coat and trousers. A breeze was coming from the north, exactly the direction I wanted to go, and it made my walk colder. A weak sun was poking through clouds and warming my back. I strolled into the park in plenty of time to meet the girl as planned. Ragged little boys with shrill cries were playing a rough and tumble game of rugby. Beside the path was a green bench. To pass the time I watched the children at play, marveling at how they could fall on their faces and spring to their feet unhurt. I waited and wondered if my mystery girl would show. She had said walked in the park on Sundays and would perhaps see me there at a certain time. It was not an ironclad promise.

Well, I would wait and see. If she didn't come, nothing would be lost. I would simply return and finish my schoolwork. The shadowy apparition that had spoiled my sleep would become only a memory. I waited half an hour, squinting down the path every few minutes. A slender figure quite suddenly was walking toward me. She wore a form-fitting coat and a perky little hat. Her skirt swung to and fro and swept the gravel as she walked. Approaching the bench, she didn't look at me. She was looking across a broad expanse of park at carriages in the road. I began to feel the rich-looking carriages were far more interesting to her than the lanky college boy on the bench. The people inside were strangers and wealthy and belonged to a world she could never enter. I too was a stranger and from a world far different from hers.

2

I could see that she had slowed her pace as she came closer, and rising from the bench I ventured a cheerful greeting.

"Hallo! I'm awfully glad to see you. How are you this chilly day?"

She nodded and looked at me with dark, indifferent eyes carefully made up to accent the smooth paleness of her face.

I wanted to call her by name but didn't know her name. So quickly I followed with another remark about the weather.

"Nippy this afternoon. Do you think spring will ever come?"

As soon as I said it I felt foolish. I chastised myself for not coming up with something clever that might impress her.

She stood in front of me and looked me over, pausing a moment before speaking. Her girlish utterance was nasal on some accents but not unpleasant. She seemed to be fully aware of what she was saying and how it would affect me.

"Why do you sit there in the cold?" she asked. "Sitting on a bench in this weather ain't good. Why didn't you walk along the path to meet me? Don't you college boys have any common sense?"

She didn't sit down, and I didn't invite her. The muted insolence in her tone of voice, cold as wintry daylight, surprised me. I had hoped her speech would be sweet and serene, passive and musical. I couldn't remember with any degree of accuracy how she sounded in night shadow. I did remember sadness in expressive eyes, and I saw that now; but it faded when her sensual lips formed a faint smile.

"Well, are you gonna stand there and freeze? I'm obliged to walk in bone-chilling weather. I wouldn't of come 'cept I was curious."

Cheerfully I agreed to walk with her and took her arm to place beside mine. I had read gentlemen escorted ladies that way and thought it the right thing to do. She quickly withdrew and walked apart from me. She swung her hips as she walked and her long legs seemed rather stiff. My first thought was to ask her name, but instead I invited her to a coffee shop where we could get out of the cold and chat.

"Oh, I don't mind," she answered, "but I can't stay for long. My aunt don't like to be left by herself on Sunday. When I had a job she never complained workdays but wanted me with her Sundays. We don't go to church y' know. Never went, don't feel wanted. Did you say something about a coffee shop? I despise coffee, but I'll take a spot o' tea with you. What harm can it do on a cold day?"

In Grafton Street we found a small café run by a Frenchman and his wife. The girl hesitated to go in, saying she felt uncomfortable around foreigners. She preferred bustling restaurants where couples go to eat economically surrounded by a noisy crowd. This was an unpretentious

establishment where working-class people came in for scrappy meals
eaten rapidly and where a scruffy French waiter, thin as a rail, was trying
to learn English. His Gallic accent amused her and she relaxed. The
balding, obsequious owner with menu in hand led us to a table apart
from the other patrons, and that pleased her.

"I don't like sitting too close to other people in restaurants," she
confessed, "and I never quite trust these foreign places, but this is nice
and not at all what I expected. It's streets ahead of other places like it.

3

The lean waiter stood over us with a little pad to take our order. Dressed
in black with something white around his neck, I couldn't help but think
he looked a little like a vulture.

"Pot of tea and a muffin for the lady and coffee for me," I said.

"Oh, wait just a minute, please! Will you wait just a minute?"

She was looking at the menu, running a slender finger with a painted
nail down the column that listed the most expensive dishes.

"Do you mind if we eat something more than a muffin? I know we
didn't come here for dinner, but I had to skip breakfast this morning I
was in such a hurry."

I had taken the precaution of bringing money with me, and so
graciously I allowed her to order whatever she wished. It was the *bifstek
aux pommes*. To my surprise she knew exactly what she was getting. To
top off the meal she ordered with an air of gaiety a paupiette stuffed with
sweetmeats smothered in a savory sauce.

"Do you drink wine?" I asked when she was silent.

"Indeed I do! Almost always with dinner. I like a good burgundy
with steak and a good white wine with fish or fowl."

The waiter was hanging over us unmoving. "A bottle of your best
burgundy, please, with glasses."

"Mais oui, M'sieur!" exclaimed the sallow fellow with a little bow.

"Oh, he speaks delightful French, don't you think? I wish I could!"

She was smiling now and her faintly red lips, slightly parted, revealed her finest feature, near-perfect teeth. They were clean and white and evenly set. They caught the light and sparkled.

The wine was expensive but I was glad I had ordered a full bottle. It made the dinner more festive and allowed for banter and laughter. We began the meal with a complimentary *amuse-bouche,* a basket of puffy brown rolls, and a ramekin of butter. As we were beginning to eat, the waiter placed in the middle of the table a finger bowl filled with perfumed water. Then came two thick and juicy steaks with potatoes on the side, green peas swimming in a rich French sauce, and a salad of romaine lettuce. In the salad were seasoned croutons shining in a mixture of olive oil, lemon juice, and raw eggs. The girl was eager and alive now, and her eyes were shining. She was hungry.

We had found quite by accident a place with a palpable air of romance. It had a subtle semblance of young bohemians eating on checkered tablecloth by candlelight. We thought we might see a strolling musician to complement the scene. Finding no such person, we turned to our dinner with gusto. Squeamish from childhood, I tried to ignore the way she ate. She was pretending to be genteel, daintily wiping her lips after every bite, but chewing with sound. She drank the wine with her little finger extended and gnawed the steak to the bone. Then with obvious delight she dipped her fingers in spiced water, sniffed them, and dried them on a napkin. The skinny waiter brought in wedges of Camembert cheese with bacon, and she ate her portion rind and all. It seemed to me she had skipped more than breakfast. When I realized I was treating the girl to a meal she really needed, my snobbish dislike of her table manners turned to warm acceptance.

I began to enjoy watching her eat, her dark eyes gleaming with satisfaction. We had a big dinner and drank the bottle of wine and talked as if all talk would end tomorrow. She claimed to be an orphan with few relatives but of good family. She had worked more than a year as a waitress, as I already knew, and she expected to work as a shop girl soon. In the meantime she had to make a living, and the world didn't really care how she did it. With eyes downcast but with no detectable remorse, she admitted she had turned to prostitution to survive. I was dismayed to hear her speak so nonchalantly about selling her body to any stranger willing to pay. I tried without succeeding to understand the gravity of her predicament. Did she really have to go that far to survive? The tabloid press in Manchester had printed lurid stories of desperate prostitutes that I found hard to believe. Now it appeared I was face to face with one of those creatures and listening to her story. Her name, she said at last, was Muriel Marie Porter. She didn't like the name and asked me to call her Merle when I knew her better. I never did.

CHAPTER FIVE

The Money Problem

I was eighteen when I met Muriel Porter in the early months of 1876, and she was seventeen. As I sat with her in the restaurant, observing the way she conducted herself, conflicting emotions goaded one another. At school in Cheshire I had begun to look at girls with more than a passing interest, but only from a distance. Breckenbow was a Quaker boarding school for boys situated in a village of a few hundred Anglicans and a handful of dissenters. Most of the residents had lived there for generations and tended to view the schoolboys and those who ran the school as interlopers. Though efficiently conducting their business and loving peace and quiet, the Quakers were seen as outsiders and seldom invited to homes or even public events. The village daughters were told to keep their distance and not get involved with the boys at the school. So all the time I was there I didn't meet a girl I could get to know.

I had grown up with two younger sisters and wasn't afraid of girls, but implacable circumstance sent me through adolescence without so much as kissing a girl. At fourteen or fifteen I realized I was fiercely heterosexual and desired relations with girls, but they were off limits. I was in love with soft female beauty, the supple female body in light summer clothing, and I concocted in my daydreams a heavenly partner. I would take a bright and pretty girl in my arms, hold her tight, and gently kiss her rosebud lips and ivory face. I would feel the warmth of her body against mine, breathe her special scent, and hold her tight. She would respond with rare and titillating good humor. Then suddenly we would become the center of attention at a fancy-dress ball. Other

31

celebrants would fall back to give us the floor. To my amazement, I would find myself dancing expertly with the girl of my dreams, whirling her around the floor gracefully to wild applause.

When school was boring or the weather dreary, I wanted to talk about the dark and forbidden sensations that schoolboys discuss in whispers, but found no sympathetic companion to listen. At Thatcher College in Manchester I knew as much about sexual instinct as any person my age but had never been close to a girl. Except for my sisters, I had rarely talked to one. I could only look at them in clothing that covered them from chin to toe and imagine what lay underneath. On occasion I had spoken to female clerks in shops, and to waitresses in restaurants, but had no social interaction. Then on nightly excursions Bobeck and I began to prowl the streets of Manchester, and finally I met the young woman who called herself Muriel Marie Porter. Still in her teens, she was more girl than woman but with knowledge of life in the raw.

In time I came to know her life was lonely and turbulent, her past sordid. I suspected she was selfish, a liar, and manipulative but ignored the hints. Burdened by nagging uncertainties but yielding to sexual instinct, I was drawn to her like a fly to honey. Conquered by the passion and naiveté of first love, I listened gravely to all she had to say and decided to help her any way I could. I believed she was an unwilling victim of an uncaring society, struggling to stay afloat in a stormy sea. With the dreamy idealism of youth, I thought I might be able to toss her a life ring and bring her to firm ground. Believing rescue could take a long time, I was unprepared when our thing began to move at breakneck speed.

One evening we found ourselves alone in my rooms. I had bought a bottle of her favorite bubbly wine, and she was drinking it like water. Tipsy, holding a half-full tumbler in one hand and the bottle in the other, she hummed a music-hall tune and did a sensual little dance.

"Why don't you bring your glass to the bedroom?" she purred, turning swiftly to complete a pirouette and giggling.

"Well, all right. But what do you have in mind?"

"You'll see!" she chirped, dancing away from me.

I followed her into the larger space that served as my bedroom and bathroom and was surprised to see her dropping her skirt to the floor and removing her blouse. Then seductively and calmly she removed her undergarments: her petticoat, chemise, and lacey drawers. In the stuffy room the scent of newly washed linen reached my nostrils.

I stared at her with open mouth. I had never seen a naked woman before. It was a new, overwhelming experience that had come to me so unexpected I hardly knew how to react. I simply stood and stared. Unabashedly the girl struck a pose, nude with slender hands on narrow hips, her small breasts thrown forward, her chin tilted upward. She was smiling and beckoning. With great saucer eyes I stared at her. I could see she was tall and thin but well formed with clear skin that seemed to shine. Her shoulders, breasts, and arms had no blemish and were very white. Her legs were long and shapely, her waist slim, and her belly flat. Her face in profile displayed a classic outline of feminine beauty.

With that odd little laugh I would come to know well, she laced her tapered fingers in mine and pulled me toward the bed. Quickly she removed my clothes and put my quivering hands on her body. I had never touched a woman's flesh before, and it was smooth like velvet, warm and soft. For the first time in my life I kissed a pretty girl, embraced her, had coitus with her, and fell madly in love with her. I did not feel, as in the French novels I had read, wave upon wave of passion. Nor did I feel, when the copulation was over, an insatiable desire to repeat the act and be with the girl forever. All the same, I knew the attraction was real and strong and more than a passing fancy. For almost an hour Muriel Porter gratified a gnawing hunger that had plagued me for years, often interfering with my studies. Generously she gave herself to me. How could I possibly not love her with all my heart and soul?

2

Six weeks went by and then came a day crowded with incident. I learned I had won with honor several coveted prizes in English and Latin. Also to my surprise, I received the highest score of anyone in the college on the matriculation examination for the University of London. The officials of the college personally honored me, shaking my hand and wishing me well. For a few days I walked on dirty pavement as though it were air. With that news and the work I was eager to do, a promising future seemed assured. I would go to a great university, master the classics of Greece and Rome, and teach in one of the colleges of Oxford or Cambridge. I would publish books on classical antiquity, well-written books that would find a wide audience. My name would be that of a leading scholar in the academic community. To honor my father who had died too soon, I would work hard to achieve distinction.

Soon after hearing about the achievement, Dylan Crenshaw paid a visit to celebrate my good fortune and invite me to dinner. Through the rain and drizzle of an April afternoon, wearing a bully sweater but no raincoat, he walked the three miles to my rooms and offered hearty congratulations. We sat before a tiny fire, balancing cups of green tea on our knees, and conversed amicably with animation and banter. Somehow Crenshaw knew about the Sunday afternoon when I dined in style with Muriel Marie Porter, and the conversation soon turned to that.

"I hear you and that girl are pretty thick these days."

"I suppose you could say we're close by now. We've been seeing a lot of each other. I'm really fond of the girl. I got her off the streets and bought her a sewing machine, and she gave me a recent photograph."

Crenshaw examined the image of a slight but shapely girl with long dark hair and youthful good looks. Her hesitant smile revealed perfect teeth, even and white. The artificial smile seemed to say, *"The world is a sad and lonely place, and hard. The weak falter and go under but not me!"* My friend thought she displayed a worldly air beyond her years.

Dylan Crenshaw had a way about him that was neither subtle nor sensitive but knew he must tread lightly.

"Do you think maybe you and she are moving a bit too fast?"

"I like her and feel obliged to help her. I believe she's a victim of circumstance. No one cares at all whether she lives or dies. She was driven to the streets by forces beyond her control, I tell you, by the sheer need to survive in an uncaring society. If I don't help her no one else will, and she'll fall apart like a rag doll left in the rain."

"Eloquent, old boy! Vivid image! You should become a writer! Is the girl using the sewing machine you bought her? Is she working with the machine to earn a living?"

"Well, no, not yet but I think she will in time."

"I'm certain you sacrificed to buy her that machine. Now you tell me she isn't using it? I don't understand."

"She plans to go at it from noon to night as soon as she finds a supplier. Right now it's bloody difficult because so many other women are trying to get the same kind of work. Competition, you know."

"Listen to me, Blue, look at me!" Crenshaw exhorted. "That girl will never work as a needlewoman. Her type will never do that kind of work. I hope for your own good you'll stop seeing her."

"I can't," I replied, visibly upset by what he was saying. "I just can't. If you knew more about the thing between us, you might understand. I can't walk away from her now. It's too late, too late for that."

"Would she work as a servant? I'm sure you know middle-class women advertise for domestic help every day. You read *The Times*."

"I asked her about that, but she said women of her social class find serving at the bid and call of another woman degrading."

"That's ironical, isn't it, old boy? Even laughable. Service in a middle-class home is degrading but harlotry in a vice den is not?"

"She told me she hated the life, was unfit for it, would do anything to get away from it. She's really not that kind of girl, believe me. I'm hoping she'll find a good place at a shop or maybe a restaurant. Both require much standing, and she's not in the best of health."

"That seems evident. She looks pale even in the photograph. But let's talk more over dinner, old man. Will you let me buy you a meal? It's my way of congratulating a good friend for doing a good job. A ripping achievement, y' know. Everybody's talking about it."

We went to our favorite trattoria, shared a bottle of Chianti, and ate linguini Bolognese, savoring the rich and meaty sauce. With lusty appetites we devoured a loaf of crusty Italian bread, thick slices of ricotta, and a knob of piquant asiago. Muriel was draining me of the small income I was receiving from my scholarships, and for weeks I had not been able to buy nourishing food. I ate the dinner with bombastic enjoyment but soon admitted I was broke.

"I don't have a shilling I can call my own," I said, looking up from my plate and wiping red sauce from my lips. "She demands more to live on. Says she can't live on less. Threatens to go back to the old life if I don't find a way to give her more. I pawned my father's watch to get money for her. The heirloom you know, that Mother gave me when I went off to boarding school. I remember saying I would keep the watch all the years of my life and pass it on to my son. Now it's gone."

"I know about the watch and I don't like to hear this," said Crenshaw, his open face showing deep concern. "You sound sad and desperate."

Suddenly aware I was spoiling the gift of a good dinner from a good friend, I forced a smile.

"No more of that," I said, affecting a cheerful tone. "Let's drop the subject and enjoy our time together. Thanks for the dinner, my friend! Now tell me how things are going with you."

We were young but not too young for the twisted black Italian cheroots that complemented the meal. We smoked in a blue haze and went on talking. Again Crenshaw expressed his concern and pleaded with me for circumspection and caution. "I'm worried about this thing," he said.

Puffing on the narrow cigar and blowing a smoke ring that hung like a halo over the table, I assured my friend as best I could.

"Don't worry, Crenshaw, I won't kill or steal in a foolish effort to help the girl. I really have no inclination, no intention whatever, of doing anything you would call foolish. You have my word on that."

3

During the month of May, as warm breezes and sunshine came to Manchester, I gave much time to Muriel. Somehow I found the money to take her to the music halls where she laughed at stale jokes and clapped her hands with childish delight. Afterwards, over and over, she hummed the tunes she had heard. When I had no money to spend, we took long walks together and returned always to my rooms. She refused adamantly to take me to her lodgings, and the claim she lived with her maiden aunt soon evaporated. She lived alone, she said, in quarters too poor to receive a college man. I asked her several times about the sewing machine. She had taken it to her room and had set it up for use near the window. A supplier would be sending her work soon. Then she would make the machine hum all day and into the night.

A month later I found out she had pawned the sewing machine for less than half its value. Though I was gravely disappointed, I forgave her. What else could I do? She said she needed a new dress and had to have money to buy it. And with the dress she would need a new hat. Her rent had increased and she needed money for that. And of course a lady had to eat. She accepted all that I gave her as though it were her due, a fair payment for services rendered. As for me, even though I was poor and my income tiny, I loved to spend money on her. Every shilling I placed in her hand gave me a little thrill of joy and pride. Then before I knew it she was asking for pounds instead of shillings, and that kind of money was well beyond my reach.

"I just don't know where the money goes," she lamented one evening. "I just don't know. I have it one day and it's gone the next. It just slips through my fingers, Lovey. All the girls I once knew told me I'm not a penny-pincher, and I have to believe it."

"It's all right," said I. "You know I'm happy to help you any way I can. I don't have much as you well know, and I can't expect more coming my way. But I'm willing to help you, want to help all I can."

I could never be sure where or how she squandered the money. I didn't know how she spent her days and nights when she wasn't with me. At times I half believed she had wandered back to the streets. More than once she knocked urgently on my door, her face drawn and spent, her makeup smeared, her hair in a jumble. On one occasion she appeared in my doorway with her right eye black and swollen. Her face was thinner than usual. Both eyes were tired with eyelids drooping, robbing her of youthful prettiness. She explained that she had been hurrying along in the street when she slipped on something and fell to the pavement. I was unsure how she could get a black eye from such a fall but didn't have the courage to pry.

Then one day in great anguish she came to me insisting she needed more money. Her voice was shrill and she slurred her words. I asked why she had such a critical need for money of a sudden, but she merely laughed, scoffing and flashing her white teeth.

"I'm always in need of money!" she cried. "You promised to support me! Well, some support you're giving! My college boy don't have a pot to pee in but wants to support the likes o' me! You are not keeping up your end of the bargain, Lovey!"

By now she was sobbing one moment and shrilly laughing the next. I could see that she was drunk, and she smelled of cheap gin. Somehow she had gotten money to buy alcohol, or some "gentleman" looking for excitement had paid to get her drunk.

"I can't live this way!" she cried. "If I can't pay my rent I'm out on the street. Do you hear me? My greedy landlady don't have one shred of mercy and no decency. You fail me, and I'll have to find a way to make my own money. Do as I've always done!"

I knew it was a veiled threat and it frightened me. I couldn't bear to think she would abandon me and return to a vile life of danger and degradation. But as winter finally released its grip and warmth flowed into the dreary streets of Manchester, she seemed to be doing exactly that. For days I never saw her. Ignoring my personal safety, I went looking for her in the streets of neighborhoods she often talked about. They were formidable places: squalid, crime-ridden, and dangerous. I looked all over for her, pestered denizens in dosshouses, but couldn't find her.

Then suddenly and without notice she was knocking on my door again, disheveled, pale, and miserable. Whimpering, weeping, and wiping her dribbling nose with a tiny wet handkerchief, she was behaving like a whipped puppy seeking forgiveness.

"Where have you been?" I asked as calmly as I could.

"I was sick, awfully sick," she wailed. "I didn't want to bother you."

I knew she was lying but idiotically went on loving her. I found it difficult to believe her story and wanted to end the affair, but try as I might I couldn't dismiss the tender feelings I had for her. As the weeks passed I made a fatal decision. I would steal money from the coats of fellow students. I would steal even their coats if I could find a way to turn them into cash. Driven by acute desperation, I was now willing to risk losing everything gained as a diligent student. I had tried fervently to give my girl all the money she needed. Becoming a thief for her would prove my devotion with even greater clarity. Moreover, stealing from a debased society to save an unwitting victim was surely no wrong. A cruel, indifferent, irresponsible, and feckless abstraction was to blame. It would not be a criminal act to lash out against it. Rather than lose the girl I loved and see her sink into utter depravity, I would do whatever I could to help her. I wouldn't kill for her as I had said to Crenshaw. That I knew absolutely. But if I had to steal to save her from herself, I would do it.

CHAPTER SIX

Shame and Disgrace

At the college I had easy access to the room in which my fellow students left their coats and books before going to class. I looked over the cloakroom more than once before I finally summoned the nerve to act. No persons were nearby that day in mid-afternoon, and so I rummaged through the pockets of a stylish black coat. I found not just a few coins, but paper money of considerable value. As I strode quickly away I felt no guilt whatever and no fear. The owner of the coat would believe that somehow he had lost the money. A few days later I searched through the coats again but found nothing of worth. So I decided to seize some books and sell them or pawn them. When several days went by and nothing had occurred to cause alarm or even caution, I grew bolder. This time I walked away with several coats, knowing I could easily pawn them or perhaps sell them for cash. Later, however, the owners of the coats bitterly complained to school authorities.

And then it happened. A detective hired by the college caught me stealing marked money from a garish but well-made coat and charged me with theft. The man had hidden himself in a little alcove and stepped forward the moment I took the money. I was eagerly counting my prize when the detective seized me firmly by the arm. I froze as he touched me, could stammer no defense, and said nothing. Mumbling only a few words, he quickly put my hands in cuffs and led me away. We passed several students as he marched me off campus, but they didn't appear to see that I was under arrest and miserable.

Jonathan Blue, promising student who had won numerous awards for excellence, was in deep trouble. To put it briefly, I was tried, convicted, and sentenced to one month in prison at hard labor. The captain of the prison guards, a tall, dry-looking man with drooping eyelids, and a birthmark on half his face recorded my appearance in the official logbook: "*five feet eight and a half inches tall, slender of build, weight ten and a half stone (147 pounds), light complexion, male features, boyhood freckles, moderately long hair light brown, eyes gray with flecks of blue.*" Without complaint I endured the month of punishment with plenty of time to think. I knew I had committed a petty crime but firmly believed it was not so grievous it would ruin my life.

Though it saddened me to see a bright academic future fall into ruin, to hear about the crime was sadder for my family. My mother and sisters in Harrogate and my younger brothers at school in Wilmslow were mortified. Nora Blue, on hearing the dreadful news, was seized with panic. Her heart, I learned later, beat against her rib cage like a pigeon in a trap, and her pain was more intense than when her husband died. In deepest misery she wept in her pillow. Her talented son had thrown away his chance to gain respect as a man of learning in a life well lived. Her favorite son had become a thief and a convict.

2

I gave my family a brief explanation of what had happened, leaving out many details and saying nothing of Muriel. I placed no blame on the girl and didn't mention her name to anyone. Officials in a bully pose interrogated me for hours, seeking a motive. They never got it. Though my love wasn't able to understand the magnitude of my crime and its repercussions, she was flattered I had taken so drastic a step for her.

"It shows me plainly you really care about me, Lovey. I'm sure you know I love you too, more than anything."

"What happened puts us both in a painful situation," I said, "but it's only a temporary setback. We'll get over it and move on."

"Of course we will and later we can have a good life together. It's only for a month in that dirty old prison, and you'll manage. You won't forget me while you're there, will you?"

"You know I can't and won't forget you. Any plans I make for the future will certainly include you."

I was dismissed from the college without a degree and forced to relinquish all plans to become a scholar. All my life I had dreamt of becoming a university don, teaching and doing research, and making a name for myself in the academic world. My colleagues would respect me, and my students love me. Now the reality of life, a stupid blunder not even related to intellect, had utterly destroyed that dream of life. Students at Thatcher College couldn't believe that Jonathan Blue – accomplished, and soft-spoken – had created a scandal. How could one so intelligent prove so stupid? I was asking myself the same question.

In the tavern where they often gathered, Bobby Bobeck who loved the limelight and had trouble controlling his tongue, spoke of me rather negatively in the past tense, and every syllable got back to me.

"Blue was intelligent enough but grievously lacking when it came to women. I could see that the first time I roamed the streets with him. His imagination worked overtime. It led him to gawk at women as if they were from another planet. Then he chanced upon those lovely ladies of the night. They sidled up to him with seductive smiles, wiggling their hips and showing cleavage. He gawked with drooling open mouth and became reckless. I warned him but he wouldn't listen."

Bobeck, of course, was lying through his teeth. Only Dylan Crenshaw had attempted to reason with me, and more than once. Routinely he had left my rooms knowing he had failed.

"Beware of maidens in distress," he had said, framing a metaphor. "Women who need to be saved are more dangerous than dynamite. A young woman looking to be saved is more explosive than the bomb of a crazed anarchist. Beware, my friend, and take care."

He wanted me to stop seeing the girl, end the affair at once. I stubbornly refused. Muriel had become the central focus of my life. It was unthinkable for me to live without her. So Crenshaw's cries of warning went unheeded. Romantic illusion drowned the voice of reason.

Inbred rectitude and circumspection fell by the wayside as I began to steal. Becoming too confident, I was caught and branded a thief and scorned by the entire college. I was forced to suffer disgrace and shame from all quarters. Wise men tell us there are tragedies in life that a person can never overcome. In spite of my upbeat remarks to Muriel as I went off to prison, perhaps this was that kind of tragedy. My dream of life had become a monstrous illusion to rend and tear.

3

During the trial no one doubted I had stolen from other students, but the question the court wanted answered was why. A contingent of college Pooh-Bahs, sitting stiffly in black gowns and displaying dignified attention, demanded to know. I was pressured to reveal why I had resorted to thievery. Was it truly a case of need? Was the income from my scholarships so little that I was driven to commit a crime? Did I steal to support some needy person? Rumors were rife that I had. Tight-lipped and obstinate, I refused to give satisfactory answers. I had decided to cooperate with them, but in no way would I implicate Muriel. Even if it meant a year in jail, I would take the blame and keep her name out of it. College authorities seeking resolution stared at me. On every face was a deep shade of disgust. A promising student had let them down.

The summer of 1876 was a time of loss and hurt but also a season of fundamental change. I endured with stoic indifference the agony of disgrace and the shame of prison and emerged saddened but with all faculties intact. I performed the hard labor of my sentence in a quarry nine hours each day and didn't buckle. In the hot sun that burned my skin I pounded rock into pieces for road improvement. Belleview Prison displayed no beautiful view at all, only ugliness and hardship. I lived with felons serving time for serious crimes, including rape and murder. In the early weeks older convicts pointed me out as prey. Others saw me as a petty thief too stupid to dodge being caught. Some flicked obscene gestures in my direction and made fun of me. They relented when I kept to myself, kept my mouth shut, and did nothing to offend them. I did what I was told and wasn't punished beyond the law. When released exhausted and sick, I went home for a month to recuperate.

During that time I laid out meticulous plans to escape the past and begin again in America. Mother reluctantly gave me the money for the voyage from her savings, saying I could pay it back later. With the optimism of youth, I wanted to start over in a new place. Goethe's sage advice, *"Amerika ist hier oder nirgends,"* meant nothing whatever to me. In my own country after prodigious struggle I had failed miserably. America with its teeming masses, wide-open spaces, and ample opportunity offered high adventure to an English lad with ambition. Muriel, my first love, I left behind. In mind and heart, however, I took her with me. Her slender form stood before me day and night, more substantial than a shadow but wavering and incorporeal. Even in the direst of circumstances I was unwilling to abandon the wraith that had haunted me when most vulnerable and conquered me.

CHAPTER SEVEN

A New Beginning

I bought passage in third class on a ship of the Cunard Line. With all my earthly possessions in a valise and small trunk, I sailed from Liverpool in August. None of my relatives came to see me off and Dylan Crenshaw was at work in another city. Alone and lonely, I boarded the ship, found my place in its bowels, and braced myself for a long and sickening voyage. However, though scores in third class groaned with seasickness and made a mess, I didn't get sick even once. Day after day the steamer moved sedately along in pleasant weather. For eighteen days when away from my bunk my world was one of sea and sky. Good weather in time gave way to bad. High winds and high seas buffeted the ship for three days. At the peak of the storm I ventured on deck, clung to the rail, and stood in awe at the size of the waves. The ocean in storm reminded me of a verse I had read somewhere, and I mumbled its lines. An old salt after weathering a tempest was speaking: *"Now she wears a placid face. But I have seen her lacking grace. And I have rued the change of mood."*

In bright and sunny weather and a tame sea, a school of porpoises rode the rushing bow wave. They leaped above the water and seemed joyous as they dropped behind to frolic in the surging wake. They followed the vessel for several days, gorging on its garbage and cutting somersaults to entertain the ship's passengers. I wandered the decks to catch the sea breezes (steerage was stifling), and found myself charmed by the sea. One day I caught a glimpse of a sea turtle. It seemed as large as the ship's wheel. At night I studied the sky to identify the North Star and the constellations. It seemed as though I could reach up and touch the starry sky. I regretted I had no book to explain the heavens beyond my schoolboy knowledge.

This new experience, crossing the Atlantic for the first time, was exhilarating. But it wasn't enough to erase the sadness and loneliness that settled upon me after a week at sea. I ate unsavory food ladled from a cauldron and plopped on a tin tray. I took my meals alone and seldom spoke to other steerage passengers. In the midst of many distractions, my thoughts were on the searing event that had placed me among them. When days were cloudy I sat moodily in a wooden deck chair, staring at the blue-green sea. Passengers strolled by in animated groups, but I tried not to look at them. The pain within, salted by loneliness, inspired me to scribble verses of saccharine sweetness dedicated to my lady. Another person in a situation so dreary might have thought of suicide, but Jonathan Blue thought only of Muriel Porter. My imagination spurred by isolation idealized and lifted to a higher plane a tawdry girl with intense eyes and perfect teeth. She became a tender flower blooming bravely in the deepest recesses of my hidden heart. On the high seas and later in America I struggled to find poetic phrases to express my feelings for the loved one I had left behind.

The vessel docked in New York at the beginning of September. It was late in the afternoon, and the mellow light of the autumn sun filtering through clouds made the shadows soft and long. A young man in rumpled clothing descended the gangplank and stood for the first time on American soil. His sandy brown hair was carefully combed, and he carried a shabby valise. Surrounded by scores of people who paid him no heed, he felt entirely alone in that new place but curious and alive. He went through customs, found his trunk, and made his way to a cheap hotel. Later he would go by rail to Boston. Before leaving England he had decided to make his home in that city and look for work as a teacher or newspaper reporter. His dream was to become a writer.

I wasn't sure I liked New York. I told myself I would stay there just long enough to see the main part of the city and perhaps return later. Manchester had congested streets at certain times during the day. Night and day the streets of New York were full of people and vehicles. A cabbie, speaking English with a strange accent, hustled my trunk into a well-used hansom and asked me where I wanted to go. The man was a Serb from Croatia. He said even though his English wasn't good after a year in America, he liked the way it rolled off his tongue. He was very talkative and advised me to bunk at a small hotel nearby.

"Three bucks all night," he said. "They gonna give you good breakfast come morning. You donna go wrong stay there, you betcha."

I didn't know the hotel paid the cabbie a small sum each week to offer such advice, and I readily agreed to go there. It was a shabby place, but the bed in the tiny room was clean and the food I got for breakfast lasted all day. The view from my window was another brick building so close I could almost touch it. That didn't bother me because the little time I spent in the room was for sleeping or reading. I remained in New York for three nights and roamed the city by day. I liked my new country, read its newspapers eagerly, and was able to neutralize the dark mood that had galled me all summer. This was a new opportunity in a new country, and I was beginning to feel almost cheerful again. As a new week began I bought a ticket for Boston, hoping to find work on a magazine or newspaper. I traveled more than two hundred miles in a noisy and smelly railway car that impressed me as huge. I was amazed to find that I could walk through the cars from one end of the train to the other in perfect freedom. As I walked, I could even buy refreshments from strolling hawkers and could study the faces of everyday Americans.

2

In Boston I found a boarding house in a quiet neighborhood and ate the abundant food on its sagging table with gusto. It was tasty and filling, and I found myself growing stronger by the day. For room and board I paid only ten dollars a week. My family in Harrogate, though shocked and saddened by what happened in Manchester, was standing by me. I knew Mama would like to hear all about the good food I was eating. So in some attempt to ease her suffering, I described in detail the sumptuous boarding-house table.

"You won't believe the many kinds of vegetables here. At dinner we have squash, white potatoes, sweet potatoes, tomatoes, green corn, spinach, beans, cauliflowers, and turnips. Mrs. Craigenstock, a widow who owns the house, will have no one go hungry. She loads each plate with meat, vegetables, several kinds of bread, cranberries, and fruit. We eat cranberries with our meat, and sometimes we have a very sweet dessert. For breakfast we have meat and potatoes with eggs and waffles and coffee. Sometimes she puts a pitcher of thick white milk on the table, and I always drink a big glass. It's a splendid boarding house. There are about ten other people living here, all very pleasant."

One person in the house was a woman who introduced herself as Myra Medlock. She was thin and plain but had a pleasant smile. A year or two shy of thirty, she was the daughter of a city official with a good income. She worked long hours in a milliner's shop at low wages. Her dark hair was neatly parted in the middle and fell to the nape of her neck in ringlets. Her pale cheeks were artificially colored and her dark eyes restless. Her sensual lips were a curious contrast to a straight and severe nose and a singular coldness of manner. She got her clothing wholesale and dressed more fashionably than the other lodgers. Better educated, she affected social graces the others didn't presume to have. She took a liking to me and always tried to sit next to me at dinner.

"I do believe you're English," she said, shyly glancing at me with a sheepish smile. "I can tell by the accent."

I was filling my plate to satisfy a hearty appetite and looking at a dish, passed to me by another boarder, that I didn't recognize.

"Oh that's succotash!" she explained. "It has sweet corn, lima beans, red peppers, carrots, okra and other vegetables. Also bits of bacon for flavor. Try some, I think you'll like it."

I put a helping of the colorful dish on my plate and passed it on to her. She smiled primly and placed a little on her plate beside an ebony chunk of pot roast oozing juices and covered with gravy.

"I like succotash," she remarked, but I never eat large portions of anything. It's so easy to gain weight at this table."

I noticed that she had plenty of meat but few vegetables.

"How long have you been in this country?" she asked.

"Not very long, only a couple of weeks. I came from Liverpool to New York and then here. I'm looking for work but spend too much of my time in your free library. I like to read."

I did indeed. I didn't read always with eagerness or enjoyment but invariably with speed and perseverance.

"You have a glorious public library here," I said to Myra, "and it's free for anybody to use. We don't have that sort of thing in England."

"Yes, we do have a good library. And it has so many books they don't have room for them all. There's talk of expanding the library."

"I find it hard to believe that I can go there and sit in a warm, well-lighted room and read any book, newspaper, or magazine that catches my fancy for hours and hours and pay nothing."

"Well, you can, Mr. Jonathan Blue, that's why it's called the free library," Myra retorted with a sense of pride. "You will have them soon in England, I believe. New developments take time."

"Yes," I said as I tasted the succotash. "We have talk in England of free libraries, but nothing accomplished as yet."

"You're in America now, and one of the finest cities in America."

"I know," I replied. "I like it better than New York."

I had not been in New York long enough to make that comparison but felt she wanted to hear good things about her city.

"We're proud of our public facilities," she offered. "We have the library, of course, but also excellent museums and art galleries and parks to enjoy in summer. Also a university as good as your Oxford. Perhaps when the weather improves I can show you some of the sights?"

"That would be capital," I replied, glancing at the woman's thin face.

A little frown creased her brow, and I attempted to muffle my British accent. I suddenly realized that I was using English words seldom heard in America. I didn't want her to take offense.

"Do you know about the telephone?" she asked, abruptly changing the subject. "It's a wonderful invention. People can talk to each other over several miles. They even say it may supersede the telegraph, make it antiquated in a few years."

"Yes, indeed. I've read about that. Before long Mrs. Craigenstock will have a telephone in her kitchen and will use it to buy groceries from her grocer and meat from the butcher. She won't even have to leave her house. Also people will write their letters on the new typing machine, and we shall enter a forum to watch pictures that move."

"Well, I can't believe all that will happen anytime soon!" she replied with a trill of laughter. "But science and the arts are improving every day. Boston has become a testing ground for all the new things before they go out to the rest of the country."

In a way Myra Medlock with her provincial pride was like my sisters. back home. I couldn't be sure I liked her even though she seemed pleasant enough. In the weeks that followed, as I struggled to write an article for a local magazine, I got to know her better. We walked and talked in the evenings but were never close. However, the impression she made was strong enough to influence a story I was planning. A matron of high standing in the community, a worldly woman of experience, would take interest in a young man and attempt to polish his manners to make him a gentleman. I'm glad Myra Medlock wasn't aware I viewed her as too old for me. Also it would have hurt her to know I was thinking of her as source material for a fictional character. I believe she liked me and perhaps wanted more than friendship, but that was out of the question. I never said a word to her about Muriel.

One spring day she left the boarding house, where she had lived for three years, and took up with a traveling man. He was a salesman of barbershop supplies and moved up and down the eastern seaboard. In the beginning she traveled with him, but after a few weeks he deposited her in a hotel room in White Plains and later in lodgings. She found a job in a shop and looked forward to his arrival in town every other month. Gradually his visits became infrequent and finally stopped altogether. Most of the time, burdened by a large black sample case, he traveled by train to small towns and large. On occasion he went by wagon to places away from the railroad. He had a schedule to follow and worked many hours to meet his quota in towns south of New York City. He never got as far as Boston again or to White Plains. In time Myra Medlock found another man, an industrial engineer, and married him. I heard he was a good man with a good income and they raised six children.

3

Another boarder was a freckled young man with copper hair named Alan Cooper. He worked as a clerk in the Postal Service and seemed to wear the same dark clothes all the time. At table he was known as a ravenous eater but never added an ounce to his thin and rangy frame. His baritone voice seemed too strong for one so slightly built, but he was affable and agreeable and people liked him. He knew that I was looking for work and thought he might help, but nothing ever came of it. We talked about politics and the presidential election of 1876. The results were delayed and contested, and that made for an air of excitement. I went with Alan to a telegraph office in heavy rain, and we saw an amazing sight to tell the others at dinner.

"It rained cats and dogs," said Cooper, "but Tuesday night was fun."

"It was indeed," I added, looking around the table. "They had this device they called a stereopticon, and they used it to report election results. They threw the returns in big black numbers on the side of a building where the crowd could read them."

"To please the crowd, as they waited for the returns," added Cooper, "they used the magic lantern to project funny sketches of the candidates. Hayes had a beard bigger than his head, and Tilden an enormous nose. Beastly weather for early November but good entertainment!"

I found Boston very much to my liking and thought I might stay there for the rest of my life. I hoped I might earn a living as an author, but in the meantime I would look for something more practical. I was spending money faster than usual, even thinking about traveling across the entire country by rail, when I realized I was nearly broke. Then my luck turned and fortune smiled upon me. I was hired to teach English, French, and German at the high school in nearby Waltham. It was a position, not merely a job. A local newspaper reporter interviewed me on my arrival. I took that as a mark of genuine respect, and the politeness of my students surprised me.

They were attentive and orderly but giggled when I first opened my mouth to speak. They soon grew accustomed to my accent and liked the way I shared my knowledge. To reach them more effectively, I began to use the Yankee equivalents, of *splendid, capital,* and *scholar.*

"Settle down, scholars!" I cautioned one morning on entering the classroom. To restore order, the masters at Breckenbow had often used that term, and it seemed appropriate.

A roar of laughter greeted me in response. It was the cue I needed to loosen the fetters of English academic life and speak a more informal American dialect in a more casual setting.

"Your recitation was splendid, Ralph, but try giving your French a more nasal quality and place stronger emphasis on the verbs."

Another rumble of laughter, whooping, and giggling.

"Oh, I meant to say that's real good, Ralph. Just keep at it."

More laughter, but this time appreciative and no longer critical.

My classroom had ranks of sturdy desks standing like sentinels with dark and forbidding rigidity. I wanted to move them into a circle for face-to-face discussion but discovered they were bolted to the floor. The air in the stuffy room was stale and smelled of pomade, mothballs, and starched clothing. When I tried to open a window for a whiff of fresh air, I found it was nailed shut. In those days in America there was little thought of ventilation, and the windows were secured against prowlers and cold weather. In a heavy sweater and breathing air that hurt my throat, I stood before a blackboard five and a half days a week teaching three languages. I filled the board with neat but chalky handwriting hard to read from the back of the room. My feet and legs ached when I finally got home. Sometimes I was too tired even to eat. But in letters to my family I assured them I liked my job.

"*A high school teacher is a very important person here,*" I boasted, trying to install a bit of humor. "*My salary is adequate and allows me to live comfortably in a spacious room I rent in a private home. For room and board I pay eight dollars a week. They treat me as another member of the family, and I rather like that.*"

The winter was one of the coldest on record. Ice and snow covered the streets and roads, and sleighs replaced wheeled vehicles. The thermometer read zero and below for days and days. I had to be careful not to let my ears freeze, but found the cold invigorating. Later in life I would hate frigid weather, but at nineteen and not much older than my students, I found walking briskly in the cold surprisingly pleasant. One evening in the dead of winter we teachers and thirty students formed a sleigh party and went to a hotel in a nearby town. There for several hours we amused ourselves in harmless frolic before returning home. Other teachers on the staff were also young, and several of the women were pretty. My eye rested on one of them with interest. Because Muriel governed my behavior, nothing came of it. Even though my work consumed most of each day, I found time almost every evening to write long letters to her. I promised I would not forget her and would send for her as soon as I could. I loved that frail girl-woman with flaming desire for reasons beyond my understanding.

I had suffered dreadfully in England, but in Waltham I enjoyed every hour of every day. I liked being a teacher, sharing my knowledge with eager youngsters who showed me respect. I liked the look in their eyes when they heard from me something entirely new to them. Unlike many schools in England, where masters endured harsh conditions in silence, the faculty in this school had a voice. Every week or so we had meetings to improve the school and working conditions. It was a pleasant place and soon became my second home. I spent many hours there of my own volition. Not once did I feel I was overworked or underpaid. Not once did I feel I had no future there. Though I was in my element at Waltham, too soon I discovered I couldn't escape the past.

One Friday afternoon when classes were over and the school empty, I was called into the principal's office. Elmer Bilderson was a stocky man with gray hair and pale blue eyes. He spoke thickly in muffled tones as if he had a cold but with authority.

"Please sit down, Mr. Blue. I have before me something of importance. School policy requires us to investigate the background of our teachers, and I've received a disturbing letter concerning you."

He looked down at some papers on his desk, ran his fingers over one he selected, and studied my face. He saw anguish, hurt, and dismay but also sad resignation. Instantly he understood his popular and competent language teacher knew he was being fired. Word had come from England that I had stolen from fellow students, had been tried and convicted, and had spent a month in prison. I was unfit to teach impressionable youngsters. I would have to go.

"I'm truly sorry," said Principal Bilderson, apologizing for lack of anything better to say. "I'm sorry to see you go."

"I'm sorry too, sir, but understand. I shall clear out my desk immediately. I wish you and your school the very best."

An hour later young Jonathan Blue, not yet a man by English law, was walking heavily to his rented room with a box full of books and papers. I was tormented by this turn of events but not surprised. Fate and the sorry scheme of things had shattered my hopes and dreams once more. The malignity of matter had caught up with me a second time to tear and punish. A cold wind whipped my legs and back. The skies were forlorn and gray. A dog so thin I could count his ribs, yelped feebly as I met him in the road. He stared at me with sad eyes and scurried away.

CHAPTER EIGHT

Westward to Chicago

From the time I came to New York and rode the railway cars to Boston, I had dreamt of traveling all the way across America by train. I knew the country was enormous, and I thrilled to the thought of spending a week or more in the clattering cars, moving night and day to San Francisco. It wasn't a dream beyond my reach, but in March of 1877 I decided to go only as far as Chicago. I had heard that unknown authors were sometimes published in Chicago newspapers, and the city offered numerous opportunities to any person willing to work. In the days following my arrival I couldn't be certain I liked Chicago. It was cold and windy, and the people on the pavement walked with collars turned up and faces turned down. After two nights in a seedy hotel, I found a cheap rooming house not far from the center of the city and settled down to write. In Boston I had written about English life in a manufacturing town, drawing upon my knowledge of Manchester, and had sent it off to a magazine. After a month the piece was rejected as not fitting their content. Now I would try short stories and send them to local newspapers.

My first story was published in the *Chicago Tribune* only a week after my arrival. Though it bore the title "Fathers and Sons," it was a tragic love story. On my second day in the city I went to the newspaper asking for work. An editor said they might buy a short story for a section of the paper that featured fiction. I wrote the story in two days under adverse conditions. It was too cold to write in my bedroom, and so I went to the common room where several brawny men sat before the fire smoking, quarreling, and playing a card game. I found a table at one end of the room, blocked out the noise, and began writing. The men grumbled I was too hoity-toity to associate with them.

"Writing a letter, huh?" grumped a hulking workman with a beard and baldhead. He hovered over the table, casting a heavy shadow.

I went on writing without answering. I was in the middle of a sentence and didn't want to lose it. I didn't look up to acknowledge the man, and he roughly took offense.

"I asked you a goddamn question, boy. Didn't you hear what I said? You do speak English don't cha?"

He was a cross-grained man, a day laborer stung by poverty, and rough as nails. His voice was gritty, and his anger produced spittle that fell on my writing paper. I wiped it off, stood up, and looked him in the eye. I was agitated, almost angry, and unafraid.

"I'm awfully sorry," I explained. "I was in the midst of a sentence and concentrating. Will you please repeat the question?"

The workman detected an accent very different from the local drawl he had been accustomed to all his life and laughed harshly. He slammed his big fist on the table and glared at me.

"Why don't you go back where you came from, boy? We don't need your kind here. Only workingmen in this house and jobs ain't plentiful. We don't have no work in this town for people from other countries, especially boys with soft hands and snobby manners."

All my life I had dreaded quarrels, and I hoped to placate the redneck with a few well-chosen words. I was about to reply with a conciliatory gesture when his companions called the big man away.

"Pete! It's your turn, goddammit, get over here!"

The bearded man shrugged his massive shoulders and lurched away, returning to the group. He was holding up their poker game.

For one who went out of his way to avoid confrontation, that sudden encounter was raw and unpleasant. But if I wanted to eat nourishing meals for the next few days, the writing job had to be finished. I pushed the ugly reality out of mind and went on scratching words on a yellow pad as fast as they came to me.

It was a long story. It filled three columns of the newspaper, and I drew without restraint upon my own life. For the first time I told the world in fictional disguise how I met and fell in love with Muriel Marie Porter in Manchester, England. I explained even though we loved each other deeply, things from the beginning didn't go right with us. So initial joy gave way to despair. Clumsy, melodramatic, sensational, it was not a good story. But it showed an inclination to reach intuitively into my own experience for fictional material. I would do that for the rest of my life as I tried to produce a long and thoughtful novel each year. Scarcely without knowing it my literary career had begun.

The piece idealized Muriel as a latter-day Laura and me as a stalwart and suffering Petrarch. Laura's intense dark eyes and lush black hair, *"all unkempt and streaming over the shoulders,"* surely belonged to Muriel. As the unhappy Laura drifted toward prostitution, her lover urged her to earn her living by sewing. But as Muriel had rejected that idea in life, so does Laura in fiction. The story ended with the lost girl clinging to her man, falling into a river with him, and holding on as both sink beneath the water. That image of sinking downward, downward haunted me at that time. When days were darkest, I felt Muriel Porter had surely dragged me downward to rot. Nonetheless, I knew I was a survivor and would somehow conquer my troubles.

I was paid eighteen dollars for "Fathers and Sons," and that allowed me to keep the wolf from the door long enough to write another story. Day after day I labored, serving my apprenticeship as a writer of fiction without knowing it. The men in the common room cast glances in my direction and muttered taunting remarks but left me alone. I wrote eleven stories for Chicago newspapers, and the income allowed me to remain in the city four months. One day I bought a little notebook to jot down my ideas for stories. Several pages I filled with persistent brooding over Muriel's impact upon me. In them was an outline for a sanitized version of the Manchester episode. Stung by what had happened and pointedly ashamed, I attempted to make the sordid details respectable. So into the notebook went this: *A naive young man meets and marries a vain and selfish woman. Her expensive tastes drive him to commit a crime. He is caught and must pay for his crime, but the repentant wife offers loving support.* No story was ever fashioned from the outline.

2

When summer came to Chicago with cool breezes off Lake Michigan, I was living on a dollar a day. A dollar in those days had some worth, but I was eating only bread and cheese and scraps of meat. My curiosity would not allow me to stay inside in good weather, and so I walked the streets mile after mile. It was good exercise and kept me fit, but the long walks that became a life-long habit burned calories that scanty meals never replaced. On rainy days or when the weather was too windy, I drew upon what I had seen and wrote about it. But one after another the stories of local color were returned with pink rejection slips. Almost overnight the income from my fiction dried up, and the money in my wallet dwindled to a few dollars. When I fell behind on my rent, the landlord demanded money I didn't have. Knowing it was a foolish thing to do but unable to think of something better, I pawned my winter clothing to pay him. I had very little left for food.

Reluctantly, for what I planned to do seemed close to begging, I went to the office of the newspaper that had published my most recent story.

"Will you give me a small advance on my next story?" I asked the editor. "I'm a bit strapped at present and could certainly use it. You will have a good and moving story in a few days."

"I wish I could do that," replied the genial editor, "but the company won't allow it. Also we have a good supply of fiction for our purposes and won't be needing any more for some time."

Winston Perkins was a stout man with a florid face, bronze hair, and a big smile. The weather was warm now and he was in suspenders and shirtsleeves. He tapped a yellow pencil on his desk as he talked, and a trickle of sweat rolled down his broad neck. His face grew serious when he saw that I had fallen on hard times.

"I wish we could buy another story from you, Mr. Blue, just to help you out. But we can't just now. And you know I can't advance money for something we've never seen."

"I understand, sir. I was just hoping against hope I guess."

"That story you submitted to us was reprinted in a paper in New York State in a town called Troy. I know it's a long way from here, but maybe they were impressed by your work and could find you a job. It's really the only help I can give you."

On the edge of a perilous cliff I might call Utter Desperation, I seized upon the editor's suggestion. The next day I left the windy city to travel eastward to Troy, New York. The journey of 800 miles was memorable for its discomfort. Children on the train were rowdy and unsupervised. Fat men with fat cigars filled the car with a haze of blue smoke that burned my nostrils and turned my stomach. An old man in dirty clothing and with a hacking cough was hugging a burlap bag filled with live chickens. A frowzy woman in clothes that looked like they were made for someone else was eating fried chicken and other goodies. She lifted each piece from a large tin bucket, gnawed it to the bone, licked her stubby fingers, smacked her lips, and began devouring another. The odor of fried food had always made me ravenous. I was faint with hunger and for an instant thought I might ask the woman for a biscuit. She had several in her bucket and could surely spare one, but something within me, stubborn pride I guess, stood in the way. I was very hungry, perhaps starving, but I couldn't bring myself to beg.

In the trash bin of the toilet I found a discarded apple with one bite taken from it. I could see the imprint of teeth in the white flesh, and I dribbled water over the apple to clean it. I ate it to the core and then ate the core. I told myself I would have to save the few dollars in my pocket for a rainy day. That meant eating whatever and whenever I could. So I put down the fastidious impulses cultivated in Harrogate and convinced myself the apple was filling and tasty. It was big and juicy but hard and sour, and it made my stomach ache.

In Troy I rented a room for one night, made myself tidy the next morning, and went immediately to *The Hellespont Herald*. Clean and neat after a week without a bath but in clothes clearly showing wear,

I asked the editor for a job. I would take anything available and work hard. As for credentials, I was a published author but would gladly work as an office or errand boy.

"We have nothing for you," the bespectacled editor with thinning hair brusquely replied. "We are not looking to hire."

"You published my story. Doesn't that mean something?"

"We pick up a lot of material from other newspapers. It's the practice of all newspapers today. We use it to fill space."

"But that was a piece of creative writing. I was paid for it but retained all rights. Are you not legally obligated to pay me for it?"

The editor laughed nervously and glanced at a co-worker at another desk. Without saying a word he stood up and walked with busy attention in that direction. The journalists had nothing to offer me, not even a soupçon of courtesy. They turned their backs on me and went on with their work. It was obvious they viewed me as an interloper and something of a troublemaker. I left them feeling sick to my stomach and weak from hunger. In the shade of an elm tree I sat on a bench to rest. I was tired and confused and needed to sort through my thoughts.

I had always been poor but any situation in which I would not have enough to eat had never occurred to me. It was beyond the range of my experience, not the sort of thing my family in Harrogate had ever worried about. I was vaguely ashamed of myself for sinking so low. The pain I suffered, more emotional than physical, overwhelmed me. I thought of throwing myself in the nearby river, but as soon as the thought came to me I rebelled against it. My brain told me the misery in my stomach would cease in time. The pain inside couldn't last forever. I had but one life to live and happy or not, I would live it as long as I could.

3

Desperate and half sick, I spent four memorable days in Troy. My classical studies accentuated the irony of the situation. In Homeric legend Troy was the mighty city of King Priam, besieged for ten years by the Greeks during the Trojan War and finally conquered through trickery. The town in New York had Greeks. I lived on peanuts in the shell bought a pennyworth at a time from a street vendor who called himself Alexander Kostopoulos. The man was tall and swarthy, thin but strong, dour in manner and appearance but talkative. He had relatives in the old country and was proud to be Greek. Though in a predicament that didn't allow for classical allusion, I was pleased to find a Greek in Troy. Sensing my situation after my first purchase, the vendor gave me more and more peanuts for a penny. I remember his kindness and generosity even now. I remember his name, Alexander Kostopoulos. He had so little to give but gave. He was in all respects a prince of a fellow.

I was down and out in a struggling little town on the Hudson and Mohawk rivers near the state capital. I walked along the towpath beside the river and looked into the swirling water and once more had dark thoughts of self-destruction. As before, it was not a solution I considered seriously. When I was placed in cuffs and charged with theft at Thatcher College, my anguish had been so great I wanted to die. I had no such emotion now, only a dull ache in the pit of my stomach and a leaden dread of what the next day would bring. I felt an intolerable loneliness and was fearfully tired. In my rambling I found a patch of grass and lay down for an hour, the June sun warming my face. I wanted to rest there longer, even spend the night there, but knew that a policeman with a billy club would demand I move on. I spent my nights in an abandoned building sleeping on a concrete floor under an oily tarpaulin.

Troy seemed oblivious to whether I lived or died, but really the town went about its business without even knowing I was there. Years later, reading in the British Museum, I came across an article speaking of Troy as the birthplace of Uncle Sam, the national symbol of the United States. A man named Samuel Wilson, called "Uncle Sam" by admiring employees, owned a meatpacking plant in Troy. When the War of 1812 broke out, his company received a large contract to supply the troops. The shipments went out in barrels marked "U.S." for United States. The abbreviation was not yet common and people asked what it meant. Wilson's proud employees told them it stood for Uncle Sam. The strong, bearded figure behind the sobriquet eventually came to personify the government of the United States. I read the article with pleasure mixed with pain as I remembered hard times in Troy. In Boston, had I known these facts, I would have told the story expansively to amuse and amaze my fellow boarders. I wondered what had happened to the good people who became my friends there.

I was starving and desperate in Troy but too proud to ask for help. Then on the fourth day when my belly was quite empty and I was feeling too faint even to walk, I chanced upon a traveling photographer who needed an assistant. Geoffrey Barnes had grown up on a farm in Pennsylvania, had worked it, and knew all about hardship. A slightly built man with a large head and hollow chest, he seemed to have too much energy for his thin legs. He was always on the move.

We went to a tavern and ate thick summer sausages with beer and bread and a succulent salad. The food was very simple and very good. We talked at length about the job I would do.

"I won't be able to pay you even a living wage," said Barnes apologetically, "but I can assure you of one thing: you won't go hungry."

"That will do," I replied. "I'm down on my luck and will be your assistant for whatever you think necessary. In time I hope to get back to England, but we can work together through the summer. How long have you been in the photography business?"

"I've been doing this for five and a half years. I've had some bad luck of my own, but slowly I found that work will numb the pain and confusion and help a person get back on track."

"I most certainly agree with that. Thomas Carlyle said work is man's salvation, and I was raised to believe it. He said if you find your work and do it, you won't have to ask if you were happy. Did bad luck hit hard when it came your way?"

"It did. My wife and son died of diphtheria." He was hesitant and laconic. "It wasn't a good time for me but worse for them. They suffered terribly. Couldn't breathe, couldn't swallow. And then came heart and nerve damage and they were dead. I sold my farm to Mennonites, everything but two horses and a wagon, and started traveling."

"I'm really sorry to hear you lost your wife and son, Mr. Barnes. Your story is far more tragic than mine."

"Call me Jeff, please. What's done is done. We can't undo the past. Hey, you ate only two sausages! I've already had three. Take another and have more beer, more salad. We have traveling to do and work."

The spiced sausages were tasty and I thought I could eat at least five, but then I discovered my deprived stomach wasn't ready for more than two. Before night came we were on our way to another town.

Barnes went out of his way to feed his assistant well. He found a good bed for me almost every night, even paid me a small salary, and bought me new clothes. With our bulky equipment we traveled in a sturdy wagon from town to town through upstate New York and New England. We took photographs of the comfortable burghers of the region, processed them wherever we happened to be, and were paid a good price. We worked together through the summer and did well. I was able to eat meat and potatoes again, restore my strength, gain some weight, and save a few dollars. In September I said goodbye to Geoffrey Barnes and went again to Boston. I made my way to Mrs. Craigenstock's boarding house, and there I was able to get a loan to buy passage home. My new beginning in America had lasted exactly one year.

CHAPTER NINE

Eastward to England

In the autumn of 1877 Henry James and Mark Twain were traveling in luxury on the great steamships that routinely crossed oceans. They slept between crisp linen sheets in private cabins, ate delicious food under crystal chandeliers, and enjoyed respect and recognition among passengers in first class. Jonathan Blue, with dreams of becoming a man of letters, had to borrow money to travel in third class. Passengers in that class were crammed deep below decks close to the rudder. Steerage was dimly lit and poorly ventilated. It was lacking in privacy, crowded and noisy, and smelled of unwashed humanity. The food was atrocious and three toilets served a hundred people. Poorly ventilated, the stench was stifling, the atmosphere rowdy, and petty crimes occurred daily. It was the second time I had spent weeks on a steamer in the company of the poorest passengers; it would not be the last. Both times I went under a cloud of depression born of failure. I had failed to achieve my goals in England as I went out the first time. Returning to England, I had failed to do the same in America. I would soon begin again, hoping it wouldn't be another calamitous false start.

This time the new beginning would take place in London, and this time I would have the companionship of the one person I loved most. In America I had written poignant and passionate letters to Muriel, and I knew she would be waiting for me. Also in America, while traveling with Geoffrey Barnes, I had given a lot of thought to the future. Now while crossing the ocean, I hoped I was putting the finishing touches on my plans. In Chicago I couldn't be sure what I wanted to do with my life, but as I walked the decks of the steamer I knew exactly what the future would hold. I had been a writer of fiction and I would be a writer again. In the notebook bought in Chicago I had jotted down outlines for stories, lists of characters and place names, notes on the structure of a story, and aphorisms to become or support the theme. In America I was a teacher and an author, and so the year wasn't entirely lost. I could build upon the American experience and benefit from it.

The ship docked in Liverpool on a Wednesday afternoon in the first week of October. Skies were gray and a light rain was falling. A hint of winter was in the air. I spent one night in Liverpool and early the next day boarded the train that would take me to London. I was certain Muriel would be waiting for me in a place we had agreed upon in our letters. It was a well-known pub and restaurant in Watling Street called the Bell and Whistle. Asking for directions, she would have no trouble finding it. When the train pulled into the station, I went to the eating-house in a cab, an extravagance I couldn't afford. Inside I scanned the faces of people dining and saw no one I recognized. Feeling faint, I went outside to breathe fresh air, then back inside. Muriel wasn't there.

"I'm looking for a young woman," I said to the barkeep. "Tall, slender, abundant dark hair to her shoulders, large eyes, pale skin, pretty face. Have you seen her?"

The portly bartender wiping a glass shook his head and sighed. "We get a lot of tall, slender, pretty ladies coming in here," he piped in a metallic voice. "But I ain't seen no specific such lady."

"She was supposed to meet me in this restaurant. We planned to have dinner here. I'm just in from Liverpool. The name is Jonathan Blue. Perhaps she left a message?"

"No, can't say she did," said the man. "Ain't seen no such lady."

In several letters I had urged Muriel to meet me in London. At first she was unsure she could leave Manchester but eventually complied. She would come to London, find a place to stay, and meet me *"with joy in my heart"* on the day of my arrival. It was already late in the afternoon and would soon be dark. I took a seat at the bar, nursed a glass of wine, and waited. At nine she had not arrived. By then I knew there would be no joyous meeting after a full year apart. I returned to Victoria Station, picked up my luggage, and found a place to spend the night. I was tired to the bone but slept fitfully. I asked myself how could it happen that on so important an occasion we could miss one another? What had gone wrong? Was she all right or was she lost and confused and sick? Then it occurred to me that perhaps she had failed to show on purpose. Quickly I dismissed the thought. She wouldn't – couldn't – betray me.

Rising early the next morning, the first thing I did was go back to the restaurant. A cook, the manager, and a waitress were there but the place was not open for business. I waited more than an hour before I could go inside. The waitress said a young woman of Muriel's description had come in just as they were closing at ten and left a message. Scrawled on wrinkled paper, it read: *"Sorry, love, things didn't go right. Come to 38 Collier Place to see me."*

"Do you know this address?" I asked.

"Can't say as I do," she replied, "but Mr. Hawley has a map."

The manager, a dapper little man with a thin mustache and an eager air to help, unfolded a large map of the city. After a few minutes he put his finger on Collier Place.

"That's near the bottom of Tottenham Court Road," he announced.

I would have to cross the river and go south a few blocks to a poor neighborhood of decaying buildings that had seen better days. Muriel had come to London as planned and had rented shabby rooms near the British Museum. My people in Harrogate knew nothing of the arrangement. With all her heart Mother wanted her wanderer to live at home. But that was something I couldn't do. I knew she would never be able to accept the girl, and I knew with equal certainty I could never reject her. Moreover, I had given up the faith of my childhood and could no longer breathe the heavy Puritan atmosphere of provincial Harrogate. London offered more freedom and more opportunity for a young bloke willing to work hard to make his way in the world.

2

In 1877 London was a city of four million people ranging in wealth from the very rich to the very poor. It had well-appointed houses in pleasant and protected neighborhoods for anyone who could afford them. It had royalty living the high life in palaces. It also had some of the worst slums in the world where thousands of working people lived in want, disease, desperation, and squalor. The slums were overcrowded, unsanitary, unsafe, and stark with human misery. Crime was a fact of life. Struggling artists with uncertain income ignored personal safety and drifted into the slums to live there on very little. A garret or bare room could be got for a pittance, and cheap eating-houses offered coarse but edible food for only a few pence. Muriel Porter had found her way into a slum district to rent two rooms. They were on the second floor of a mean but tolerable lodging house in a picturesque, vermin-infested neighborhood. We would live there as man and wife for almost a year.

As I was sailing into the port of Liverpool and getting ready to disembark, Muriel was looking for a place to live in a city she had never visited. For hours she wandered the streets not knowing where to turn. Then a kindly policeman pointed her in the right direction, and eventually she found a lodging house she thought "respectable." In the cool of an autumn afternoon, I walked up to the respectable house. The mellow sunlight clothed the old building in a soft and pleasing color. A boy and girl who should have been in school scampered in the road playing kickball. A stout woman with gray hair pulled to the back of her neck was sweeping her stoop. Her beady eyes, like black coals in a red and wrinkled face, looked me over with the suspicion of her profession before she replied to my inquiry.

"You looking for Muriel Porter, are ye? Up there," she said, pointing to the second story, "right above me own lodgings."

I entered the building and made my way to a living arrangement too small to be called a flat. Its only door opened into a narrow, half-dark hallway. I tapped lightly on the grimy, yellow-brown door, paused for a moment, and knocked harder.

A woman behind the door called out. "Who's there? Just a minute! Be with you in just a minute!"

I could hear movement and waited longer than ten minutes. Then suddenly the door opened and Muriel flung herself into my arms. I drew her close to me, and she kissed my neck and face.

"I'm so thrilled to see you, Lovey!" she cried. "Did you have a good trip all the way from America? Did you have any trouble finding my place? Did the pub people give you the note I left?"

Her clothing was a flimsy dressing gown that revealed a slight, almost skinny figure. She managed a wan smile under tousled hair that fell freely down the ivory neck to thin shoulders. Just as I remembered, her perfect teeth were even and white. I looked into her pale face, swollen from lack of sleep, and kissed her lips tenderly. Her eyes were tired but intense, her face strained but happy. Later she told me she felt a high degree of happiness the moment she saw me, but also a hammering in her head that made her want to cry.

With nervous repetition she explained she had become ill just after moving in. The next day had dragged along hour after hour, and she found herself too sick to get out of bed. As night came she had blurred vision and a terrible headache, but somehow summoned the strength to go out. She arrived at the restaurant shortly after I left and scribbled a note for me. They could see she was sick and sent her home in a cab.

For an entire year I had seen in vivid imagination a tall and fresh and pretty girl who grew more beautiful as the months passed. The woman who now led me into the stark and plain rooms that would become my home for a year was guardedly pretty in the soft autumn light but tired and worn. She was in pain she confessed when I asked about her health, suffering from migraine headaches that came without notice and robbed her of sleep. The story of her whereabouts during my first night in London was riddled with inconsistencies, but I believed every word. Loving her with the rapture of first love, I felt jubilant to have her back in my life again. I would look after her with deepest devotion, and she would be the only companion I would ever need. We would live each day as a special gift and cherish every moment of every day. It didn't matter that the rooms had battered furniture, no carpeting, an alcove for a kitchen, and dingy windows fringed with frayed curtains. We had each other now, two against the world, and that was all that mattered.

3

In the early morning in deep embrace we awoke to the clanging of a bell. I threw off the covers and jumped out of bed. Muriel sat up with only a pillow in her lap. In the rumpled bed she looked very white and clean. I peered outside and saw a bakery cart lumbering slowly down the street. Quickly I jumped into my trousers and ran downstairs to buy two gigantic rolls with little tubs of butter. When I returned, flaunting the golden rolls as a captured prize, Muriel in her dressing gown was heating water for tea. We ate the buttered bread at the little table in our sitting room, laughing and making jokes and delighting one another. The autumn sun with its special coloring was already casting a pattern on the bare floor.

"We shall find a carpet to cover the floor, something you like."

"Oh, don't you bother yourself with that, Lovey. We have to think of necessities right now. Any luxuries like carpet will have to come later, maybe when we're sixty."

We laughed at that and I leaned over and kissed her forehead.

"I feel so light and limp," she said, daintily sipping her tea. "Limp as a wet dish rag, I would say!"

I lost my habitual reserve and burst into a great bellow of laughter. "Shhuhh," she cautioned, "the landlady lives right beneath us."

"I know!" I laughed even louder. "She told me!"

All night long we had made ardent and uninhibited love. The release I felt was engaging, relaxing, expansive. Muriel's passion matched mine and placed us in a realm not quite of this world. In that one vivid phrase she expressed her feelings exactly and also mine. Then suddenly, even before we left the table, her mood changed.

"We're going to be living in sin, y' know," she said with a little whimper of protest, a troubled expression clouding her face.

I really believe she was selling her body in the streets of Manchester even when I was sending her love letters from America. But in her special way of viewing reality she reasoned that was work and therefore no sin. Now she would be living out of wedlock for the sheer pleasure of it, and the thought was mortifying.

Again I laughed, thinking she was making a joke. When I saw that she was serious, I mentioned a concept I had jotted down in the American notebook. It wasn't original. Browning had used it in more than one poem, but now it had a personal application. I leaned across the table and placed her slender hands in mine. I wanted her attention.

"Now listen to me. If an unmarried woman is really and truly in love with the man she has chosen, she is worthy of more respect than the married woman who lives with a husband she doesn't love."

It took a full minute for her to digest what I was saying. "You mean it's a sin to live in marriage with a person you despise?"

"Yes, you could put it that way."

"Then I'm here to tell you my papa and mama lived in sin! They couldn't stand each other!" Her eyes blazed and she was laughing.

She seized immediately upon the idea and made it her own. It was a good excuse for living a bohemian life until she could persuade her man to marry her. In the meantime the landlady and anyone else she came across would know all the details of how we met, fell in love, and were married in a grand ceremony at Brighton by the Sea.

Muriel quickly made friends with our landlady, giving her an elaborate but mendacious account of where and when we married and what her handsome husband did for a living. The stories she invented gave her pleasure, and she showed a certain fertility working out the details. She soon revealed a keen interest in gossip and told me all about the woman who called herself the landlady even though others owned the house. She knew all about the lodgers in their rented rooms and what the butcher said under the seal of secrecy last Thursday. I knew her stories rested on fabrication, but if she wanted it that way it was all right with me. As a writer of fiction wouldn't I be doing something similar?

Her flaws of character didn't go unnoticed, but I loved her

nonetheless and was willing to make any sacrifice to keep her in my life. She loved me as much as I loved her, I thought, and she was entertaining and funny. To earn a living I would tutor as many students as I could find and write fiction in my spare time. I wasted no time getting started. Chicago had taught me that a publisher would eventually take my work and pay me for it. At the end of October I began to put together a long novel, using special paper bought at a special price and a good pen.

November came with fog and icy rain and near the end of the month I turned twenty. In excellent health, I had plenty of energy to work from dawn to dust and beyond. In more affluent neighborhoods I put up little advertisements for pupils. Within a month I had three boys and saw them daily for two hours each. The first came at nine in the morning and the third at three in the afternoon. I allowed myself an hour between students and the last of them left at five. After supper until midnight I had time to give to my writing. On most evenings I shut myself in the bedroom, locked the door, and wrote from nine until midnight. When time came to review and revise my work, I read each word of every sentence carefully. Then I read my revision rapidly to get a notion of the whole. More than once I destroyed all I had written, calling it puerile tripe. My literary labor in London was making slow progress.

I earned a pound a week from my tutoring, and we could afford a good dinner once in a while. So on occasion we went out to eat and lingered over the table to chat, sipping the burgundy Muriel liked. Then to her alarm, because she believed it was a wild and dangerous game, I began to experiment on how cheaply I could eat without losing weight. First I resorted to vegetarianism and discovered the lentil. It was high in protein and could be made into a rich and nourishing soup. Muriel liked the taste at first, especially when boiled with onions, and for a time we made it a staple of our diet. Then I found I could buy a bucket of grease from a restaurant for less than three pence. I brought it home, heated it almost to boiling, poured it into bowls, and dipped chunks of bread in it. The bread so treated had a meaty taste and filled the stomach. But the brown grease left a metallic aftertaste. Also flavors of fish, foul, beef, and pork were not exactly harmonious. Muriel tried eating the greasy bread, liked it until it gave her a bellyache, and then pronounced it disgusting. In a pique she got rid of the grease in the water closet.

Bread and butter she liked, especially with a dollop of jam, but butter was expensive and jam was a luxury. Coals were expensive too, and the tiny fireplace throughout the winter had merely a flicker of fire carefully tended. Sometimes we went to bed before bedtime just to keep warm. On some evenings, when I wanted to work at my writing, my fingers were too stiff and cold to form the words. I wore my overcoat in a room so frigid I could see my breath. At times I caught a whiff of whiskey on Muriel's breath, but she swore it was medicinal and only a nip of vinegar. The vinegar, she said, tended to keep her warm. Maybe so.

CHAPTER TEN

Bohemians in a London Slum

The New Year – it was now 1878 – came in with a blast of cold air that rattled the windows. I finished the first volume of the long novel begun in the fall. Writing in the three-decker tradition, I had two volumes more to go. When days were dark and dreary, I went to the British Museum to work in the warmth and comfort of the Reading Room. I was thankful we lived within easy walking distance of the museum. In February, in a letter to my brother Quentin, I said I hoped to finish my first novel in little more than a month. I was young and strong and wrote swiftly with little effort though with not enough time. It pleased me to know I could fashion a believable world of my own invention populated with people worth knowing. I exulted in the creative power that came from some mysterious source within. Writing fiction with characters thrown into conflict to make a good plot helped me forget the scenes of real and sordid conflict around me.

When pushing a pen across paper and filling it with tiny words, I was able to ignore the squalor of the slums, the noise, and the stench. Muriel's nasal fugue, which irked me at times, became part of the cacophony of rooming-house life I was able to tune out. Living among poor people and closely observing their daily behavior, I believed I was in close contact with the real world. Rambling through unsafe streets to gather material from life brought me closer to the realism I wanted in my novel. At peace when writing, I had no way of knowing I was creating for myself an unreal world that in time would make the everyday world a bitter pill to swallow.

The lodging houses, overcrowded and teeming with raw humanity, I came to know well. In my neighborhood I saw entire families living in a single room at the mercy of shrewd and unforgiving landladies. The shabby rooming houses, affordable to those with small income but off limits to the destitute, crawled with vermin and reeked of alcohol, urine, and worse odors. Desperately poor and with little hope for anything better, lodging-house denizens were often drunk and disorderly. Foul language was common, and the flimsy walls didn't conceal the screams of abused women and children or the sounds of lovemaking. In the middle of the night I could hear moaning and groaning. In daylight, male voices were often cursing and complaining.

Family functions for most of these people were confused and chaotic and lacked privacy. Domestic conflict could suddenly turn violent, and sudden desertion was common. The angry breadwinner walked into the jumbled crowd and disappeared, leaving a family of guileless and gullible children to shift for themselves. At night the halls and stairs of these pestholes sheltered the homeless who were often destructive. It was dangerous to live in those surroundings, but I viewed them as grist for the creative mill. Indifferent to discomfort and often ignoring common safety, my senses grew keen as I observed the hardship around me. It was a time of exhaustive physical activity but unparalleled spiritual and mental growth. Of first importance to any writer, I was finding my subject and my voice. Even though I had published nothing since arriving in London and was often hungry with little more than a shilling in my pockets, I felt I was becoming a writer that England and the English-speaking world would soon know.

In February I was suffering stomach pain, probably from malnutrition, but took it upon myself to go to Westminster Abbey to witness the marriage of Alfred Tennyson's son. I went to the ceremony expressly to see the great poet, and I saw other grand people as well, including Princess Beatrice. Easily I recognized Herbert Spencer among the celebrants and unmistakably Tennyson himself.

"I knew him in a moment," I informed the family in Harrogate. *"He wore the same cumbersome cape-coat you see in his portraits. His son was remarkably like him."*

I didn't make a habit of seeking out famous people merely to look at them, but Tennyson and Spencer were different. I had grown up on Tennyson's verse, often recited by my father. I had read every line the poet had written and eagerly read his current publications. Even though I despised the jingoism and imperialistic sentiment often on display, I knew some of his poems by heart. I disagreed with many of the ideas expressed by "the voice of Victorianism" and yet, like thousands of middle-class readers, I revered the old man who later became a lord. The poet was a hero to a youth who loved the printed word, and so was Spencer. In 1878 I saw Herbert Spencer as *"perhaps our greatest living philosopher."* Then as prevailing opinion swung against the man, I revised my own opinion. In later years the dust would lie heavy on Spencer's unread volumes.

In May I took on another pupil in Latin. He seemed bright enough, and I gave the boy three hours a week from eight in the evening to nine. For those three hours of tutoring I received only four shillings.

"People will not pay more," I lamented in a letter to my brother Will. *"It's a shame I earn so little, but my novel progresses."*

As the summer began, with high hopes and fingers crossed I sent off the completed novel to a well-known publisher. He held it for three weeks and respectfully rejected it. I sent it to another and received a rejection, and then another. No one would buy it.

"Just what I anticipated," I said in a letter to Quentin as fall was coming. *"They held the manuscript for weeks and weeks before letting me know they didn't want it. The next book will have to be better."*

"Is there no way you can sell your present novel?" asked practical-minded William in one of many letters. He worried that his brother was working himself to death while slowly starving to death.

"I'm sure it can be," was my guarded reply. *"Someone is sure to take it sooner or later. And don't worry, Will. I'm not starving yet."*

However, to my chagrin the novel could not be sold. I had

devoted hundreds of hours to the book and had written it under the most trying of circumstances, *but it could not be sold.* It was later destroyed, its title and subject matter forgotten. I burned it one evening to save a few coals. Afterwards in regret I decided I would keep abortive work, but it didn't happen. Over the years I lost many full-length titles.

2

When the middle of September came with the promise of another severe winter, Muriel and I moved to a single room in Islington. Before we could hustle our meager belongings into the cheaper abode, the landlady laid down the law. She was a squat and square woman with yellow hair, dry skin, and a dry cough. She spoke with a cockney accent in a hoarse but voluble monotone as if from a script. We were to have no visitors except "respectable" people. We could not send out our washing or do it ourselves. Washerwomen in the basement of the building would do it at extra cost. We could have meals sent up to us on occasion but also at extra cost. We would respect the furniture and the walls and floor and damage nothing. Once a month a cleaning crew would inspect and clean the room at extra cost. The family in Harrogate was appalled when they read these rules. Muriel had heard it all before and wasn't surprised. As yet she was unknown to the family.

My brother Will was now working fifteen hours a day as a bank clerk in Manchester. He confessed that he often came home to poor lodgings so tired he went to bed without eating to sleep through the night. His intention was to rest half an hour before preparing supper. Even though his own health had troubled him for years, he worried about the health and welfare of his older brother. Will was up to date with new opinions on ventilation, and he cautioned me to open the window in cold weather a few minutes each day. He was unaware of London's blue haze that stung the nostrils as one walked in it.

"*It is very bad only having one room,*" he wrote. "*You must of course do everything possible, even in winter, to keep it fresh.*"

On reading that remark I remembered the nailed-shut windows of my stuffy classroom in Waltham, Massachusetts. Teaching there hour after hour in stale air had given me blurred vision and headache. I said to Will I would surely take his advice and open a window even though it was costly and could mean risking a cold.

"Do you consider it best to remain in London?" he asked in one of his letters. *"Perhaps a milder climate would be more to your liking."*

"I must remain in London," I answered. *"I will most definitely remain in this city as long as body and brain hold together. To make it in the literary world I must remain here and tolerate the bad weather."*

I was there not for a picnic in the park, I went on to say, but to find the work best suited to my talent. I made it clear to Will I didn't like living as a poor person any more than anyone else, but hoped to use the poverty around me to my advantage. I assured him that when I became a published author I would be able to overcome it. As I recall, I used *proletarian novel* to describe the work I had in mind.

"I shall write about my experience among the poor," I said to Will, *"and the world will see them as they are. Few middle-class people, even the leaders of this nation, really know how poor people manage to survive in London. It is my opinion they will surely pay to find out."*

Will was apprehensive. He knew I had always been ambitious, but now I seemed to be taking on more than I could chew.

"I earnestly hope you don't lose yourself in fiction and lose any ability to cope with the exigencies of the real world," he said to me in a letter showing anxious and loving concern.

"I know the difference between fantasy and reality," I curtly replied, *"and I am presently seeking a mastery of both."*

Uncertain weather had come again. Muriel was suffering from "thin blood" and complained of a chill in our room. We cleaned out the fireplace, removed all the cinders left by former tenants, and went out to buy lumps of coal. Laughing and joking, we brought the expensive coals home in a scuttle provided by the landlady. We used the black chunks of fuel sparingly but enough to keep the room comfortably warm. Then came the day we had long anticipated, November 22,

1878. The date was circled in red on our kitchen calendar, my twenty-first birthday.

I attained legal majority on that day and received my share of a trust fund left by Father. It came to five hundred pounds, not a mean sum for anyone in those days and a fortune for a struggling couple living in a single room. Even though we continued to live in much the same way as before, we now had a buffer between us and the gaping maw of poverty. I used some of the money to reimburse my mother, who had paid for my passage to America. Another sum went to Boston to pay back the loan I had received to return to England. Mrs. Craigenstock answered with warm thanks and sad news. She had read in a newspaper that Geoffrey Barnes was killed by a train while crossing the tracks in his wagon. His horse was also killed, and his photographic equipment destroyed. The good woman knew he had been my employer whom I respected as a good man. His unlikely and untimely death saddened me for days.

I tried to keep the remainder of my inheritance in escrow to accrue a small interest, but slowly it dwindled. Its main effect for about a year was to make us feel better about ourselves when our poverty became heavy and biting. We could say we were not as poor as the day laborers who stood shivering on windy street corners in semi-darkness waiting for work each morning. Some of them got up before daybreak to be foremost in the throng, hoping to increase their chance of being chosen. A man on a cart would point to the men he wanted, and they would move away from the others. Those who were not chosen endured another day of hunger, worry, boredom, and empty pockets. Strong, proud, and active men were being reduced by the times to idleness and lethargy and loss of hope. The tragedy of their lives was no work to fill the day. They had children to feed and hard muscles to use. They wanted to work but were too often idle. With large families they lived in a single room like animals in a den and had little hope for anything better. I was living also in a single room but with only one person. Unlike the workingmen with no jobs, I had two that consumed all my time. I had as well some high expectations and money that was soon gone.

3

The New Year – 1879 – came with the wintry weather I was beginning to dread. I wanted to walk, but the air was cold and the streets wet and slushy. I left our room to buy a book now and then and to frequent the warm shops that Muriel liked. In a second-hand bookstore I met a young German intellectual named Günter Kurtz. He was four years older than I but looked younger. His close-cropped hair was blonde, his eyes blue and set wide apart, and his body stocky. His eyebrows above a fleshy nose were light brown, almost blonde, and he wore a beard that obscured his mouth and lips. Of average height and weight, his shoulders sloped noticeably from a strong neck. He was soft spoken and reticent in manner and clearly interested in books.

His English was so fluent he spoke almost without an accent. Within minutes I could tell that my new friend was studious, awkward, poor, lonely in a country not his own, and in love with literature. The man had a real feeling for good literature and hungered to share his passion with others. He could throw himself into rare sympathy with a writer, see the best in him, and talk about the best with fluency and understanding. As for practical affairs, he was even more inept than I was at fourteen or fifteen. Quickly we formed a friendship that lasted many years. If posterity by some fluke should remember me, so will it remember him.

Günter Kurtz was the first of my friends to meet Muriel. Dylan Crenshaw had seen her photograph in Manchester but didn't become acquainted with her until later. I had put off introducing Muriel to Crenshaw but thought Kurtz would be able to accept her on equal terms. So before we went off to a lecture together Kurtz had tea in our room and chatted amicably with us. When we returned in the cold of a January evening, Muriel immediately took a liking to my friend and insisted that he stay for supper. Our table built for two was really too small for three people, but somehow we managed.

The supper was a thick soup of lentils, chickpeas, potatoes, and bits of ham scraped from bones given by the local butcher. It was easy to put three bowls and three teacups on the unsteady table, but Muriel cautioned with her throaty laugh that elbows could topple it. We brought the table close to the fire and huddled around it. She was anxious to make herself pleasant. I had only a few friends, and she wanted this quiet-spoken, fair-minded, bookish German to be my friend. In a general way she distrusted all foreigners, but Kurtz was different and she liked him. Maybe it was because he was unassuming and very poor. She put the soup on the table and sat down but couldn't think of anything to say. Then as we began to eat she remembered the bread.

"Oh, the bread!" she exclaimed with the odd little laugh that showed her white teeth. "We can't eat soup with no bread. Heavens!"

"It's superb soup," Kurtz assured her. "It's so good we don't need anything at all to go with it. Save the bread for another day."

I nodded a signal and Muriel went to a small armoire where she kept a tidy supply of groceries. Her thin hands quickly found a thick, brown loaf and she brought it to the table.

"You must have bread with your soup, my friend," I insisted.

"Of course you must have bread!" echoed Muriel. "Soup's no good without bread. It must have bread to stick to your ribs."

All day Kurtz had eaten very little and was quite hungry. But the young German knew his friends were as poor as himself and didn't want to impose upon us. I liked the sensitivity shown by the man's refusal, but cut him a very large slice. We ate the bread and soup and talked. Interjecting clever witticisms whenever we could, we discussed the lecture we had heard. Muriel was bored with talk she couldn't understand but tried not to show it. Kurtz slipped into a vein of nostalgia. He loved his native land and regretted his exile from Bismarck's Germany but found it impossible to return. Then he began to talk of future plans.

"Have you heard about what Thomas Hughes is doing in America?" he asked. "It's a utopian experiment in the hills of Tennessee. He's building a farm community there on the money he got from *Tom Brown's School Days* and other books. He's calling the place Rugby, Tennessee and expects it to thrive in three years. The soil, I'm told, isn't very good, but they expect to grow tomatoes and vegetables and sell them."

"Well, naming the place Rugby is fitting," I laughed, "and ironic too.

If not for Rugby School he couldn't have written the book, and if not for the book he couldn't be sponsoring social experiments."

"I know," replied Kurtz, sharing my laughter. "But to be serious for a moment, I'm thinking about going there. They want young, disenfranchised men like me to come and grow tomatoes and build houses and study in the library, and perhaps meet and marry a pretty girl and raise a large family. I'm told Hughes is bringing together a fine library to be used by all the community in their leisure time."

"When would you go?" I asked with hesitation.

"Well, I plan to teach in a girl's school to raise the money for the trip. I will go perhaps in a year or two, maybe in the spring of '81. I think maybe I could do some good there."

"I won't try to dissuade you, my friend, but I know from firsthand experience that America is *not* the Promised Land. I spent a year there and nearly starved. I really believe your poet Goethe was on target when he said, *Hier oder nirgends ist Amerika.*"

"Said what?" interrupted Muriel, who didn't understand German. "Now, Lovey, I don't want you speaking gibberish I don't understand."

"America is here or nowhere is a rough translation," I replied.

"Maybe a better rendering," added Kurtz, "would be '*America is here in your own back yard or nowhere.*' As you know, the poet is emphasizing one's own little place as the land of milk and honey. Not an original idea. Voltaire and others used it before him."

Idealistic and hopeful, Kurtz would travel to utopian Rugby in the summer of 1881. He didn't know the colony would suffer a typhoid epidemic in that year and wrestle with legal problems. Two years later he would return to London crestfallen and confused. The Tennessee experiment didn't work out as planned. Although the town gained as many as 400 residents, by 1887 most had died or moved away. By 1890 Rugby was crumbling into ruin. All that remained years later was the library, the name, and a few diehard residents with vague memories.

CHAPTER ELEVEN

First Novel Self Published

Winter passed and slowly gave way to spring, and spring eased into summer. In peak condition during the warm months, I tutored every day and worked in my spare time on another novel. I thought I might lecture for a small allowance, but the workingmen who would be my audience couldn't pay for what I had to say. Reluctantly I had to abandon the project. Muriel was beginning to feel neglected but tried to support my dream of becoming a writer as best she could. She was often warm and encouraging one day but cold and moody the next. Already I was beginning to see a hint of instability in my life's companion but thought little of it. More than once she hinted we couldn't go on year after year unmarried and living in sin. Wherever we happened to be she assumed other women viewed her as the loving wife of the good-looking young man walking beside her. She wanted to make the imaginary tableau real, and it was never out of her mind.

"I just know that couple looking at us believe we're married. They see us as happy people leading a prosperous life. Oh, if they only knew!"

"How could they know anything about us?" I pointedly asked. "And why would they want to know? They are strangers, Muriel, and they have no interest in us whatsoever."

"Oh, that is just your opinion!" she would reply, pouting.

In August in fine weather we fell into the habit of taking long walks to explore parts of the city we had never seen. In a festive mood we visited fashionable neighborhoods such as Richmond, Twickenham, Strawberry Hill, and Kingston. In some places we paused to watch street artists at work, and we admired the gardens with gorgeous flowers and exotic plants. We stood in front of grand houses and asserted we would live there one day. We thought we might take a steamer on a weekend to Ipswich or Yarmouth, but then we discovered the cost was far too expensive. In a few years, I promised, we would do that and more. Established writers, I told her, live well.

I gave as much time to Muriel and leisure activity as I could while continuing to make progress on the novel. Before the middle of August I had finished more than twenty chapters and was trying to decide the fate of a villainous character.

"Don't you worry," I assured Muriel after summarizing the action of the story, "Wildethorn will come to a bad end. He's a diabolical scoundrel and deserves what's coming!"

"I'm eager to read your story when it's done," she said with that odd little laugh. "I can't wait to read the unhappy ending even though I like happy endings better. I sure hope it's going to be a big success, Lovey, and will bring us some money."

"I expect to finish in three weeks or a month. I'm fairly certain the manuscript will go to a publisher sometime in September."

"And then we marry in October and celebrate in a fancy restaurant!" she exclaimed. "I'll wear a white satin dress and a new hat and a veil! And we'll have the best chops in the house! Maybe we can leave London for a few days and go to the seaside if the weather is warm and sunny. You won't forget now, will you, Lovey?"

From the time we became a couple in Manchester until she faded from my life, Muriel had called me Lovey. Not once as far as I can remember did she call me by name. I never knew why but didn't inquire. I assured her the marriage would take place on what I hoped would be a fine autumn day to complement our happiness. The weeks went by rapidly, and we found ourselves in the middle of October. I wanted the wedding to be simple and spontaneous, perhaps coming as a sudden surprise in the afternoon. Muriel insisted on knowing the exact time and date. Simple or not, our wedding would need planning.

An ancient civil servant married us on Monday, October 27, 1879.

Muriel Marie Porter of Manchester, now twenty, became the lawful wife of Jonathan Thomas Blue, almost twenty-two. Günter Kurtz, our German friend, was the only witness. The bride was radiant in a satin dress of white with lavender trim, and the groom wore a black suit with a white tie and a pleated white shirt. The weather was not good. The skies were gray with dark clouds and a chill was in the air. That meant no honeymoon in another city. Instead the three of us had a small celebration in a modest restaurant. The family in Harrogate knew nothing of the marriage and would learn nothing until I summoned the nerve to tell them many months later. We were living at 44 James Street in a single room at the end of a roach-infested hallway. To that room, after our celebration and after saying goodbye to Kurtz, we returned. I unlocked the door, lifted my bride into my arms, and carried her gallantly across the threshold. She was light as a feather and giggling.

The room was chilly and smelled of powder and perfume. The scent had lingered from earlier in the day when Muriel made herself beautiful for her wedding ceremony. With haste but carefully, we removed our wedding clothes and tumbled into bed. A candle beside the bed flickered far into the night and burned out. When morning came we awoke and made love again. The autumn sun filtered through the dusty window and made the room golden. On the street below a vendor was setting up shop. All was right with the world at that moment, and we were happy. Before noon we returned our wedding clothes to the rental shop. We agreed it was prudent to rent garments to be worn only once.

2

Through the month of October to the time of our marriage, I struggled to put all the pieces of my novel in place. After the ceremony in the glow of gentle support from Muriel, I crafted the rough draft into a manuscript of 450 pages containing forty-six chapters. I was certain the book would be cast into three volumes and become expensive to print. Because of the expense, publishers might hesitate to take on the project from an unknown author. I was calling the novel *A Faraway Place* but changed the title before publication to *Workers at Sunrise*. I read the narrative aloud to Kurtz, taking four days to do it. My German friend listened as one entranced and was enthusiastic about all he heard.

"Impossible not to find a publisher!" he cried. "It will be the book of the season! I forecast a change of fortune for you, my friend. Good fortune for you and your lovely wife from now on!"

Chatto & Windrum returned the manuscript with a polite letter regretting they couldn't fit it into their requirements. Even though Muriel and Kurtz were hurt by disappointment, I was calm and stoical.

"I'm not surprised," I assured them with a grim smile. "It's really what I expected. If they had accepted the manuscript, it would have been a piece of extraordinary good luck. That's a rarity among unknown authors and a rarity for me as a person. I have never been a friend of fortune. Most luck that comes my way is bad luck."

"Oh don't say that, Jonathan. Remember to keep a stiff upper lip, as you British say. A little optimism goes a long way, you must surely know, and good luck can fall to anyone!"

"I'm not a lucky person, Kurtz. Hap and Circumstance and fickle Fate are not exactly in league with Jonathan Blue. In my dry and dusty domain, I know from experience, good luck invariably surrenders to bad."

"Unhappy thoughts make for unhappy people," said Muriel to console me. "I read that somewhere and believe it."

'Yes, I agree!' asserted Kurtz. 'Tell him that again!'

She repeated her remark laughing, and Kurtz laughed with her. Then he offered advice. "View this thing, my friend, as just a temporary setback, a little bad luck perhaps that could change instantly."

I couldn't resist repeating a witticism I had hidden somewhere in the many pages of my novel. "If I didn't have bad luck," I said with a frozen smile, "I would have no luck at all."

They laughed and Muriel filed the remark away in memory. She had never heard it before and thought it clever.

Without delay I sent the manuscript off to Smith & Richards. They sat on it for weeks before returning it with a polite but critical letter of rejection. "*It possesses a great deal of graphic power and some humour, but it is deficient in dramatic interest. As a series of scenes the book is good. As a tale it fails to meet the requirements of the reader of fiction.*"

I shook my head in amazement. How could anyone calling himself a critic spew such nonsense? I wanted to tell them I didn't write the book for that enigmatic creature, *the reader of fiction*. All the time I was writing I never expected to please that worthy abstraction, and so the publisher's asinine comment I found unacceptable. The book was deficient in dramatic interest only because it avoided the sensational plots of Victorian fiction and depicted real life. I hoped my book would be read by thinking people who would discuss it among themselves and be driven perhaps to correct some of the social abuses seen in it. If it fell into the hands of movers and shakers, that could happen.

By now the manuscript was worn and wrinkled, but off it went to a third publisher. Stone & Haverhill returned it in less than two weeks with an equally foolish criticism. "*The book is very ably written, according to our reader, but we are sorry to say he does not recommend it to us on account of its rationalistic tendency. We do not believe in fiction being the proper vehicle for conveying doctrinal opinions.*"

I was truly amazed at that. I wanted to tell them the novel's narrator preached no doctrine whatever, but possibly the characters and the way they lived their lives hinted at doctrine. I didn't bother.

"And yet the narrator does interject opinion," said Kurtz quietly one evening as we talked. "Maybe that's what they mean."

"Perhaps," I replied. "But you understand it's a novel detailing social problems that cry out for solutions. The principal characters are earnest young people striving without success to improve a sour society in the dawn of a new phase of our civilization."

"It seems they are shaping a doctrine as they try to realize their aims, but of course that's not the same as preaching. And fiction can no longer convey opinion? What garbage!"

"The doctrinal content is reflected in the title. Maybe their reader didn't get beyond the title. Anyway, I'm fond of *Workers at Sunrise*. I believe when the book is published it will attract attention."

"I like the title," Kurtz replied, "and you know I like the book. Publishers can be unpredictable and ignorant too. And we know the reading public can be fickle. But optimism, old fellow, optimism."

"Yes," I retorted, "that stiff upper lip you mentioned has to be worn all the time in this business, and one must have a heart of oak."

"Oh, absolutely! Did you English invent the phrase, or does it belong to the Americans? No bother. It fits you, my friend!"

In the early months of 1880 I sent the manuscript, now becoming dog-eared because many had handled it, to several publishers in London. All rejected it for one reason or another that was never quite clear. When I asked for clarification, I got no response. Redfield & Hall acknowledged receiving the manuscript and promised to give it *"early and careful consideration."* They returned it a month later without explaining why. That led me to think of publishing the book at my own expense. In March I signed an agreement with Remington House and paid them all that remained of my inheritance, about 150 pounds, in three installments. They agreed to print 277 copies of my first book in a three-volume set. The price would be one guinea, fairly expensive for the time. I was three months beyond twenty-two, and told myself I had done the right thing. My novel would be *live* on the shelves of bookstores, according to the publisher, sometime in May. The year was 1880.

3

As the date of publication approached, I couldn't resist talking about the book. Muriel listened politely most of the time but ignored me when I went on and on. Sometimes she interrupted me in mid-sentence and hooted with that quirky laugh of hers when I showed annoyance. I was certain the book had some good ideas worth thinking about, even worth implementing in the real world. Its structure could have been tighter, but its style reflected the forceful discourse of a mature man of experience. The book was well written and readable, I thought, but others would have to reach that conclusion.

"Ordinary readers will get little from it," I said to Muriel, thinking out loud. "The book's desperate seriousness will surely depress them. But people of intellect might appreciate the ideas woven through the text, and so I'm hoping for some notice."

"I liked some parts of it," she assured me, "but then we both know I'm not your ordinary reader."

That brought a smile to my face. Often her off-hand remarks made me realize I was too serious, too earnest for my own good. I hoped I had a sense of humor to equal hers, and I wanted to take each day lightly, but I had to think of the future and making a living.

"If I'm ignored, I shall think seriously of taking a job as a clerk. Just recently I read in *The Times* of an opening in a hospital. I might be able to get something like that."

"Your family would be horrified!" she exclaimed with that odd little laugh punctuating her remarks. She knew about middle-class prejudice and how clerking in a store or even an office was viewed as a job beneath one's station. She was trying to make light of the situation.

"I'm not exactly the shining hero of my family," I replied, "and I don't live with them any more. So it wouldn't matter."

"You will have to do something soon, Lovey. Our buffer against poverty was spent on the book. We don't have anything to fall back on now. I guess you can see I'm a little scared."

I had placed us both in a precarious situation and knew it. So immediately I began a regimen of hard work on a new novel. My German friend, intellectual and eager to help, gladly read the first volume.

"It's even better than *Workers*!" he exclaimed. "It's a tighter story. It catches the reader's attention and holds it firmly! It moves the reader along on a current of kinetic energy!"

"You sound like an engineer!" I laughed. "Let's not run headlong over a cliff, old boy. I know you want to encourage me, but kinetic energy?"

He responded with a shrug and a laugh, "Well, I like to tell myself I'm not entirely ignorant of science and physics!"

I moved easily into the second volume and expected to finish the third in record time. But then tragedy struck. At Easter time as 1880 moved into spring, my brother William died suddenly of tuberculosis at the age of twenty. It was a terrible blow to the entire family and especially to me. I had explained the Thatcher College debacle to Will in many serious letters, reaching a special understanding with him. Then suddenly my brother, my best friend and confidant, was gone. His untimely death left us all in a state of calamitous shock.

Leaving Muriel in London, I went alone to Harrogate. I was there three days and tried to console all members of the family. But the loss of my brother was even more cutting than the loss of my father a decade earlier. The sorrow I felt was intense and genuine. I knew the others suffered too, but the death of my beloved brother brought on a grief so profound I couldn't shake it. Will was only twenty and innocent and believed in God. Quentin and I had drifted away from the old religion, but not Will. How could a loving God allow him to die so young? I believe it was then I truly began to deny the existence of God or any kind of god. I had called myself an agnostic but in shock became an atheist.

I remembered the jolly times Will and I had shared in boyhood. I thought of all the letters we had written to instruct each other, some of them pompous and filled with sage advice but many plainly amusing. It pained me to think we would never talk again, never reveal our inmost thoughts to each other, and never complain of the present as we looked forward to the future. On the third day I returned to London and to the manuscript in progress but could make no progress. Day after day, to Muriel's dismay, I did nothing but mope and stare at a blank sheet of paper. The delicate machinery that created fiction seemed broken.

Workers at Sunrise, rejected by a dozen publishers, was published at my own expense in June. Even though it was given a fairly long review by the *Athenaeum*, few people took any notice of the book. Expensive and by an unknown author, affluent readers thought twice before buying it. Also, because of the unsavory subject matter (the lower classes of London presented with unrelenting realism), no lending library would buy it. At the end of summer only twenty-nine copies had been sold. In Harrogate, Quentin attempted to sell a few copies to friends and neighbors but with little success. He explained it was not a book for the faint of heart and expensive. I sent a few copies to prominent people in London, including Lionel Chandler, a well-known writer though not of the first rank. He had won notoriety when he raised the hackles of Matthew Arnold with a shallow definition of culture. He seemed to know everyone of importance and had many friends in powerful places.

Chandler received the book one afternoon in July and stayed up past his bedtime to read it. The realistic account of life in the slums incited enthusiasm, and the next day he dashed off a letter to the author:

"Whether prostitutes, thieves, and debauchees talk as you make them talk in the night houses of the Haymarket, I do not know nor wish to know. But there can be no doubt as to the power of your book. It will rank amongst the best of these years. My wife tells me there is enough stuff in the book to make six novels."

It was a long and rambling letter brimming with Victorian prudery but also high praise. I rejoiced on reading it and quickly sent off a copy to my sisters. When Chandler returned to London in August, he invited me to dine with him. Later he introduced me to people who could help me get a foothold in the publishing world. It seemed the tide had turned for Jonathan Blue, and the grinding poverty I had lived with while writing the book would soon fall behind me. However, I felt awkward in the presence of influential men who lived in fine houses, and I soon cut sociable ties with them. Also as the year wore on, my marriage seemed to be in trouble, and that alarmed me.

CHAPTER TWELVE

Muriel in Storm

The summer of 1880 was hot and humid. I mourned the death of Will but pushed myself to write every day. My tutoring was taking up a lot of my time, and sometimes I envied the privileged boys who came to me with light hearts and no worries. They were happy and bursting with energy, and I did all I could to make them believe I was happy too. They consumed too much of my time, valuable time I needed for writing. But they were my bread and butter and my only source of income. So I gave my best to them, winning their admiration. In the evenings when Muriel wanted me to stroll the streets with her and visit the shops, I was trying to write. I could tell she was becoming more distant, but there was little I could do about it. When I could stand on top of the mountain I was climbing, I told her, our life together would certainly improve. In the meantime she would have to be patient.

Even though difficulty at every turn threatened to overwhelm me, I took Kurtz's advice and was cautiously optimistic. I would do my work as a writer even if I had to take a job as a clerk or laborer to earn money for a living. I believed heredity had given me a talent that had to be cultivated and used. My brother Quentin, of the same heredity, was dreaming of literary endeavor too and would become a writer. The entire family valued books, and for me creating a book was in my blood. My father, clinging to a shaky faith as he pursued intellectual interests, had loved literature as well as science and had published a small scientific volume. Now the son hoped to perpetuate his father's name by publishing not one important book but many.

In my early teens when I went off to school, I was slowly rejecting the religious beliefs of my family. The vigorous rationalism of the books I was reading was in conflict with intuitive religion, calling into question even crucial doctrines. Did an all-loving God truly exist? And was there life everlasting? And the Bible, was it really the word of God? I doubted religious doctrine and shortly after Will died, doubt became unbelief. If I could no longer pay allegiance to a Puritanical religion, what might take its place? Years went by before I found a substitute.

In London, searching to fill the void, I replaced the old religion with the Positivism of Auguste Comte. For a time I was a devout disciple, even dating my letters according to the Positivist calendar. Though I later discarded this "religion of humanity" with its focus on the individual as savior, it governed my thinking and behavior during those early years of struggle. I was trying to find a system of thought to replace the lost religion of my childhood, but had found only ephemera based on scientific principles. In time, discarding Positivism, I lost all faith in religion of any kind but kept unimpaired the morality that was part and parcel of organized religion.

In a pompous letter to Quentin, sent shortly after the death of Will, I spoke of the brevity of life and echoed some of Comte's ideas. *"I must sternly face the fact that only a short time may remain for me to develop what intellect I have. The day cometh when no man can work, and I must keep that injunction ever before me. Do I show myself an ignorant and foolish man? Or do I show myself as one bent upon using my faculties to the utmost? I prefer, of course, the latter."* Keenly aware of the value of sustained hard work, I believed myself liberated from Puritanism and ready to win the approval of powerful middle-class liberals.

The long hours I gave to my teaching and writing, the poverty that pressed upon us, and a future that seemed uncertain gradually began to wear on Muriel. As the days went by she found herself alone and fighting boredom. On some days she went to several markets to buy the cheapest food she could find, carry it home to cook, and wait for her husband to join her. On other days we had no money for food, and she could feel a gnawing hunger that made her quick of temper. A dram of whiskey or even a little vinegar mixed with water calmed her belly and made her feel better. This weakness for alcohol had ruined her life once before and now threatened to do it again.

A weekly paycheck earned by a working husband might have helped her avoid temptation. A daughter of the working class and knowing only that way of life, she was not able to understand how a man could labor at anything and not be paid. Only my tutoring brought us just enough to live on, and she believed I gave less time to that than to my writing. Before long she convinced herself that I cared more about winning recognition than retaining her love. That state of mind led to thoughts that brought on destructive behavior. Immersed in my own defiant struggle, I failed to notice the subtle changes taking place in the girl I had married. I didn't see the negative changes until it was too late.

2

The first anniversary of our marriage came on fast. We planned a small celebration in a good restaurant. I remembered how Muriel had enjoyed our first dinner together, and I hoped we might recall and relive the fun we had. We would go to the same restaurant and be served perhaps by the same waiter. I hoped her dark eyes would sparkle again with delight, but she was becoming unpredictable in her behavior and told me plainly she was not inclined to go anywhere with me. She was no longer the loving girl who saw me as her savior. She was often sick and in pain, complaining of everything in her life and causing trouble. Every day her body grew thinner. When we could afford a good dinner, she had no appetite. Her milky complexion soon became pallid and pimply. The large, intense eyes had a doleful look as if a loved one had died. The abundant hair she had long prized went unwashed and scraggly, falling uncombed to her shoulders. The life around her continued to be part of her life but to a lesser degree. In time except for the landlady whom she liked, she fought with the lodgers and made friends elsewhere. On the day of our anniversary she was away from our rooms visiting a friend.

Two weeks later, after a long day of work and study in the Reading

Room of the British Museum, I returned home to find my wife drunk and disorderly. She had scattered my personal papers all over the bare floor. In frenzy she had seized priceless sheets of manuscript and ripped them to shreds. A hundred torn pages created by countless hours of labor cluttered the floor. Some of my favorite books lay utterly destroyed, their pages ripped out and their bindings broken.

"What in the world is going on?" I asked in amazement.

Her clothing rumpled and soiled, she was slumped in a chair staring at nothing. "Jus' what you see!" she hissed, becoming animated and combative. "Life ain't worth living no more, especially with a bloke like you! I have no life with you and you know it! All you ever do is stick your nose in them rotten old books and scribble stuff. You call it work but what does it bring us? Nothing! Nothing!"

"I hope to do better, but teaching and writing take up time."

"You pushed me out of your life, and you know it! You were gonna take me to that little French restaurant and treat me to a good dinner on our anniversary, and what happened? Not a goddamn thing!"

"Don't you remember, Muriel? You refused to go. You were not even home on that day, and there was nothing I could do."

"My friend Susan was sick but you wouldn't believe me. You think I'm a liar. You never listen to anything I say and you think I'm a liar."

I was staring at the mess she had made, hoping I could salvage some of it, and said nothing. She continued her tirade, spitting out vulgar words and sobbing as they hit their mark.

"You went off to a fancy dinner not long ago and left me here alone with only stale bread and moldy cheese to eat! Then you had the gall to tell me all about the fine gentlemen you dined with, and the wine you drank, and the fancy food you ate!"

"Those were people trying to help me, Muriel."

"Trying to help you? What about me? No one is trying to help me!"

"I know you're miserable, but things will improve if you give me time. That's all I'm asking for, just time to get a foothold."

"Hah! Fat chance that will happen! I can't give you time! I'm all out of time! I can't give you anything! Even if I could you wouldn't want it."

She was sobbing uncontrollably now and screeching profanities. My attempt to comfort her and avoid a scene had not worked. I worried that the neighbors would hear the noise and fabricate juicy gossip. But as soon as she began to scream she fell from the chair and collapsed in a heap on the floor. Seeing her like that alarmed me.

"Here, let me help you get out of that dirty dress and into bed."

I got no response from her, and she didn't resist when I removed the dress she had worn for several days. It now had yellow vomit on it and smelled of urine. I balled it up and tossed it into the food hamper. Then I scooped her off the floor and carried her unresisting to bed.

She had made friends with our current landlady, and that worthy person had sold her a bottle of whiskey. Some of the money she was given to buy food went for alcohol, and imperceptibly she was backsliding into drunkenness. She had managed a fragile sobriety from the time we began to live together, but she was now becoming alcoholic and sick. Once more I made up my mind to save her, but in the meantime I would have to work at what I knew best. I was tutoring in the homes of my pupils now, and that meant seeing her less and less. Without close supervision she could sink into irretrievable alcoholism, and I knew I wouldn't have the money to seek professional help. Should I lose just one of my pupils, it could mean a return to lentil soup for supper instead of meat and potatoes. I needed a steady job but worried about qualification.

"*I ought to be exerting myself very seriously to find some fixed kind of occupation,*" I said to Quentin in one of my letters. "*I fear I must give up hopes of the book bringing anything in, and my position is getting troublesome. But what kind of work am I fit for? They won't take me in a business office. I know nothing of such things. The outlook is gloomy.*"

I was convinced that a second book would go far to get my name recognized, but now with the manuscript pages destroyed I would have to start all over again. I would choose a subject close to me and write about what I knew. Inevitably for dramatic impact I would draw upon my troubles with Muriel. I felt I had struck out a path for myself in fiction that was fresh and different. I called it "utmost realism," nothing like the syrupy pap of most Victorian novels. In a letter to my brother towards the end of 1880 I explained what I had attempted to do in my first novel and what I would do in the second. *"I mean to bring home to thinking people the ghastly condition (material, mental, and moral) of our poor classes. I mean to show the hideous injustice of our whole system of society, and to offer a plan of altering it. Above all, I intend to preach an enthusiasm for high ideals in this age of unmitigated egotism and shop."*

I knew exactly what I wanted to do, what I felt I had to do, but the world was indifferent and my personal life brutal. With a drunken wife to care for, I had to curtail my writing and research in the British Museum and stay home. I managed to see a few pupils in their homes, but had to let some go. That meant less income, no luxuries whatever, and coarser food. To do any writing at all, I had to shut the door that separated the two rooms we lived in and lock it. I hoped to write for two or three hours but had to check on Muriel. Sometimes I found her gone.

3

In the jaws of winter, Muriel spent most of her time at home. With the coming of spring she found her way into the streets and pubs again. Early in April a faltering sun struggled through dark clouds to bring warmth. Dylan Crenshaw was back in town and eager to talk about his latest adventure. Without hesitation he made arrangements to spend an evening with his oldest friend. He walked from the station to visit us in Lambeth and knocked loudly on our door. A moment later he knocked again with less energy.

"Just a moment," I called. "One minute, please."

A female voice of high pitch was whimpering and quarreling, and I knew he could hear movement inside. After a few minutes I threw the latch and flung open the door.

"Come in, old man, come in!" I cried, vigorously shaking my friend's hand. "So good to see you! Let me take your coat."

We had not seen each other in more than a year, and the world traveler – "a soldier of fortune" he was now calling himself – was as robust as ever and had much to talk about.

"I brought along some wine," he said, placing the bottle in my hands. "It's not the best in the world, to be sure, but potable I dare say."

I selected two glasses from a little cupboard and brought them to the fire where Crenshaw had found a chair. We held the glasses, red with thick wine, to the firelight and made a toast. The ritual went all the way back to our college years.

"To health and good living!" said my friend, raising his glass and pronouncing the toast. His voice was loud and strong.

"To health and good living!" I intoned with less exuberance.

From the bedroom came another voice, complaining but incoherent. I had made Muriel comfortable and was hoping she had fallen asleep. Crenshaw's exuberant toast had awakened her just as she was drifting off. She was now complaining of too much noise.

"I'm awfully sorry," I muttered, visibly agitated. "My wife is sick and a little drunk. I was putting her to bed just as you were knocking. Please excuse me while I look in on her."

I knew he could hear voices crisp with anger behind the closed door. Then of a sudden he must have heard a loud thump on the wooden floor. Muriel in a drunken stupor had fallen out of bed, and I was struggling to put her back and calm her down. I returned to my friend seeking composure but with a stricken face. We sat before the fire and drank our wine and talked. Crenshaw had much to say of his travels, and I confessed with some reluctance that living with Muriel was becoming problematic. He had known her from the time we were students at Thatcher College in Manchester, and he had reservations about her even then. So anything I revealed now was no surprise.

"Just last week," I hesitantly said, "she had a seizure in a chemist's shop and had to be carried home through the streets. She attracted the attention of the police who brought her here. You can imagine my chagrin when they showed up at my door."

"From the little I know," replied Crenshaw thoughtfully, "she seems to be losing control. Could you plead poverty and commit her to an institution? That way she might be able to get the care she needs."

"It's a good suggestion, old man, but she would never go willingly.

She likes this place. The landlady is coarse, arrogant, grasping, greedy, and manipulative, but Muriel likes her."

"Of all the places in the world to live, she likes living here? And she likes the landlady of this magnificent edifice?"

"She tells me she enjoys the woman's spicy conversation, her strong independence and bawdy gossip. She likes the way the landlady lives her life in a difficult world. The woman grates on my nerves and I try to avoid her whenever I can, but Muriel has taken a liking to her."

"Sounds as though she's found a friend, someone in common."

"That's the word for it all right, *common*. I'm afraid it very aptly describes her. She's sick too. Even if I could afford hospital care, and I'm convinced she needs it, she wouldn't leave this place willingly. I would have to force her to leave and cause a scene."

Muriel suffered from rheumatism, an eye condition, neuralgia, poor nutrition, and convulsions. She was suffering too from feelings of inferiority, class conflict, and neglect. To escape the pain that plagued her, both mental and physical, she drank heavily. She had begun with nips of vinegar as a child. It wasn't long before she was gulping gin and whatever she could get her hands on. Shortly after we met she told me she had become an alcoholic at fifteen or sixteen. Under my guidance she gained some control but was now drinking again. I tried to help her, tried to keep a close eye on her, but she spiraled downward.

She was drawn to the gin joints where denizens of vice and low life gathered. Deaf to her husband's protests, she walked into the night to find people of her own kind. Once docile and compliant, she was now combative and loaded with venom. In new lodgings she went out of her way to make friends with the landlady, but often they were soon quarreling and almost coming to blows. She tried to become the friend of other lodgers, people her husband ignored, but routinely she fought with them. Those scenes of unbridled anger on the edge of violence increased as time went on and left me shaken. They caused us to move from one shabby lodging house to another. Always packing and unpacking, our lives were constantly in disorder and turmoil.

Towards the end of July in 1881, shortly after Günter Kurtz left for America to become a farmer in Tennessee, we moved to 15 Gower Place. It was the same slum neighborhood we had lived in earlier, but in quarters with a bedroom, sitting room, and kitchen. The income from tutoring and from articles I had written for a Russian journal was enough to keep food on the table but little else. Yet we managed to keep a bird in a cage and a lovable old cat we named Grimm. In letters to my sisters I tried to sound a note of mellow domesticity – *"Old Grimm waxes fat and sleeps much on the hearth rug"* – but to my brother I complained of circumstances that often interrupted my work. We had found no way to escape the poverty that plagued us. Muriel was increasingly dissatisfied with me in her life and causing me pain. Her behavior was unpredictable and stormy. She was also sick and needing expensive medical treatment I couldn't afford. That too caused pain.

CHAPTER THIRTEEN

Muriel Consumed

In a letter to my sister Emma near the end of 1881, using a figure of speech I thought she would like, I spoke of the struggle for existence in London: *"This survival thing is very much like holding yourself up after a shipwreck. If you come in contact with another poor wretch, it's to fight and struggle for a piece of floating wood."* I went on to say that for people who don't have to worry about tomorrow's dinner, life in London could be pleasant and rewarding. *"Otherwise it's a cruel sort of business."* London for me had become a Darwinian jungle where only the fittest survive. I knew myself to be a survivor but worried about Muriel. She had always been tough and resilient, but now she was yielding to temptation and rapidly losing every good quality she ever had.

The faultless rooms in Gower Place turned out to be unsanitary. Out of sight in the moldy walls and feeding on the filth left behind by generations of lodgers, vermin were breeding and posed a health hazard. So once again we pulled up stakes and moved from comfortable rooms into something less comfortable. In March of 1882 I decided to live closer to my pupils, ten in all, so that I could be with them in their homes from nine in the morning until six at night. After six I trudged homeward to a dinner of bread, soup, and cheese and later worked on my writing until midnight. Except for the walking (which I rightly saw as good exercise) and for Muriel left alone, the arrangement was a good one. My wife's fondness for alcohol and her behavior becoming more unpredictable by the day made it too risky to have students come to me.

One rainy afternoon I returned earlier than usual and found her sitting on the bare floor, her long legs fully exposed, weeping. Her hair fell over her face to the floor, and I pulled it aside. She was bleary-eyed and sallow, shivering, and ranting.

"I have no life and no love," she sobbed. "I'm lonely and sick and angry all the time. No one cares to talk to me any more, not even the landlady, and least of all you! It hurts to be alone! It kills!"

I looked at her with astonishment, as though I had never seen her in that condition before. Then quickly I became the caring, solicitous husband. With tender words and clumsy caresses I thought only of calming and consoling her. I knelt down beside her and took her in my arms. Her shoulders were thin and bony to my embrace. I stroked her fevered cheeks and her wet, tear-stained face.

"Please, love," I said, my anxiety mounting. "Please get up and have something to eat. Then I shall put you to bed. You need food to keep up your strength and you need rest."

She didn't seem to notice I was there and went on sobbing bitterly, wailing like a wounded animal. I had never heard a woman weep with such total abandon. It was painful to see her like that and my heart, though made harder by past events, was torn. I felt of a sudden a deep pity for her wasted life, the same emotion I had known in Manchester years earlier. At that time the feeling was seasoned with an abundance of love, but now I felt only pity. She wouldn't eat. She stared at the bowl of soup as though it had a something nasty in it. She wouldn't touch it or the milk I poured for her. I stripped her to her underwear and put her to bed. She tossed for an hour and then slept fitfully many hours.

Somehow in the midst of these troubles I managed to go on writing. I had published my first novel in 1880 before the misery began and was now working on what I hoped would be my second. I thought I had chosen a compelling subject: Victorian prudery and the restrictions placed on authors. I had fashioned strong and talented characters in conflict with middle-class rules and rigidity. I had devised a plot with a series of twists and turns, and the novel was moving right along. Every evening from five until nine I locked my door to prevent interruption and scribbled in a neat but tiny hand page after page. Then from eleven till well after midnight I read the classics in Greek or Latin.

The two hours between nine and eleven I set aside for Muriel, but in warm weather she was spending few of her evenings at home. She loved the streets and the night and the crowds of shadowy people seeking pleasure. Because she had lived in one room most of her life, she disliked cramped quarters and sought freedom in the streets. Much of my fiction at this time was never published and was eventually destroyed despite the promise I had made earlier to keep it. Many pages of manuscript I burned in the grate for warmth or used them to start a fire. After ripping one manuscript to pieces in a fit of rage, Muriel never touched my papers again. For that I was thankful. An immense amount of literary labor consuming hundreds of hours often came to nothing, but I could blame only myself. Each failed attempt, however, gave me insight and direction for subsequent books. The hours I put in trying to write a good story also provided some escape from the ugliness of my world. I was happy only when I was working and maybe sleeping. More than once I felt on awakening that my life of incessant labor and hardship was nothing more than a dreary dream from which I would soon awake.

But it wasn't a dream. During the spring of 1882, as I toiled sixteen hours a day at tutoring and writing, Muriel returned at intervals to her former life of sensual indulgence and debauchery. Left alone to shift for herself, she would slip away at night, ply her trade near the winged statue of Eros in Piccadilly Circus, and lose herself in the vice dens nearby. Several days later, defeated and repentant, she would straggle home. With huge tears streaming down her gaunt cheeks she would beg her husband to remember his marriage vows and forgive her. Time and again I did, but rapidly in warm weather she sank into irretrievable dissipation. Drunk and disorderly, she lived on the streets or in dosshouses. For a month or more I would hear not a word from her and begin to think I was free of her. Then bedraggled, wracked by disease, and smelling of doom, she would sneak into the lodging house and knock on my door again. I despised her by then and wanted to be rid of her. At one time I had loved her dearly in spite of her flaws, but in the early months of 1882 I felt only a dull disgust and aching pain. Losing her after trying so hard to save her was unaccountably tragic. Again I placed most of the blame on an uncaring and dissolute social order.

2

The tension created by Muriel's behavior posed a very real burden. I feared it was not only hurting my health but would in time weaken or destroy my creative power. I was becoming so agitated that I dreaded hearing the doorbell ring, or the postman's knock. To Quentin I confided in a tone verging on despair that I had lost all peace of mind and lived in a miasma of conflicting emotions: *"I am getting most frightfully nervous."* My work had suffered interruptions that delayed all progress, and I was losing the last shred of sustaining hope. I spoke of costly illnesses consuming Muriel, embarrassing seizures in public, shrill and violent behavior in the streets at night, descent into chronic alcoholism, and unspeakable depravity. I said also, despite the cost, I had decided to commit the woman to a medical facility in Hampstead. She viewed that benign place with its mission to rehabilitate alcoholics as a cruel and noisome prison. Loudly sobbing and threatening a scene, she begged me not to send her there. But what could I do?

In June of 1882, after being at the clinic only a few days, she put on a nurse's uniform she found in a closet and walked away. The next day she went to live with friends unknown to me. The tales she told them were bizarre distortions of the truth. With vivid and unrestrained invention, she apparently vilified her feckless husband as the cruel villain of a reckless melodrama. In her mind I was not above persecuting an innocent flower-like victim. Her cronies in spite and anger sent me abusive letters crudely scrawled in pencil on soiled paper. Though I cannot understand why, I gave in to her coming home in October. Soon afterwards she strayed again into the streets and found mean lodgings elsewhere. Although in 1883 she was living within walking distance of my rooms, I saw her in the streets only once.

One evening near the end of summer in that year, I walked up to Piccadilly Circus for exercise. It had rained during the day, and the streets glistened in the lamplight. The public houses and theaters were closing, and people were stepping around puddles left by the rain. I looked idly at the fluid crowd and suddenly saw Muriel. For weeks she had been out of my thoughts, and now I was looking directly at her. She was crossing the wide street, dodging the traffic with no eyes for anything else, and didn't see me. She wore a tight skirt, a large hat with feathers, and a low-cut blouse that complemented the skirt. From only a few feet away in the half-light of evening she appeared to be a well-dressed lady separated in the crowd from her male companion. I didn't wish to speak to her but wanted to know where she was going at that hour. So I stationed myself at the top of a concrete stairway to keep an eye on her.

She walked slowly down the street to the corner, turned and walked back toward Piccadilly, turned again and walked to the corner. I couldn't figure out what she was doing. Maybe she was waiting for someone, a friend perhaps. She overtook a man strolling slowly in the same direction and gave him a sidelong glance. She walked onward a few steps, came to a street lamp, and waited. When the man approached her, she appeared to speak to him. He stared at her for a moment, firmly shook his head, and walked swiftly away. Without a doubt on seeing that, I understood what was going on. I turned and walked in the night rain as fast as I could. I wanted to run.

In her absence, though lonely and agitated and not eating well, I slowly regained my peace of mind. But in September of 1883 a policeman came knocking on my door. It had happened before and was always embarrassing. With a flourish of self-importance, clipboard in hand, the constable informed me that Mrs. Jonathan Blue had gotten into trouble and had given my name and address as nearest of kin. He spoke in a low, confidential voice and seemed concerned though puzzled.

"Is she really your wife, Mr. Blue? We had to take her in, lock her up. She was disturbing the peace, brawling in the street with two drunken whores. It was one-thirty in the morning."

"Yes, she's my wife but we're separated. I'm not surprised by what you say. She deliberately seeks the company of harridans."

"She was drunk and disorderly and cursing like a sailor. Screeching dirty language real loud. A fierce one, I tell you, and violent."

"You are not revealing anything I don't already know, officer. She's an alcoholic and a whore and madly out of control. I've tried often to help her, but it all comes to nothing. I can't do a thing now."

"As her husband you may come to Magistrates Court in Bow Street and argue for her release. She claims you're the only person in this entire city who has a reason to be interested in her."

Once more in distress, she was reaching out to me, her protector and savior, waiting for rescue. After days of fretful indecision I didn't go to the Bow Street court. She remained in jail to serve her time. The food, I learned, was barely edible, but to my surprise she gained some weight. Upon release she was allowed to shift for herself and melted into the populace. For weeks I thought she would come pounding on my door demanding entrance, but that didn't happen. As fall moved into winter, she dropped out of my life entirely. It was then that I felt the misery of my existence as never before. I was alone but legally married. I was in bondage with no escape. Outdated laws insured it.

Body and mind told me that my unhappiness would go on forever. Night after night I tossed in a rumpled bed unable to sleep. One indisputable fact disturbed me: my life was a dull litany of tedium and pain. Insomnia was making the situation even worse. Lying there in darkness and staring at the ceiling, I thought of my father's untimely death, my loneliness and isolation at Breckenbow, my disgrace and dismissal from Thatcher College, the wretched days of near starvation in America, the death of dear Will at so young an age, and the searing torment of the moment. Maybe I would wake up when the long, dark night was over to find myself an innocent, cheerful, laughing child. Perhaps fate would favor me for once, and I wouldn't awaken at all.

3

In a brown study but free of Muriel at last, I put behind me the misery she had spawned and went back to my writing. I had destroyed my second novel when no publisher would buy it. Now I began to read through the first, and while the book was rough in places on the whole it wasn't all bad. I had written *Workers at Sunrise* as a novel of social protest. In method it was a drama of everyday life among the poorest denizens of London. Its purpose was to present a free and open flow of ideas that might improve the lives of London's poor should the ideas be acted upon. Its theme called for influential idealists of both sexes to work long and hard to achieve lasting change.

For practical reasons I accepted the conventions of the Victorian novel; so in structure the book revealed little originality. However, the presentation of poverty and slum life with stark and unerring realism was something new. Refusing to limit myself to moments of crisis, as earlier social novelists had done, I examined hour by hour the daily lives of poor people. In so doing I captured the rhythm and texture of their lives and gave them meaning as suffering people. I dared to deal with all of human behavior, not merely sanitized pap demanded by the middle class. I later discovered some of my portrayals of the poor and the way they lived their lives were as accurate and believable as the reports of social scientists of the time. However, some readers found my presentation of life in the raw disturbing and my strident authorial commentary unsettling. In later novels I polished and refined the realism and curtailed intrusive authorial comment. I let the story tell itself. Even the critics called it a big improvement.

Readers quickly noted that my female characters were strongly rendered. Carrie Wilson was based on Muriel and is believable in every detail. Meredith Albright, a character I couldn't sketch from life, is not. A wealthy philanthropist, I portrayed her with seriousness that quickly became heavy dialectic. The young woman is compassionate and idealistic and eager to alleviate the misery of the poor, but comes forward as a bluestocking who can hardly speak a syllable without sounding pompous. This, for example, is how she states her mission: *"I shall endeavor to gain the personal confidence of these poor people, so that they will freely impart to me their difficulties and allow me to help them in the most effectual way."* Though set against a background of dark and effective realism, my portrayal of Meredith Albright oozed syrupy idealism born of youthful inexperience. I didn't see it when writing or revising. Kurtz might have seen it but said nothing. In that first novel my presentation of upper-class women grievously missed the mark. Later, as I came to know wealthy women who divided their time between town and country, my characters in their likeness would trill an easy flow of language to reveal vibrant and believable personalities.

Invariably the women who came into my life went into my novels. Muriel's influence upon my books is therefore not surprising. What does surprise is the prediction in this first novel of events that would decide her fate. Set down when our marriage was calm and happy, the prediction is a dark one of dissolution and destruction. In *Workers at Sunrise* earthy, emotional Carrie Wilson is similar in appearance to Muriel and has a similar personality. The fictional character shares with her real-life model the same attitudes and emotions, and both go downward the same way. The chapters portraying Carrie show a young woman caught in a vicious downward spiral. They examine in detail the same forces that would destroy Muriel. Yet the book was composed when she and I were young and hopeful. We faced adversity in those days with courage, laughter, and youthful optimism. Why I could have seen her sinking downward is beyond my understanding.

During my year in America, I had brooded on the fallen woman in Victorian society, that "priestess" as a leading historian called her, sacrificed for the sins of the people. Now I carefully traced Carrie's slow descent after her seduction by a clergyman's son. For a moment I thought the girl herself might possibly be to blame, but that unsettling speculation I quickly dismissed when I placed all blame on her seducer. Though raised in religion as the son of a minister, the man couldn't resist primal urges and so became a predator to corrupt the innocent. I believed, from what Muriel had told me, that loss of innocence triggered careless behavior in girls of unstable family. In our pillow talk she described her first encounter in terms so vivid I could never forget it. Her mother's lover forced himself upon her when she was thirteen. She got no recourse from her mother who insisted she was lying.

When Carrie Wilson enters the common room of a night house in

Piccadilly, tall and showily dressed, she cuts a fine figure. Heads turn and salacious men gawk at her, knowing she belongs to *"the aristocracy of the demimonde."* For a time she is much in demand but soon catches a dread disease. Shunned by those who formerly sought her, she sinks rapidly downward. Then Arthur Cooper, the novel's protagonist, appears on the scene to save her. He puts her up in rooms better than she has ever known, nurses her back to health, and eventually marries her. But the experience of the streets, *"the period of wretched vagabondage,"* has left an indelible stamp upon her. To get money for gin, she falsifies household accounts, pawns any object that will bring a few pence, and returns to prostitution. The pattern of Carrie's behavior, created before 1880, exemplifies in detail that of Muriel Blue after 1882.

Carrie's experience illustrates the fear-ridden despair of any sick prostitute in London. The girl in a brothel or walking the streets could support herself only so long as good health and good looks remained unimpaired. Some girls, ravaged by disease, resorted to begging when they couldn't entice a customer. Once when I was walking the streets to gather material for a story, I met a girl who looked like a middle-class milliner of good family. On closer view I saw that she was unsteady on her feet. When I turned to walk away, she began to beg.

"Please, sir. You can spare a shilling, can't you? I'm sick and can hardly walk about, but I have to get money somehow. If I don't my landlady won't let me sleep in her house. I'm safe but a little sick."

"As I said, I'm as poor as you, but take this and go home." I gave her all the money I had. It was enough to buy a good dinner.

In *Workers at Sunrise* Arthur Cooper goes in search of Carrie. He finds her simulating nudity on a stage in a London vice den. Risking assault by the male customers, he seizes her and takes her home. Two months later as spring is coming she dies of syphilis. Though flirting with melodrama when dramatizing Carrie's death, I was clearly drawing upon my tumultuous life with Muriel.

CHAPTER FOURTEEN

Beatrice Gossam

I completed another long novel in September of 1882. When it was done I moved to a neighborhood near Tottenham Court Road where I lived alone for two years. That ended the sordid shuffle from one squalid lodging house to another. Moving from place to place with Muriel had gone on with clockwork regularity, but now the cycle was broken. I quickly made my new address known to publishers. Smith & Richards returned the manuscript, saying the book was too painful for people to read at leisure and would give affront to members of Mudie's Select Library. Immediately I sent the novel to another publisher who sat on it for a month and turned it down with no comment.

In the meantime I had taken Muriel to a hospital for an eye operation. The procedure didn't go well and she lost part of her sight. Instead of coming home after recovery, she went to the lodgings of another patient. Two weeks later I received a telegram urgently asking me to come and take her away at once. She had assaulted the person who had befriended her. In October we were together again in mutual domestic rancor and misery. Even though the eye operation left her unable to see clearly, I couldn't keep her home. Nervous, restive, and combative, she insisted on walking the city streets. I had to hire a woman to walk with her. Eventually she wandered alone into the night and didn't return. Shutting out the ugliness, I worked diligently on a new novel.

In December, the day after Christmas, I informed Quentin that Heath & Company had accepted my novel and would pay fifty pounds. It was hardly more than a token fee, but getting the book published for any fee seemed reward enough. As it turned out, my great expectations were premature. The publisher found objectionable material in the book and asked me to revise it extensively. I consulted Lionel Chandler who advised me to make the changes, but the publisher held the book in limbo for almost a year. Then at last he sent me a moralizing letter with a long list of passages to be revised. Reluctantly I devoted six weeks of labor to bowdlerizing the book. I returned the altered version, expecting it to be published in a month or so, but it didn't happen. Though set in print for proof reading, the long novel in three volumes never saw the light of day. It was eventually lost.

While waiting for the publisher to make up his mind, I was writing *The Outsiders*. A small publishing house accepted that book in 1884, and it became my second novel. Four years had gone by since I had published at my own expense my first novel. In the meantime I had written three additional books that no publisher would accept. I would have given up the struggle but for a native tenacity that kept me working. Also I believed in myself, believed in spite of it all I would soon be published. Somewhere in the back of my mind was a shadowy notion that eventually someone would see quality in my work and place it before the reading public. At last after four long years that someone had come forward, and the dream was becoming reality.

The main plot of *The Outsiders* develops a theme of choice between two girls of contrasting values. Dexter Waymark, the protagonist, must choose dreamy and religious Maud Ganderby for a life partner or Ida Stellaron. Maud with her romantic delusions is a product of the middle class. Ida, on the other hand, has risen from hardscrabble poverty and belongs to no distinctive class. In her struggle to find her own way in the world she has become a self-sufficient and pragmatic woman. Dexter Waymark, Ida Stellaron, Julian Castillo, and Harriet Littleton are the outsiders. They are young bohemians who attempt to live their lives according to a standard of thought and behavior not in keeping with Victorian propriety. That alone in a sternly moralistic society brands them as outsiders. Harriet Littleton, modeled after Muriel, is similar to Carrie Wilson in *Workers at Sunrise* but with few positive features.

Together they form an authentic picture of my stricken first wife.

They are tall with dark hair, shapely, sensual, and morally obtuse. Carrie has a smooth and attractive face, but Harriet has features of "sickly hue." Both women are outgoing and sociable, make friends with coarse and bawdy women of suspect reputation, and get into trouble when their landlady complains. Neither one knows how to make use of her time, is painfully bored, believes she lives too much alone, and quarrels with the respectable husband. Furtive in their glances and sensing the hostility of the world around them, they are nervous, restless, discontented, and quick of temper. Both yield to physical urges at an early age, become drunken prostitutes, fall into wanton depravity, and die before the age of thirty. Carrie depicts Muriel Blue in the early years of our marriage. Harriet is the coinage of her after I came to loathe her. While Carrie is pathetic in her weakness, Harriet is drawn without sympathy. Against a background of vivid realism, she is shown as bitter, hateful, peevish, cunning, and corrupt but not evil. I was a post-Darwinian moralist when describing her, and I saw the woman merely as weak.

Some aspects of Harriet's personality seen by readers as evil really show strength. Her cunning, for example, places her in a position of advantage when dealing with others. To get her way, she can be cruel and manipulative. At another time, depending on her mood and mission, she may show herself as meek, ingratiating, and docile. Influenced by current ideas of heredity and reversion, I described Harriet as *"miserably weak in body and mind,"* and yet her temper is sometimes a weapon she uses with great skill. From her parents she inherited *"a scrofulous tendency"* that tainted her moral sense and pulled her downward in life. Serious symptoms of this diseased heredity took the form of convulsive fits. Returning home one evening, Julian Castillo found her sprawled on the floor thrashing about and foaming at the mouth. In a letter to Kurtz, I described Muriel's seizures in almost identical terms.

While developing a fictional character, I was thinking of Muriel as unregenerate from the moment of conception. Beginning with the opinion that she was a hapless victim of society, I came full circle to believe she was naturally corrupt and therefore beyond help. Any attempt to reach out to her, any attempt to save her from herself, was doomed to failure. Her existence was directed not by circumstance, not by social forces, but by natural law. Her behavior, I came to believe, was dictated by the inherited chemistry of her own body. In this way I excused myself of all blame. A decade later, in a novel focusing on the middle class, I would have a woman of maturity and experience pose a question and provide an answer: *"How can anyone drive a girl into a life of scandalous immorality? She took to it naturally, as so many women do."* Maybe so. But the world she lived in, uncaring and indifferent, chipped away at Muriel's resistance and pulled her down.

Fashioned in deliberate and pointed contrast to Harriet Littleton is Ida Stellaron. Intelligent and good of heart, Ida was forced into a life of degradation mainly by economic circumstances. One bleak and simple choice lay before her, life or death. Even as a negative heredity worked against her, she chose to live. The daughter of a prostitute, she inherited qualities that made her vulnerable to forces other women might have resisted. She is my rendering of "the noble prostitute," a stereotypical character of the time. I came to admire her, even though some perceptive readers insisted she wasn't admirable at all. They saw Ida as superior to Harriet but not the superb woman her creator envisioned. She hopes to meet a generous man of wealth who will take pity on her and claim her. So I provide a young idealist who promises to love and support t her. Readers claimed that was selling herself again. I had falsely interpreted Ida's opportunism as the universal struggle to survive.

To make herself worthy of Waymark and socially fit, she performs a ritual of cleansing and rebirth. It is a passage the publisher wanted expurgated as exceeding Victorian propriety, but somehow it remained. On the beach at night Ida removes her clothing, walks naked into the sea, and washes away the unclean past in the foaming surf. She emerges from this symbolic baptism a shining example of feminine purity. As she steps from the water, rising above the ugliness of her past to confront a cruel world with calmness and strength, I wrongly insist she has always been clean of mind and pure of heart. She is perhaps an idealization of Muriel not as she was but as she might have been.

Though I was trying to forget the pain of living with her when she was slowly falling apart, inevitably Muriel came into the novel. In retrospect it was no surprise because women were to influence my work profoundly in later novels. As I began to get a foothold in the literary world, I shifted my focus from the poor to the middle and upper classes, but always I paid careful attention to the women who lived in the worlds I created. Some I adored and some I despised, but every one of them brought color, drama, and life to the story.

2

Though professionally published and promoted, *The Outsiders* went beyond late-Victorian discretion. The critics called it lurid, and so readers mired in Puritan morality hesitated to buy it. The book was advertised near the middle of June in 1884, but during the summer only a few copies were sold. Pressed even harder by poverty, I moved to a single room at 62 Spenser Street near Regents Park. Günter Kurtz had returned from Tennessee disappointed and discouraged, but believing he could write a book about the experience that would make him a rich man. In April he went back to Germany and began a correspondence with his English friend that endured many years. With Kurtz no longer around, though the weather was warm and bright, I was lonely and depressed. The failure of my second novel convinced me to relinquish all thoughts of a literary career. Losing hope by slow degrees, I felt I would have to stifle my ambition to become a man of letters and take a steady job to supplement the meager income from my teaching. I would forget about writing and merely read what others had written.

I thought of becoming a clerk in a hospital or charitable institution, or even a shop and endure the stigma. Unable to rid myself of middle-class prejudice, it seemed dreadful to become a clerk or a draper's assistant. Muriel was right on target when she once said my family would object to my becoming a clerk and feel shame. Then without notice my daily life began to change for the better. I was invited to gatherings at my pupils' posh homes and quickly accepted each one. I met influential people who heard I had published two novels. They asked me to visit them as a dinner guest in their homes. Soon I was eating well but too busy to create another book, and that worried me.

In August I spent two weeks with the Chandlers in the lake country, the region made famous by Wordsworth. There I climbed hills, strolled along the shore of Lake Windermere, and went on long walks with the family. After the palpable silence of rural scenes, the noise of Spenser Street assaulted the ear. A week or two later I met Mrs. Ronald Gossam and spent a weekend at the family's stately home in Gloucestershire. I came as a tutor to examine her sons but when invited to remain as her guest, I warmly accepted. In luxurious surroundings a world away from my grubby room in London, I found it difficult to relax but enjoyed myself. My hostess was a well-traveled woman, born in India and fluent in the exotic languages of the East. She knew many accomplished people and maintained friendships with persons of rank and title. After I returned to London, Beatrice Gossam remained in steady contact with me. When fall came she told me she would divide her time between a town house in the city and the manor house in the country.

In London our friendship progressed rapidly. Her son David, only thirteen, soon became my favorite pupil. He arrived at my place in mid-afternoon and left at eight in the evening. Sharing my knowledge with the boy was at first rewarding, but the long hours soon left me hard pressed to find time for writing. After acquiring several more pupils, I taught all day with only one hour reserved for lunch and rest. By suppertime at eight or later I was finally alone. After a scanty meal I worked at my writing until midnight. Early the next morning I began another day of tutoring. The *"pupil business,"* as I called it in a letter to my brother, was robbing me of valuable time and becoming tiresome, but I had to make a living somehow just to pay the rent. Also I liked David Gossam and particularly the boy's mother. In a letter to Kurtz I described her as *"one of the most delightful women imaginable."* Gracious and lively of manner, genuinely interested in my life and work, this mature married woman with children seemed to me more desirable than any woman I had ever known. I was starved for feminine companionship, and with admirable efficiency she filled a void in my life. Her husband was often away hunting with his cronies in Ireland and didn't complain when she began to live her life as she wished. On my first visit to her home in the country, she asked me to call her Beatrice.

She appeared to be in her early to mid-thirties but was actually ten years older. The passing years had been kind to her, leaving her well preserved and happy. She had married a wealthy man when quite young and had been a popular member of Anglo-Indian society. Her tales of faraway places, told with humor in a well-modulated and musical voice, amused me and left me laughing. As we grew closer she invited me to supper parties, dinner parties, and even tennis parties. At heart I didn't enjoy such gatherings. I felt socially inept in the presence of upper-class people. In time, however, I came to believe that most of them were quite shallow, flitting like butterflies across the surface of life.

When my sister Maggie visited me in London, I spoke of invitations coming to me in the mail everyday. "Here is one for a tennis party next Monday. Games in the afternoon."

"But Jonathan," she said in that sisterly tone she always used to instruct me, "you don't play tennis. I've never seen you run. As a boy you galloped by the river with your brothers but not when you were older. Tennis, you must know, requires running."

"I run sometimes," said I defensively. "When walking a country lane I sometimes break into a slow trot."

"Where people can't see you, Jonathan, and slow. When people play tennis, they run very fast and other people watch."

"Maybe by watching I'd learn how to play, but really I consider the game a waste of time, and I don't have a moment to waste."

"That sounds exactly like you, dear. I know you never waste time."

"Well, there's a line to be drawn somewhere," I said with a grin. "It's flattering to receive the invitation, but I really can't accept it."

"I'm glad you have friends here in London," said Maggie with a heavy sigh as if she were not glad. "I'm happy for you."

I was flaunting my newfound popularity, bragging a little about my good fortune. The chance to complain of too much attention delighted me. I went to the party after all and sat on the sidelines and watched my supple new friend move with the grace and liveliness of a young girl. In a tennis costume showing no more than a bit of leg in black stockings, she played a fast and vigorous game. I was surprised to learn the game required special shoes, and I thought her costume was too restrictive. It could have been shorter and lighter. Stockings, bodice, and tennis apron needed to go. But hypocritical Victorian prudery ruled the day.

When I first became acquainted with Beatrice Gossam, I was living at 62 Spenser Street, a locale similar to the Grub Street of Samuel Johnson's day. After she came to live in London and began to visit me regularly, I moved to better quarters to entertain her. At Christmas time in 1884, I leased for three years (later extended to six) a good set of chambers in Marylebone Road. The two rooms and a kitchen were clean and comfortable. In the kitchen I was able to do more than prepare a pot of tea. I was soon eating soup with bits of meat, cheese, bread, and vegetables. I liked the convenience of the place and my neighbors seemed respectable. Above all – and this delighted me – I was no longer subject to the thralldom of landladies. I was glad to be rid of those riotous women even though in my fiction I would remember them as grist for the mill. In several novels, as time moved on, I would present London landladies against a background of humorous satire.

3

While living at 7-K, I tutored fewer pupils and was able to give more time to writing. Often I labored on a manuscript nine hours a day and was able to resolve knotty problems even in sleep. Determined to do what I thought I was made to do, I lost myself in literature and the creative process. In January of 1885 I quarreled with *Punch* on the question of frankness in fiction. Mindful of a barbed retort, I declared that Thackeray and others had betrayed their artistic integrity when they meekly surrendered to the false modesty of the people. Instead of yielding to the prudery of public taste, they should have had the courage of their own convictions. As I expected, the guardians of public morality took issue with that. One of the hacks at *Punch* roundly lampooned me in a tasteless reply, but the shabby treatment on the front page of *Punch* didn't bother me at all. The hack had repeated my name several times in capital letters, and that made me laugh with glee. Any fool could see it was good advertising. I should have thanked him but didn't.

Through the winter and into a wet and slow spring Beatrice Gossam came to my apartment on a regular basis. I liked her and she liked me, but there was no intimacy between us and no impropriety. We knew a lasting friendship was better than a fleeting affair, and I felt I could learn from her. She was a woman of worldly experience and had many rich stories to tell. It pleased me to see her take an interest in my life and work. She encouraged me to talk about my writing and listened carefully. One afternoon she examined my photograph album and made kind and thoughtful remarks about Mother.

"You get your good looks from that lady, don't you?"

"I'm not sure of that. People say I look more like my father. But I do think Mother has a face that shows character."

"Yes, I believe so, and she has a mind of her own too."

"That couldn't be more correct," I asserted. "She goes about her business indifferent to war, revolution, social upheaval, natural and man-made disasters, and anything else you can name. Her home was always her haven when raising her children. It's her world even now and sacrosanct. She was a good wife and continues to be a good mother."

"She appears to be a strong woman who knows what she must do and does it. She raised a large family knowing exactly what to do."

"She has always been a strong woman, but I can't say with full honesty that I really know her."

"Why in the world would you say that?"

"She seemed to change after I came back from America. Became more distant and never accepted the girl I later married. When we try to talk to each other regarding serious matters, we say only a few words and the conversation ends. I have a passion for discussion but little tolerance for small talk. By contrast Mama thrives on chitchat." I saw no reason to divulge why I went to America.

"Mothers are often like that. My own mother was charmed by gossip but rebuked me for being a social butterfly. Scolded me for associating with the native people in India. They were beneath my station, she declared, and she thought it a waste of time to learn their language. We could never see eye to eye on anything. We quarreled a lot."

"And yet you turned out all right, I dare say, by the looks of you!"

Beatrice gave me insights into her world, which I could use in my fiction, and she was often in my thoughts. Her warm personality struck chords never touched by any of the few women I had known, not even Muriel. In times of stress I took comfort in the thought of her. I could see in my imagination her woman's face and refreshing smile. I could smell the aroma surrounding a proud and capable woman, and I could hear her musical voice even when walking the noisy streets. Her easy, mature femininity and the wholesome way she embraced life impressed me and left me vulnerable. Dylan Crenshaw believed our passionate friendship became a love affair. In all likelihood it would have become a torrid affair if I had not chosen to run.

In early June of 1885, beside my window on a rainy day, I brooded over Mrs. Gossam while trying to write. Her image distracted me and prodded me to look for an easy way out. I was ready to reject this lively woman of wealth even though she had become a close friend. I wanted more from her but knew romantic overtures would generate serious problems. There was a line to be drawn, one I could never cross, and it brought a gloomy mood. I was tired of London and the bad weather and the hard work to establish myself as an author. I yearned for the broad skies and open spaces I had seen on my way to Chicago. Perhaps I could return to America and labor as a farm hand. That way I would grow strong in the sun and forget I had ever been a struggling writer who had peeked into the world of polite society.

Running was a pattern that would recur time and again throughout my life. Invariably when I met a woman of wealth and education, instead of being drawn to her I thought of flight. Before the summer was over I was attempting to sever relations with Beatrice Gossam. Perversely I wanted to slam shut the doors of opportunity she had opened for me, and I couldn't quite understand why. Though it seemed I was punishing myself for wanting to end the friendship, the rational part of me presented persuasive argument to close it.

As early as October of 1884 I had complained in letters to my family that Gossam's world of endless parties was stealing too much of my time. *"I used to suffer from loneliness. Now the difficulty is to get any time at all to myself. I am beginning pugnaciously to refuse invitations."* In the summer of 1885, fretting over time lost and literary work not accomplished, I felt I would have to make a clean break with her. To support the wisdom of my decision, I began to find fault with her friends. Those ladies and gentlemen who once seemed so lively, congenial, and witty now fell short of my expectations and were disappointing. Their interests were shallow and frivolous and their conversation empty chatter. Though free of drudgery and masters of their time, they seemed more concerned with style than substance. I was finding it difficult to tolerate the artificial tone they affected in airy conversation, their insistent display of unsullied happiness in their own little world.

I placed high value on my time and couldn't bear to lose so much of it in frivolous and unproductive activity. The premium I put on time and work puzzled my new friends of the leisure class. Their aim was to pass agreeably the hours of each day and sleep well at night, nothing more. They claimed some knowledge of Carlyle, who had preached the doctrine of work, but they knew little of struggle and the fruits of labor. By the end of 1885 my friendship with Beatrice Gossam and her upper-class friends had run its course. I had entered their world as if beckoned by fate and initially had enjoyed the novelty very much. Then of my own volition I left that rarefied sphere inhabited by ladies and gentlemen of leisure, and left it abruptly. Although in later years I would know affluent people in the literary world, I wouldn't return to the haunts of those idle people. I had heard from a good source that some women of Gossam's class cultivated authors as a hobby. Under no circumstance would I become a skittering monkey or dancing bear to entertain them. My stubborn self-respect wouldn't allow it. Yet fond thoughts of Beatrice Gossam lingered in memory for a dozen years.

CHAPTER FIFTEEN

Holiday and a Telegram

In 1885 I authored two books: *Emily Claremont* and *Comes the Morning*. The former was published in 1886, and the payment I got was an unbelievable fifteen pounds. The latter title didn't appear in print until three years later. Neither book was anything at all like my first two novels. They depicted middle and upper-class life and had little to say about poverty, London slums, or social reform. By the time I was reading the proofs for *Emily Claremont* I had another long novel well underway. I was working around the clock, seizing all the spare time I could find with only moments to relax. Dylan Crenshaw, who popped in from time to time to check on my health and well being, began to call the product of my compulsive regimen "the genre of nervous exhaustion." He was joking in his affable, easygoing way but clearly hitting the mark.

The family in Harrogate thought I was working myself into an early grave. In June my sister Emma spent several days with me at 7-K. With her doing the cooking we ate better than was my custom. We chatted and laughed and explored parts of London. When she left I complained of loneliness. At that time I was recasting *Emily Claremont* into two volumes. I was also working on the first chapters of *The Populace*, and three weeks later I wrote the early chapters of *Comes the Morning*. To juggle three books at one time was a new experience for me but challenging. Sustaining the literary labor and making it less tedious was my desire to gulp down all the great literature in several languages. Any time I was not writing or sleeping I was devouring one or two books bought cheaply at a second-hand store.

At the beginning of 1886 I was telling Emma that *Emily Claremont*, slated to appear in 1885, would be published in February. As it turned out the book didn't become live until May. The delay irritated me even though I was happy to be returning to my special line of work. I finished *The Populace* early in 1886 and made up my mind to publish the book anonymously. I felt it was not good to have two books published in a single year under my own name. In March I sent off the last of the proofs and was paid £100. It was the largest sum for a single book I had ever received. Reputable journals advertised the book, and favorable reviews appeared in print. Chandler, who liked to think of himself as my mentor, sent a letter praising the novel. *"Your book looks like it's going to be a striking success. The advertisements are phenomenal and there is talk of mysterious authorship."* It was better received than any of my earlier novels, and by the first week in May had sold 500 copies. Gerald Foster wrote to Chandler with good words about the novel, asking if it were Jonathan Blue's. *"I suppose so. There is some masterly work in it. One page describing the East End graveyard contains a passage that is one of the most beautiful in modern literature. And there is genius throughout."*

That amazing compliment prodded me to work harder for bread and cheese and a taste of fame. In a letter to Maggie I said I was toiling fearfully over the construction of a new book. Its heroine would be a working-class girl named Elaine. *"I have to go to a hat factory, a lunatic asylum, and other strange places. I wander much in the slums to absorb atmosphere and tone and gather materials. Every book is harder than the one before, but the next shall also be better than anything preceding."* In July and August I was spending all my spare time in the slums of Lambeth. *"I am doing my best to get at the meaning of that strange world, so remote from our civilization. I have the strangest people and scenes floating in my mind. Tomorrow, a Bank Holiday, I must spend in the street. On such days there is much to pick up."*

I wrote enough script to make seventy pages in print, but then I realized the book was not moving in the direction I wanted. So reluctantly I destroyed all that I had written and started over. Again I spent the entire day in Lambeth, not returning home until two in the morning. *"Ah, but you will see the result! I have a book in mind which no one else can write. It will contain the very spirit of London working-class life. Little by little it has been growing. I feel it is far better than anything I have yet done. I write with fever and delight, and I'm nearing end of third volume."* I titled the book *Elaine of Lambeth* after its heroine. She and her sister, factory girls in the district, would carry the story forward and support its theme. I really believed that within a few years they would become two of the most delightful and memorable characters in English literature. Sadly, that didn't happen. Quietly and quickly, as the book ceased to be read, the sisters dropped from the public's memory.

To absorb my subject as thoroughly as catching a cold, I roamed the narrow, litter-strewn streets of Lambeth daily. At times I paused to view window displays of wholesome food I wasn't able to buy. There behind the glass was a wedge of cheese beside a tasting knife, a bowl of succulent fruit, a boiled ham on a white platter, thick slices of American beef, and fat German sausages that made my mouth water. Meat was expensive and most of the time not part of my diet. The pleasure I took in describing a well-laid table in my novels was largely vicarious. However, the people I came to know were depicted with uncompromising realism and candor. Charles Bayfield, in the initial stages of a monumental study of the laboring classes in London, praised *The Populace* as one of the few novels he had ever read that presented an accurate picture of working people in London. Bayfield could have praised in similar terms *Elaine of Lambeth*. I sometimes exaggerated the plight of working women for dramatic effect, but in that book, even more so than in *The Populace*, I viewed factory girls with detachment and accuracy.

2

In January of 1887 I finished *Elaine of Lambeth* and congratulated myself on a job well done. It was another realistic novel of slum life, but an offhand comment I made upon completion suggests the book's realism was tempered with idealism: *"Elaine herself is one of the most beautiful dreams I ever had or shall have."* I had become emotionally involved with my story and its main character, even tearful as I wrote certain chapters near the end. I valued the book above anything I had written. The reading public appeared to like it when published in the middle of 1887, but the reviewers were less than enthusiastic. A clearly stated narrative, they conceded, but a weak plot. I could have told them my intention was not to construct the usual Victorian plot with its twists and turns and melodrama but to present in the manner of Zola an authentic perception of working-class life in London. I didn't bother to tell them anything.

Unlike my earlier novels, critics could find nothing morally objectionable in the book. So Mudie's Select Library, notable for never buying a book that could bring a blush to a maiden's cheek, took eighty-five copies. That surprised and pleased me. Perhaps in time Mudie's would take 2,000 of a new Blue book, as it often did with popular writers, but that of course was wishful thinking. A year later *Elaine of Lambeth* had sold 400 copies, a fair number but falling far short of the total copies printed. Readers didn't see it as a better novel than *The Populace*.

As the Lambeth novel slowly made its way into public recognition, I began work on a story I was calling *Dust and Dew*. I liked the title and felt it would be a strong and important book, but when I saw it wasn't developing as intended I crushed its pages and tossed them away. The work was not good enough, not better than my latest novel, and so I trashed it. To gain a reputation as a serious novelist, I believed sincerely that each book made ready for publication had to be better than the one before it. Also each book would have to be distinctly my own, recognizable by readers even without my name on the cover. *"I cannot and will not be reckoned among the petty scribblers of the day,"* I said to Quentin. *"To avoid it, I must issue only one novel a year. Each book must have a distinct character, a book which no one else would be likely to have written."* With its close examination of factory girls in the slums of London, *Elaine of Lambeth* was that kind of book. It was done with a light hand but with real sympathy for its subject and with gentle satire.

Lotty Lanfallow likes her life as a factory girl so much she refuses to give it up for a more secure existence offered by a relative. She is keenly alive, boisterous, outspoken, earthy, warm-hearted, laughing, and seldom overworked. Convinced that her independent way of life is right for her, she is happy and wholesome and eager to accept whatever comes her way. Always humming a tune, she is a lover of crowds and vigorous activity and enjoys being jostled on the sidewalks. She glances at men with a coy expression of innocence abandoned and with inward laughter. In her prime and eagerly embracing life, she participates in noisy festivities that gather momentum to become joyous expressions of human happiness. At times my portrayal of the factory girl seemed more romantic than realistic. The scenes of young men and women laughing, singing, flirting, and dancing remind one of similar scenes in French and Italian operas. Yet the studies of the new social scientists corroborated my realism. Lotty Lanfallow in real life could be seen on Sunday afternoons promenading arm in arm with girls of her kind.

As winter slipped into spring and spring into summer, I turned my back on the real world and lost myself in my writing. Living with characters of my own creation assuaged my loneliness and isolation and lifted my spirits. Some of my characters really came alive on the static page, and I liked them. When I could find the time, I sat by the window and read through my earlier novels with an unwavering eye. Often I shook my head and frowned, wondering how I could have written so poorly. Paragraph after paragraph seemed to cry out for revision. Good writing was hard work, and yet my salvation was work. In time it became almost a religious experience for me. I dined with my publisher on occasion but didn't actively seek new acquaintances. In warm and pleasant weather I rejected invitations to social events even when I knew I might enjoy them. My mood was pensive and solemn. Social gatherings demanded smiles and small talk. I wasn't good at small talk.

In the middle of summer I spent a few pleasant days in Eastbourne alone with my thoughts. Afterwards I visited my family in Harrogate and strolled leisurely beside the river. Walking had long been a favorite pastime, but already I was feeling a shortness of breath on returning from a long outing. In London again came news that Heath & Company had accepted "Clement Dorricott," finished in April of 1887. I felt it was not a worthy successor to *Elaine of Lambeth* and suggested serial publication. Heath returned the manuscript posthaste with not a word of explanation. Disappointed but not bothering to inquire, I tossed the manuscript on a heap of abortive work to become lost.

3

Eastbourne in Sussex near the end of January 1888 was almost as cold as London. I was there in the summer of 1887, liked the old town, and wanted to return. It was a strange choice for a winter holiday, for the weather was far from pleasant. Even so, the old-fashioned town offered quiet and privacy. It also had affordable accommodations where I might be able to work. Unable to write in London, I had rented a bedroom and sitting room for half the rental rate in London. There at a little desk the landlady provided I began one novel after another. Writing far into the night and smothering the sheets of paper with diminutive script, I went to bed exhausted but satisfied. The next day as I read through the text, squinting anxiously at every word and syllable, nothing seemed to go right. I was aiming for a goal I couldn't reach, something beyond my ability. Browning had said a man's reach should exceed his grasp, and so I struggled to extend my reach. Day after day I wrote page after page, choking each page with hundreds of words. Hours later after careful scrutiny I destroyed it all and started over.

The wind whistled around the eaves of the old house and under the windowsill, exacerbating my feelings of unease. The futile effort to create a believable story beyond the mediocre left me with headaches and sleeplessness. That and a nagging loneliness – only the landlady was in the house – made it impossible to work. So I asked a friend to join me for a few days. Dylan Crenshaw accepted the challenge, and the two of us went for long walks in blustering winds, ice, and snow. In the middle of a frigid February we walked across the downs to East Dean, bracing ourselves against a fierce easterly wind and plunging defiantly through snowdrifts on the sunken road. The exercise and companionship of my oldest friend drove the headaches away and left me feeling better. Earlier I had complained of unreliable health and depression. I had found myself unable to complete the third volume of the novel I had worked on for months. That brought on misery worse than mere depression. The tradition of the three-decker novel, dating back to Walter Scott, was still in vogue at the time. It was slowly giving way to novels of one volume that could be read at a faster pace on trains and hansoms and in parks. I had begun my career in the three-volume format and was finding the habit of writing expansively hard to break.

For more than a week Crenshaw and I spent our days walking and talking. Home again after hiking through the snow, we huddled in overcoats in front of a tiny fireplace and constructed elaborate disquisition. Into the wee hours of the morning we talked of art and literature and life. When we were not parsing Greek verbs and complaining of the cost of coals, we argued over the merits of Burne-Jones, Cailleibotte, and William Morris. In our mental jousting we aired our different opinions of George Meredith, Matthew Arnold, and Walter Pater. The latter had recently published *Marius the Epicurean,* and we spent an hour discussing the probable impact of the philosophical novel on impressionable readers. About a man in ancient Rome who admired beauty for its own sake, in just two years the novel had become enormously influential in liberal circles while others condemned it. We also spoke of the multitude of current novelists struggling to make a name for themselves and agreed they had nothing to say. Not one seemed promising.

When Crenshaw returned to London, I found myself alone again. To stave off loneliness, I made slow progress on a book I thought I would call *The Insurgents.* I finished the first volume and read it through and thought it better than anything done earlier. Then I read through the script a second time and couldn't resist making alterations to improve it. These "improvements" led to another beginning and a rewriting of the first volume. By then I was thinking of a new title and jotting down notes for the second volume and deluding myself into thinking I was making progress. On the last day of February – 1888 was a leap year – I broke off my writing to take a solitary walk through the snowy afternoon to Lewes. Returning to my rooms, winded and chilled by the long and raw trek over rolling hills, I found a telegram waiting for me.

It read: "**MRS. BLUE IS DEAD. COME AT ONCE.**"

Astonished, I stared at the brief message with its blurred capital letters on yellow paper. My face, tinted rosy by the cold afternoon, turned whiter than a sheet. The elderly landlady saw it happening.

"Are you all right, Mr. Blue?" she asked.

"Yes, Mrs. Withers. I'm all right. But I must leave on the 7:45 for London. Something has happened that requires me to be there early tomorrow morning, something not entirely pleasant."

"After walking all that distance in the cold you must be hungry. Will you have time for supper before leaving?"

"No, I'm afraid not. Maybe I can grab something at the station."

"I shall bring you a sandwich with hot tea," she said, moving toward the kitchen. "You can put the sandwich in your pocket and eat it later, but drink the tea now, please, to fortify your blood. You don't want to go all the way to London in a cold train with nothing warm inside."

I put the telegram in my shirt pocket, and sipping the tea I began to pack my luggage. My head spun with confused and agitated thoughts. My heart was pounding so hard I could feel a piercing pain in my chest. Though I had not seen Muriel for several years, I was suddenly required to pocket all shame and behave as her husband. In that identity I would be looking after her again perhaps in death. With a feeling of shock it occurred to me she wasn't even thirty years old. Perhaps she had fallen into desperate trouble and had sent the telegram to the one person in all her life who once had loved her. Having no one else to turn to, it was perhaps a last cry for help. I knew she was capable of that, and I would have to be careful. I ate half of the fat sandwich, the gift of my generous and caring landlady, and put the other half in my pocket. I gulped down the last of the tea, thanked the woman for her kindness, and got to the station just as the noisy train with its bright light came puffing and whoosing to a grinding halt.

February 29, 1888 came with cold and blustery winds. The train was headed northward from Sussex to London. It was moving at good speed but clattering with tiresome monotony on worn rails. In wintry weather I was traveling in a third-class car that was unheated. I wore a sweater under a heavy coat and was warm enough, but my feet were cold. Feeling hungry, I rummaged in my pockets, found the remainder the sandwich Mrs. Withers had given me, and ate it. Opposite sat a florid man of middle age reading a newspaper. Over the edge of his paper he looked at my auburn hair, pale face, and full mustache. My eating didn't seem to bother him. To pass the time and not disturb him, I tried also to read in the dim, flickering light. The movement of the train caused the small print to dance before my eyes and jerk out of focus. I folded my newspaper, put it on the seat beside me, closed my eyes, and sought rest. I tried not to think of the thing I had to do the next day. I dreaded even the thought of it and was nervous.

CHAPTER SIXTEEN

Dead at Twenty-Nine

It was near midnight as I fumbled with stiff fingers to unlock the door of my flat near Regents Park. I had walked from the Baker Street Station in icy drizzle and was chilled to the bone. It was too late to build a fire, too late even to heat a bowl of soup, and so hurriedly I got into my nightclothes and jumped into bed. Cold and hungry, I shivered under the heavy blanket for half an hour before I was warm enough to sleep. I was thinking that maybe the telegram was a ruse, just another of Muriel's tricks to bring me back into her miserable existence. I knew she had drifted back to the streets, and maybe she wasn't dead at all but sick and suffering a common disease. Maybe she was hungry with no money to buy food or pay the rent. Perhaps she was in trouble with the police again and needing help from the only friend she ever had.

I remembered I had lost sight of her in 1883 and had not seen or heard from her in five years. So after all that time, working as a prostitute and spending all she earned on cheap gin, maybe she really was dead. The thought alone made me catch my breath, and a vague discomfort invaded my stomach. All day I had eaten very little and so maybe the dull pain came from hunger. Then I thought the pain could be the visceral reaction to knowing that after years of bondage I was possibly free. As I slipped into fitful sleep, I was thinking of Coleridge and that wonderful poem. The albatross was falling from the neck of the ancient mariner into the sea. Perhaps my albatross had let go of me too.

My alarm clock sounded at 6:30. I was already up to bathe and dress and eat a spare breakfast. In the kitchen I heated water for tea and a shave and spread some butter on a piece of bread. As I ate I looked at the telegram again and found Muriel's address at the bottom. She was living in a dreary neighborhood of small shops and poor lodging houses that I remembered from my years of dire poverty. I could walk the distance and be there in less than an hour, but the weather was rude and blustery and so I hailed a cab. Inside with both windows closed it had a peculiar odor of unwashed people and stale oats. I could understand why body odor might linger, but why oats?

Not ready for an ugly encounter so early in the morning, I decided to exit the cab as it approached 16 Wilson Street and walk, observing anything that might be out of the ordinary. If I found Muriel alive, despite her condition I would leave immediately. I dreaded looking at her again, either alive or dead, but knew it had to be done. Slowly I made my way to the shabby lodging house. The cold seemed to crawl along the pavement as if alive. The sordid street was littered with trash. An old newspaper glued itself to my knees. I bent over and peeled it off. Decaying and dingy houses stood on either side of the street, huddled together as if for warmth. Smoke from the chimneys, pungent and pale blue, swirled in the wind. Scruffy little shops were opening for the day. Ragged children played kickball in the road. I pulled the brim of my hat down and the collar of my overcoat up. I stood in front of the three-story dwelling and saw nothing to cause me to turn away.

In the gray morning I ascended the steps slowly and gingerly, as an old man would do, and knocked on a door with many layers of paint. When no one answered I pushed it open and entered the small foyer. It smelled of cheap alcohol and some kind of cleaning fluid and was as dirty as the street outside. On one wall I saw a bank of mailboxes belonging to tenants. The boxes displayed common English names except for one that had no name at all. Then of a sudden I realized the landlady had already taken the liberty to remove Muriel's identity.

The keeper of the house came from a seedy room on the left and addressed me. She was square and thick with thinning gray hair and a red, fleshy face. Her height was not more than five feet. She wore a loose-fitting brown dress with rust-colored stains. A cheap necklace had left a thin green line around her unwashed and sagging neck. Her careworn eyes above leathery cheeks squinted as she viewed her visitor. The small black eyes, like beads in the face of a stuffed doll, were red around the rims but shrewd and alert.

"Are yer lookin' fer someone, sir? A room is it yer wantin'? I can let one in a day or two, but doubt one such as yerself wants accommodations in this 'ouse. Only poor people live 'ere." She paused, and peered upward to read my face. "Maybe hit's business that's bringin' you 'ere?"

The woman spoke with a cockney accent and with the abbreviated language of landladies in that part of London. She was trying to sound pleasant and polite, but her raspy speech was slurred and loud. Her hoarse, gin-thickened voice reminded me of the past when I wasn't free of slum landladies, and it made me shudder.

"Yes," I answered, "I'm here on business. This telegram I have in my hands. It reached me somehow, and I came right away." I unfolded the slip of yellow paper and showed it to her.

"Oh, then yer Mr. John Blue, the 'usband!" she exclaimed, squinting at the telegram. "Police went to yer place as I understand it. Talked to yer neighbor there and sent the wire."

"Jonathan Blue," I corrected.

"Oh, yes! Right, sir! Right this way. It's a dreadful business to take care of. I'm 'opin' yer up to the burden."

2

We climbed a flight of stairs and went down the dim corridor to Muriel's room. A native delicacy prompted the woman to leave me. The door was slightly ajar and I opened it with apprehension. The squalor of the room in which my wife had died at twenty-nine struck me like an unexpected and vicious blow across the face. In freezing weather there was no ventilation, and the stink was strident. The grubby room was fetid with the smell of death, unwashed clothing, and human waste. The emaciated body, in a damp and flimsy nightgown, lay on a sordid bed half covered with soiled and dirty rags that passed for blankets. Under the bed on the bare floor were the only shoes the woman had owned, a pair of cheap boots. Hanging on the back of the door was a tattered, mud-splattered dress and a threadbare coat.

In the room was a bed, a small table with a chair, a battered tallboy, and an old wardrobe for clothes. I opened its doors and found nothing more than a summer dress with an oily substance on the hem. In the last days of her life she had pawned every item of worth she owned, including her clothes. Smudged and wrinkled pawn tickets, half hidden among other items on the grimy table, gave proof of that. I looked into the dead woman's face and was conscious only of one emotion: pity for her wasted life. She had brought only rain and storm to her moment in the sun. When she departed, it was as if she had never lived. Not a person in the entire world mourned her passing. As the landlady had said, her death as well as her life was a burden.

I stood in the middle of the stinking room, swaying slightly. My head began to swim, and I found it hard to breathe. I removed my coat and tried to open the window. Old paint had sealed it shut. I threw open the door to hear the ugly noise of the squalid house. A baby was crying, a woman was whining, and a man was cursing. I slumped on the wooden chair and rested my throbbing head on the table. I closed my eyes only to have visions of the past invade my senses. For a moment I remembered all the misery I had suffered on this woman's account and all the pain. So painful a memory I couldn't endure, and quickly I forced myself to stand and move about.

I knew I would have to inspect the room carefully and later talk to the landlady. Somehow I found the strength to look into all the nooks and crannies. In a drawer I found a few scraps of stale bread and some rancid butter. It was the only food she had to eat, and the room had not enough heat to soften the butter. In another drawer I was surprised to find the letters I had sent to her during my year in America. They were neatly stacked and tied with a thin pink ribbon. She had saved them all, and I could tell by their condition that she had read them often. In their midst I found a faded photograph of a younger me. A tiny hole at the top told me she had pinned it on the wall at one time or another.

Near the pawn tickets were three "pledge cards" thrust upon her at different times by temperance workers in the streets. On each grubby card was a printed promise to abstain from alcohol. Unable to resist the well-meaning efforts of the temperance women, Muriel had signed each card with a palsied hand on the proper line. Minutes later she could have thrown the card away but had taken it home to toss it on the table. The pledge cards tendered mute and pathetic testimony of the struggle she had lost. I interpreted the cards as proof that she had tried to resist at least one of the afflictions that killed her before she turned thirty.

In the stinking room I began to see a pattern of behavior I wanted to forget. Weak and desperate from tuberculosis and other ailments, she had become addicted to alcohol and possibly drugs. To pay for the habit and keep a roof over her head, she sold her sickly self to strangers. Any money she was able to earn had gone to buy oblivion in cheap gin or pain-killing drugs. It made her tainted life easier to endure and left her unwilling to ask for help. When she might have called out to someone, she was too sick, too near death to bother. I could see, as the putrid walls closed in upon me, that she had died in a bleak and hostile place with no friendly care from anyone.

In my conversation with the landlady, the practical and necessary talk to sort things out and make decisions, I learned of sordid events in the last weeks of her life. Muriel had been out of control, creating one disturbance after another, and in conflict with all who knew her. With clenched fists she had attacked a female tenant on the floor above her, and the district police had come to arrest her. She had caused the exasperated landlady enough trouble to bring impending eviction, but then she fell ill and was confined to her room. Nearing death, she had become the worst of the landlady's tenants, irredeemable and combative, and no one offered to take her to a hospital. On her deathbed, dying by slow degrees, not one person had come to assist her. She had a few friends – the talkative landlady called them "associates" – but they were so vile in appearance they were not allowed to enter the house. Only a doctor had come to sign the death certificate and state the official cause of death as *acute laryngitis*. I was confident of other causes.

Attempting to sustain a gentility not rightly her own, the landlady divulged that Mrs. Jonathan Blue, during the three months she had lived in that house, had been wild and unlawful and bent on self destruction. Within a week after coming there she had alienated all the other tenants, and more than once they had insisted she be sent packing. But she, the landlady, was too kind-hearted to evict her. She allowed the poor woman to stay because she managed to pay her rent and had nowhere else to go. But rules were rules, sir, and . . . With visible impatience, I listened to the woman's diatribe and nodded my head. Years ago a doctor had reprimanded me for giving Muriel a dread disease. I knew she had told the man a blatant lie, but all I could do as the angry physician berated me was nod as I was nodding now.

3

I went back to the room to be sure the door was closed. Looking into her face, stark and cold, I found not a shred of femininity or even humanity. It was the face of a waxy old mannequin, not the volatile and vital girl I remembered. I couldn't be certain I recognized the features as belonging to Muriel. I wanted to look into the dark eyes, but they were closed and bulging. Only the fine white teeth remained the same.

I grieved for her, for what she was and for what she might have been. The thing that troubled me most was the absolute futility of her life. Only a handful of people knew that she had ever lived, and they had viewed her with contempt or as a commodity to be bought and sold. Yet in one brief encounter her life had touched mine and changed it profoundly. Perhaps the change was for the better, but who could tell? Who among us can read the future? Certainly she had caused me to suffer, and from the suffering did something grow? Philosophers have said suffering makes for a better artist, but how could I be sure? Of one stark perception I could be sure. That thing which had been a woman and now was nothing had lived and died in bleak and painful confusion.

The next day I screwed up the courage to see Muriel for the last time. Her corpse had been laid out with skill. Her face, unrecognizable the day before, was delicate and almost beautiful. The pale skin, tight and translucent over prominent cheekbones, accented the closed eyes that in life had flashed with intense emotion. The sensual mouth, painted a glowing red in life, wore a clean and natural hue. The pain she had inflicted upon me rushed into mind and heart with a burning sensation, but I did all I could to put it down. She was dead now, my first love, let her rest.

I was saddened by her death but couldn't persuade myself to go to her funeral. I paid for her coffin and all the funeral expenses and even paid a sum I couldn't afford to hire mourners. The landlady for another fee took care of the details. She informed me in earthy language that people in her neighborhood loved a good funeral and viewed it almost as a festival. Even though Muriel had angered most of them and lived among them as someone to be despised, they were eager to attend her funeral, peer into her coffin, and speak kindly of her. It made them feel better about themselves. It made them human.

I retrieved the letters and the photograph and sorted through the tattered pawn tickets. Nothing else in the squalid room had any value whatever. Without knowing why, I redeemed the gold wedding ring she had pawned for half a crown. Holding the ring in my hands and looking it over, I was drawn into a strange and lucid mood of exultation. My chains had fallen away. I was free! The heavy albatross that had clung to my neck for almost a decade had quietly slipped into the sea. On a sunny day a month later, walking across a bridge spanning the Thames, I took the ring from my pocket and flipped it into the river. It sparkled in the sun and made a tiny splash.

CHAPTER SEVENTEEN

Aftermath and Travel

After Muriel's death I tried to lose myself in work but found it impossible. I wrote to my sister Emma, asking her to visit. She came to my flat chirpy and cheerful and spent a few days there, sleeping on a rented cot. I liked the sound of her voice and her facial expressions and the way she laughed when I made a witty remark. My mother and older sister in their cold reserve never laughed when I tried to make a joke. Emma always did. Her presence chased the blues away, but after she left I sank downward again into dreary depression. To make matters worse, I suffered from a bad cold and couldn't answer her letters. When finally I did write, it was to tell her that I was idle and unhappy, confused and lonely, and at the end of my rope as a writer. *"I took up a pen but couldn't frame a sentence. In blank misery I sat for half an hour staring at the sheet of paper. Then I turned to stare for hours at the fire. All day long I do absolutely nothing, I don't even read and rest is beyond me."* She replied I was losing myself in self-pity, and of course I was. She advised me to take a long walk, brew a pot of tea on returning, and write.

I thought the air in that part of London was killing me, and so taking a long walk couldn't be done. The fumes wafting from the Baker Street Station were damaging my health. They were making me weaker by the day even though I was only thirty and had a mountain of work to do. I would have to get away if only for a short time. I needed a change of scenery, a change of climate, but what good would that do if I remained perpetually alone? I viewed myself as a hermit living in a bleak desert, and I took my desert with me wherever I went. It was an affliction I had

136

never been able to cure. It dogged me year after year, and I could find no anodyne. Then I got to thinking maybe there was a remedy after all. I was a writer with a number of full-length books behind me, and I would continue to write. The dull mechanic exercise of putting words on paper would be my salvation. It would help me forget the misery of the present and the bittersweet past. At times I had lived intensely as I hammered a new novel into shape, and I would do that that again. I would focus on recent events and write.

After three weeks of unhappy idleness, of staring for hours into the fire and mulling the meaning of Muriel's life and death, I began to write with unprecedented fluency. Though the weather continued cold, winter was losing its grip and spring was on its way. The novel I was calling *The Insurgents*, begun in the middle of 1887 and nearly finished before the end of that year, I put aside to be lost or destroyed. It was one of many abortive books I would labor on prodigiously and never publish. Now I was writing a novel of human suffering, lost souls mired in poverty and misery, and I was working with a steady hand. I had a good outline and even a good title, *The World Below*. On the first day I wrote six pages in five hours and felt satisfied. The second day I wrote twice as many and had to venture out to buy more ink. The third day I wrote from nine to noon, filling page after page, and from three o'clock to ten. Not a single page required rewriting. My imaginative power that had failed me for an entire year had returned stronger and more inventive than ever. I finished the book in only four months.

To keep up my strength, I began to eat thick slices of fat bacon for breakfast instead of toast and marmalade. A daily dose of cod liver oil was making me more energetic. I was exercising with dumbbells and walking when I could find the time. Two years had gone by since I had sold a book. It wasn't because I had ceased to write or become lazy. It was because I firmly believed I had lost creative power. Quite simply, I couldn't write well enough to satisfy my expectations. Every attempt was frustrating, painful, and producing nothing. I had gone to Eastbourne thinking a change of scenery would help, but that location was no better than London. The bracing walks in snowy weather eliminated my weariness but didn't boost my ability to create. Then came the fateful telegram and the need to act. It sent me to 16 Wilson Street where in reeking squalor I stared at Muriel's dead body. The shock I felt in every muscle and vein threatened disintegration and collapse. Yet the ugliness of it all somehow gave me focus and energy.

As I wrote about the imprint of poverty on young girls, I began to feel a renewal of indignation. I had felt that way at eighteen when I got to know Muriel Porter in Manchester. I couldn't blame myself for the way she had thrown her life away, but I was unwilling to blame her. At fault, I believed, was a callous society, *"a vice inherent in the nature of things."* I would dissect and analyze the forces that destroyed her, and I would thrust into the teeth of the world a severe indictment against them. My mission would be to reveal in powerful fiction the misery of the disenfranchised, and Muriel would help me more in death than she had hindered me in life. Every day, as spring weather came with bright air and flowers, I put tiny words on paper until my eyesight blurred and my wrist ached. Hour after hour as the sunlight made its way through the dreary windows of my sitting room, as the gas lamps flared on the street outside, I strove in solitude and silence. But on occasion I found time to walk with my eyes wide open through the streets and squares and poor neighborhoods of London to absorb the ambience.

I went to Clerkenwell at the end of March and to Shoreditch and Spitalfields in April. In Marylebone Road I admired the working girls who skipped along in high spirits, laughing and yammering. I spent a day at the Crystal Palace and bought a couple of books in Grosvenor Square, but the jaunts in fine weather intensified my loneliness. Springtime and couples walking hand in hand made my isolation bitter. *"This life I cannot live much longer,"* I noted in my diary. *"It is hideous."* As May passed and summer came, I was fretting myself into headaches but expected to frame an end to my novel in July.

Curiously, at thirty years of age I began to think I wouldn't live much longer. Muriel's sad death at twenty-nine reminded me of my own mortality. She had told me as early as 1880 that she suffered from tuberculosis, and I knew the disease was contagious. My dear brother

Will had died very young of tuberculosis. I was haunted by the idea that I would die also while young and of the same affliction. I never coughed without putting a finger to my mouth for the telltale scarlet. When on occasion I had the luxury of a handkerchief, I looked into it after use for spittle mixed with blood. Not finding any was only temporary comfort.

On the whole my health was good and I remained active. One evening in June of 1888 I went to a gathering in a fashionable home where I chatted amicably with cultivated people. At the party hosted by my publisher, I had a long conversation with a woman in her sixties. She knew all the living writers with a claim to greatness and spoke of their foibles with amusing fluency. She told me a story about Browning and how a man of some renown, well known in political circles, had never heard of the poet. Her amazing tale reminded me of my neighbor, the Queen's printer, who had never heard of Charlotte Brontë.

My host had entertained Charlotte in his house some forty years earlier and had wonderful stories to tell about her. He invited me to sit with him on the balcony after dinner, where we drank delicious coffee and smoked cigars. We talked about current events, politics, and literature. A full moon lit up the night, and the street below was silvery in the fine air. Someone spoke my name – Jonathan Blue, the novelist – and people gathered round me. With pleasure I answered questions about *Elaine of Lambeth*. A young woman asked if *Workers at Sunrise* would be published in a new edition, and that pleased me. But the question that gratified me most came from a gentleman who wanted to know when my collected works would appear. Through the summer I remembered his name with satisfaction. Could it really happen? Never, I thought, never in a thousand years . . . and yet.

2

I went back to my writing with renewed vigor, and by the middle of July the novel of slum life spurred on by Muriel's death was nearly done. One Sunday it rained all day and the weather turned cold. In the afternoon I lit a fire, as though it were December, and planned the last three chapters. The next day I went to Mile End Waste to attend a meeting of the match girls planning a strike. I wanted to study their faces and get a notion of what they were thinking. I was disappointed to find only a few standing passively behind a middle-aged dowager. It was a cause dear to the hearts of the match girls, but middle-class jackdaws seeking attention had taken charge. The scene made me wonder how much longer workers would submit to having so-called activists lead them by the nose. How much longer would they suffer in silence? When would they find a leader and develop a voice of their own? If that should ever occur, would it spell revolution for England?

Near the end of July I wrote from eight to eleven in the morning and from six to eight at night to finish *The World Below*. In four months I created a dark novel in three volumes dealing with the plight of the poor in a wealthy nation. I had done the job with high emotion because the subject was close to me. I wrote at times with anger and pity and distress. Completing the book helped me come to terms with the years of sacrifice and pain and all that reminded me of Muriel. I could now put behind me the bondage and misery of the past and look forward to the future. Perhaps I would find compatible companionship, even a quiet domesticity, in a comfortable home. In later novels I would focus on social and political issues crying out for solution. I would put aside the poorer classes to probe the problems of the middle class and the nation. In the meantime I was able to do what I had dreamed of doing for years: travel to Italy and the classical past and enjoy a respite from writing.

Shortly before I finished *The World Below* and sent it off to my publisher, I met a man of German origin named Lucas Bauer. He was a thick, big-boned fellow with huge arms and feet and a small head on a wide neck. His cheeks were red and plump and his blonde hair was clipped short. He had a habit of rubbing his hand across his stubby hair and blinking his blue eyes. My longtime friend, Günter Kurtz, was a German and the most congenial man I had ever known. I was thinking Bauer could be similar, and we exchanged addresses. Then one afternoon in the autumn of 1888 Bauer came to my flat brimming with excitement. He announced he would soon be going to Naples by way of Paris.

The more he talked, the more I wanted to go with him. An hour later we were planning to leave England at the end of the month for a lengthy tour of Italy. Bauer had little money and welcomed the chance to share expenses with a fellow traveler. He advised me to buy a frying pan and some other utensils for simple cooking. That way we could save on the cost of restaurant meals and conserve our money for seeing the sights. Aware that he too had just enough to get by on, I happily accepted Bauer as a lively, resourceful, and interesting person. Traveling together we could share memorable adventures in new places at moderate expense. And traveling with a companion was far better than going alone.

In late September we were in Victoria Station waiting to leave London. Dylan Crenshaw with a friend in tow called out to us. Sporting a raffish, broad-brimmed hat with a plume, a dashing rust-colored cravat with a huge knot, and a flowing cape slung romantically over one shoulder, he approached with long strides and quickly caught our attention.

"Hullo, Blue! You didn't think you could abscond like a shadow in the night without saying goodbye, did you?"

His manner was genial, loud, and cheerful, his greeting warm and friendly. He had heard from my neighbor that I was leaving for the Continent and was going by train to Dover for a Channel crossing. Delighted to see my old friend after many months, I let go with a guffaw of laughter and introduced him to Bauer. Crenshaw thrust out his hand for a hearty handshake, but the German merely nodded and stepped away. Though rebuffed with obvious incivility, my friend was amused.

"Well," he joked with a wink, "I'm jolly glad to see you have an affable companion going alone with you! And I do wish you well!"

Crenshaw and friend were planning a hiking trip into Scotland. They had visited my flat hoping to persuade me to join them. If they had come a day or so earlier, I would have gladly accepted. Now the train was pulling into the station, and I would board it with this person I knew so little about and be in Paris the next day.

"How long will you be away?" Dylan cried above the noise.

"I don't really know!" I shouted. "Probably a couple of months!"

"Well, give my respects to Rome! You'll love Italy!"

When we were seated in the train's small compartment and facing each other, Bauer rubbed his big hand over cropped hair, blinked his blue eyes, and asked whether Crenshaw and I were close.

"The best of friends," came the reply, "my oldest friend, and a capital fellow! Our friendship goes back to college days."

Bauer looked at me with a faintly supercilious air of disbelief. "College days, huh? I never went to college myself."

"I did but left short of graduation." I didn't explain why.

As soon as we arrived in Paris we went looking for a suitable room. To my surprise we couldn't agree on where to stay. Bauer insisted on spartan accommodations in a seedy hotel and was obdurate. Suffering from a sore throat and longing for rest in a better hotel, I ended the argument by offering to pay more than my share. Bauer accepted the arrangement without any show of appreciation. I was beginning to see quite early that my traveling companion was a penny-pinching, uncivil lout but tolerable. I didn't want a conflict of personality to put a damper on our adventure, and so I tried to believe Lucas Bauer meant well. But instead of finding a room we could share and thus save on expenses, after contentious discussion we rented separate rooms.

3

I soon discovered that traveling with this man would try my patience as well as my pocketbook. He was a moocher and an egotist and knew very little about art or anything else. All he could do in the presence of great art was jabber egotistical nonsense. When I wanted to study a painting for its subtle excellence, or luxuriate in the ambience of natural beauty, my companion behaved exactly like the philistines I had scorned in my novels. Sadly, life was imitating art and making my days in Paris not as sunny as I had hoped. On the second day we planned to have dinner together in a good restaurant. I suggested a pleasant boulevard restaurant near the Seine, a place we had passed earlier in the day, but Bauer insisted on something cheaper.

"Let's go in here," he said, pointing to a cheap eating-place that catered to street people with very little money.

"Sorry, old boy, not that place," I replied. "It's dirty and smelly and filled with street urchins. We're here to enjoy the sights and sounds of the City of Light, not to go slumming."

"Ah, hah!" the German snorted. "You are just as I thought! English people with their shameful class system are snobs and hypocrites anywhere they happen to be. You wrote a book called *The People* and I thought you were one of the people."

"*The Populace*," I corrected, showing no anger. "I don't want to quarrel with you, Bauer, but why must we deprive ourselves of basic comfort and decent food? You know as well as I we'd be out of place in there."

"All right, have it your way," said Bauer, blinking his blue eyes, "but remember next time we choose an eating-place it's my turn."

Reluctantly my companion agreed to enter a little restaurant advertising "world-famous cuisine." We dined with none of the camaraderie I had hoped to find, and the "cuisine" tasted vaguely of raw fish. I rapidly came to the sad conclusion that Bauer could never be a congenial fellow traveler. The man was stingy beyond belief, cheating when we divided the day's expenses, and lying about it. He was stupid and vulgar and blind to anything that required thought and sensitivity to appreciate. He claimed to be an artist, but after getting to know him better I noted in my diary: "*I understand the man now; he is not an artist but an artisan. He aims merely at decorative house-painting.*" That would have been all right, for I knew from the beginning he was no gentleman, but he was also dishonest and not to be trusted. Even so, I couldn't find it within myself to confront the oaf and part company with him.

A week went by and I received a letter from Smith & Richards. They offered to buy *The World Below* with all rights for £150. My books were not selling, they claimed, and so they couldn't offer more. *Elaine of Lambeth* had been well advertised at great expense, they said, but had sold only 400 copies. This book showing a mastery of my craft promised to do better. So they would take a chance and hope for the best. I knew the sum was not enough for an established author with six full-length novels to his credit, but I couldn't expect more. So without hesitation I accepted their offer. It meant I could now go on to Italy and live there for as long as a year. In sunny Italy I could free myself of drudgery and the daily grind to make a living. I would also find a way to sever all ties with Bauer. Meanwhile I would bask in knowing for an entire year I would be free to enjoy life in pleasant surroundings. When the weather turned cold for a day, I pegged away at Italian grammar to brush up on the language. I wanted to immerse myself in Italian culture past and present.

In good weather I went on a long and solitary walk to explore Paris. The city and its river delighted me. Mile after mile I walked beside the Seine on both sides, taking in all the sights and listening to a medley of sounds. The river flowed eight miles through the heart of Paris, and I found bridges I could cross to reach the other side. I returned to my room feeling tired but found time to read about the Seine. The next day I wanted to take a boat ride down the river, but Bauer called it a waste of time and too expensive. I had become exasperated with him, tired of the daily rounds for tourists, and eager to get on to Italy.

In any event, I went to the Louvre and Notre Dame with Bauer and was repelled by the man's ignorance and lack of taste. I couldn't believe he could speak negatively of the Mona Lisa and feel rapture looking at gaudy flowers advertising soap in a grocer's shop. By now I despised my companion and wanted to part company without rancor. We were not saving money by sharing a room, and his presence began to oppress me. Yet I couldn't bring myself to defy the boor or even displease him. I listened to him complain and later regretted I had nodded in agreement. Bauer could never be my friend, and I wanted to be rid of him.

In Paris longer than expected, I found excuses to explore the city on my own as often as I could. I spent my days visiting museums and galleries alone and attended lectures alone. At the Salle des Conférences I listened to a speech by a leading feminist who showed signs of intellect but looked like a fishwife. I made an effort to understand her rapid and fiery French, catching most of what she said, and studied her mannerisms. I thought I might be able to use her in my fiction some day, should I choose to write on the woman question. In the Louvre I spent happy hours observing the paintings of the masters and taking notes. On another day I went to the theater and saw an adaptation of *Crime and Punishment*. It maimed without shame the great novel I admired as a marvelous book. I wondered how so many self-important people could be so inept in a clumsy enterprise they mistakenly called art. The adapters had butchered the intricately structured long novel to fit its main events into a couple of hours. The actors spoke their lines mechanically and without feeling. It was clear they didn't even know what they were saying, nor did they seem to care.

A few days later I arranged to leave Paris from the Gare de Lyon en route to Marseilles. From there we would go by steamer to Naples.

"It's good you're so efficient at these things," said Bauer as we were eating dinner, "but I'm remaining in Paris. I'm compelled to do so."

I thought my companion was joking but wanted to be certain. "You're staying? Why didn't you tell me this before I made arrangements?"

"I have artistic work to do, important work, and it must come before mere travel. I hope you understand. You won't be upset if we spend a few more days in Paris, will you?"

"This comes as something of a surprise. How many extra days?"

"Oh, three or four, maybe six at the most. I have sketches to do."

"I shall try to undo the schedule for two and go on without you."

"Oh no, my friend. You can't really do that. You'll lose a large sum of money. If we postpone leaving we don't lose a centime, not even a sou. We just go to the station and change the date."

"If you wish to stay in Paris, that's your business. I'm going to Italy."

When I stood firm and wouldn't postpone the departure, Bauer relented and came along. Before we left he bought some difficult works to read, explaining that with so little time to devote to reading he was compelled to peruse profound treatises. He had no time at all for reading novels. They were written to entertain, and he had to get more from his reading than mere entertainment.

"I'm a disciple of Herr Kant," he crowed. "I judge everything with the touchstone of Pure Reason. I feed upon his complex and convoluted doctrine. I gorge myself on the Categorical Imperative."

I laughed inwardly at this pompous little speech. The German philosopher had not only gone to Bauer's head, but the gorging went to his waistline as well. Pure Reason, from the looks of the man, had to be as highly caloric as pure lard or red meat. I wanted to say that Bauer was spouting nonsense but held my tongue.

"I have no time for frivolous books," he repeated with a heavy sigh. "I shall never read the stuff you write. Art is long but life is short."

"The real problem," I said to him, "is that you . . ."

I didn't finish my thought. The real problem was Bauer's inability to concentrate longer than ten minutes on any book and fewer than five minutes on Kant. I believed the man could benefit from knowing that but decided I wouldn't be the one to tell him. Let someone with equal boorishness tell him. Early in our so-called friendship I learned to keep my mouth shut. The fellow wasn't interested in anything I had to say, or in anything anyone had to say. He lived in his own little world, the center of the universe, and not a thing beyond mattered. I made up my mind, in spite of not wanting to travel alone, to rid myself of him as soon as I could. I had longed for a congenial companion with whom I could share the excitement of Italy, but he was surely not the one.

CHAPTER EIGHTEEN

Italy Past and Present

In the third week of October we hurried through cobbled streets to the railway station. From there we went by rail to Marseilles. We had spent an entire month in Paris and would soon be in Naples. I sat by the window through the afternoon and took in the view. Bauer wanted to chat, but the noisy train gave me a good excuse for not responding. Because of time constraints we saw little of Marseilles. I strolled along the city's main street near ten at night, however, and was impressed by its cleanliness and bright lights. From my room at bedtime I could see an extensive garden of beautiful cypresses, and from the garden came the song of a nightingale. The next day we embarked for Naples at nine in the morning and arrived at four in the afternoon. The late-autumn day was like summer. The legendary Mediterranean Sea was choppy, but diamonds on its surface sparkled in the sun.

As soon as the ship entered the harbor, dozens of little boats came out to meet us. The boatmen in bold and colorful costumes, standing in the tiny craft to be seen, called out the names of hotels in a language I couldn't understand. For once Bauer was able to help. He had made the acquaintance of two Italians and had become good friends with them. He persuaded them to haggle with porters to place nine pieces of luggage in a small boat. They convinced the porters and the boatman that we were local residents and wouldn't pay the inflated fees reserved for tourists. In that way Lucas Bauer saved enough money to buy a good dinner for two, and for days he bragged about how clever he had been. On shore a shabby little carter who knew fluent English hauled us to an inexpensive hotel. He shook our hands effusively, crying out "thank you" in Italian, German, and English. We paid his fee without haggling, and that brought undue excitement. Viewing us as chumps and shrugging his shoulders, he scurried off to find another mark.

A few days later we rented rooms in the house of a German woman recommended by Baedeker. Bauer went nowhere without his Baedeker, and I soon discovered how accurate and thorough were the German's guidebooks. Our landlady was known to the entire city as Frau Paffenroth. She was a merry little woman with gray hair pulled back in a bun, spreading hips, and a large bosom. When she laughed her breasts and stomach shook like jelly in a bowl. Lucas Bauer found her amusing and spoke German with her. Later she confided to me that he spoke passable but vulgar German. He had taken pains to have his traveling companion believe he was fluent in several languages, and now I was discovering that even his German was suspect. So what language did he really speak as his native tongue? His English was acceptable in the streets and parks of London but not in the drawing room. His French was clumsy, and when it came to Italian he knew only the basic phrases. I was not surprised to learn that he spoke no language well, and anything he said in whatever language lacked substance.

As the days went by, he put away his artistic pretensions and began to display an aggressive philistinism. Wherever we went he made it clear that he knew the price of everything but the value of nothing. Now more than ever I wanted to explore Italy alone. Without delay I entered into the life of Naples on my own. I had come for its classical associations, but instantly the human activity in the precipitous city captured my interest. I complained of having always to climb hills but loved the sights and sounds and katzenjammer of the streets. There was a grace and hullabaloo all around me.

In all my life I had found nothing like that in England. The streets teemed with goats, donkeys, horses, dogs, cows, calves, children, monks, nuns, priests, jurists, soldiers, panhandlers, pickpockets, hawkers selling their wares, and all sorts of people buying and selling. Riding on the warm and bright air, so different from the heavy haze that smothered

England, was a constant uproar: street carts crunching on the pavement, drivers yelling, barbers calling, dogs barking, donkeys braying, bells tinkling, and the occasional barrel organ grinding out folk tunes. Adding to the cacophony and making it ripe and sensuous were the church bells that tolled on the hour every hour.

I liked the happy atmosphere of the streets. It flowed into the restaurants where I ate cheap but good food and where I drank wine with each meal. Sometimes I ate a juicy pear while strolling, or grapes and figs just off the tree. In nearby Pozzuoli I sat for an hour in a public garden on the waterfront, enjoying the sunshine and the sea breeze and dazzling colors. Old fishermen were basking in the sun, and some were mending their nets. A spirited organ grinder was making lively music. The sea tempered the heat, and I could feel an invigorating tonic in the air. It was laden with the salt of the sea, and that made it keen and sharp. Under a tree silhouetted against the blue sky sat a lovely girl with a slender waist and long legs. She was reading a book. I glanced at the girl, and she boldly returned my glance. I looked at the tree branches. They reminded me of a Japanese print I had seen in the British Museum. The girl herself, slim and fit in colorful garments, called up a painting of a young woman I had seen in the Louvre. It was dated 1650 and over the centuries natural feminine beauty had remained the same, unchanged and constant. In tune with the surge of lively activity around me, I was a world away from the wintry streets of London.

In November in warm and sunny weather I visited Pompeii, going there by train on a Sunday when admission was free. I viewed the remnants of antiquity with a deep-seeing eye, my imagination investing them with the life and color of the distant past. A classicist from my college days, I stripped away the centuries to enjoy the era of Horace and Virgil. I had expected Pompeii to be little more than a tourist trap but was pleasantly surprised when it went far beyond my expectations. I noted how the lizards ran along the ancient walls seeking the sun, how the houses were arranged along very narrow streets, and how all of Pompeii was carefully preserved with pride. My only thought of literary labor came on November 15, 1888 when *Comes the Morning* was published as a book in London. I viewed that novel as a failure even though it had appeared in serial form near the time of Muriel's death. Many Londoners who had never heard of Jonathan Blue read it as a magazine feature, and as a book I expected a few more readers. One or two might send me a letter by way of my publisher.

2

Before leaving Pompeii I came upon a group of German tourists in animated conversation at a small inn. My German was not good enough for me to understand every word, but they were laughing and joking. One of them was speaking German with an accent that seemed oddly familiar. Later I discovered the person was an Englishman from Yorkshire, my own native ground, and looked the part. He was short, large of waist and belly, and in his early fifties. He wore muttonchops on each jaw. They were fuller and darker than the sparse hair on top of his round head. His cheeks were tan and weather-beaten. He wore on his chin a salt-and-pepper beard. His laughter was jovial and loud. I learned that Algernon Portman had been in Italy for seventeen years and now lived with his Italian wife and large family near Sorrento. Portman was fluent in four languages but spoke each with a distinct Yorkshire brogue. He took a liking to me and invited me to his home to meet his family. Curious about the life and habit of a Yorkshire man in Italy, I accepted the invitation on November 23, the day after my thirty-first birthday.

In a little cart pulled by a donkey and gaily painted, Portman and I went up to a trim little house in the middle of a lemon orchard. Inside we found a strange assortment of people in the midst of clamorous disorder. Portman lived with his young wife Catarina, their four draggle-tailed children who spoke not a word of English, her aging parents infirm and illiterate but feisty and talkative, and his half brother Ernie, who claimed to be a poet. He had once been a medical student in Edinburgh but failed to pass his examinations to become a doctor. He was now a hopeless drunkard dying of an unknown disease and able to eat only bread and salami once a day at night. Any food consumed in daylight he vomited.

Ernie had a room in the cellar, which he shared with me for the night, and we talked for two or three hours.

"I know I'm going to die," he said rather plaintively, shrugging his thin shoulders. "I can't eat, can't keep anything down, can't sleep, but I would like to publish my poems before I go."

He had once been round and fat, he said, but was now thin as a shadow and looked yellow and leathery. His age was not more than thirty-five, but his skin was loose, wrinkled, dirty, and with splotches of white. His clothes hung on him like they belonged to someone else, and his bony hands trembled as he talked.

"I eat little these days. I'm very sick just about every morning. I'm pretty sure I have cirrhosis of the liver, and that's a killer, y' know. Only the thought of publishing my poetry keeps me alive."

"Do you have enough poems to make a volume?" I asked.

"More than enough. I write a little every day. It's the one thing that keeps me going. Sensual pleasure has no appeal any more. The Italians say the only way to live is to forget you're going to die, but I can't subscribe to that. The only way to live is with purpose. That's why I cling to the hope of publishing my poems."

"I can offer no assurance, but I shall ask a friend to help you find a publisher in London. He may not be able to do it, but he will try."

Later in a letter describing the beauty of Naples, I asked Crenshaw to help the man if he could. My friend replied, saying he couldn't find a publisher willing to take a chance on the poetry of an unknown expatriate. By then I was out of touch with the family in Sorrento. And yet thoughts of a dying man living in a cellar away from Italian music and sunlight haunted me. I wanted to know the end of his story, but it was hidden in the future. I hoped I might visit the family the next time I came to Italy. If the fates allowed it, I would surely come again.

For two or three days I worried about the Portmans and their plight, knowing there was little I could do to improve their situation. To overcome the depression I felt, I spent two days on the isle of Capri and then returned to Naples. At the end of November I took the night train to Rome, leaving Lucas Bauer behind. Without quarreling and boosted by silent understanding we had agreed to part company. I traveled all night in third class and got no sleep but was entertained by the antics of a harlequin boy piping music on a wooden whistle. In Rome I quickly found a room with a small kitchen and rented the place for a month.

Though weary, I couldn't resist leaving my new abode to view the Forum and the Colosseum. Then I walked along the Tiber and back to my rooms to rest. I remembered it was one of the longest rivers in Italy. It came down from the backbone of Italy, and ran through Rome to the Tyrrhenian Sea. It also meandered through Rome when it was the center of the world, and the thought pleased me. By association it brought into memory the Seine in Paris and the Thames in London. Once when I was too hungry to sleep I rambled to the middle of a bridge and looked down on the Thames to view the dawn in misty water. The color of blue steel gave way to pale gray, and for several minutes, as the sun was rising, the river sparkled with golden nuggets.

3

Rome was cold and not at all like Naples. The streets were quieter and the populace more dignified than the Neapolitans. I could walk without street urchins pestering me, and with my Baedeker in hand I wandered happily away from modern Rome into ancient Rome. Part of my second day I gave to England, visiting the graves of Keats and Shelley and noting details in my diary. In that quiet place I found pine and cypress trees and roses still in bloom. I touched the gravestones and read the inscriptions, sadly noting that Keats's famous epitaph – *here lies one whose name was writ in water* – was being obliterated by time. In the next month I divided my time between modern and ancient Rome, finding much of interest in both. Almost every day I encountered blonde Germans living in Italy and energetic Americans touring the country. The latter amused me with how little they knew about anything. They reminded me of a recent encounter with one of their kind.

On the ship sailing to Naples I met a man from Missouri who was finding *Don Quixote* rambling and convoluted and difficult to finish.

"Are you reading the book in the original Spanish?" I asked.

His congenial reply was brusque and loud: "Oh, no! Not me! It's hard enough in English. Was it done in Spanish too?"

"Yes, I believe it was. I've read the book many times in English. One of these days I hope to read it a few times in Spanish."

"I'm not sure I can get through it in English," the man sighed, "but I like Quixote's sidekick, Sancho Panza. He's really a funny little guy."

Recalling that scene caused me to remember another incident with an American. At the foot of Vesuvius, the most famous volcano in the world, I had visited a little inn surrounded by rolling vineyards of wine grapes. There I met an attractive American woman with skin as white and smooth as alabaster. She was separated from her companions, was distraught and hungry but unable to speak or understand Italian.

"Do you speak English?" she asked plaintively.

"I do," I replied, "it's my native tongue."

"Oh, I'm so glad! I really need your help. Will you help me, please?"

I had never been able to resist a lady in distress, especially one so attractive as she, and so I readily offered to help her as best I could.

"My group went off to the mountain without me," she explained. "I've been waiting for them to return. They should be here by now."

"Surely you will see them soon. Is everything all right with you?"

"Not really. I need food. I'm famished. I don't know how to speak to a waiter. They don't understand English."

I ordered for the woman a succulent beefsteak with potatoes, green beans, sliced tomatoes, and buttered roll to receive her undying gratitude. Later at the Forum in Rome I met an affable and talkative American who couldn't speak a word of Italian. Without knowing it, the man was being swindled wherever he went. In European cities, and particularly in Italy, Americans of both sexes were seen as fair game.

The days passed rapidly and before I knew it I was in the midst of the holiday season. As a thunderstorm raged outside, I attended Christmas services at St. Peter's simply for the beauty of the ceremony. I was not in sympathy with the doctrines of the Catholic Church, nor with the teachings of any church. For longer than I cared to remember I had been an agnostic, losing every shred of religious faith at an early age. At St. Peter's my Protestant roots caused me to feel a bitter contempt for the richly clad priests performing arcane rituals. A moment later, viewing those same priests as representing an institution of power, intellect, and endurance, a feeling of reverence swept over me. Then I remembered reading about priests in times past molesting nuns and even children, and I wondered whether evil in the Church persisted in the present.

Just before the end of the year I went to Florence. On a Sunday when admission was free I visited several art galleries. I was impressed by my first view of Florence. However, the city lacked the famous antiquities of Rome and the colorful sights and sounds of Naples. Unlike the sunny and warm iridescence of Naples, the air was raw and cold and the mists obscured any vista of the city from the hills. As in Rome, I suffered from loneliness but was glad to be free of Bauer. If I ever came back to Italy, I told myself, I would travel with someone who could share my interest in the glory and grandeur of Italy's past.

Near the middle of January, 1889 I began to think about the novel I would write when I returned to England. For ten years, beginning in 1878, not a day had passed that didn't require me to labor on a writing project. When I tried to relax on rare holiday, the work of the moment weighed heavily upon me. When I strolled through the streets for exercise and relaxation, I found myself taking mental notes for use in my work. But the journey to France and Italy broke the habit and gave me respite from my chosen line of work just when it was becoming drudgery. At the end of January I went to Venice. There as in Florence I was reminded of the Renaissance, which I viewed as a rebirth of ancient learning at the beginning of modern times. Venice with its monuments was therefore merely an echo of antiquity. Except for its unique watery setting it wasn't truly interesting to a lover of the classical past.

To my mind the Greek temples at Paestum were grander than Renaissance art and architecture, and more real than the dirt and grime of the present. But lovely Venice with its canals and gondolas and street music, its special lighting at night, its lagoons and seagulls wheeling in a blue sky, was vastly pleasant. In Venice I began to outline the plot and theme of my next book, which I thought I might call *The Puritan* after one of its main characters. It would deal with a group of English expatriates in Italy slowly surrendering to its siren song. I would have them living in some of the places I had visited, particularly Naples.

Near the end of February, the morning dull and cold and my bones aching, I began the long trip homeward. I went by way of Milan and Brussels and returned to London at nine in the morning on March 1, 1889, exactly one year after viewing my wife dead. The weather was windy and cold and the streets were thick with slush, so very different from the weather in southern Italy. My flat, closed tight all the time I was gone, smelled of dusty and leathery old books. I liked the smell, but every inch of the place needed airing and a good cleaning. I would have to do it on my own the very next day. The cleaning woman I had before leaving was no longer available. She had found a job as a custodian in one of the new department stores.

Trying to get my affairs in order, I scrutinized my rent bill. I was being charged for an empty flat all the time I was gone, and the bill was enormous. Maybe I should have sublet the apartment, but how could I expose my books and all that I owned to strangers? I was lucky enough to have an understanding landlord who learned from my neighbor I was away in Italy and would soon return. With no thought of eviction he allowed me to pay the money I owed him in monthly installments. It was an expense that had not crossed my mind even once when traveling free of worry in Italy. The debt was paid in full just as fall was coming.

CHAPTER NINETEEN

Home Again and Talk

A week later I boarded the 1:30 train for Yorkshire to spend a few days with my mother and sisters. In my letters from Italy I had often said I wanted to talk about my adventures rather than scribble words about them. Now I seized the opportunity and relived the best moments of my trip with the people closest to me. When they listened with a show of interest, I spoke with excitement about all the things I had seen and loved in Italy. However, as we were having dinner I assured them that one thing was certain: I wouldn't go there again in winter.

"Why not?" Maggie asked. "I've always heard that Italy has a mild climate and a special sunlight that makes the colors intense."

"Well, yes, the southern cities are that way, and the coloring of any scene on a sunny day is marvelous. No wonder Italy has produced great artists for hundreds of years."

"Then why do you complain about the cold, dear brother?" she asked with her usual persistence.

"A person can't explore the northern cities with any comfort in winter. I thought the whole country was warm the year round until I went there. Now I know better."

"Couldn't you dress warmly and forget about the cold?" asked Emma. "Surely the weather there in winter isn't as bad as here."

She was young and when she wanted to do something outside, she paid little attention to the weather. In the springtime she often walked in the rain, lifting her face to it. In winter she welcomed the snow.

"I did dress warmly," I replied, "but you can't see things in the open air unless you tolerate a biting wind. You can't spend time in galleries and churches either – too cold. My month in Florence was all but wasted because of bitter weather."

"A pity," said Maggie. "I didn't know the buildings had to be heated. I guess I've always thought the southern sun warmed the houses."

"It does, but not enough in winter. The poor in the southern part of Italy suffer greatly during the winter. They have no fire for warmth, only for cooking. I was fortunate enough to have a grand lord of a stove to pay humble obedience to, but not them."

They laughed as they grasped the image – a big, commanding stove sitting grandly in the middle of the room demanding homage on a cold day. A shivering human all too eager to obey.

"No, no, not on your life," I asserted smiling as the laughter ended. "It must not be winter the next time I go to Italy."

Mother nodded in a knowing way, but my sisters shook their heads in disbelief. I was only thirty-one, a young man in the prime of life, they were thinking, and yet I was talking like a doddering old man with thin blood and palpitations. With that frame of mind they wondered how long my health would hold. But Mother had known for years that I was sensitive to wintry weather. She believed it went back to my boyhood even though I had said in letters from America that I liked the blasts of winter when living in Boston.

After spending a few days with the family, I was back in London to begin the work I had put aside for five months. I tried to write in March but made little headway. At the beginning of April I sat down at 3:30 in the afternoon and wrote until 9:30 in the evening. At the end of those hours I had written two and a half pages and had worked myself into a headache, the first in many months. A few days later I labored from three to eleven and filled four and a half pages. I finished Chapter One of the book I was now calling *The Liberated* and went on to Chapter Two. Before the end of April I had completed several chapters of the first volume but went back later to rewrite. It was almost an obsession, the endless rewriting. I frequently complained that it hindered my progress grievously, and yet I believed it made my writing better. The current project was a new kind of book taking me away from grinding poverty in mean neighborhoods to well-off people in a different country. It was therefore harder to plan and write even when the scenes of life in Italy triggered pleasant memories.

My novel, *The World Below*, had been released in March, and complimentary copies had gone to my relatives. Emma confessed that she felt a sense of horror on reading the book. Its depiction of unrelenting poverty disturbed her. I explained I was writing in the realistic mode and had taken pains to make my scenes exactly as I had found them. I added that fidelity is of first importance in a novel depicting realism, and I was happy to see she understood what I was saying. Maggie said bluntly the book was not to her liking. She couldn't identify with any of the female characters, and she wanted no part of their world even though Clara Pruett had caught her attention. I replied I was proud of the way I handled Clara's tragic story. My brother Quentin, slowly gaining a precarious reputation as a chronicler of country life, praised the book, insisting it was the best thing I had done.

The World Below was about working-class people wanting to work but often having no work and forced to live from hand to mouth in boring idleness. Central to the story were strong, able-bodied men desperately needing jobs to support hungry families. Their women, of equal importance and strength, worried with them about making ends meet. I knew that working women in London were confronted daily with insecurity and harsh treatment. Some of them managed to find a morsel of happiness, depending on circumstance and disposition, but many sank into despair and untimely death.

Except for rare exceptions, working-class women with ambition and desire to move into a higher class were doomed to failure. Clara Pruett in my novel exemplified a longing to move upward with egregious results. She personified ruthless ambition, struggle, and ultimate defeat. Her story underscored my conviction that social class in England has always placed ambitious persons in uncertain bondage. I knew from my own experience how easy it was in the British system to sink to a lower class, but climbing above one's class was all but impossible. To be born lower class was the luck of the draw. An unlucky card doomed persons of intelligence and talent to poverty and hardship.

2

As Clara attempts to escape the working class, she is penalized in ways she cannot understand. At seventeen she has worked three years as a needlewoman and is sick of it. Her father can see what is happening to her and is worried: *"The girl can't put up with it any longer. It's ruining her health, and it's making her so discontented she'll soon get reckless."* In time she abandons the workroom and becomes a waitress, but the new job brings no improvement. The hours are thirteen to fifteen a day with no chance to rest. Day after day she is on her feet, moving quickly from table to table loaded with heavy trays. The place is noisy, crowded, and smelling of unwashed humanity. It is little more than a factory for the production of human fodder. The people who labor there as cooks and waitresses are overworked and underpaid.

Of a sudden and without notice, Clara quits and goes in search of other work. Quickly she learns that only menial jobs at very low pay are available to one in her position, and the world is uncaring as to whether she lives or dies. Torn by anxiety and seething with anger, she enters at that time into *"a feud with fate."* Unseen forces, mindless but seeming to act with malice and direction, strike out against her. One afternoon she breaks a cracked pane as she flings open the window of her room. The glass cuts deep into her palm. Spellbound by the sight of her own blood, she watches it trickle to the floor to form a scarlet puddle. She throws herself on the bed and sobs in despair.

After a night of sleepless agony, she tells herself she understands her unseen opponent, the brutal force struggling against her. Why had she suddenly quit her job? Why at that time rather than countless other times? *"It was not her own doing. Something impelled her, and the same force – call it chance or destiny – would direct the issue once more."* She decides not to resist, and though fate remains her enemy, she finds herself relieved from the stress of resisting. Despair gives way to an amorality that makes her laugh at convention, at social rules that govern human behavior. She has discovered that only the law of the jungle demands obedience, for she lives in a state of nature where only the fittest survive. Accepting that challenge, she must think only of self.

For a time Clara drops out of sight, and the reader is left to wonder what kind of life she is living. Later we see she has become an actress, but the glamorous new life has brought few rewards. The work is hard and competitive, and behind the scenes not glamorous at all. Bitterly she recalls her struggle and concludes: *"There's no such thing as friendship or generosity or feeling for women who have to make their way in the world. We have to fight, to fight for everything, and the weak get beaten."* In that state of mind she seizes without hesitation and without compunction her chance to wrest the leading role from another actress. Destiny tells her she can't afford to think about the pain she has thrust upon a colleague. If their identities had been reversed, the other woman would have done the same to her.

On her way to the theater she is not exulting in the new role she is to play, but thinking how the next role will have to be bigger and better. Near the entrance a veiled figure steps from the shadows and flings liquid into her face – *"something that ate into her flesh, that frenzied her with pain, that drove her shrieking she knew not whither."* Defeated by the woman she had betrayed, her pretty face severely burned by acid, she goes home to the slums to spend the rest of her days in a darkened room. Clara Pruett had dreamed of becoming a popular and talented actress. She wanted to escape the oppression of the working class, achieve wealth and recognition, and climb into a higher class. She dared dream of glamour and leisure and even some degree of power.

But things in the world below, *"the sorry scheme of things,"* had other plans for her. Where drudgery was the order of the day, to dream of escape was to commit an effrontery that angered fate. To expect more than basic survival in such a world invited disaster. An element of retributive justice was also present. Willing to victimize others, in time she herself became a victim. As I told her story, I was mining a vein of fatalism that owed a debt to John Stuart Mill, Thomas Hardy, and the German determinists. In other novels I had tried my hand at fatalistic presentation of characters in conflict and was pleased with the result. In later years I turned increasingly to the dark and unpredictable role that fate plays in human life, viewing it always as a mysterious force beyond understanding and beyond human control.

Inevitably as I wrote about these women, echoes of Muriel came into the novel. The squalid room in which she died becomes the room of a woman destroyed by drink and hardship. The temperance cards found in Muriel's room turn up in the fictional room. The wobbly signatures on the dated cards, each more unsure than the one preceding, reflect a steady decline similar to the one that seized Muriel. The death scene of Margaret Bascombe is another reminder of the room I was compelled to visit in March of 1888. On entering the death room Margaret's husband reacts as I had done. Shaken by what he sees, he feels profound pity for the poor woman. He stares at her stricken face, looking for something he can recognize, and he mumbles to no one in particular: *"Do you remember what hopes I had when we married? See them now – look at this bed as she lays on! Is it my fault?"*

Another man burdened with an irresponsible wife and complaining of callous deception, mimics my dilemma with Muriel: *"At last she began to deceive me in all sorts of little things; she got into debt with shop-people, she showed me false accounts, she pawned things without my knowing. Last of all, she began to drink."* The experience of Sukey Barton later in the novel is still another echo of Muriel. For reasons her friends and relatives cannot understand, Sukey abandons herself to hard liquor, takes up with mean companions, leaves her caring husband, and sells her youthful body on the back streets of Shooter's Gardens to get money for drink. Starkly put, *"Sukey had strayed on to a downward path."* Once the descent began there was no calling her back. Like Muriel, she found perverse pleasure in a wild and careless life that promised freedom. Writing the book in a fever of painful reminiscence, I purged myself of all that reminded me of Muriel. At last I was free.

One evening near the end of March in 1889 Crenshaw paid a visit to hear all about Italy. The wind was whistling around the eaves of the old house and we built a small fire. Near ten o'clock I heated two fat scones, and we ate them with butter and cherry jam. Sipping black tea scented with bergamot, we conversed into the wee hours of the morning. Afterwards, rather than walk home through neighborhoods that put him at risk, Crenshaw slept on a pallet near the fireplace. Nothing pleased me more than to have a sympathetic and knowledgeable listener as I spoke of my travels. My friend had been to Italy more than once, and so we could share experience and compare and relive the good times.

"I do believe you're happier pouring out the details of your stay in Italy," laughed Crenshaw, "than actually being there. It's the mark of the storyteller, of course, and not at all objectionable."

"Well, I can tell you this, old friend, the details are selective. I won't mention the bitter weather I endured there or other unpleasantries. You know it's always good to run through one's travels with a traveler."

"Yes, the recollection means savoring the highlights of a very memorable experience. One's memory is indeed selective."

"Reminiscence puts the imagination to work and clothes everyday scenes and ordinary activities with a sheen like new paint."

"It's the glimmer of romance. And you call yourself a realist!"

"Even though I write realistic novels, Crenshaw, I'm not altogether a realist. You know me better than that."

"Yes, I do know you. I've been in your life a long time, and I probably know you better than your mother. Oh, I'm sorry I couldn't help that poet you found in Sorrento. I spoke to several publishers but they all shook their heads. Adamant about refusing."

"Oh that doesn't surprise me. I knew the poor man had a very slim chance of ever getting published, but I wanted to give him hope."

"What in the world ever happened to him?"

"I don't know. I lost contact with the family after I left them. If I ever get back to Italy I hope to visit them again and learn more about him."

"And you went to Pompeii? Tell me about it. I never got there."

I told Crenshaw all about Pompeii and was thankful my longtime friend seemed to take a genuine interest in my travels. Also he offered provocative insights as we talked. The man was a genial egotist and self-centered but knew how to maintain a friendship.

With the coming of spring we saw more and more of each other, and enjoyed the give and take of lively conversation. On one occasion the robust behavior of Dylan Crenshaw (who had developed a wild side in America and Australia) rather disturbed me. We had planned to meet near the middle of April for lunch at a little bohemian restaurant he had found. As I was waiting for him to appear, a messenger came with the news that he had been arrested! I walked briskly to Marlboro Street Police Court and found Crenshaw in a cell. He was sitting there with a half smile on his broad, expressive face and with an air of total nonchalance. As I approached he stood up to grasp the cell bars and greet me.

"Hullo, Blue! Sorry to bother you, old man, but I couldn't think of a better way to let you know what happened. I got into a fracas, a donnybrook y' know, and I didn't want you to eat without me, or wait for me to show. So I sent li'l Pete to explain. Glad he found you."

"You're a rotter, Crenshaw," I joked. "We could be eating at this moment, savoring bread and cheese and sipping a good red wine, but here you sit in jail! What in hell is going on?"

"Well, it's a long story and I don't have the time to do it justice."

"How in the world did you put yourself in this predicament?"

"It's like this," he paused and took a breath. "I'll try to make it short because in a few minutes I have to go before a judge."

We stood there on either side of the bars facing each other. I wore a slight frown but Crenshaw continued to grin. He seemed to be enjoying the absurdity of being arrested like a common criminal, and I know he really liked telling a good story.

"I was walking down the street minding my own business when this fellow came from behind, pushed me roughly as he passed, and began to walk in front of me. I had two or three books in my hand, spectacles on my nose, and was carrying an umbrella. Maybe he thought I looked upper-class and too peaceful, and so the bugger clobbered me pretty hard on my left side and seriously interfered with my strolling gait."

"Are you sure he did it on purpose? Couldn't be an accident?"

"Well accident or not, I caught up with him and stepped on his heels just to let him know I was not unaware of his rudeness."

Looking at me from behind bars, Crenshaw laughed heartily. "The bounder turned and called me names and asked me what I proposed to do about it. I didn't propose to do anything, I did it!"

He paused and laughed again, this time even louder. "I hit him hard with my umbrella and knocked him down. He tried to get up and I hit him again. With amazing accuracy I might add! Finally the ugly blighter got up and found a policeman and charged me with assault and had me arrested. Can you believe it?"

A turnkey came and unlocked the cell door and led Crenshaw away with me close behind. I sat on a hard bench in a drafty courtroom and listened to the proceedings. My friend was up on charges of assault, and in a few minutes it was over. The fine was three pounds, and I was required to pay it. Anticipating a fine and with only a few shillings in his pocket, Crenshaw had hired a boy to run to the restaurant with a message. When it was all over he laughed and laughed and commented on the sweet, sweet taste of freedom. In spite of no small degree of worry, I shared his laughter. I hadn't sold a book in months. My savings account had dwindled to almost nothing. I was almost as poor as Crenshaw, and I had lost three pounds to his reckless behavior. In the next few weeks I would have to practice a severe economy to make up for the loss.

A few days later I had to put down my dismay to entertain Lucas Bauer. His short blonde hair was darker now, but the habit of rubbing it with a beefy hand was still there. His waist was thicker and the pale blue eyes duller. He was dressed in better-looking clothes than I remembered and appeared more prosperous. As always he gushed a merry fountain of rodomontade. An uncle in Berlin had died and left him a sizable legacy he could live on for years. He was newly arrived in London from his European travels and had taken lodgings better than the old ones.

Now settled in clean and comfortable rooms, he decided he would see his old traveling companion again. He was in high spirits and jaunty even while assuming a languid air. Speaking rapidly but with measured excitement, he hinted of scabrous intrigues and steamy love affairs. He spoke of a mistress he had kept for a month in Rome.

"Ah, Roma, capitale d'Italia!" he exclaimed. Speaking three languages as clumsily as ever, he sputtered without shame: "Benissima, that lady! Une belle fleur! A delicate flower, but oh what a flower! We met at the opera, you know. Well, to be honest, just outside the opera in the square. We hit it off. To save money she moved in with me. We had fun!"

Though beside himself with the pride of conquest, his story was meant to amuse. But because I knew "the lady" was a denizen of the night, the perception caused an image of Muriel to swirl in my brain. Bauer offered to treat me to a fine dinner, saying he didn't have to worry about money any more. I would have liked nothing better than a good meal in a good restaurant but recalled in Paris, famous for its cuisine, the man had chosen the cheapest eating-house he could find. Even though he claimed to be in clover at present, he would probably seek out a place with greasy plates and foul food. As mind and heart struggled with stomach, I summoned the strength to decline his offer. He left mumbling to himself shortly afterwards. When suppertime came I found a tin of tomato soup in my little pantry. I ate it hot with some cheesy crackers newly introduced to the market.

CHAPTER TWENTY

Emily Singer

April came and went and the spring of 1889 moved into May. In London's lush parks the afternoons were fresh and sparkling with a stirring in the air. Under a blue sky the shrubs and trees were budding. Nature was alive and one could feel a rustle in the earth. In warm and sunny weather painters and carpenters descended on my place of residence to spruce it up and give it a fancy name. To get away from the noise and distraction, and a gnawing loneliness that always came with pleasant weather, I went again to Harrogate. I brought along a valise stuffed with a change of clothes and sixty manuscript pages of my current project. I hoped to finish *The Liberated* with its theme of Hebraism slowly being absorbed by Hellenism in a house that favored Puritanism. I found a sturdy table in the upper portion of the house and went to work. Day after day as the weather grew too warm for comfort, I covered page after page with tiny script until the job was done.

Writing to my friend Günter Kurtz in Potsdam, I said the book was going well in *"this home of Puritanism."* I knew the phrase could refer with equal accuracy to the household itself and the town. I could observe the Puritanism, an important force in my book, inside the house and outside among the townspeople. My mother and sisters, devoutly Protestant, endorsed the Puritan attitudes pervasive in my novel. The town of Harrogate for more than two centuries had been a home for dissenters of every stripe and a refuge of Puritanism. What better place, I told myself, to write a book satirizing Puritan rigidity while admiring its strength and tenacity? Proximity to my subject was exactly the impetus

I needed. It allowed me to work unimpeded without time-consuming false starts and even provided a bit of inspiration. I saw it as a strong story full of color and passion, and I wrote with delight. The title of the book referred to a group of British citizens living in Naples who eventually were able to free themselves of Puritan morality. Specifically the title referred to Hester Bowes, beautiful but sternly Puritan, who gains a larger apprehension of life and reality after living in Italy.

Although both of my sisters influenced the character, I was thinking mainly of Maggie as I created Hester. However, when Emma read the book in 1890, she angrily accused me of using her as the model for my fictional character. *"Nothing of the kind,"* I replied, hoping to placate the angry woman. *"You have grown up in a more liberal atmosphere."*

For the sake of peace in the family I was willing to compromise. If Emma fell short of emancipation as defined in the book, she was certainly more liberal than either her sister or Hester Bowes. Four years younger than Maggie, Emma had been more receptive to my instruction, had read more widely, and retained more. I was able to talk with her more openly on suspect subjects, and as the years passed I wrote more letters to Emma. On the whole I considered her more enlightened than her older sister. Yet both had been reared in a stronghold of Puritanism, and neither had been able to throw off entirely the dogmas of the past to live freely in the present.

In the first chapter of the novel with its echoes of my Italian experience, Hester Bowes is seen writing stern and gloomy letters beside a window that overlooks a scene of rare beauty. The shimmering Bay of Naples and the city of sunshine have done little to energize her sense of beauty. *"You need not envy me the bright sky,"* she tells a friend back home, *"for it gives me no pleasure."* In the more favorable climate to recover from a stubborn illness, her deep-seated Puritanism will not permit her to show interest in anything Italian. She is not able to enjoy the street sounds and the music, not even the legendary sunlight. She is there only for warmth not available in England.

The ringing of church bells is to her a sad reminder of a centuries-old adversary, Catholicism. On Sundays there can be no walking the streets to mingle with the citizens and admire the sights, no piano playing or use of any musical instrument, no reading for entertainment, no casual and careless chitchat at table, and no laughter whatever at the dinner table. As her health slowly improves, she works on plans to build a chapel in her hometown. In time, however, as the subtle influences of her surroundings play upon her, she puts the chapel plans out of sight and becomes more flexible in behavior.

Gradually the beauty around her awakens and intensifies her love of beauty. She finds herself reading Dante on Sunday, raptly listening to Italian folk music, and experiencing the pleasure of long walks in the sunshine. Her severe Puritan attire slowly gives way to colorful and comfortable clothing. Her frown evolves into a smile, and she gives up her *"silly desire to build a chapel."* Instead she will use the money to build public baths in her hometown. Hester's spiritual journey from Hebraism to Hellenism runs through many chapters. The transformation is slow, meticulous, and far more subtle than any summary can show.

I wanted my sisters to follow a similar path. If they could free themselves from what I considered a restrictive religious faith and become more worldly, they could attain in time their full stature as women in the modern world. In Emma I saw greater promise than in Maggie. But to a liberal mind such as mine at that time, both fell short of the goal. Though on the surface they seemed more enlightened than women of their region and class – both were schoolteachers – at the core where it really mattered they were staunch Puritans. That was obvious in any conversation that revealed their ideas and beliefs. It was obvious too in the way they conducted themselves.

I wanted my sisters to become acquainted with current intellectual opinion. I wanted them to show a wide range of reading and gain a reputation for being liberally educated. Reading widely, as I had done, would exercise their minds and stimulate their imaginations and leave them with little time for the sour religious tracts I despised. But when I thought about their intellectual progress, I suspected they would never become truly liberated. On holiday with Maggie I enjoyed the sensuous beauty of Sark and Guernsey, but found myself becoming irritated with the cast of mind my sister often displayed. *"My sister is a Puritan,"* I confided to Kurtz, *"and we can talk of nothing but matter of fact."* My tone, as Kurtz noted, was one of weary resignation.

It was impossible to talk with either of my sisters about anything that had to do with the private acts of one's life. Their innate Puritanism prohibited any reference to sex in any context. It stifled even the innuendo permitted other middle-class families and demanded periphrasis or verbal games, which I found intolerable. My sisters viewed the human act of reproduction as foreign to their world and naughty. They viewed the necessary act of defecation as nasty beyond words. They were prisoners of Mrs. Grundy with their roundabout phrases, and their talk irritated me. While I was reading Ovid on the island of Guernsey under blue skies that reminded me of Italy, Maggie in her late twenties plodded through some dirty little pietistic work. I was reading in the original Latin the witty and sophisticated love poems of a classical poet who would die in exile. She was attempting to digest poorly written pamphlets on how to become a better Christian. Her reading tastes rubbed against my senses, and I wondered with leaden sadness whether my teachings for a decade had not been wasted on her.

2

The summer of 1889 was hot and muggy but went by rapidly. In September I was back in my London flat and feeling lonely again. Workmen had improved the looks of the building, but the management had given it a pompous name I didn't like. Near the end of the month I went to Chiddingfold in Surrey to visit an upper-class intellectual named Emily Singer. She had appraised my social novels in *Murray's Magazine* in an essay that placed Jonathan Blue and Roger Leland side by side to reach a conclusion that neither had a workable solution for the conditions we described. With some reserve I evaluated her discussion and found it competent. It came from a person who knew the poor neighborhoods of London and the misery of human life there. Even though her article had been prepared too early to mention my most powerful novel of poverty, she had shown a genuine interest in my work. Later she read *The World Below* and judged it abundantly better than any other book I'd written. That began a hesitant and polite correspondence, which led to my visit. She shared a small house in a picturesque village with another young woman who just happened to be away on holiday.

In casual dress appropriate for the season, diminutive Miss Singer greeted me with a smile and a throaty welcome, extending her right hand. Was I supposed to shake that hand? If so, it was beyond the pale of current rules governing polite behavior between a man and a woman. Possibly she placed herself among the ranks of the new women who believed shaking hands demonstrated and promoted equality, but apparently she was less aggressive than most new women. I was relieved when she lightly touched my fingers and withdrew her hand.

"I'm so glad you could visit," she said with a show of pleasure.

In America I had met women who seemed quite beautiful until they opened their mouths to speak. Then I found their voices were metallic, nasal, unpleasant. A grown woman speaking with the squeaky voice of a little girl grated on my nerves even then. Since that time my ears had become attuned to the sound of the female voice in maturity, and Emily Singer's spoken word pleased the ear. Though pleasant, it lacked the timbre of Mrs. Gossam's voice and couldn't be described as musical.

"I'm delighted to be here," I stammered. "It's a beautiful autumn day and the scenery along the way was stunning. I enjoyed my trip."

"We're not so far from London as people believe. The city reaches out to border the county to the north, but of course Chiddingfold is in the south of Surrey and closer to Sussex."

"When we came to the River Wey, I could see it flows northward into the Thames. I understand the River Mole flows in the same direction."

"Yes, the rivers here are delightful in summer. The boatmen drift with the current all the way to London. But getting back can be a problem! Shall we have luncheon? Later we can walk and talk and I'll be your guide for sightseeing. I'm sure you must be famished."

"Oh, not at all," I lied. "I had a big, hulking breakfast before I left."

We ate smoked beef and cheese on savory bread, a tangy salad with nuts, and a tasty dessert. She had placed a finely carved bowl of big and juicy grapes on the table, and they reminded me of Italy. Later when the sun was lower and the shadows longer, we explored the countryside and enjoyed a vast amount of talk. I returned to London recalling the pleasantries of the visit and feeling glad I had gone. As the train took me homeward, I exulted in the beauty of the place. The downs were blue against a gray sky, some flowers were still in bloom, and the foliage dazzled the eye with bright colors. I had seen a tree on which every leaf was a brilliant scarlet. It was unique and so was Emily Singer. In a letter to Kurtz, I described her as a small, attractive woman of twenty-eight – *"Jewish, intellectual, cultivated, and wealthy."*

She was a lively young woman known for her independence, wit, and ability. An heiress of high social standing, she had chosen an active life of the intellect in preference to tea parties and idle dignity. When I met her, she had already become a fledgling writer. Eventually she went on to publish studies of the French Renaissance and the French Revolution, and she tried her hand at biography. Her wide-ranging intellectual interests were similar to mine. She knew classical Greek and read Plato and Sophocles in the original. She was a student of modern literature and a lover of poetry. She adored Tennyson's musical verse but was appalled by his old-fashioned ideas regarding women and their place in society. She was active in social reform among the poor in London's East End, practicing a personal philanthropy there. In later years she established a home for orphans and helped rehabilitate men in prison,

Such a woman was certain to win my admiration. In November I paid a visit to her flat in London and was impressed by the sumptuous interior. I learned she had inherited £20,000 from her father, had invested the sum wisely, and was free of financial worry. As we talked I looked her over carefully and filed away mental notes. Later I confided to my diary that her face and manner were quite pleasing, more so than when I first met her. Gazing at her as she prepared tea, and not missing the smallest detail, she was in a special way quite beautiful. Alone in private rooms with the woman and observing how she conducted herself, I was surely drawn to her. However, I felt troubled when I compared her social and economic position to my own. Our meeting in Surrey, pleasant and relaxed in the open air, had awakened my sensitivity to nature and the colors of autumn. Our second meeting in a luxurious London apartment set me on a course through perilous emotional waters that had to be navigated with meticulous care.

The way she lived caused me to compare my poverty to her wealth, my insecurity to her independence, my austere life to a life lived in luxury. The result was a feeling of painful inadequacy. I found it impossible even to think of a romantic relationship with her. All I could hope for, if I dared hope for anything, was a casual friendship. I had convinced myself that only the rarest of women would risk living in poverty with a struggling writer. Also no author worth his salt would marry an heiress for her money. My sense of honor, painfully and tediously restored after the fiasco at Thatcher College, stifled even the promise of happiness with such a woman as Emily Singer. The people close to me – they could be counted on the fingers of one hand – all agreed that when faced with worldly decisions, I repeatedly chose to suffer hardship and deprivation rather than compromise my code of ethics.

The lively correspondence that sprang up between Miss Singer and me allowed me to classify and categorize her by type. I could see immediately that she was something of a new woman, for she had all the characteristics of that person. She was well educated, active in social reform, busy with a wide array of interests, and beginning to make her voice heard in a tumultuous and noisy world. She was also a good example of that particular type of woman who paid little attention to religious doctrine, accepting for spiritual guidance a broader sense of morality. That was the subject of the novel I was writing when I met her, and my acquaintance with this liberated new woman helped me apply similar characteristics to my fictional women. After I came to know Emily Singer, she influenced my image of the advanced woman in much the same way my sisters had shaped my view of the dogmatic woman. She helped me make my portrayal of the new woman less severe of line, less harsh, and more graceful than in my early novels.

3

Emily Singer knew a multitude of people and had many friends, but for a time she took a personal interest only in me, Jonathan Blue. I was thirty-two, tall and slender, well spoken and well mannered. My sisters said I was courteous, thoughtful, well read, talented, and good-looking but worried too much. Miss Singer admired my literary endeavor and saw steady progress toward maturity with every novel. She wanted to be my friend and perhaps more, but in the summer of 1890 I made up my mind never to see her again. At that time, according to my diary, I rejected entirely the prospect of finding a wife belonging to the middle or upper classes. As I was declining invitations from Singer, I confided both to Kurtz and Crenshaw that I had little hope of finding a female companion in England. I had concluded that my chance encounter with a sympathetic, intelligent, educated woman of secure financial and social position had brought me more pain than pleasure.

With women of her stamp I felt strangely inferior. In their presence I was awkward, reticent, and not true to myself. I thought they viewed me as a well-known author and expected urbane, witty responses from me. I felt they could never accept me as an ordinary person with ordinary faults and simple needs. And so I was stiff and artificial and not myself. Emily Singer had come uninvited into my life and for a time had put down my terrible loneliness, but she was no match for that feeling of unworthiness that made me run from her.

In October of 1889 I began a new novel, which I called in preparation *The Head Mistress*. The plot centered on middle-class life in a provincial town and the faulty education of girls in the new high schools. Later I placed the setting in London, thought about changing the title, and was certain it would become a savage book. In a few days I finished outlining the story and went on to select the character names. I was thinking the protagonist of the novel, a female character, could echo Miss Singer. She would be the truly educated woman standing in contrast to falsely educated women. But two days after visiting her in London, I was off to Greece and the work was laid aside. I had said I would never travel to Italy in winter, but Greece was farther south and I hoped it would be warm and sunny. My travels took me away from my story for three months. When I picked it up again after all that time, I had only a vague recollection of the patterns I meant to weave. Reluctantly I abandoned what might have been a strong novel. The remnant I tossed onto a growing heap of abortive books.

In the middle of November I was crossing a rough sea in heavy winds that threatened storm. With some difficulty the old steamer docked for the night in Genoa. Early the next morning under blue skies it set out again, sailing down the coast of Italy and through the Bay of Spezzia past Livorno. I remembered that was the body of water where Shelley had drowned when his small sailboat capsized in 1822. Though it happened a lifetime ago, the poet's untimely death saddened me. But the Gulf of Genoa, as splendid as the Bay of Naples, dazzled my senses. The next day I managed to make out the faint outline of Vesuvius spewing clouds of smoke. Then at three in the morning we passed Stromboli with its volcanic activity turning the black sky crimson. Later we sailed southward and eastward into the Ionian Sea. Just as the sun was setting I caught a glimpse of Mount Etna on the coast of Sicily. As the steamer approached Piraeus, the chief port of Athens five miles southwest of the city, I promised myself I would never spend another winter in England. I would go southward and find sunshine even it meant living on a few pence a day. After a journey of nine days, during which I made friends with a young Greek who spoke English, I reached my destination. It was a place I had long dreamed of visiting.

I was surprised to find that Greece was still on the old calendar and was behind Europe by twelve days. It had a strong Eastern flavor, and Greeks spoke of "going to Europe" as if they were not part of Europe. The customary traffic was between Constantinople and Asia Minor, not Europe, and the public markets were called bazaars. The weather in November was like an English midsummer. The sky was a deep blue even when the wind blew hard. In places where I found no wind, the sun on my back was like fire. The climate was incredibly arid. Except for a few carefully watered trees and shrubs, Athens could boast very little grass or green foliage. Where there should have been expansive greenery, I found only bare ground baking in the sun and clouds of dust.

The sunsets seen through the dust were unspeakably beautiful, and the Acropolis in the dying sunlight glowed with a rich amber. It occurred to me that the landscape had changed little in three thousand years. The early rulers of Athens, living on the high ground of the Acropolis, saw the same natural beauty, the same splendid vistas as I was seeing now. I planned to be there a month and then sail for Naples.

Modern Greek was difficult to understand, but I could read the newspapers and speak it well enough to ask questions. The waiters always spoke Greek but resorted to a few words in French and Italian when pressed. They served exotic dishes swimming in oil. I learned to like some of the food, but the red wine I had loved in Italy had a resin taste in Greece. One morning at breakfast a waiter brought me a newspaper in English. That pleased and surprised me because most of the people I met were impolite and brash. Many of them tried to swindle me but not with the finesse of the Italians. All of them were bent on making money. Regretfully I heard no street music in Athens, and that reminded me once again of the warm Neapolitans who knew how to make life melodious. While I looked forward to returning to Naples, I would do all I could to enjoy Athens. In daylight, as in Rome, I spent my time in the places known to ancient Athens. In the evenings, as in Rome where I read Horace in Latin, I read Aristophanes in Greek.

As Christmas came I visited Naples for the second time and felt as joyous as on my first visit. I was in the midst of sunlight, color, warmth, uproar, and music! I was again in Napoli, Napoli! Bagpipes moaned and groaned in the streets and church bells tolled. The weather in the southern city was delightful, beyond description. My room at my old address had a wonderful view, and I felt at home. Letters had been forwarded and were waiting for me. The food in Italy was tastier than anything I had eaten in Greece, and the city of sunshine was glorious at Christmas. I was back in my element! Among the letters I found a tattered postcard from Algernon Portman, asking me to visit.

CHAPTER TWENTY-ONE

The Portman Family

I went again to Sorrento and found the same dirt and disorder as before. Sitting around a large oval table devouring peasant food afloat in a rich sauce, they talked about Ernie. The failed medical student who yearned to become a published poet was dying in a nearby clinic. A derelict in decay who was drunk every day, who ate only at night and lay retching in a squalid cellar away from the healing sunlight, was too weak, they told me, to be the terror of the family any more. His one ambition was to see his poems published, but that never happened. In the confusion of the unhappy household the children gathered up his manuscripts to kindle a fire. When he heard what had happened, Ernie became enraged, swore he would kill every one of the little angels, but suffered a heart attack. The four little girls were older now and more rambunctious. They chattered all at once in the local dialect and tugged at my clothing to get my attention. Their parents and grandparents had not aged at all and were in good health despite their troubles. All of them, except for the children, spoke with an annoying whine and worried about a bleak future. Not one person in the strange family appeared to be unduly sad in regard to Ernie's misfortune. He was dying, nothing more.

I spent a week with the Portman family, buying groceries for them and learning more about them. Algernon told me at the dinner table, speaking English, that he wanted to emigrate to Connecticut. It was a dream he had long nourished, but he was certain his family wouldn't come with him. His wife wouldn't think of leaving Italy without her parents, and they were too old to establish themselves in another country. The children were young enough to go anywhere but spoke not a word of English, never learned to read or write, and couldn't be torn from their mother. So he would have to go alone, if he went at all, and that meant losing all he had ever gained in Italy.

"I'm trapped here," he groaned with a comical touch of exaggerated anger, "trapped like a prisoner in a dungeon! When I came to Italy years ago I thought I was coming to sunshine and freedom. Now a no-good family won't stand by me when I want to do something with my life. Ernie dreamt of doing something with his poor wretched life, and look where it got him. It's gonna be my fate to die just like him."

"Have you thought of selling your place here and moving to the city? Perhaps you could find a job as a clerk in a city of your choice or find work as a translator and make a new start."

"I could never be a clerk and I can't sell this place. Clerking is beneath me and the place belongs to Catarina. Her parents put up the money to buy it and that's why they live with us. When you live with old people, friend, you have to give up your dreams. I love my wife but she always sides with her parents, and they are squeezing the juice out of me. I would like to go back to England, back to Yorkshire if I could, but I can't even dream of that. I'm trapped, my friend, trapped!"

Listening to Algernon Portman complain about his squabbling family made me thankful I was solitary and free. I disliked domestic conflict and felt I would never marry again even though I suffered from loneliness and need. I wondered why a man couldn't find a female companion and live with her because he liked her and part from her if he grew to dislike her. Why did a couple have to tempt a punishing fate merely to enjoy each other? Why did so many couples, and the Portmans were a good example, fall into a web of inextricable misery soon after marriage? I asked myself those questions but got no answer.

As the days passed I could feel the tension in the household, even among the children. When Algernon entered the room the little girls grew quiet, looked at him with sad eyes, and scampered away. He explained with theatrical lamentation that in all likelihood their mother was turning them against him. Her parents were in on the dirty deed too, and he was only one poor wretch against them all. One evening when her husband went to the outhouse, Catarina cornered me in the kitchen and told me her side of the story. In her singsong Caprese dialect, most of which I couldn't understand, she sputtered painful anguish through salty tears.

"Believe me, Mr. Jonathan Blue, I speak the truth. Algernon Portman never knows from one day to the next what he wants to do. He has no rudder, that man, no helm my papa says, for steering a course through life. All he does is drift without purpose or direction whenever the wind blows. He cares only for himself at the expense of his family."

I decided all I could do was listen sympathetically. After all, what could I say to improve her lot even if she could understand me? Also it seemed to me she wanted to unburden herself with talk. She wanted to be heard only and expected no helpful response.

"His own pleasure, his own comfort, is all he cares about. Ernie terrifies the children, maybe even molests them, and what does he do? Nothing! It's all he's capable of doing. That Ernie, that most peculiar man, terrorized my family! Threatened to kill my girls! And Algernon stood by with a silly grin on his hairy fat face and did nothing!"

"Does your husband mistreat you?" I ventured to ask.

"Mistreat me? Mistreat me? Hah! If only the world knew!"

She was almost screaming in her agony, and large tears rolled down her cheeks. "Sometimes in his rages he beats me! He threatens me with knives! He calls me a slut and a whore and tells me to go home to my family. Will you listen to that? He tells me to go home to my family! They live here, right here in this house, my house, and the crazy man tells me to go home to my family! He doesn't want me or need me any more, he says, but I know for sure he would die without me!"

I could see that Portman was a passionate fellow and half believed all she said. With mounting emotion and little restraint she lamented as in an Italian opera the misery of her life.

"I am doomed to live in dirt and discomfort and fear until I die. And my poor little girls, what in heaven's name is going to happen to them? Well, at least that crazy Ernie is gone! And good riddance! But every day this wretched house gets more wretched. I tell you, Mr. Jonathan Blue, I don't know what I can do, what anyone can do!"

My heart went out to the woman, so emotional and so full of pain, and yet somehow comical as she blurted a crescendo of misery almost operatic. Speaking rapidly as large crystalline tears washed her face, she wrung her thin hands and twisted her black hair into a tangle. I tried to comfort her, touching her trembling shoulders and brushing her cheek, but she had worked herself into frenzy and was beyond comfort. The moment her husband walked into the kitchen she ceased complaining, grew quiet, and vigorously began to wash the dishes.

I left the strange family the next day. "Torna a Surriento!" Portman called to me. All eight of them, smiling broadly, waved goodbye.

2

The visit to the Portman house was a sad interlude in the midst of happy travels. I grieved for them and the agony they had brought upon themselves, but I could think of no way to help them. Even if I tried they wouldn't accept the help, for they had conditioned themselves to a way of life that nurtured their distress. They fed on one another, took comfort in their mutual misery, and were fiercely loyal to each other. Portman would never go home to Yorkshire nor travel to Connecticut. That was only a gossamer dream. His family in the trim but disorderly house was more than that and all he had.

I went back to Naples, expecting to remain there through January of 1890 and then return home. I worried about a flu epidemic that had begun in Siberia in October, had reached Berlin and Paris by November, and was pandemic in Italy, Spain, and England by December. I told myself that should I become sick I hoped it would be in the warmth and sunshine of Italy, not in the cold and cloud of unfriendly London. I never fell victim to influenza, but was lying ill in bed when I should have been sailing homeward. I suffered from congestion of the lungs; a condition I thought was brought on by a bad cold or something more serious. A German doctor skillfully treated me. He didn't charge me anything at all, and later to show appreciation I sent him a copy of *The World Below*. I had a high opinion of Dr. Limberger. The man was a gentleman with an easy, affable manner and a good physician.

Returning to England by way of Gibraltar, I saw one day in late afternoon a glorious rainbow arcing above the Mediterranean Sea. It rose gracefully from the dark blue water to curve with bright and glowing colors across a dappled sky. Looking eastward, I stared at a truly beautiful and moving natural sight.

"It has seven colors from red to violet," said a fellow passenger, leaning against the rail. "We don't see rainbows at this time of year in England, you know, mostly in summer after a shower. A rainbow isn't a physical thing. You can't touch it. It's made of sunlight and raindrops. It's nothing more than a pattern of light, a reflection, on moisture."

"Really, sir?" I asked with a show of not understanding. "When I was a boy I thought if I could find the end of a rainbow I would romp in the sparkling colors and maybe even carry home the pot of gold."

The man looked puzzled and moved away. For an instant his myopic spectacles reflected the rainbow, the glow and glitter of sunlight on raindrops. I laughed inwardly for a moment and then began to feel sad as I remembered what Keats had said about rainbows. Surely the poet was reacting to this same breed of person when he wrote: "*There was a rainbow once in heaven. We know its warp, its woof, its texture. It is listed in the dull catalogue of common things.*"

At Gibraltar the weather was rainy and a storm was brewing. The top of the great rock, a landmark for centuries, was covered with cloud and mist. Gusty winds were beginning to blow and the waves were building. I stood on the slippery deck, clinging to the rail, until the rock was no longer visible. Opposite Gibraltar lay Africa, mysterious and foreboding. I had heard of its wild mountains, wild animals, and unpredictable people. I had a longing to go there but knew I never would.

The wind was howling and cold as we crossed the Bay of Biscay, and the vessel rolled and pitched in rough seas. Storm clouds stretched their arms across the sky, blotting out the sun. Every point on the compass threatened weather not likely to improve anytime soon. I stood at the rail to study the sea and feel its power, but as the wind increased I went below and found a chair in one of the corridors where passengers gathered. The ship's parson in clerical garb approached and spoke to me.

"I hear you are a celebrated author," he said with a friendly smile. "I mentioned your name to some of the passengers in first class, and one of them recognized it immediately. The woman said you've written several novels that read very well."

"Well, thank you for the compliment," I said to him after a moment's hesitation. "I have a dozen years of writing behind me and eight long novels to my credit. Come spring my latest book will be in the shops. I hope you will read it."

"I shall make a note of that and look for it," said the parson with a pleasant chuckle. "In the meantime I hope you'll mingle and let the good people on board know of your work."

"You tell me the people in first class already know me," I remarked. "Sometimes I wonder why it's my fate to be known by first-class people when I must travel in second or third class." I smiled as I spoke, making light of the situation and taking pleasure in the irony.

The parson, a genial man who had never been burdened by poverty, couldn't be certain the young author was serious or joking. He chose to interpret the remark as a witticism, as an intellectual play on words expected of an author. He was chuckling as he hurried away.

"I shall make it a point to read some of your clever books, Mr. Jonathan Blue. Indeed I shall!"

He didn't ask for titles. Despite his parting words, it seemed obvious to me that he would never read even one of my books. And yet I rather liked the man. He had a kind heart.

3

The year 1890 came in with cold and sleet and snow. Near the end of the second month I was home again and complaining of slippery streets and slush. A month later the snow and ice turned to rain and fog, equally oppressive, and a biting wind began to blow. One of the first things I did after arriving in London was to write to my publisher to ask why *The Liberated* was not being advertised. My mood improved when the book was published in the spring and promoted extensively. Also I took comfort in the sound of a barrel organ nearby. To my dismay the authorities in Naples had banned them at the height of the Christmas season, and that alone made my visit less pleasant than the year before. In London, even before spring had fully taken hold, a lively tune from a barrel organ was reaching my ears. It lifted me from the depression I always felt on returning home from a trip. I thought I might hire an organ grinder to play in my rooms by the hour as I tried to plan a new novel, but then I thought of my neighbors. They were quiet and respectable people and might complain, interpreting the music as raucous noise.

At the end of March I was working steadily on a new book with scenes to be set in Guernsey and Sark. My sister Maggie, who was with me in those places, worried that I might bring her into the book and subject her personality to satirical thrusts. The sisters did not like seeing themselves as targets of satire. It seemed their brother was making fun of them. They wanted me to succeed as a man of letters but not at their expense. Both were relieved when the book, like so many others, proved abortive. In the middle of April we went to Paris to spend ten days there. The spring weather was not as good as we hoped it would be, and seeing Paris as tourists was expensive. However, we managed to eat French cuisine in some good restaurants and see the usual sights. We strolled the streets and boulevards and visited museums and art galleries. In Montmartre in good weather we were privileged to see musicians, painters, and writers at work.

One evening we peeked inside the Moulin Rouge, hoping to enjoy a close-up view of the rowdy dancers in gaudy costume. The club was loud with music and chatter, packed with all sorts of people drinking and dancing and flirting. I wanted to see that strange little man who was making the place famous with his bold and colorful posters. I asked a waiter who motioned in the direction of the window. Another waiter, pausing for only a moment, told me that Toulouse-Lautrec was not to be found at his favorite watering hole that night. Without taking a seat – my sisters were a little frightened of the saucy place – the three of us withdrew. I knew I would have to reckon with the strait-laced behavior of my sisters in Paris. I would have to put behind me any thought of viewing the naughty nightlife of the city. It was a compromise, I told myself, but worth it to see the delight on their faces as they began to feel the special magic of Paris. Each day we took in the sights, at ease with one another and laughing. When evening came we went searching for a suitable restaurant before returning exhausted to our hotel.

After two weeks we were crossing the Channel again. I was moodily silent. Summer was coming, and I dreaded returning to London to work in solitude. To keep that pesky wolf from the door, I had to have another novel ready for a publisher before the end of summer. As early as March I had made a start on a new one but had put it aside in frustration. Now I thought I might work faster and better in the home of my mother and sisters. During the summer months, in the company of my family, I felt I could write three to eleven each day and be with them in the mornings and early afternoons. I couldn't expect stimulating conversation from them, wine at every meal, witticisms to draw laughter, but we would be in the same house and I wouldn't be alone. Through the first weeks of May, in the stuffy little room set aside for me at the top of the house, I made what I thought was good progress on the new novel. With memories of Greece, Italy, and France to sustain me, I worked without faltering. But soon I desired rest and companionship and found myself succumbing to anxiety and doubt.

The specter of endless labor in that pedestrian place began to trouble me. I felt I couldn't endure more of such a life. In my early thirties, I wanted to relax and enjoy the years I had left. I wanted to laugh and talk, savor good food with good wine, listen to music, and make love to a young woman. Brooding on the matter, I felt that life was meant to be lived. Let someone else write about it. Yet each day demanded I become a writing machine to sustain life. Somewhere, perhaps in the writings of Charles Bradlaugh, I had read a powerful statement that really came home to me: "*I pity the artist, whether he writes or paints, who must live by his art. You will hear people say that poverty brings power to the artist.*

It does not; it eats into his soul. It drives each day a nail into his coffin." I memorized those words, for they absolutely applied to me.

Scribbling words on paper meant isolation and solitude even when my imagination was most active. When I had to endure one painful false start after another, when it seemed my talent had crept away to cringe in hiding, I felt the burn of torture. Yorkshire, moreover, was in the grip of bad weather and the town of Harrogate, brashly conservative, was not the right place for me. Also I was mortified to learn that my keenly satirical novel, *The Liberated*, had failed to show its satire to shallow critics who pronounced it a failure. My friends had called it the best thing I had ever done, even better than *The World Below*, but foolish men who couldn't recognize irony in any form were heaping vituperation upon it. What did they want from me?

Even though one reviewer detected "subtle touches of humour" and called the book "clever and amusing," I suffered from alienation and a mild paranoia. There seemed to be afoot a cynical and deliberate attempt on the part of persons unknown to silence me as a writer. I knew that my novels were better than most of the stuff that poured from the presses every day, even that receiving high praise. And so I couldn't understand why novel after novel invariably failed even as contemptible hacks became wealthy. As I struggled to put together my ninth full-length novel, the days were gloomy and lonely and the nights sleepless. I began to convince myself that serious changes would have to take place in my life if I were to get on with my work.

To survive as a writer and as a man with normal human needs, I would have to leave England in search of a mate. I would have to find a female companion on the Continent to assuage my loneliness and feed my hunger. I couldn't be certain I would find her in Germany, France, or Italy but find her I would. I was ready to make an exhaustive search. To my family I said nothing of the parched emotional desert I was desperately attempting to cross. In letters to Günter Kurtz, a struggling writer in Germany, I spoke of indecisive plans and mounting frustration. Kurtz replied that he was in much the same predicament. All day each day, though tired and hungry, he worked at writing a book better than the one before. Neither the publishers nor the public seemed to notice what he was doing, much less to care. He was as isolated and alone as I. When approaching a woman in the streets, she invariably looked away from him. Not once, he confessed, had any woman ever looked him full in the face. Not once, even in America, had any woman shown a passing interest in him. The future for us both looked bleak indeed.

CHAPTER TWENTY-TWO

Raw Emotions in Summer

June came and went with fair weather that grew warmer. I was thinking I'd be able to finish my latest project by the end of August. But one failed attempt after another drained my creative power and left me exhausted. With each sheet of paper filled with script but tossed into the wastebasket, the job became more impossible. When August settled upon Yorkshire, I was angry with myself and depressed. Confused and frustrated, I was suffering an emotional slump that bordered on despair. The condition was affecting my health as well as my career, and my sisters were beginning to show concern.

"Let's go for a walk, Jonathan," Emma said to me one morning, as we were finishing breakfast. "You could use some exercise and fresh air, and we can talk as we walk."

"I would like nothing better," I replied, "but it's my turn to wash the dishes. Perhaps after the chore is done?"

"Oh, go on now the both of you," Mother insisted. "Maggie and I can do the dishes. It's a fine day and you want to go out and use it."

"Well, all right," I said to Emma. "I'll get my hat and some comfortable shoes and meet you out front."

In the early morning we walked through the town and into the countryside. All my life I had enjoyed walking in a natural setting far more than on the hard pavements of London. During my early years there, in the throes of insomnia, I had prowled night after night through neighborhoods inhabited by rough and dangerous people. Unlike Dylan Crenshaw, who sometimes boasted of getting the best of thugs who wanted to harm him, I had never been accosted. In those years my clothes and appearance were no better than those of any other denizen in the poor districts of London. Down-and-out muggers, looking me over, thought I was one of them and left me alone. It was the one stroke of good luck that came my way in those years. I'm certain I prowled the same neighborhood as Jack the Ripper with no fear of trouble.

"So how is your latest book coming along?" asked Emma, interrupting my thoughts. "Are you making good progress?"

"Not really. I'm having trouble as usual. I compose with good speed at times, and the words that go on the paper seem exactly right at the moment. Then later I make changes, wonder if they made the story better or worse, and end up crushing the sheets and tossing them away. At the moment I can't seem to fall into the rhythm I need. And I know I'm putting down more than I should. A good novelist should know what to leave out, and I'm having trouble with that."

"Is something else bothering you? Mother says you worry too much about money. She says maybe you couldn't afford the trips to Italy and Greece and our holiday in Paris. You insisted on paying for just about everything. Is it about money?"

"Oh, no, not a'tall. I really enjoyed treating you and Maggie. I could have saved the money from my last book, but why? I really needed to take those trips, and they did me a world of good."

"So is that your pattern for the future, Jonathan? Write a book, get a handsome sum for it, travel and get restored, and write again?'"

"Ah, Emmie, that sounds like perfection. It sounds marvelous to me, though not achievable. My books don't bring a handsome sum and never will. I'm told they appeal only to a limited audience."

"At dinner last night you mentioned traveling to Germany sometime soon to visit your friend. You know the climate isn't the same as Italy, and this warm weather will be over soon."

"I do want to see old Kurtz again. It's been a long time and we go back a long way. Also I want to meet people on the Continent."

"Why there and not here? Do you think people in other countries are more friendly, might help further your career?"

"Possibly, but probably not. Kurtz has been trying to help me in Germany, but unless my books are translated I see little hope for readership. I hear I'm getting readers in the United States where they pirate my work. Maybe eventually the English-speaking world will read me, though I doubt it. As for friends, Kurtz is a good and close friend. In London I have only one, and half the time he's off to America or Australia or some other faraway place. He's a good man, Crenshaw, but I want to move among cultured people, intellectuals if I can."

"You wrote to me once about visiting a woman in Surrey. You described her as accomplished, intellectual, and close to your age. What happened with that, if I may ask?"

"Yes, all of those adjectives fit Emily Singer. Bright, attractive, engaging, and wealthy if you want more," I answered with a chuckle.

"Well, what happened? Maggie and I were thrilled by that letter and prayed she would match your intellect and be your type."

"Thank you, Emmie. You and Maggie both have good hearts. I know you want only the best for your brother. But the world seems to have other plans, villainous plans involving incessant struggle in solitude."

"Oh, come on, Jonathan! That heavy pessimism doesn't become you. Why do you say such things? Why not say you're depressed at present, down in the dumps, but will soon overcome it?"

"I'm depressed at present but will soon overcome it."

That lightened the mood and we had a good laugh. "Well, what happened?" she persisted. "Did it end suddenly without explanation, like a bad novel or bad play? Did she say *never darken my door again?*"

"No, nothing quite so melodramatic. I broke it off. She was an heiress and wealthy. I was penniless. I knew it could never work. Even if we had fallen in love and thought of marriage, I could never have lived off her money. So I declined her invitations and broke it off."

Generally I said nothing to my sisters about my private life. But now that Emma had bought it up, I went on talking. "Crenshaw urges me to live abroad, flee England altogether. For whatever reason I can't make friends in London, or any other place in England."

"I know about that, and I could never understand why."

"Maybe it's what I do for a living, how hard I work and how little rewarded. I become despondent too often and bitter. Though loving England, I despise the English system and the English populace. Yet in Italy I rather loved the people, even the rough ones."

"I don't understand. You said about the same thing years ago in your letters from America. You had friends there and seemed happy."

"I was . . . well at least for a while. Then my unkind past caught up with me and the specter of starvation raised its hoary head!"

I chuckled at what I thought a witticism but she didn't respond. She had been reading my American letters and had found a cheerful outlook in most of them. Several mentioned the good food I was eating. No letter said anything about starving, but later she heard the whole story.

"I'm more myself when abroad. Maybe it's because I don't expect people to recognize me as a published author, and so I can be just a man. Does that make any sense to you?"

"Well, of course it does. But a fine English girl would fall in love with you if you gave her half a chance. I think you know that as well as I."

"Not a middle-class girl, Emma. No woman of the middle-class is willing to live with a struggling author in penury. Those women remain single by the thousands rather than marry any man with less than 400 pounds a year, and many demand 600. As you know, my income is half that, even less. My plan is to move about on the Continent where money goes further and perhaps some day find a wife there."

Again she didn't respond. She wouldn't admit it, not even to herself, but seriously she didn't want her brother to marry a foreign woman. Too many English gentlemen were doing that. While she would never openly express prejudice of any kind, she was a soldier in the ranks of conservative women. I didn't press the issue further, and as we began to return home a gentle rain was falling. We stood under the branches of a sheltering elm until the shower passed. In the little room at the top of the house I went back to my writing but made little progress.

2

When August came I was sick of the daily struggle to put together an intricate story of lasting worth. I hoped with all my heart that I might stumble upon a sustained inspiration to electrify a savage novel. Each day for several hours I covered sheet after sheet with script, but the following day destroyed just about everything I had written. In the bosom of a loving family, I suffered from acute loneliness. Then out of the blue I met a local girl named Connie Henson and promptly fell in love with her. I had heard from Maggie that Connie had shown an interest in my writing, and so we visited her home to give her *Elaine of Lambeth*. The next day Maggie and I were invited to dinner. The evening with the Henson family – Connie had a brother and sister – was filled with music and laughter and good-natured chatter.

"That young woman sang quite well, wouldn't you say?" I asked Maggie as we made our way home.

"Yes," came the curt reply. "She did. I could see you were smitten."

"Oh, no, not smitten," I laughed, "but I did like her music."

Later I went to Connie's house alone and enjoyed myself vastly. Again I listened to the music of the girl's piano and her father's violin, a mellow and melodious duet. With a hearty appetite I ate their food, drank apple juice instead of wine, and shared their laughter.

Once more, on returning home, I had good things to say about Connie and her family. My sister Maggie was certain I had fallen in love.

"Let's hope something good comes of that visit," murmured Emma under her breath as I relaxed in the parlor.

"We can hope," said Maggie much louder, "but don't be surprised if your big brother runs like a rabbit."

She was directly on target. Within days, for reasons I myself couldn't understand, I abruptly cut all ties with Connie Henson and never saw her again. Sorely disappointed, the sisters sought some sort of explanation. In a tense conversation with Emma just before I left for London, I tried to explain my behavior. I knew Maggie wouldn't understand.

"This solitude, you must know, this unendurable isolation in a place inimical to all my thoughts and feelings is killing me."

Emma tried to be sympathetic but was quick to show impatience with a person who could speak so negatively of his native place.

"You grew up in this town, Jonathan. As a boy you loved it!"

"Yes," I replied, "I did love Harrogate as a boy. But now in maturity I can't stomach the town, not for another day."

"Do you think London, or any other place, will be any better?"

"In London I'm lonely too. I've been thinking about finding a decent work girl who may be willing to live with me. I'm too poor to marry a middle-class girl, and the time has come when I can no longer live alone. I need the supportive companionship of a good woman."

"I think you need companionship too," Emma bluntly replied. "But believing you can't marry a middle-class girl is balderdash and you know it. Quentin is poor but living in harmony with a good wife. He's a poor and struggling writer too, but he married a middle-class woman, and they seem to have a good marriage."

"Quentin, dear Emmie, is the lucky one in this family. He has a law degree and could use it for a good living, but he prefers to dream of fame as a country chronicler. Of his own free will he has chosen to live in poverty. This older brother of his at no time made that choice."

"Don't you dream of fame and wealth as a writer too?"

"Not any more. As time passes one's dreams fall by the wayside."

"Not mine!" she remarked firmly. "And not Maggie's either. One of these days Maggie and I will open our own school and make a go of it. The school will help us earn a little money, perhaps, but mainly we want a rewarding reputation in the community."

"Hang onto to that dream and make it come true, Emmie. You have the time. Will, on the other hand, ran out of time. He had dreams too but somehow offended fortune and died too soon. I'm also unlucky. I know it only too well. That girl Connie would surely suffer if she were foolish enough to become involved with me."

Emma fell silent, knowing the futility of trying to argue with her brother. I never mentioned Connie Henson's name again, not even to my old friend and confidant, Günter Kurtz. As I had done with Emily Singer and Beatrice Gossam, both wealthy and upper class, I was running now from a woman of my own class who might have loved me.

Back in London I worried about my lease coming to an end when the year was over. I was undecided whether to renew it or not. The rent after improvements had become too expensive. Also I felt I needed to live deeper in the city's slums to gather fresh material for my fiction. My novels of the middle class had not been received as well as expected, and so I was thinking of going back to the genre I began with, the proletarian novel. I needed a female companion to make my life tolerable, but I couldn't afford to go in search of one until I sold another novel. When October came I had scrapped the book I was calling *Hilda* and was working on a new novel with a temporary title, *Victor Ross*. Its focus was on poor and struggling writers like myself. Not satisfied with the early title, I was soon calling the book *New Bleak Street*.

The image of Connie Henson was at work in my imagination as I was writing the early chapters. I began the book soon after our meeting, and the girl entered unbidden into its pages. Whipple, a character similar to the author in many respects, is a talented but struggling novelist specializing in the new realism. At one time he had been very much in love with a gentle, intelligent, attractive, middle-class girl. However, because of his poverty, he couldn't expect to have his love returned. He couldn't even dream of establishing and sustaining a relationship with such a girl. So in headlong flight he ran from her. Sentimental and sensitive, a woman's love was for him an unattainable ideal.

Another character in the novel, a poverty-bitten would-be novelist named Barksdale, was engaged to be married four times. Each time the girl jilted him because he was honest enough to reveal his poverty. He hopes to meet another girl from the working class or from the country. With her he may not be so open. In a short story that I published later, the main character gives vent to similar thoughts. *"Perhaps it's my long years of squalid existence. Perhaps I've come to regard myself as doomed to life on a lower level. I find it impossible to imagine myself offering marriage or making love to a young woman such as those I meet in the big houses."* In a letter to Kurtz, I penned these same thoughts as I searched for an answer to my own dilemma.

3

The early fall weather of 1890 was crisp and bracing. The autumn air produced a euphoric sense of freedom and brought many people out of doors. The skies were golden and the iridescence of the air gave a soft and pleasing color to the streets and shops of London. Life flowed at a slow pace, and people smiled and nodded as they jostled one another on the pavement. Driven by an urge to walk, I rambled alone through parts of the city. I never spoke to other strollers but sometimes touched the brim of my hat or nodded with a half smile. For seventeen days, except for my cleaning woman who came once a week, I spoke not a word to anybody. In all of London there was no one I could visit in comfort. Dylan Crenshaw, planning to go abroad, had gone to the seaside to relax and write an itinerary for his trip. My publisher was also out of town. Emily Singer had come up from Chiddingfold and wanted to see me, but I was determined not to renew my friendship with her.

On two separate occasions, in a feminine hand on engraved stationery, she sent me polite invitations to visit her. After much agonizing, indecision, and hesitation I rejected both. Writing a polished refusal, I remembered her strong personality, her lively conversation, her sumptuous apartment, and the delectable refreshments she had served me. On one occasion she had urged upon me an ornate dish filled to the brim with strawberries covered with rich and sweet chocolate. It was a treat I couldn't resist. My supreme satisfaction amused her as I tasted one of the strawberries and screwed up my face in delight. She laughed and pushed the entire bowl into my hands. It was all I could do to eat only a few. I was fond of Miss Singer and the memories associated with her, but now despite my loneliness I denied myself the pleasure of her company. I wanted an uninhibited and uncomplicated female of the working class. She would assuage my loneliness and satisfy my needs.

With restored energy I went looking for a female partner. I wanted a healthy girl who might come and live with me out of wedlock. If Muriel had been alive and living elsewhere, I would have said we could live together and go our separate ways if trouble developed. But Muriel was dead and the safety net of an earlier time had been removed. Now the girl might hold out for marriage. Even so, if she had no close family ties and was perhaps in economic difficulty, she might consider such a proposal. The morality of the lower classes, I knew from experience, was often in tandem with survival and not so rigid as that of the middle class. Also it was not inconceivable that a girl might want to improve herself by living with a well-educated author. My friend Kurtz, living alone in Germany, agreed that solitude and sexual deprivation could undermine a man's health. Yet he urged me to think twice before choosing a girl I might have to marry.

It was dangerous to become involved a second time with a woman of the working class, but there was no hope of marrying anyone of a higher class, no real hope whatever. I persuaded myself that my low income required me to search for a working girl who could adjust to my genteel poverty without complaint. Walking with Emma in Harrogate, I had said that educated English girls wouldn't tolerate poverty after marriage. Anything under £400 a year they saw as unacceptable. In 1890, after publishing eight full-length novels, my income was only £150. I did the math and convinced myself that no girl of the middle class, no provincial girl such as Connie Henson even if she were magically in love with me, would be willing to marry me. It didn't occur to me, as I considered my problem, that deep within I felt unworthy of any woman. I continued my search, hoping for something to happen, and it did.

Towards the end of September, in the neighborhood of Marylebone Road outside a shop, I met a young woman named Natalie Garwood. She was exiting the shop as I was entering and we bumped into each other. The sudden encounter got a conversation started. She was the daughter of a small shopkeeper, a cobbler who sold shoes and repaired them, and she worked as a waitress. She was tall and thin and no older than eighteen. In a couple of months I would be thirty-three. Some instant calculation told me I was fifteen years older, but I saw no problem with the age difference. I spoke to her several times after our initial meeting, and began to take my evening meal at her place of business, a restaurant catering to working men and women. Over time a cautious flirtation arose. When she took my order and tossed her head as I mentioned how pretty she looked, I grew bolder.

"Do you suppose we could walk together when your shift is over?"

"Why, sir! Why would you even ask me that?" she exclaimed, pursing her lips in a frown that quickly faded. "I don't know you from Adam!"

"You know I come here often to eat a monkish meal," I chuckled, trying to make light of her remark. "You know I'm a well-behaved fellow who is never drunk and never causes trouble."

She was pretending to write my order on her pad as she spoke. "I must tell you I can't talk about personal things. It's against the rules of the establishment. My boss would fire me. Also my papa tells me never to get chummy with the customers."

"Well, it was just a notion I had. Maybe some other time."

I had already accepted a curt rejection when she spoke again. "I know you look and talk like an upstanding person, but that's all I know."

"Then you will walk with me to know me better?"

"Well, maybe," she said, smiling and affecting coyness. "I guess it can't hurt and I don't mind. I'm pretty sure you're not that Jack the Ripper come back to rip again. Well, are you?"

Just two years earlier everyone in London was talking about Jack the Ripper. Moving in fog and darkness in the same neighborhood as this, he murdered and mutilated five unfortunate prostitutes with surgical precision. Scores of policemen, citizen patrols, bloodhounds, and even fortunetellers tried to chase him down, but he was never caught. I understood the drift of her joke but didn't laugh. Yet I felt a need to respond somehow, and with a friendly smile quickly replied.

"If I were Jack the Ripper, I would be on the prowl in the dark looking for my next victim. Instead you see me here in this well-lighted place asking you to walk with me. When do you get off work?"

"I'm off at nine," she said after some hesitation. "Meet me out front. We can walk a little, but I have to be home by ten."

She was graceful in movement and her manner of speaking wasn't unpleasant. She was marginally pretty, but sexual instinct thrusting me close to her made her very attractive. More than once as she moved with a large tray on her shoulder I had seen a sensual quality that seemed to speak to me. I could tell she liked my looks and the way I conducted myself and believed she already knew me. Though gaunt from months of agony and near panic, she told me later that I was better looking and more mannerly than other men who made overtures.

I ate my food in silence, left a generous tip, and paid my bill at the counter. A heavy, morose woman fingered the money carefully and put it away. Outside I waited until Natalie left her station. We went to a small café near the park and talked over steaming cups of tea.

An hour later, gathering her skirts in a flurry and rising, she cried, "I must go! Papa will be angry and worried. I can't stray from my schedule too far, y' know, 'cause my papa is very strict."

"Will I see you again?" I asked, hoping to convey interest.

"Of course, silly!" she replied with a muffled laugh. "I have to work, don't I? And you have to eat."

Her slender fingers were fumbling with her coat, and I helped her put it on. "You won't let on to the girls I work with that we talked, will you? They can be so catty and they just love to gossip."

"Of course not! I won't say a word to anybody. My deportment will be the same as always. Tomorrow, then, at the usual time?"

"Your *deportment!*" she exclaimed, emphasizing the word. "You are such a talker! What in the world does it mean?" Before I could answer she was gone. I liked the way she moved.

CHAPTER TWENTY-THREE

Natalie Garwood

When Dylan Crenshaw heard I was prowling the streets to find a female, he thought his friend had reverted to the behavior of his college days and had picked up a prostitute. Alarmed and worried, he postponed going abroad and came immediately to 7K to get the full story. I prepared a pot of tea and we drank it with buttered muffins and talked.

"So what's going on with you, my horny friend?" Crenshaw asked, trying to keep it light. "I gather you're frustrated and lonely like half the men in London, but when you go looking for diversion – for lack of a better word – you of all people have to be careful."

"Yes, I'm obliged to be careful," I blurted. "But I couldn't stand it any longer. So I rushed out and spoke to the first woman I came across."

"You did what?" asked Crenshaw incredulously. "You did what?"

"Well, that's exaggeration but it's the gist of what happened."

"Details, old man, give me the details."

"I don't remember exactly where I met her, maybe Tottenham Court Road or in Marylebone. We bumped into each other and got to talking. She didn't hurry away or pretend not to hear when I apologized. Another woman might have. We chatted a few minutes."

"You mean to tell me you met the woman as you walked the streets? Somewhere on the pavement? Maybe a shop? Where exactly?"

"I think it was outside a chandler's shop. I was there for candles and she was exiting, and we collided. I apologized and we began to make small talk. She told me she was on her way to work. I asked what sort of work, and she said she was a waitress in a restaurant nearby."

"And then my horny but honest friend became her best customer!" Crenshaw exclaimed facetiously with laughter.

"Well, not exactly but you're not entirely wrong either. It's a cheap little restaurant in Wimpole Street. I went there after we met and was there a few days ago. I was feeling miserable, and so I asked the girl if she would walk with me when she finished her shift. She was defensive at first, said her father wouldn't approve. Then because she had seen me often and I wasn't a stranger to her, she agreed to sit and talk in a little café I know. That's how it started."

"That's how it started?" Crenshaw repeated. "There's more?"

"I looked into her background. I know where she lives. I've talked with people who know her. The family is respectable and she's had a strict upbringing. Her mother is dead. Her father is a tradesman of good reputation and looks after her. She has an older sister who works as a nanny for a middle-class family in the midlands."

"I do hope you know what you're getting into, old boy," said Crenshaw with a look of dismay as he tried to light his pipe. "When you tell me things like this, I always think of Manchester."

"This girl is nothing like Muriel, old friend, believe me. You'll see that when you meet her. As I said, a strict and moral upbringing."

"I do hope she's nothing like Muriel. And for your own good I hope you know what you're doing."

I could feel no love for Natalie Garwood, only a tender feeling for having her in my life. I described her to Crenshaw as lively and interesting with a refinement I never expected. While she chose her words carefully and was never vulgar, she breathed sensuality. All I wanted, I assured my friend, was her companionship. If it led to a quiet domesticity and sexual release, so much the better. The girl had said she liked me better than the workingmen she had met. They were coarse and too pushy, she said, and too demanding. But I was different, polite and patient, and such a talker. I amused her and made her feel at ease (as they did not), and she felt comfortable being with me.

She knew I came as a visitant from somewhere beyond her experience but seemed willing to live in her world among her people. We began to see each other just about every day. By the end of October she was hinting she might live with me somewhere in the country. She had spent her entire life in the city and was curious about the country. She had heard one could find peace and quiet in the country. It didn't occur to me that she wanted to leave a job that kept her on her feet many hours every day and threatened to undermine her health. If she wanted to live in the country with me, I wouldn't renew my lease when it expired at Christmas. I would leave London and find a place in Exeter and persuade her to come to me later. I was hoping as I made these plans that she wouldn't insist on marriage. After Muriel even the thought of marriage made me sick to my stomach. I was down on the very idea of ever getting married again.

"I must consider nothing but mere physical need," I confessed to Crenshaw that evening when we talked.

"Activity can curb physical need, my friend. That's why I travel the world! Come along with me, Jonathan, and get involved and forget this messy stuff. I'm thinking the step you're about to take is dangerous. It could result in untold misery, and you know it."

"You speak as if I plan to marry the girl. No, Crenshaw, absolutely not! There will be no marriage. I will say that emphatically, *no marriage and no misery!* Nothing even resembling the Muriel fiasco."

Notwithstanding that assurance, Crenshaw worried and so did Kurtz who heard about the affair. Both men knew that when it came to women their longtime friend lost entirely the reasonable control that characterized him most of the time. They knew that I had fallen into a deep abyss when as a very young man I met and fell in love with Muriel Porter. I had made a fool of myself with a dissolute girl not worth my time, and I had paid dearly for it. Now they believed their friend was about to embark on a similar course. They could see it was a case of body suppressing mind, warm blood vanquishing spirit. Simply put, my masculinity demanded femininity, and neither my friends nor I were in a position to oppose the thrust of natural urges.

2

One balmy evening in October, not more than three weeks after we met, Natalie made her way to my apartment and surprised me. "Hallo!" she squealed when I opened the door. "Guess who!"

She was standing in shadow, covering her face with gloved hands and giggling. After work she had changed into a dress more suitable for summer than fall, but it flattered her figure and I thought she was stunning. She wore a little rouge to heighten the color of her cheeks and lips, and her abundant dark hair was elaborately dressed.

"Come in, my dear!" I cried with genuine astonishment. "I'm so happy to see you! I never thought you'd come here on your own. And against your papa's wishes? What a wonderful surprise!"

I had been sitting at my little desk hour after hour trying to scratch a few inky paragraphs on paper. The job was not going well, and now I had a good excuse to chuck it.

"Oh, you were writing," she said, frowning as she looked at the papers on my desktop, "and inconsiderate me interrupted you. I don't really want to do that, y' know."

"At the moment, Natalie, you come first. The writing can twist in the wind for all I care. Come, let me take your coat. Have a seat and make yourself at home. In a few minutes we can have buttered crumpets and tea. Welcome to my humble abode!"

"*Twist in the wind*, you say? *Humble abode*? You are such a talker!" Her laughter was metallic but not unpleasant. "What peculiar expressions tumble from your mouth! I just love the way you talk!"

That was the beginning of cozy evenings in the privacy of my flat. She liked my sitting room and found it comfortable. She peeked into my bedroom with its bed and bathing stand and quickly withdrew. She laughed when she saw the tiny kitchen and the pots I had hung from the ceiling. I was thrilled to see her moving about in the lonely emptiness of my rooms, but then I found she was not so easy of virtue as I had hoped. When the talking dwindled and we sat on a bench in front of the fire, I put my arm around her and tried to kiss her, but she resisted.

Later in the evening, sensing my urgency and perhaps taking pity on me, she allowed me to hold her gently in my arms and kiss her cheeks. Any behavior beyond that was off limits, and quickly she made it clear to me that she disliked innuendo. For bodily functions and all the facts of life she spun elaborate euphemisms, rejecting any common word that seemed coarse. She told me she thought the sexual act was necessary to create a family, and perhaps necessary to show affection in marriage, but otherwise indecent. Out of wedlock the act was something animals did and scandalous. She cautioned her suitor not to speak of such things in her presence. Papa had taught her well.

I wanted to meet her father. I believed if I could talk with the man we could perhaps become friends. But each time I broached the subject she found excuses, saying her father was a hard man to know and not likely to invite a stranger with soft hands and clean nails into his home. He was a shrewd workingman, she explained, keenly conscious of class and able to detect even from a distance one's place in society. He worked fifteen hours a day on shoes, and his fingernails were always dirty and blunted. He ate spicy foods and broke wind backwards. After work he drank cheap gin that made his breath unpleasant but never enough to become drunk. A protective parent, he worked hard at his trade to provide a comfortable home for himself and his daughter.

The man quickly sensed that my intentions concerning the girl were somewhat less than honorable. He had heard the sordid stories of lascivious gentlemen preying upon naive working girls, and he was rightly suspicious. For several weeks he refused to meet the tall and slender alien from another sphere who seemed to be unduly interested in his daughter. In time, however, we met in a drinking place frequented by workmen. The meeting didn't go well. I was polite, even humble in his presence, but he bluntly declared I wasn't welcome in his home. He accused me of chicanery because I didn't have the workingman's look. Yet he didn't object when his daughter came to visit me alone in my rooms several times a week. More than likely, he didn't know. I asked Natalie if she came with his approval but got no answer.

Seeing each other so often, the relationship advanced rapidly though not to the goal I was seeking. *"Our relations are as yet platonic,"* I had to tell Kurtz after the New Year, *"and if anything is to come of our connection it will have to be marriage."* I had apparently forgotten what I had said to Crenshaw: no marriage and no misery.

The girl was surely listening to her father. He was a man of the world, a businessman dealing every day with people who tried to cheat on the little money they owed him. More than once he had told his daughter to keep her treasure chest securely locked.

"Don't you dare give the key to nobody, not to any man that just wants a temporary fling. You'd be plain crazy to do that, girl. You gotta hold out for matrimony, or you dump him fast."

"Yes, Papa, I know. And I'll remember the advice you give me."

With teachings such as those firmly instilled from the time she entered puberty, Natalie was not willing to live unmarried with any man. In little ways she let me know she liked me lots, but she also made it clear that if the relationship were to go further than snuggling, I would have to think of marriage.

"No hanky-panky," she firmly declared, "and no benefits beyond a kiss without a wedding. I'm not that kind of girl."

"Ah, come on now," was my response, "listen to your heart, Nattie! Follow your feelings, sweetie! I know you better than you know yourself. You are just as sex driven as I am."

"P'raps so, but little you know!"

In all likelihood she was, but her father's conditioning wouldn't allow her to cross the line with any young man who wanted her. And why should she? With a little patience and persistence, she could marry the man, avoid all stigma, and be protected by the new marriage laws. The woman was flawed in a number of ways but not stupid.

3

My friend Dylan Crenshaw claimed Natalie Garwood was not very attractive of face and figure and had only her gender to recommend her. In hindsight I believe he was correct. But when I finally summoned the courage to ask her to walk with me, her sexuality was all that mattered. Night after night I had prowled the streets and squares in search of female response. On one occasion I caught up with a slender woman who seemed to be window shopping and commented on the weather. She glanced at me apprehensively and quickly entered a shop. Another time as people were leaving their clubs and the theater, I spoke to an attractive young woman who proved a bit too open and friendly. She looked like a well-dressed shop girl, but within minutes to my dismay she was offering her services as a prostitute.

After meeting Natalie I went almost daily to her workplace just to look at her from a distance. I felt alive all the time I was trying to seduce her and not entirely disappointed when I failed. She alone had chosen to come to my flat so we could be together, and with the first kiss I felt I had won her. When she cautioned me to relax and move slowly, I began to see the spiritual side of the young woman. She appeared to have more than the sensuality that drew me to her initially, something subtle beyond the physical that perhaps I could develop. During those early years in London I had written intense letters to my sisters, hoping to improve their education. Now I thought I might be able to enrich Natalie's internal life. I would have to be subtle in the attempt, for I knew without a doubt that she was proud and stubborn.

We took long walks together, talked and laughed, and shared simple meals. On occasion we enjoyed a bottle of wine as a special treat. I read to her some narrative poems I felt she would like, and she seemed to respond thoughtfully and with sensitivity. Later she admitted she didn't understand much of the poetry she was hearing but enjoyed the way I read it and the sound of my voice. She told me stories of her childhood, happy stories mainly, though some were gloomy. She had grown up in a poor neighborhood in London and while still a schoolgirl three boys had tried to assault her. She ran home to tell her parents, but they could do nothing about it. The police said it was the burden of every good-looking girl. Boys would be boys and it happened all the time. Her papa yanked her out of school at thirteen to work in his shop after her mother died of tuberculosis. At sixteen when she wanted to train to become a hairdresser and cosmetician, he said the schooling was too expensive and wouldn't pay for it. So she left his business and worked for a time in a chandler's shop and later became a waitress. She didn't like being a waitress. It was too hard on her feet and back. The hours were too long and the pay too low. She was a talkative person but quiet at times and almost pensive. That, I thought, was a good sign.

I liked her docility and gentleness and thought I might be able to mold her in a slow and gradual way to look upward. She had what it pleased me to call "a certain natural refinement," and it seemed to me that in time she would be able to move comfortably among middle-class people and even the upper class at a rare soirée I might attend. I knew she had little formal education and read virtually nothing, but she was intelligent and teachable. She appeared to be flexible in attitude, and that encouraged me. I was moved when she said she wanted to read my books and other books I might recommend. It delighted me to learn she was willing to work hard to please me, and so I began to have thoughts of marriage. My friends and family once again expressed concern but were powerless to interfere.

We were married in 1891 in the last week of February, the same day my letter on the correct pronunciation of Greek appeared in *The Times*. In a brief civil ceremony with only her gruff and silent father in attendance, Natalie Garwood became Mrs. Jonathan Blue. We had no money for a wedding dress and even though she merited the symbolism of a white gown, she went to her wedding in casual clothes. Back on the street and waiting for a cab, she wore a spray of flowers her father had given her and a golden wedding band from her husband. I did not inform my family of the event, nor did I say anything to Crenshaw. In letters to my German friend Kurtz I gave a vague notion of the change about to take place in my life but offered no details. My plan was to work hard in a quiet and peaceful domestic setting to achieve fame as one of the leading novelists of the day. In the meantime I would enjoy the comfort of a well stocked home and the companionship of a wife and children. Socially I would keep a low profile.

From the ceremony we drove in a fog to Paddington and caught a train to our new residence in Exeter. It was the first time Natalie had been on a train and the first time for her to live anywhere away from London. I thought she would like the country but couldn't be sure. She was, after all, a young woman born and bred in the city. The weather was cold and murky with little promise of warmth or sunshine. It was emblematic of our future together.

CHAPTER TWENTY-FOUR

Domestic Life With Natalie

Because I found it impossible to write in a vacuum, Natalie Garwood had a tremendous influence upon my work. In October of 1890, just a week after meeting the young woman, I made a new start on the novel that would become *New Bleak Street*. The project went smoothly and rapidly in sharp contrast to the numerous false starts of the summer. Sheets of paper crammed with tiny script began to form a stack of good size on my desk. Chapter after chapter went into the manuscript with little hindrance and without extensive revision. To my surprise I completed the novel in early December. On average I wrote four thousand words a day in a neat but barely legible hand. I could read the script myself with no trouble, but my publishers invariably complained. More than once they tried to persuade me to have my manuscripts typed before submitting them. But competent typists were hard to find in those days. Also the machine was newfangled and unpredictable, and a typed manuscript was expensive. So I relied upon pen and ink and sturdy paper that would accept the ink as evenly as I could make it. Casting the manuscript into print required a keen and special eye. Even then the proofs often had many errors to correct.

Through it all Natalie was patient and supportive. She didn't free me entirely from the isolation and frustration that had left my earlier work in a shambles, but she did assuage my loneliness. During the months of autumn and into winter she was a sympathetic companion. She gave me warm support to help me replace a devastating depression with emotional strength. She extended solace to a troubled spirit, and that was enough to open the gates of my creative power. She gave me the peace of mind I needed to seize and bring forth my best talent. Most of all, I received from her the calm assurance that I was a man and not a bloodless, mechanical writing machine. We were not intimate before marriage, but just the promise of gratification made me feel alive and masculine and confident. After working all day in solitude I never learned to like, I could look forward to the company of a willowy girl abloom with youth and chasing a dream.

She had some trouble appreciating my wit, savoring the sardonic amusement that often flavored my comments, but she understood my sense of humor and laughed at my jokes. As I planned and wrote the chapters of my most famous novel, Natalie's influence was immense and pervasive. Yet even as I made good progress I knew the long and tedious months of preparation had not been entirely wasted. The materials I had thrown away in disgust returned in bright moments to be reshaped by a rekindled imagination. They came to me when needed, and the result was a rapid completion of three volumes.

Early in 1891 I was going through the proofs of *New Bleak Street* and was surprised at how well the book read. *"There are savage truths in it,"* I said to Quentin, promising to send him a copy. The book was published in April and received favorable attention in major journals. Even so, I asked acquaintances not to send me reviews. It quickly became known as the best of all my work, and many readers were asking who is this Jonathan Blue? I sold the book unconditionally for £150 and got no royalties when it went through several editions. While the publishers made money on many of my books, I never did. Even so, I felt I could live for an entire year on £150 and then publish another novel. If I could establish a reputation as a thoughtful and readable author with a large audience, I might ask for more. I remember telling my friends that *New Bleak Street* was created in utter prostration of spirit while I was deep in misery, but the remark referred only to the many false starts before meeting Natalie. Also when it came to human suffering, my own in particular, I admit I was exaggerative and theatrical.

Kurtz was enthralled by the book and sent glowing praise. In long letters he assured me I had reached my maturity as a novelist and would soon be recognized as one of the best in England. Natalie liked it too. I informed Emma that she read my novel and called it *"the most pleasing of any book she had ever read."* Though intended to be taken as a harmless bit of humor, my sisters saw the comment as a flaw in my character and rebuked me. During her time in school Natalie was exposed to a few books and must have read them but left school early. In later years she read only magazines and penny novelettes until after her marriage. Now she was eager to offer emotional support by slowly reading her husband's lengthy and weighty novel and listening sympathetically when he talked about it. However, instead of being grateful for a gigantic effort on her part, said my sisters emphatically, I was poking fun at her. Both of us wanted our marriage to work, but I was already exhibiting smug superiority. I'm sad to say they read my character correctly.

Through the summer and into the fall *New Bleak Street* was causing a stir and bringing recognition. Readers found it to be a novel about the hazards of writing a novel and trying to sell it. It was new in tone and subject, and powerful. The major theme was authorship, but an important supporting theme was the survival of the writer with artistic impulses in a crass, buy-and-sell commercial age. It was a time of intense competition in the business world. Publishers and the lending libraries viewed the writing of fiction as a business to entertain the masses. Charles Edward Mudie, who bought no book that couldn't be read aloud by a maiden in the presence of her family, was the force behind Mudie's Select Library. The firm ordered new novels by the hundreds and became a power in the publishing world.

When a novel was judged unsuitable for the adolescent daughters of middle-class burghers, no order came from Mudie's and the book languished. So for many years the library was influential enough to enforce limits on the subjects that could be safely treated. For that reason alone publishers rejected the book that might have become my second novel. It went against the grain of Victorian morality and the wisdom of the establishment. Because I refused to buckle under to Mrs. Grundy, symbol of Victorian prudery, most of my books brought me very little money. Late in my career, after attaining widespread recognition, I was saying in letters to Kurtz, *"I earn so little, so little!"*

2

New Bleak Street denounced those commercial interests that viewed authorship as a trade. From the time I had tried to sell my first novel in 1880, I had found the business of publishing not to my liking. Most publishers were honest, I thought, and yet they tried to make money on an author's labor while giving back very little. A decade later, as I wrote about the problems of authors and publishers, my book became intensely autobiographical. It revealed far more of myself, in the person of Basil Leonhard, than I ever intended. The suffering protagonist, a timid man in conflict with himself, is similar in many ways to me. Both grow up in a provincial town; both get a good classical education; both come to London hoping to write for a living; both live in squalid lodgings among the very poor; both spend their days in the Reading Room of the British Museum; both believe they must take a job as a clerk when they find themselves without money; and both endure great agony when they sit down to write. Both men struggle to create a lasting work of artistic integrity but live in dire poverty when they can find no market willing to accept it. Basil Leonhard shares with me, Jonathan Blue, the same mentality, the same temperament, and the same cynical attitude.

For a long time Leonhard has been struggling to write a powerful novel but has destroyed everything he has written. Then as if to confirm his worst fears, he enters upon a period of spiritual dryness, creative paralysis, and can't write at all. His materialistic, middle-class wife advises him to view his art as a trade and write for the market, but to prostitute his talent is unthinkable. He tells his wife he would rather starve than drag his precious work through the commercial mire. Of course my friends and family easily saw I was writing about my own predicament. They insisted if I wanted a comfortable income, I would have to forget about creating masterpieces. If I were to study

209

the market and write for it, my income would increase threefold in as little as two years. But I was stubbornly unwilling to sell my talent to the highest bidder. In that respect author and fictional character were one and the same, but with a big difference. Basil Leonhard gave up writing and spiraled downward to despair and death. Jonathan Blue somehow found the strength to survive and continue the battle for another decade.

In January of 1891, before Natalie came to live with me, I spent much of my time getting to know my new surroundings. The winter weather was mild in Devonshire, and I was able to ramble through scenes of great beauty and variety. One day I strolled along the banks of the River Exe all the way to Dawlish, and later in a biting wind I walked beside the sea. Even in the bleak winter light, the coast with its red sandstone cliffs was strikingly beautiful. Its strata so impressed me that I began to study geology and borrowed Lyell's *Principles of Geology* from the free library. Then later I discovered a village on the Exe so perfect and so picturesque that I imagined a special plan afoot to keep it that way. Inland I found quiet farms, rolling hills, winding valleys, and a spiny furze in yellow bloom along the road. The two longest rivers, the Tamar and the Exe, flowed southward into the English Channel. Others in the county were the Taw and the Torridge. I would have liked walking beside them down to the sea, or floating in their current in a rowboat.

While living in Exeter was agreeable, Natalie had kept me waiting for more than a month, and I was beginning to lose patience. Finally I wrote to say the wedding ceremony would have to take place in February or not at all. It came at the end of February, and within a week we took a set of rooms on the second floor of a house with a garden. At heart a tame domestic creature, I began to enjoy my new home and its predictable daily routine. My depression disappeared and my health improved rapidly. As we came to know each other better each day, I felt myself becoming cheerful, expansive, even optimistic. However, within a month I was sounding an ominous echo of my first marriage: "*Intellectual converse is of course wholly out of the question.*" I was asking virtues of Natalie not in her power to give. In time she would see that and bitterly resent it. Also gnawing at her sense of well being was whether I truly loved her or merely wanted her as a sexual partner.

In my defense, I had entered into the marriage driven only by emotional and physical need. For a time in the 1870's, in those halcyon days of youth and hope, I had loved my first wife, a girl-woman of little worth, with desperate intensity. By contrast, the feeling I harbored for Natalie Garwood in the 1890's was based mainly on desire. My sisters, though Puritanical and tight-lipped in matters relating to sex, knew I suffered in a way they could never hope to understand. So when I told them I was taking a chance on a second girl of the working class, they were alarmed but said little. They understood that the girl though poor was respectable, and so the marriage could possibly succeed. One could cite any number of examples where men of accomplishment had married milkmaids to live in happiness. William Blake, a major poet and visionary, had married such a woman.

And there was Ben Weatherstaff. He imported goods from the Orient, owned a large company, and was one of the richest men in Harrogate. He lived handsomely in a fine house on eight hundred a year and had married his cook. She had come to live with him after his wife died, and she became an excellent second wife. However, my sister Maggie had a vision one evening of her brother drowning in a murky sea of despair. It forecast a future that could be as dismal as any time in the past. She grew fearful and pleaded with me to think twice about what I was doing. Becoming involved a second time with a woman who could hurt me deeply was a risk I couldn't afford. I listened to her reasonable plea and thanked her for her concern, but already I had made up my mind.

To allay any fears my sisters might still be harboring, I had words of praise for Natalie in my letters: *"My wife does very well,"* I said after we were settled in Exeter. *"She improves much in every way. Her cooking isn't the best, but she has many very good qualities."* They were happy to hear that even though it troubled them. Big brother, they told me later, was describing his wife in much the same way he would have described a good servant. To Quentin I said the same thing in much the same tone, but went on to suggest that Quentin's wife might like her. *"Natalie, as you know, is uneducated, but I am more than satisfied with her domestic management. She has many very good qualities and most distinctly improves. I feel sure your wife Katie might see her now and then."*

I had convinced myself that instead of living in her world, as I had led her to believe shortly after we met, she would find it better living in mine. I told myself I wanted only the best for my good and loving wife, and I really believed I was doing the right thing.

3

Maggie and Emma were eager to meet Natalie and invited the newlyweds to spend a few days in the family home. After some hesitation involving not a little soul searching, I declined. Before introducing her to my family and friends I wanted to avoid embarrassment by knowing her better. I wanted to study her behavior, her mannerisms and movement, her patterns of speech, and the way she conducted herself in general. I wanted to know more about her past, her coming of age in London, and her associates. I didn't see myself as class conscious or prejudiced in any way, but of course I was. When a reviewer of one of my books hinted I surely belonged to the class I wrote about, I was flabbergasted and felt insulted. Now married to a woman of the working class, I would have to be careful socially so as not to offend. I was hoping that in time my wife would feel comfortable with my sisters and sister-in-law and middle-class friends. Also I felt that in time we could base our relationship on something more spiritual than physical attraction.

In the early months of the marriage, however, that alone was sufficient. To my great satisfaction, Natalie quickly lost her inhibitions and exhibited a sensuality I had not seen earlier. Also her language became more open and honest. No longer did she scent indecency in every offhand remark, and she dropped the euphemisms she seemed so fond of using before marriage. Without hesitation she undressed in front of me and was comfortable with nudity. In less than a month we were more compatible in the bedroom than anywhere else. She had no religious scruples to overcome, as with most middle-class women, and no restrictive moral code. Her intimate behavior was instinctive, natural, and normal. That pleased me enormously. The emotional and physical relief I gained was so invigorating that I soon developed affection for my bride. I would find subtle ways to educate her and thus make her even more attractive. I knew that other men of letters had schooled uneducated wives, and I began to think I might be able to do the same.

In less than a month, towards the middle of March, Natalie became pregnant. During the early months of her pregnancy she did all she could to please her husband. She listened as I discoursed at great length on subjects she couldn't understand, and she tried to read the books I recommended. She sat with no show of impatience as her husband, in the manner of pompous Victorian sages, read poetry aloud to her. She cooked for me and washed my clothes; she went on long walks with me in the countryside; she tolerated my behavior when I rejected the neighbors living on the ground floor. As Muriel had been before her, she was democratic and gregarious and liked people. She was generous in her acceptance of humankind, but if her husband for whatever reason chose to dislike their neighbors she would remain by his side. When summer came she looked forward to being out of doors in sunny weather and fresh air. She was young and alive, and eagerly she went on long walks with me, chatting all the way.

Though heavy with child and tormented by intermittent pain in her pelvis, she rambled with me – laughing, talking, hooting – in search of wild flowers. At Clevedon she heard tales of the Coleridge circle, people who were English to the bone but seemed to her somehow foreign. She remained quietly in the background as I worked on my current book. As my partner for life she felt it was the least she could do. But in the last months of her pregnancy, when she was round and grumpy, the cordial relationship we tried to maintain grew cooler each day. After the birth of a healthy son in December, Natalie began to show the first signs of bad temper. In addition to nagging physical pain, she had concluded her husband viewed her as inferior. That hurt even more.

As the months passed she ceased to speak tender and loving words to me. In the dark bedroom the sexual act was performed in silence and never lasted for more than a few minutes. When she asked me to be more considerate of her physical need, with obvious embarrassment I refused to talk about it. I viewed myself as open-minded in the affairs of life, but my behavior in the bedroom was governed by Puritan heritage. During the day, particularly when I was trying to work, my voice had an edge of command. Rather than asking her to bring me a book, extra paper, or a cup of tea, I directed her to do it. At the time I didn't know I was offending her. The pain Natalie Blue was beginning to suffer, both physical and emotional, was increasing daily and becoming intolerable. Concerned with my own affairs, I was too obtuse, or too self-centered, even to notice. Yet before the end of our first year of marriage her behavior had changed. Once eager to please, she was becoming unpredictable, quarrelsome, and quick of temper.

In the middle of July in 1891 I finished *To Live in Exile* and sent it off to Smith & Richards, asking £250. The firm coldly informed me they wouldn't pay that figure because *New Bleak Street* was fast becoming a failure. The remark alarmed and grieved me. My latest novel was doing quite well in the marketplace. A bookseller had assured me of that. My friends and relatives had praised the book without restraint. Important reviewers had called it the best of all my novels. American publishers had pirated the book to make money. I thought of finding another publisher but meekly asked for the usual £150 to be paid immediately. A few days later the manuscript was returned. In the package was a message saying my books would never sell unless I made them more pleasant. My vision of reality was too dark for the average reader. People want sunlight in the books they read for entertainment. It was the same old tripe I had heard before. They wanted a dancing monkey.

I sent the manuscript to another publisher who offered £120, falling well short of the £200 I requested. The novel, a major work by any standard, went into production near the end of the year but wasn't published until the middle of the next year, 1892. Publishers often required me to wait for months to see my work in bookstores, and that had a serious negative effect. A book with a background of fresh current events was often stale by the time it was published. I wanted to write a book, get paid for it, see it in print, and begin another for immediate publication, but that couldn't be done.

CHAPTER TWENTY-FIVE

A House of My Own

At the end of August we moved from our second-story rooms above neighbors I found objectionable to a house in Exeter. It was the first time I had been able to afford an entire house, and I breathed a great sigh of relief. It was spacious and comfortable and situated in a setting I found desirable. The rent was reasonable, far less than in London, and I felt we could live there content and happy for a long time. Instead of messy talk to resolve domestic issues, I wanted a silent understanding of our domestic routine and relationship to each other.

"I am at last in a house of my own," I announced with an air of triumph to my relatives, *"and a very satisfactory house it is indeed. It's surrounded by flowers and foliage and has a graceful view from every window. The neighborhood is beautiful, inside every convenience."*

My study was small but quiet, and I worked there without the hindrance that had plagued me before my marriage. Natalie was quiet as I worked, and most of the time I hardly knew she was in the house. But when her belly became big and her movements slow and clumsy, her emotional fuse quickly became short and her temper explosive. I had always dreaded quarrels, and so to keep peace in the household, as well as to make a living, I spent more and more time in my study. I wrote two books and several short stories in 1891, but as the year drew to an end I looked back to recall that at times I had felt the same old despair that settled upon me during my first marriage. Though I refused to admit it, my second marriage after one year was falling into ruin. It was happening even as we celebrated the birth of a son.

Natalie gave birth to our first child in December 1891. We named him Walter, but I soon found a nickname for him. After the delivery she began to suffer from sciatic neuralgia. The sharp, intermittent pain inflamed her temper and put a damper on her efforts to be the dutiful wife. The physical pain, extending from the lower back down leg to the foot, was augmented by emotional pain. Almost daily, even before our first year was over, she found herself offended by something I said or did. Her sense of humor was no longer in tandem with mine, and she believed I was making fun of her. In a subtle way I was trying to make light of her condition to help her cope. I could see she didn't understand but could find no way to explain or clarify. My demeanor of gentlemanly breeding soon began to wear thin. My aristocratic temperament rubbed against her democratic bearing and made her irritable. She responded with outbursts of unrestrained temper, behavior eerily similar to that of Muriel. With both women my air of superiority triggered a conflict of class as well as personality. It infuriated my first wife. It was now having the same effect on the second.

Though I meant no harm and didn't do it deliberately, I drew attention to their background and their lack of formal education. I thought I could help them gain an education, and naively I believed they wanted that, but my good intentions backfired. Both women interpreted my behavior as insufferable, insulting, intolerable. In time they reacted with galling anger and heaped upon me a torrent of verbal abuse. Living with Jonathan Blue drove Muriel Blue into drunken stupors and eventually to the streets. It was enough to change Natalie Blue, a passive and pacific personality when I met her, into an unrelenting shrew. Though earlier she had chosen her words carefully, showing as much refinement as she could muster, before the end of our second year together she was bombarding her fastidious husband with gutter language. Unlike my pietistic sisters who had never uttered a dirty word in all their lives, Natalie didn't hesitate in her anger to spit out four-letter words made sharp with shrill contempt. She took comfort in their effect upon me.

I wondered where she had picked up the vulgar and abrasive idiom she flung at me. Had she not displayed before our marriage a genteel refinement, which shuddered at such language? Had she not been sheltered all her life by a gruff but solicitous father who insisted on moral rectitude? On the other hand, she could have grown up in the midst of domestic violence punctuated by strong language. In various conversations, when I was probing her past, she sometimes hinted at that. Perhaps she was reprising what she had learned in her formative years, merely repeating language she had heard; I had no way of knowing. Not only were her words harsh and abusive as she vented her anger, but sometimes for emphasis she lobbed crockery at me. In several novels that came after our marriage, I depicted an enraged wife hurling objects at a cringing husband. It was art imitating life.

We were now living in a private house in a pleasant neighborhood made bright by flowers and foliage. After many years I was no longer in a squalid lodging house in a noisy city. I had realized my dream of living in the country, and yet a feeling of misery and discomfort persisted. In my diary I carefully described the mounting conflict, the constant bickering over matters of no importance, and the daily increase in my wife's ferocity. I couldn't understand the cause of her behavior and was unwilling to accept blame. I believed, as illustrated by some of the women in my early novels, that she was constitutionally weak. It was a theory I had read about and taken to heart. An unreliable and tainted heredity had left its indelible mark upon her. She was therefore inherently unstable, and there was little I could do about it. My view of heredity and its effects had changed very little over the years.

In Exeter the winters were milder than in London, but in January of 1892 my wet footprints on the bathroom floor soon became icy and slippery. A winter much colder than average was upon us. For the first half of the month, as recommended by doctors, Natalie was in bed recuperating from delivering her child. During that time she was irritable and peevish, often demanding my assistance even with bodily functions. Then as she was able to walk about again she came down with influenza, and we had to send the infant away to a couple living on a farm. By the middle of February Natalie was in stable health again, and we went on a week's holiday to Penzance, a notable seaside resort in

Cornwall. Gilbert and Sullivan had made the place famous with their satirical operetta, *The Pirates of Penzance*. I was relieved to find the weather warm and sunny and hoped to return in summer.

Home again, we walked to the Wiggins farm to see our son. We found the baby in good care and growing strong on warm milk directly from the cow. "I say it for all to hear," said plump Mrs. Wiggins, revealing the depth of her Devonshire accent and her genuine fondness for the child, "the baby is an eater, all right, a real eater. He loves milk and berry juice and sleeps well at night and grips your finger hard."

"He flourishes astonishingly," I said in a letter to my family. *"Now over vaccination and clutches at objects and wants to crawl."* It had become a hobby of mine to observe the child's development carefully. I was glad to know my son was normal and healthy. It delighted me to see rapid growth in the infant, changes almost every day. The laws of nature had always been a mystery to me, and now I could see them at work as my son grew rapidly from infant to toddler in my home.

2

Early in 1892 *Wilfred Windset*, my tenth novel, was published in London. It was as topical and timely as I could make it, but I had written it rapidly and thought it was lacking depth. To Quentin I wrote in the middle of February: *"I don't know whether to send you a copy of WW. It isn't worth much, but you can have one if you like."* Later I had to admit I was thoroughly surprised to read favorable reviews and find that most readers liked the book. My sisters away from the intellectual life of London didn't like it and eagerly explained why. They couldn't agree with my opinions on religion and the new education for women, and they attempted once more to win me over to their way of thinking. With patience and good humor I let them know I valued their criticism, but not anything they could say would change my jaundiced view of a bleak, indifferent, uncaring world. It had hit me hard when I was young.

Written immediately after *New Bleak Street* and its favorable reception, *Wilfred Windset* examined the feminist movement that was currently attracting much attention. Campaigning as the radical candidate for membership in Parliament, Windset addresses the Rotterham voters on the place of women in modern life. In the best classical tradition he opens his speech with an amusing anecdote on long hair and gets a few laughs. Then becoming serious, he acknowledges that women are demanding more freedom, greater opportunity, and political equality. But will their education allow them to reach those goals? The ordinary girl is sent forth into life with a mind scarcely more developed than that of a child. Her education is not only inadequate in the marketplace, but also in the marriage market. With little ability to judge for themselves, these girls often make monstrous errors when accepting men as husbands. There is no panacea for rendering marriages universally happy [some laughter here] but judicious training can put women on guard.

When the meeting breaks up, the townspeople gather in little groups to continue the discussion. What they say in this scene supports the main points delivered in the speech. One person, however, airs radical opinions a politician would never touch. *"Close at hand, a circle of men had formed about Mr. Chown, who was haranguing on the woman question. What he wanted was to emancipate the female mind from the yoke of superstition and priest craft. Time enough to talk about giving women votes when they were no longer the slaves of an obstructive religion."* Chown's intemperate harangue repeats the dominant theme of *The Liberated*, the novel I wrote after returning from Italy.

In the midst of another group Mrs. Waggoner, a fiery feminist, is airing her views on the subject. She is saddened by Windset's lack of courage when handling basic facts, but realizes that boldness is out of place when politicians try to please their constituents. His speech was so full of chauvinism, she claims, that it should have been called "Woman From a Male Point of View." And yet would any member of "the struggling sex" disagree with his remarks on naive girls being lured into monstrous marriages? Waggoner hints that she herself endured a similar experience in youth, but somehow managed to free herself to become a leader in the most important movement of her time.

Later she brings up the subject of fashion and how males in the industry dictate restrictive clothing for women. Pausing beside the lake, she remembers having witnessed a splendid sight on that spot some years earlier. When a little girl fell off the bank into deep water, a young man, fully clothed, dived in to rescue her. *"If we could swim well, and had no foolish petticoats, we should jump in just as readily. It was the power over circumstances that I admired and envied."* Mrs. Waggoner dares to insist that women are inherently as brave as men, a dangerous new idea for the time. She also complains of the cumbersome dress of women as too restrictive and blames it on male influence. Concentrated commentary of this sort eventually sparked a revolution in women's dress even as conservatives quietly questioned female bravery.

In March of 1892 I was correcting the proofs of *To Live in Exile*, a book with passages revealing perhaps too much of myself. As autumn came in a blaze of color, I completed in six weeks a novel that quickly became known as one of my best. Before the year was over I was working on still another book. I wasn't entirely free of the false starts that had plagued me earlier. Yet living with Natalie and little Gubsey (my pet name for Walter) helped me write with greater ease than ever before even when conditions were not ideal. I looked back upon 1892 as a time of domestic misery and discomfort, and yet despite it all I published two books and several short stories. *To Live in Exile* was released in April and received good reviews, some critics allowing that I had finally come into my own as a writer. I was now thirty-five, married and a father, but the serenity I sought seemed always to elude me. I was proud of my latest publication and mailed copies to all my friends and relatives, including my sisters. They read the book carefully and sent me scolding letters to express their dismay. For them the novel wasn't fiction at all. It was on every page open and unrestrained autobiography.

The letters bulged with unanswerable questions. How was it possible their bright and beloved brother had strayed so far from righteousness? How could I reject the foremost teachings of Christian wisdom and find so little to replace them? How could anyone disbelieve the Bible, they asked in a tone of reproach, simply because it was not written in the latest scientific jargon? How could anyone deny the existence of the spiritual world simply because it could not be seen? Why did I persist in risking the loss of eternal life? Did I not know that with views such as mine I could frizzle in hell? Maggie's stubborn piety particularly annoyed me. Emma too had failed to free herself from the dogmatic religious beliefs of her childhood, and that saddened me.

I believed it had stunted her intellectual development. But hanging on to her religion gave her a sense of security that I had lost. It allowed her to face the unknown with far greater equanimity than her brother. However, every time they found autobiographical passages in one of my novels the sisters felt I was exposing them to satire and ridicule. Private persons to the core, they believed their privacy was being shamelessly invaded. I apologized profusely, saying I had never intentionally made fun of them in any of my books, but they remained unconvinced. Despite their criticism, I thought *To Live in Exile* was a powerful book. While its structure and plot lacked distinction, many of its pages were honest and moving. To Kurtz I wrote: *"It was a book I had to write. It is off my mind and now I go on with a sense of relief."* To clarify the comment, I said I wanted honestly to reveal where I stood in the matter of faith and religion, a position far away from that of my sisters and mother.

3

In the fall of 1892 Natalie was not in the best of health but somehow managed to care for our child. Though I helped in little ways, I found time to wander the countryside with my sister Maggie and my brother Quentin. In the first week of October, a season of golden sunlight by day and a brilliant full moon by night, came news that Lord Tennyson was on his deathbed. England's most famous poet died at eighty-three in the middle of the night. His sickroom was flooded with the same moonlight that captivated me in Exeter. Newspapers eulogized the man with glowing hyperbole, and crafty booksellers quickly displayed his poems in their windows at "reduced" prices. Journalists assumed the multitude avidly and lovingly read Tennyson's work, but Edmund

Gossett, a scholarly critic and biographer, dared to set them straight. I sent him a supportive note of agreement, and Gossett replied with kind words of encouragement: *"May I venture to say with how much interest and sympathy I follow your career and read your powerful and mournful studies of life. With sincere thanks for your valued letter."*

I showed Gossett's letter to Natalie and she read it slowly. By now she was losing patience with her husband's never-ending struggle to become a well-known author, and she spoke with a sardonic frown on her rapidly aging face. "Mournful studies of life?" she asked, scorning the phrase. "What's the good of writing mournful studies of life if they don't bring us enough money to live on?"

"They will in time I hope."

'That's your problem, Jon. You always *hope* but you never *act*."

"Let's not quarrel, Natalie. I'm trying and that's all I can do."

"No, it's not all you can do. You can get a steady job as a clerk somewhere and write in your spare time."

Her remark echoed an angry admonition from Basil Leonhard's distraught wife in *New Bleak Street*, written just after meeting Natalie. To hear it now in the same context produced an eerie sense of déjà vu. I knew that any reply could trigger a quarrel, and so I ushered her out of the little study and closed the door.

On Christmas Day, feeling nostalgic, I brought out a batch of Will's letters to read over again carefully and critically. My brother's death at twenty had shaken me to the core. Reading his letters I felt a deep sadness all over again. I had cherished the warm companionship William had given me. Now I had only the memory of the young man and some of his letters. They seemed as good as those classic documents of the epistolary tradition lost in the mists of time. They could be published as a book for youngsters coming of age, but to do that would reveal too much of a friendship I held sacred.

It bothered me that Natalie was unsympathetic. "People die all the time," she said. "You have to get over it."

Only a heart of stone could speak that way. I didn't want to get over it. Later I confessed to Emma that for days and days I heard only the voices of my immediate household, and one voice in particular was not always pleasant. Happy and healthy little Gubsey, however, was a constant joy. A book filled with colorful pictures made him chortle with delight. He found a comb in the bedroom and used it to comb his few strands of hair. More than once he got hold of a brush and comically scrubbed the floor. I took the time to observe my son carefully and sent rhapsodic reports to my family about the infant who was now one year old. *"He kicks so strongly it is difficult to hold him for long. He can very nearly walk. He knows the meaning of a great many words."* The child had a kitten for a pet and was taught to handle the creature gently. Sometimes he interrupted his father's work, crawling between my feet and tugging at my trousers to be lifted to my lap. Most of the time, even at night, Gubsey was no bother.

The second half of January 1893 was warm and sunny. The weather allowed me to ramble the country lanes near Exeter while Natalie remained home with our child. I was keenly observant as I walked, even though most of the time I was thinking about my work. I had just finished going through the proofs of *Redundant Women* and had written volume one of a new novel I was calling *Gods of Iron*. I was also writing short stories, and one evening I sat near the fire and hastily scribbled "A Minstrel of the Byways" in remembrance of my long walks. I wrote it as a trifle for my own amusement, but it was later published with good payment in a magazine read by thousands.

I liked living in Exeter but felt I needed to be closer to my subject matter. I had always drawn materials for my fiction from the life around me, and now my isolation was making me dependent upon books and newspapers for literary material. I wanted the streets again and the life of the city. Natalie was longing for London too and becoming restive. That and the promise of a new public library in Brixton, the best of its kind with a comfortable reading room, made me think of returning to my old haunts again. In April came heavy rains that kept me indoors most of the time, and in May my mother visited for more than a week. She had become in her later years an autocratic woman and somewhat intimidating. Though she had declared that under no circumstances would she say or do anything to upset her son's wife, Natalie felt the woman was judging her housekeeping and finding it lacking.

"I have many good recipes," Mama said, "and I would send fair copies to you if I could be certain you would use them."

"I'm not sure we can afford the ingredients that go into fancy recipes," Natalie retorted. "Your son don't make a lot of money, you know, even though he seems to work hard. Only last month he published a new book, but it didn't bring us much at all."

"He seems to be doing all right, my dear. This is a pleasant place he managed to get for his family. You and the tot are well fed and well clothed and live in a comfortable house. What more do you want? Perhaps you could manage more economically?"

Frugal all her life by inclination and penny-pinching by necessity, Mama thought she was offering good advice. But Natalie interpreted her well-meaning remarks as criticism.

"I would rather not," she curtly replied. "Just once I would like to live from one week to the next without worrying about money."

"Oh my goodness! In these times I'm not sure anyone can do that. When Jonathan's father died we most certainly had to worry about money, but with God's help and guidance we did all right. I do hope you'll find a good chapel here to attend."

Growing up among London's poor, Natalie had never gone to church. London had many richly appointed churches, but people of the working class stayed away in droves. She didn't know how to reply to the older woman's remarks and remained silent. Mother later described her as a rather sullen young woman, defensive and stubborn. I think she really wanted to be a friend to Natalie, but it was not to be. She never found the time to visit us again. On returning home she announced she liked the house I had found at last and hoped I would remain there for a long time. *"It isn't good to be moving from pillow to post so often, Jonathan. You need to put down roots."* She was wisely correct, but London was calling and I had to answer the call.

CHAPTER TWENTY-SIX

Clara Collader

In the middle of May as the weather grew warmer I arranged to lease the upper part of a residence in Brixton. It was a pleasant place in a pleasant neighborhood, but Brixton was nothing at all like Exeter. We would be living again in South London with urban people on the floor below. From sad experience we knew that a heavy step on a bare floor could create a problem. In June when all the foliage in Devonshire was in full bloom, when skies were vibrant and birds were chirping, Natalie and I were packing to leave the house we had thought we would live in for many years. At the end of the month, after sweaty hard work that left us both out of temper, we were settled in our new quarters. We had lived in the Exeter house almost two years.

One balmy day near the end of July I left home at dawn to explore the old neighborhoods that lived in memory. The streets were fresh at that time of day, and a gray mist was rising from the river. As the sun came up the mist became a gossamer veil of rainbow colors that sparkled with gemlike brilliance. Taking a deep breath, I paused behind the rail to enjoy the scene. The air was cool and clean and easy to breathe. I was glad to be strolling beside the Thames again and felt at home. I walked briskly without fear past smelly slums, run-down factories, and quaint shops. Men going to work in the early morning greeted me with a smile and a nod. In the distance I could see the stately buildings of government. The sun was warm on my face when I turned homeward. I was back in my element again, feeling good in my charted territory. Near eight o'clock, my appetite keen, I was home for breakfast.

Redundant Women had been published in April and was reviewed by leading journals through the summer. I sent off a copy to Kurtz, who in his usual self-deprecating way made cogent comments. In reply I aired my thoughts on the woman question. *"I doubt we are greatly at variance in our views. My demand for female equality simply means that I am convinced there will be no social peace until women are intellectually trained very much as men are. Among our English emancipated women there is a majority of admirable persons; they have lost no good quality of their sex, and they have gained enormously. The 'typical woman' must disappear or become subordinate."* I said also that I was done with "questions" and "issues" and wanted to write a novel that everyday people could read for entertainment. Lacking moral purpose and heavy dialectic, the critics might even call it a work of art. The summer passed before I began to make progress on the new novel.

The reception of *Redundant Women*, the book I had written in only six weeks, surprised me. It reached out to a lot people who found it very interesting. Many segments of the population, not just the handful of intellectuals who were now following my work, found its subject close to their lives. As early as *Emily Claremont*, my third novel, I said with pronounced authorial intrusion: *"Of no greater unkindness can parents be guilty than to train as if for a life of leisure children whose lot will inevitably be to earn a livelihood by day-long toil. It is to sew in them the seeds of despair."* My portrayal of the ineffectual Maddox sisters in *Redundant Women* dramatizes that remark. Their education, consisting only of genteel "accomplishments," fails them grievously when they are required by circumstance to support themselves. Late in life they dream of opening a school but can't find the strength or the funding. Alone and confused, they fail to find their place in the world of work. Superfluous and expendable, they sink gradually downward.

My sisters, unmarried evangelicals, were surely in mind when I created the Maddox sisters. The fictional sisters, products of my imagination, share many similarities with the real-life sisters. I see them all as pietistic, conventionally educated, unmarried, and redundant. My older sister, Maggie, was already thirty, angular, and austere. Rigidly Puritanical and not in the best of health, she worried about her digestion and pasty complexion. The younger sister in her twenties still retained the bloom of youth but was rapidly aging. Like the Maddox sisters, they supported themselves as overworked and underpaid teachers. Emma complained that her life as a teacher was not as good as she would like. In fact it was becoming insufferable, she wearily confessed. The hours were long and the wages low. Unruly pupils with no love of learning and no respect for their elders were becoming intolerable. Her complaints delivered respectfully in writing fell on deaf ears.

"Yes," I replied, *it's a monstrous thing that you should work so hard for so little. Yet I suppose people will not pay more.*" I hoped in time my sisters would open the school they often talked about.

That was the dream nurtured day by day by the Maddox sisters. "*We shall certainly open the school. We have made up our minds to that. It is to be our life's work. It is far, far more than a mere means of subsistence.*" But they fail to realize their dream. Worn and discouraged and given to procrastination, afraid of losing money in a bad investment and not certain they could manage a school, they are not able to act. As the book ends the original six have been reduced to only two. Alice insists that she and Virginia will open their school soon, but the reader knows they never will. The Maddox sisters and the Blue sisters share numerous similarities, and yet Maggie and Emma were made of sterner stuff. They were cautious, indecisive, often ineffectual, but knew how to endure. They lived as unpretentious women who read evangelical periodicals, decided never to marry, suffered from indigestion and headaches, and spent most of their time at home. Try as I might I was not able to imagine a brighter future for either of them. Though decent young women, and capable of work more lucrative than teaching, it seemed to me they lacked nerve. I felt they also lacked experience and dedication. Later they would open their own school and surprise me.

2

One afternoon in the middle of summer I took a tram to Richmond, an affluent suburb of London. It was the home of a woman calling herself Clara Collader, and I had been invited to visit. I had heard of the woman in March of 1892 when my sister Emma told me she had delivered a lecture on my novels before the London Ethical Society. When she wrote in May of 1893 asking to meet me, I offered little encouragement. I had resolved to live quietly out of the limelight and have little to do with people wanting to curry my favor. It had become a habit almost, a perverse pleasure, to refuse invitations from women who had read my books and wanted to meet me. Most of the time a polite refusal ended the matter, but Miss Collader was not like the others. Undaunted, she sent me several articles she had published. One of them was about Jonathan Blue, and that softened my attitude toward her. During the next two months I declined several of her invitations, but in July I relented and visited her well-appointed home in Richmond. Later I jotted down a record of the meeting in my diary, noting that Miss Collader was younger than I had expected, intelligent, and bookish. It was a terse, oblique reference to the positive impression she had made.

She was an excellent specimen of that type of woman I had long admired. She had in fact all the qualities of the advanced woman of the late nineteenth century, characteristics of the enterprising new woman. At thirty-three Clara Collader was well educated, active in social reform, and in tune with the intellectual currents of the day. She claimed to be the first woman to graduate from the University of London with a degree in political economy and do advanced work in the field. To qualify for the master's degree, her reading included Adam Smith, David Ricardo, John Stuart Mill, and John Ruskin. I soon discovered she was also a reader of novels as well and had some training in the classics.

In 1886 she had become a researcher for Charles Bayfield, helping him prepare his monumental *Life and Work in London*. She specialized in the positions that were open to women. Job opportunities for women were increasing with each passing year, and the future was beginning to look less bleak for those superfluous women who had to support themselves. Bayfield later named her chief investigator for women's occupations. It pleased me to see that her thoughts on women's work were similar to those I had presented in *Redundant Women*.

In August, less than a month after our initial meeting, Miss Collader paid a visit to the Blue home in Brixton to meet Natalie and little Walter. She sipped tea with the family and we found her affable and cordial. A week later she and Natalie spent a Sunday boating on the Thames. They rowed the boat almost to Greenwich, laughing and joking as Natalie tried her hand with the oars. Though born and raised in London, she had never been on a boat in all her life and couldn't swim. Collader, on the other hand, rowed skillfully, using the oars adeptly. The two women were of different class and background, and yet began to like each other as they enjoyed themselves on the water in fine weather. Clara quickly accepted Natalie as her friend and equal, and the latter lost no time letting me know she liked that.

"I really do like her," Natalie said to me at the end of the day. "She's a smart woman and she seems to like me, and we had fun on the river chatting and laughing. She didn't talk down to me as you do at times."

"I don't mean to do that, Natalie, believe me. I've never wanted to hurt you, and yet you believe I deliberately seek to annoy you."

"You do annoy me often with talk I don't understand, and you know it. In all the time I was with Clara she never did that."

"I'm happy for you. You've become friends quickly, and I hope it will be a long friendship. First names already?'

"Yes, she asked me to call her Clara, which is Latin for clear and bright. She said her papa called her Clarabella because he thought it meant pretty Clara. Later they found out it's an organ stop that sounds like a flute! Then I started calling her Clarabella, and would you believe it? She squealed liked a flute! We laughed and laughed and almost upset the boat! We were a couple of schoolgirls having a good time. My name, she told me, has something to do with Christmas. Clara's not religious, however, just bookish and reads a lot. She said Blue is a very old family name, maybe Scottish, that's been around many years."

"Indeed it has been and it's fairly rare. I'm proud of the name. In Boston at the Edgar Blue Historical Museum they couldn't believe my name was Blue. People I met there thought I was joking."

We chatted without rancor before dropping off to sleep. Natalie had enjoyed a pleasant day on the river and was in a good mood. She was always pleasant when happy. Only misery made her sour.

By September, when I was quarreling with a plagiaristic parson in the newspapers, Collader had become a loyal and confidential friend. She was quick to understand the special circumstances of my domestic life, and didn't hesitate to let me know she was ready to offer help when needed. One evening she sent a note to me containing a generous offer. She would provide for Walter's support should I ever find myself without an income. From then until I left England to live in exile we remained good friends. Collader also tried to maintain a casual friendship with Natalie. They got along very well in the early months but drifted apart as time passed. Natalie was slowly becoming more angry, more unstable and unpredictable, and suspicious of everybody.

3

The summer of 1893 quickly moved into fall. October came with bleak winds promising raw weather for November. The quiet domesticity I was seeking when I married Natalie had now become raucous uproar. It drove me to rent a dingy garret for the quiet necessary to get my work done. The bare room was cold and uncomfortable and away from my books. I believed I wrote from life, drawing upon resources that surrounded me, but in that cold garret I realized how much I depended on the printed word when writing. Suffering from a persistent cough and dreading the coming of winter, I began to work on a new book at home. I was calling it *Miss Gordon of Camberwell* but soon changed the title to *Jubilee Year*. Camberwell of the first title was a district of south London not far from Lambeth and Brixton. The improved title referred not to a neighborhood, but to the Queen's Golden Jubilee of 1887, a time of national celebration. It was a precise title because much of the novel's action took place in that year.

I heard from my publisher that *Redundant Women* was selling better than expected. People were reading the book and wondering how much of it reflected the author's life. Perceptive readers had spotted autobiographical passages in earlier novels and were now looking for them in this novel. They knew I was married and were asking whether my wife came from the middle or working class. Some readers were certain she was the model for the woman Alfred Yard lived with in *New Bleak Street*. Though Yard was discontented with his lower-class wife and could see only her faults, I viewed her through her suffering and admired her. I saw in my imagination a patient, humble, loyal, quiet and calm wife with a noble heart.

Yard met his future companion in a chandler's shop when she was young and pretty, saw her take pity on his longing and loneliness, and persuaded her to share his spartan quarters. The time had come when he couldn't live without a partner, and a kind fate allowed him to find the right person. "*His marriage proved far from unsuccessful; he might have found himself united to a vulgar shrew, whereas the girl had the great virtues of humility and kindliness.*" Yard's good fortune was fictional and imaginary, perhaps wishful thinking on my part. Those who believed me to be as fortunate as my character were sadly mistaken.

Towards the end of our second year together the rewarding family life I had hoped for – a wife and child, a pet and the family hearth – was beginning to shatter into little pieces. I complained that domestic discomfort was keeping me from doing my best work. Our home was so often in uproar I found it difficult to concentrate and went to the new library for quiet. That brought complaints of neglect and more conflict. Also when not picking a fight with me, Natalie vented her temper on the hapless kitchen girl. Though my income was too uncertain to hire a servant, she insisted on keeping one. Not able to pay them a fair wage and believing she had the right to order them about, she had trouble with one servant after another. They came and went with the regularity of a ticking clock. Later I would bring the problem into my fiction and write sympathetically of abused and underpaid housemaids, but as I wrote *Redundant Women* my focus was on characters similar to Natalie.

Mrs. Tom Chitford – selfish, shrewish, and lacking affection – is the image of Natalie as I saw her at that time. Her husband is in poor health and longs for the fresh air of the countryside, but she must live in London. To dwell anywhere else, even a few miles from the city, is to force her to live in exile. Similarly, Natalie couldn't adjust to living in the town of Exeter. Its impressive cathedral dating from the Middle Ages, its reputation for being a seat of learning, and its country vistas had no lasting effect on her. Its peace and quiet made her long for urban noise.

Natalie liked the clap and rattle of traffic in the streets. It had a soothing effect upon her. A woman who had spent her entire life in the streets and squares of the city, she lived for the day when she could forget the country and breathe London air once more. Living in the country, she began to show a savage temper laced with vulgar outbursts. Her counterpart, Mrs. Chitford, also displays a fierce temper. After the death of her husband she spews venom in all directions. I suspected that my wife often spoke the same way about me, particularly when she visited relatives in London or chatted with shop people. Unlike Muriel, she had no cronies with whom she could vent her misery.

Mr. Shackleton, though a minor character in *Redundant Women*, is memorable for reflecting the distress I was beginning to feel in the second year of my marriage. The man is driven insane by having to explain his jokes to a dim-witted wife. A person of intellect who carefully cultivates wit as a hobby, he is married to the dullest woman anyone could have found. She lacks a sense of humor and cannot understand even the broadest of jokes. Only flat, simple, declarative statements are intelligible to her. If I had my own wife in mind as I described Shackleton's wife, and it seems I did, I was being unfair. Natalie may have missed some of the subtleties of my discourse, but early in the marriage she laughed when I joked and tried to appreciate my wit. She may have been slightly unstable even when we married, but she wasn't stupid.

Mr. Applewaite, another of the book's minor characters, has married a pedestrian woman whose eyes are closed to any way of life beyond the practical, materialistic, and mundane. On an outing in fine weather to view the landscape near Tintern Abbey, she complains of her incompetent servants and ruins what could have been a very pleasant afternoon. Natalie had done exactly that on a similar outing, She was always complaining of servants who could not or would not follow instructions. I believed the problem lay more with her than with them. It was a bone of contention that grew worse as time passed. Mr. Applewaite wants out, but English law has made it very difficult for him to divorce his wife. So to escape from her and avoid the specter of suicide, he becomes a restless wanderer. A friend, hearing that the man is haunting the shores of the Mediterranean Sea and living from hand to mouth, speaks his epitaph: *"A pity – he might have done fine work."*

More than once, as I listened wistfully to Dylan Crenshaw talking about world travel and its rewards, I had thoughts of chucking it all and becoming a vagabond. At one time I even thought of returning to America and giving my remaining years to working on a farm. I longed for open spaces and open air. It was, of course, only wishful speculation. Like Algernon Portman in Italy, I dreamed of a better existence in a better place. Yet for all that, I was fairly certain I would have to struggle every hour of every day to eke out a living in England. I wasn't free to wander the world, as Crenshaw was doing, or live in a country more pleasant than England. I was a family man with a wife and child to support. I would be called upon to do that for as long as I lived.

CHAPTER TWENTY-SEVEN

Monstrous Disillusion

In 1892 I had hope of salvaging my marriage, but during the next year when writing *Jubilee Year* a troubling disenchantment closed in upon me. Ada Spears in that novel embodies all the defects I had found in Natalie. Notably inept at managing a household, Ada is vulgar, pretentious, and explosive of temper. Fiercely independent and frequently violent, she is a vessel of smoldering anger. Without warning the woman's ferocity flares into fiery abuse, and she tongue-lashes her husband, servants, and sisters without restraint. Her fury is evident in the powerful climactic scene, which forces her husband to take their child and flee. Arthur Spears is vastly uncomfortable in the unquiet house he calls home, and so he spends most of his time at the office. At quitting time he can't expect to relax in a peaceful domestic setting. Each day he worries about uproar. Then one evening he returns home to find a uniformed policeman in the doorway. A servant under arrest has stolen marked money. Sent upstairs to put on her coat, the hysterical girl seizes a pair of scissors and slashes her throat. Moments later Ada stands over the bleeding girl screaming abuse.

As Arthur dresses the housemaid's wound and restores her to consciousness, his enraged wife accuses him of sexual relations with the girl. Pushed to the limit, he seizes her by the shoulders and flings her from the room. On the other side of the door she screeches insults in *"the language of the gutter and the brothel,"* a distinct echo of the tirades that came with unsettling frequency from Natalie. Arthur huddles in a fetal position against the door, his hands clasped over his ears while his child screams in terror. Ada leaves the house to file charges against the servant. Arthur bundles up his three-year-old son and runs. He tells himself he will never again live under the same roof with Ada. The devastation in the lives of Arthur and Ada Spears is another example of accurate prediction of events in my own life. Their intense and bitter story, told with uncompromising realism, reflects with fidelity my own situation. Yet final separation from Natalie didn't come until nearly four years later. As I had predicted in fiction the outcome of my wretched first marriage, I dramatized with alarming accuracy the failure of the second. Once more I was writing better than I knew. Some force within me or without, unconscious and unknown, directed me.

2

Winter came again with violent winds and brutal weather, bringing coughs and colds and general discomfort. At the beginning of 1894 little Walter, two years old and his father's favorite person, came down with bronchitis. The condition was painful and the little boy lay tossing and gasping and crying out through the night.

"We have to do something about Gubsey," I said to Natalie.

"Well, go ahead! Tell me what!" she replied, becoming upset. "Just tell me what! You're the smart one in this household! So tell me!"

"If we stay here, he may have to go into a hospital, and that's very expensive. We would never be able to afford it."

"Why does living have to be so hard? I've told you a thousand times this place is too cold in winter. That's what did it, and you know it as well as I do. But all my complaining went unheard."

"Heating a flat the way you would like it means spending money we don't have. The doctor says the boy ought to be in a better climate. I'm thinking Eastbourne. It's milder there, and the salt air will be a tonic for him. No coughing and gasping for breath there."

"If the house is cold, it won't be any better than here. And you know it. Why move to another location to live in a cold house?"

"We have to do whatever we can for the boy. If we have to sacrifice to care for him, so be it. We'll find a warm house."

So again we packed our personal items, put the furniture in storage, and moved to another location. We went to the quiet seaside town, and within days the toddler seemed on the mend. A week later the bronchitis returned, keeping us up at night and requiring us to stoke the fireplace around the clock. Then a strong east wind came off the sea and the child ceased to snore and gasp in his sleep and recovered. Natalie's temper improved dramatically, and I made good progress with my writing. When not at my desk I rambled, as I had done years before, across the downs to forgotten little hamlets dating from Saxon times.

There was something about Eastbourne, even in the dead of winter, which was stimulating at one moment and serene the next. Natalie liked the place too, and we decided to remain there until spring before returning to Brixton. I finished *Jubilee Year* in April and sent it off to my publisher. I thought I would have to be in London to read the proofs but dreaded living again in Brixton though I was becoming restless in Eastbourne. So of a sudden we gave notice to the landlady, packed the few items we would need in a new location, and moved to Clevedon. We rented the same lodgings we had when Natalie was pregnant with Walter, and the cleanliness of the place pleased us both.

By the end of June I had finished the short novel *Eve's Ambition*, written in a single month to run serially in an illustrated magazine. Also in 1894 I was publishing a steady stream of short stories and was pleased to see they were helping to bring me recognition. I had made it clear to Natalie and my sisters that my aim was to make myself known as a leading man of letters while remaining out of sight in quiet places. Thomas Hardy had taken that course and so could I. Now it seemed the dream of fame was slowly becoming a reality. Yet I continued to be at war with the world and with myself, admitting to Kurtz that the present was giving me not any more satisfaction than the past, and the future was bleak. *"There is nothing before me but steady work, a low income, and turmoil. I have been suffering from headaches which now and then interrupt my daily tasks."* I didn't say what might be causing the headaches. I was unwilling to admit, even to myself, that our nomadic way of life was taking its toll upon my family and me.

On going to the seashore I thought I would be retuning to London in a few weeks. Instead we lived in Eastbourne until late spring and then in Clevedon through the summer. At the end of August we were back in London looking for a place to live. A couple of days later I went by train to Dorking and rented two rooms, expecting my family to arrive later. Natalie objected to living there, and so in late September I went looking for a place in Epson. In that suburb of London, close to all the important places in the city, I found a house that pleased her. To end the peregrination, the restless roaming from place to place, I signed a lease for one year. My income was now improved, and Natalie insisted on keeping a servant. We hired a woman who could boil a potato and cook a joint of meat without spoiling it, but my wife's temper drove her away. I resumed writing short stories on demand just for the money. With machine-like precision, I turned them out one after another with little revision. It was the only way I could assure a steady income.

In those days Epsom was almost a part of London but retained the tenor of a small rural town. It had become a retreat from the workaday world of the city, a place to get away from it all, but close enough for urban business and pleasure. It was a very old town dating back to Saxon times, and its racetrack was famous. During Derby Week Londoners flocked to Epsom, but most of the time High Street with its old clock tower was a sleepy roadway with little traffic. We rented a house on Worple Road, a quiet neighborhood a few blocks from the main street. I liked the ambience and convenience of our new residence so much that I advised my friend Kurtz in Germany to look for a similar place on the outskirts of Berlin. There he might find peace and quiet.

Günter Kurtz at that time was writing a book about his Rugby, Tennessee experience and struggling to make it authentic. He was living alone in a noisy rooming house and complaining. Though busy with my own work, I found time to help my friend find obscure sources for adequate documentation. I was surprised to learn that a town in Tennessee was also called Harrogate. When I wasn't at work in a library

I was attending literary events in London. Natalie remained at home to care for our son. On several occasions I went to gala parties and formal dinners, but went alone. When I talked about the good times I had, she became angry and bitter. I couldn't understand why because the events were for men only. Later I understood. Her being so close to the city she loved and yet so far produced a cancer within her that slowly festered.

3

Near the middle of December in 1894 *Jubilee Year* was published to catch the Christmas trade. The novel sold more copies than usual and readers liked it, but I made no attempt to attend gatherings to promote it. As a family we celebrated the season at home even though all three of us were suffering from colds. The servant had quit without notice, and Natalie complained that all the work fell on her even when she was sick. She had lost touch with her friends in the city and was no longer able to visit her ailing father in the old neighborhood. The man for reasons unknown to her had lost his cobbler's shop and his home and had lost himself in the general population. Her sister had also moved elsewhere, leaving Natalie feeling more alone than ever. Gradually she came to believe she was sinking downward while her husband's star was rising. She didn't bother to read my books any more, saying they were too wordy and the print too small. She resented being left out of the recognition I was earning and complained of lost identity. The satisfaction I felt as I became more widely known, often expressed in a witticism, she coldly ignored. Living with her had never been easy, but each day her temper became more volatile. I had hoped she would never become bitter of tongue, and yet her behavior alarmed me. Inevitably her presence and her influence came into the novel I was writing.

In *Jubilee Year* I viewed with disgust the typical woman of the lower middle class who cared only for herself. Stephen Knight, lecturing his clueless son, speaks my thoughts: *"When you are ten years older, you'll know a good deal more about young women as they've turned out in these times. You'll have heard the talk of men who have been fools enough to marry choice specimens."* I now believed I had blundered in hooking up with Natalie and was taking comfort in supposing other men had suffered lapses of judgment too. Bristling with contempt, Knight speaks of *"trashy, flashy girls"* who call themselves ladies and consider themselves too good for *"honest, womanly work."* Unfit as wives and mothers, they have turned the traditional English home into a place of *"filth and disorder, quarrelling and misery."* His tirade runs on and on.

Instead of staying home to look after their families, the women jostle one another in the streets and shops, waste money on worthless merchandise, and chatter nonsense incessantly. They have nothing to recommend them, not even their youth. Knight doesn't include in his misogynous tirade English women of the upper class. He believes they are not so vulgar and not so ready to accept every new fad that comes along. His thoughts were mine, for I never lost my respect, even my sense of awe, for upper-class women. I admired them from a distance to the end of my life. However, when I learned it was the fashion for such women to cultivate authors as mascots, I refused to enter that world a second time. It was Puritan pride at work again, but I had no regrets.

I was now beginning to question my earlier views on woman's place in society. Even when most cynical, however, I never believed that women in any way were inferior to men. The notion defied logic and was an abomination to thinking people. However, my opinions on the worth of the feminist movement were taking a negative turn. It had fostered in my estimation a spirit of rebellion that was undermining domestic stability in fragile marriages and throwing homes into tumult. To stem the tendency, I was thinking a show of male dominance might work. A display of physical strength at the right moment could possibly tame the rebellious woman. Even a verbal warning in some cases might do the job. So Oscar Barrant in *Jubilee Year* lectures his wife Nancy to drive home the point: *"I am your superior in force of mind and force of body. Don't you like to hear that? Doesn't it do you good when you think of the maudlin humbug generally spoken by men to gullible women?"* The fictional character was able to achieve good results with just a few words, but I was too diffident, too gentle, or too weak to speak as he did when

Natalie was upset. Most of the time after a violent outburst I suffered in silence, grumbling to myself.

At the beginning of 1895 I was writing to my friend in Germany on stationery engraved with the Epsom address. It was a touch of class that I hoped would improve my image, for at that time I was corresponding with important people. For a decade I had nurtured my reputation with what I considered a select reading public. I felt it would grow steadily stronger with more readers if I could publish something of worth each year. Each of my novels since *The Populace* had been reprinted in cheap editions for sale at home and abroad. Even though I received no money whatever from unscrupulous publishers and American pirates, the mass distribution boosted my reputation as a serious novelist. My books were appearing in several countries of the English-speaking world as well as France and Germany in translation.

Slowly I was winning the recognition I had sought, and it pleased me to see my name mentioned as a well-known person in popular periodicals. I felt I was becoming firmly established as a writer of some importance, but that meant keeping my nose to the grindstone and my work in the public eye year after year. In that respect 1895 was a good year. It saw the publication of three novels in the new one-volume format. They were *Eve's Ambition*, *Slumbering Embers*, and *Guest in the House*. While I was not particularly proud of these titles, they brought me a comfortable income and helped secure my position as a man of letters. At last I was writing for the trade and making a living.

I was now a member of the Society of Authors. It brought me professional and social advantages but no detectable inspiration. Ten years old, the Society had a thousand members and was working hard to teach authors their rights while exposing dishonest publishers. Its founder, Roger Leland, viewed the production of literature as strictly a business and insisted that authors be paid according to the rules of business. The master idea was to improve the economic condition under which an author labored. So even before I joined their ranks, as the author of *New Bleak Street* I had become a figurative spokesman for the group. I was in sympathy with their aims but was disappointed when their conversation revealed a cast of mind I deplored. Creative writing for most of them was a business, merely a way to make a living. Dylan Crenshaw, who wrote to support his travels, had no trouble accepting that point of view. But for me in England and my friend Kurtz in Germany, creating a work of fiction was much more than that. Both of us were grinding ourselves into an early grave, struggling to leave behind a legacy of high merit in times that richly rewarded scribblers and hacks.

CHAPTER TWENTY-EIGHT

At Last a Man of Letters

In the autumn of 1894, when I attended my first dinner sponsored by the Society of Authors, I found it to be a gathering of petty tradesmen. I met Roger Leland at that meeting and immediately disliked him. I had read his work and had a good opinion of it, but the man himself (who would soon be knighted) lacked distinction. A month later, in a new dress suit bought for the occasion, I sat next to Leland at dinner. I tried to engage him in conversation but found him unwilling to utter more than a few perfunctory syllables. Despite his reputation as a well-known author, I formed a negative opinion of the man. *"Commonplace to the last degree,"* I confided to my diary. Leland's behavior was boorish and arrogant, but mainly I blamed him for the commercialization of contemporary literature. Most of the other men in the room, though decked out in formal wear and seated at lavish tables, also lacked distinction.

My contempt was unsparing and perhaps unwarranted, but toward the younger writers I met in private homes I was charitable and cordial. As they gathered around me I sought to convey an importance I didn't feel. To Kurtz I joked, *"I am beginning to have a literary past. In meeting the young writers of today, I feel a veteran. It is curiously entertaining to have them hang on every syllable I utter. And how strange a thing it is when, in walking about the streets of London, I pass the streets where I lived in those days of misery!"* As an author at last becoming well known, the miserable past rose up to haunt me. My journey across an unquiet sea had been stormy and fraught with peril. On a rare sunny day when the wind was calm, I felt I had reached safe haven.

It was a delusion, of course, for my domestic life in less than two years of marriage had become tumultuous and unhappy. After *Eve's Ambition* because of unsettling events in my household, I was not able to start another novel for some time. Though I told myself I had tried to make it work, my marriage was becoming insufferable. Quarreling and nagging, sharp words and bad temper were now replacing the affectionate companionship we had shared until Walter was born. Natalie's vulgarity pricked me like a thorn, and her incompetence as a mother and supervisor of servants overwhelmed me. Within a week after moving into the house at Epsom she quarreled loudly with the servant and slapped her little boy so hard his face became swollen. When this happened I wanted to end the marriage, but resolved to go on living in the same house for the child's sake. I made up my mind to dine out more often, attend literary events that could benefit my career, and befriend other writers. I would even reply to letters written by women asking for sympathy and advice. That was risky and possibly explosive, for I knew Natalie had a jealous streak and a short fuse. Each time I left the house I worried that on returning I would find my child harmed in some way and my books and papers ripped to shreds.

Often for that reason alone I turned down invitations. But now in letters to Kurtz, instead of speaking of my loneliness, I described a deluge of invitations from all sorts of people. To get away from the ugly scenes at home, I accepted many of them gladly. Though dining with cultivated people became a refuge for me, it exacerbated the domestic situation. When I was away "having fun," as Natalie put it, she was confined to a small and uncomfortable house with a wayward child and a lazy servant who couldn't obey the simplest instructions. In her mid twenties, lively, talkative, and gregarious, she wanted a social life too. But day after day she found herself living in isolation in the shadow of the city she had always found exciting. Lonely and miserable and blaming her husband for brutally neglecting his home and hearth – his wife and son – she was becoming more and more unstable and prone to violence.

One day in the spring of 1895 the servant, a pale and wispy girl on the job for two weeks, dropped a dish on the tile floor. It was a beautiful day, serene and sunny with gentle breezes and chirping birds. For the hapless servant the fine spring day quickly became darkest night and her dream of life a nightmare. Natalie heard the dish break into little pieces and flew into a rage. Dancing around the startled servant, she spewed venom in all directions.

"You stupid slut!" she screamed. "That was my one and only gravy bowl, and it had a gilt decoration I really liked. Now in your idiotic clumsiness you broke it! Get out of my kitchen, you piece of trash! Get out of my house and my sight!"

"I'm so sorry, ma'am, I really am. Take it from my wages, please."

"Get away from me, go now! Go and pack your things and leave!"

"I'm sorry, ma'am, I really am. It slipped from me accidental like."

"Stop blubbering, you idiot! Just get your stuff and go!"

In my study I heard the commotion and came out to see the girl sitting on the floor in dire confusion and sobbing. My wife was standing over her, threatening to attack her, demanding that she leave the house immediately. Unable to calm the women, I took the servant by the arm and left the house. Two hours later when I went back to pick up the girl's belongings, Natalie was still in a rage.

Incidents such as these I couldn't divulge even to Dylan Crenshaw who was thinking of chronicling my life with Natalie. But in my diary, carefully hidden from prying eyes, I found refuge and a shred of solace. I spoke of Natalie's acid tongue, her screeching tirades, and her contempt for the feelings of other people. In a tone of heavy resignation blended with an undercurrent of anger, I called her misbehavior "blackguardism." It was an old-fashioned word but appropriate.

Living with the woman, I expected a sudden outburst of anger any time of the day or night. I dreaded sleeping in the same bed with her. In my own home I had no respect and found it difficult to remain pleasant. Away from home I cultivated the image of an urbane author and gentleman. By definition, of course, I was not a gentleman. Even though with the passing of time I attained some degree of sophistication,

I was never truly a gentleman. However, my sisters and the half mirror in our bathroom assured me I was good-looking: tall and slim with a full mustache, sandy hair, and masculine features. As the years passed, I changed as all men change but gradually. In my twenties I was shy and unsure of myself. In my early thirties I was withdrawn and bitter and often offended those who made no effort to understand my caustic wit. Now at thirty-eight, mellow and respected as a veteran writer, I was feeling a decline in energy and believing more than half of my life was over.

The charisma I cultivated had its base in the unhappy situation at home. It gave me an air of resignation and reserve that others found interesting. I was also a master of the English language and its literature and well versed in other languages. My extensive education, largely acquired on my own, was easily superior to that of the gentlemen who invited me to dine at their private clubs. I conducted myself with dignity and spoke careful words in a calm and resonant voice, taking pleasure in their arrangement. At dinner parties I impressed other guests as well dressed, debonair, articulate, intelligent, and well read. But despite the appearance, I suffered from persistent loneliness. Intense hunger for the warmth of a loving woman consumed my waking hours.

2

At the end of May in 1895 Derby Week came to Epsom. The horse race for three-year-olds had been founded in 1780 by the 12th Earl of Derby and had become an annual event. People of all classes, some with titles and sprawling country estates, poured into the town for the celebration. During the day ruffians clogged the streets and lanes. When night came they shot off fireworks, got riotously drunk, and made a lot of noise. Natalie was fully attuned to the excitement and liked it, but I wanted to get away. I found it difficult to tolerate humanity in the raw, the seething throng seeking pleasure. So I withdrew from the big celebration, viewing its antics with disdain. Natalie, on the other hand, was one with the multitude and spoke of the good times with enthusiasm.

"Why can't you stay here and just enjoy what's going on?" she asked. "What gives you the right to be so snobbish? They bring a happy atmosphere when they come here, and carloads of money."

"I never receive a farthing of what they bring and not a moment of their happy atmosphere," I replied. "The business isn't to my liking. Happily it takes place only once a year."

"Oh you are so sensitive! Why do you hate people? Why can't you let people have a little fun? Why can't you and I have a little fun once in a while? Why is it we never have fun any more?"

"It's time I go to Yarmouth and scout out a place to spend our summer holiday. In this hot summer weather we should be near the coast."

"I'm gonna walk the streets with the little nipper and enjoy what's happening here. I'll talk to all sorts of people and forget the gloom caused by a sour husband. I'm gonna have some fun!"

We didn't go to the seacoast that year nor anywhere else. I thought we might go on holiday at the end of July, but an invitation came for a fancy dinner I couldn't refuse. I was also away from Epson in June. In that month I went to the home of Edward Clay in Aldeburgh and spent a gala weekend there with a pleiad of clever writers. Natalie of course stayed home, fuming that her husband was deserting her once more to be with his hoity-toity friends while she had no friends at all, nothing to do but keep house for an ungrateful husband.

Her charges were not entirely without merit. While I spent a vastly enjoyable holiday at Aldeburgh, sharing literary gossip with six other writers, she remained home with a toddler. Clay lived in a modern and spacious house near the water and owned a sailboat for the enjoyment of his guests. A caterer served delicious food, and I ate heartily while arranging with my editor to write more stories. I liked Grant Alston who had just published a controversial novel called *The Woman Who Did*. Unlike Roger Leland, the man was genial and talkative and lacking in affectation. He was a scientist as well as a writer and believed Christ never existed. He was paid a thousand pounds for the book and was receiving royalties of twenty-five pounds a week. That bit of news hit me hard and aroused envy and wonder. As we spoke in confidence, Alston said he got along quite well with his wife. Like most middle-class wives, she tended to be religious while he was not, but they compromised when necessary and lived in harmony. That was the word of advice he gave me.

"Compromise," he said, "compromise whenever you can. Most of the problems that arise between a man and his wife can be settled with persistent compromise." Mr. Alston had never met Natalie and would never meet her. He didn't know she was unwilling or unable to compromise.

Many of the writers I came to know at this time were members of the Omar Khayyám Club. It was a dinner club for literary men active in the profession, and I soon became a member. I attended my first dinner in July. That was the month I wanted to be with my family at the seacoast, but the meeting seemed more important. In fact I later decided it was the most important social event of my entire career. The dinner-club meeting convinced me that finally I had come into my own as a man of letters. It took place at the Burford Bridge Hotel near Box Hill and was held in honor of George Meredith. Now a lionized old man of sixty-seven and hard of hearing, Meredith came in after the dinner was over and greeted all the men at the table. When someone mentioned my name, he called out, "Ah, Mr. Blue! Where is Mr. Blue?" Flattered and a bit flustered, I stood for a moment like a sentinel on guard and soon afterwards shook hands with the celebrated author.

Minutes later the toasts in his honor began. Meredith delivered a brief but eloquent speech of gratitude, and then Thomas Hardy spoke. Twenty-six years in the past, as a reader for Shipman & Hill, Meredith had advised Thomas Hardy to withhold his first novel from publication on grounds that it was strident and radical. Was that good advice? He finished his speech to laughter and approval. Then I was asked to speak as another author with early dealings with Meredith. I rose and spoke a few words concerning the anonymous reader accepting *The Outsiders*, but only after much revision. I doubted the man would accept anything from me now. The self-deprecation, which I thought was awkward and lacking in wit, brought laughter. It pleased me to be the focus of attention among generous peers who really liked me.

If not for deteriorating conditions at home, the year 1895 would have been a happy time for me, as happy as a glum temperament would permit. The hardships endured in the past had receded into the mists of time but had left scars that would never fade away completely. Happiness of a high order, therefore, was not in the cards for Jonathan Blue even when things were going well. As far as my career was going, 1895 was a banner year. I had found recognition as a novelist ranked with Hardy and Meredith. I had found a stable market for my books and stories. I had a comfortable income for the first time in my life, and could expect even better as long as I was able to work. The old three-decker tradition had given way to one-volume works that made my job easier. Second and third editions of such novels as *The Outsiders* were making my name known to a wider audience. I was viewed as a veteran writer, sensible and seasoned, and was now a respected member of the literary community. I was no longer a recluse writing in lonely solitude but was actually turning down invitations to fancy dinners.

I had finished a short novel, *Eve's Ambition*, and already had a publisher for it. Some old ideas featuring women and marriage filtered into the novel. One had to do with how women viewed men with low incomes. "*When a man is sure he will never have an income of more that £150*, declares the main character, "*it's a crime if he asks a woman to share it.*" The woman expressing that opinion has a secret wish to marry a man with money. Since the age of twelve she has known only work and anxiety and fear of the future. In her twenties, Eve is glad to have a job as a bookkeeper but wants more. "*If I hadn't been clever at figures, what would have become of me? I should have drudged at some wretched occupation until the work and the misery of everything killed me.*" Her one ambition, her aim in life, is to find a young and wealthy man of the upper class, quit working, marry him, and become a lady of leisure. That would make the present endurable and the future bright. She must also think of freedom from want in old age. A proper marriage could bring that and more. Several ambitious women in my books marry for money.

One in fact, Ida Stellaron, has the same ambition as Eve. Receiving a fortune after their older husbands die, those who marry for money set their sights on men with titles. Marriage for them is a means to achieve place and position in society, and love has little to do with it.

The second work, *Slumbering Embers*, was written in two months for a new firm. When the main character confesses he fathered a child out of wedlock, he is not able to marry the woman meant for him. Later he discovers she has become a lady with a title but also a widow. So after twenty years of yearning, he finally marries the woman of his heart's desire. Unhappy for years in a marriage without love, the lady tells him she will never marry again, but the strength of his devotion wins her over. Her personality is similar to that of Beatrice Gossam, whom I knew ten years earlier. Also the theme of the book prefigures the plot of a long novel written in good times near the end of my career. I drew upon my Greek experience for the setting of the story, but some of the characters don't come forward as fully drawn or interesting. Even so, the publisher paid me £150 for the book and it sold well.

After many years I was listening to the advice of friends and writing for the market. None of the stuff was very good, and I knew it, but dashing off a short novel in a month or two and receiving the same fee as for a full-length novel was lucrative. Another novelette, a thin story called *Guest in the House*, was the third title for 1895. It was about another ambitious girl trying to rise in social class by living with a family in the suburbs. The lively, man-crazy girl has left home because she and her working-class mother quarrel constantly. Her mother has married a second time, and to achieve peace and quiet the new husband insists the girl move out. He is willing to pay three guineas a week to the people who take her into their middle-class home. But in no time the girl causes havoc in the house and is asked to leave. She reaches safe haven when she marries a man employed by a commercial enterprise newly arrived on the scene, the Electric Lighting Company.

A number of short stories written on demand and some magazine work occupied me for the rest of the year. In the midst of this labor, because I wanted to return to more serious work, I decided to refuse future requests for short stories. It was not a good decision. Some of the tightly structured stories were reaching a wide audience, and a steady income was dependent on writing more. Even so, I wanted to write another long novel, a substantial work, and needed time to plan it. When Christmas Eve came I went to bed early. As I drifted into deep sleep, after lying awake for more than an hour, I dreamed of my brother Will whose life was cut short at twenty. Hale and hearty and eager to discuss his travels, William had just returned from Rome. To my surprise, for my brother had never studied the language, we conversed in German.

3

On the first day of 1896 I began taking notes for the long novel I had in mind. I knew it would mean a sacrifice of income, but I thought I could write a powerful book not to be compared with a novelette or short story. I thought I could finish the first draft by the end of May, but the project was interrupted three weeks later by the birth of a son we named Austin. A doctor and a midwife came in to deliver our second child, and for squeamish me it was not a pretty scene. Because the servant had quit only a few days before, I was called upon to help with the procedure. In the kitchen I heated gallons of water and supplied as many towels as I could find. The doctor – a round, smiling, stumpy little man – was genial enough, but the midwife was bossy.

When finally the healthy infant was bundled in blankets and placed in a makeshift crib, I felt a deep sense of relief. Then I became aware of the fact that I would have to care for little Walter, sleep on the sofa, and prepare meals every day for at least two weeks. There would be no time for literary work, and under the circumstances I couldn't afford another servant. Natalie lay with the newborn infant in the bedroom, calling out for assistance around the clock. The doctor had ordered ten days confinement, but she grew restless after seven or eight and began to tidy up our sitting room and even do some cooking. At night she couldn't sleep and kept me awake wheezing and moaning even though I was on the sofa in our sitting room.

When our life with its quarreling and bickering was almost back to normal, a pipe fitter looking for a gas leak with a candle set off an explosion. Only the workman was hurt, but the blast caused massive damage to every room in the house. Until repairs could be made, the family had to find shelter elsewhere. When settled in another place I wanted to get on with my novel but was stymied by the temporary living arrangement. Also I had to endure endless vilification from nagging Natalie. It seemed as though some devil had seized her, forcing her with flaming eyes to bleat bitter invective against her will. In April, driven by desperation, I left Walter in the care of my mother and sisters in Harrogate. Returning home after a walking tour of Wales to collect my thoughts, I braced myself for my wife's inevitable fury. As calmly as I could I made it known to her that I would not allow my son to grow up in a house tainted with conflict and quarreling. Her frenzied response brought wailing and blubbering from the baby. I was able to restore calm only when I convinced her that the work she gave to child care would now be cut in half. And she could see her son whenever she wished. Walter would become a pupil in the school my sisters had recently established. To relieve me of worry, they assured me he would be in good hands.

Progress on the long novel was impeded by uproar at home and by other causes as well. I feared I was getting to know too many people who interrupted my work too often, and I suffered at times from a serious cough. In June I attended a dinner at the Savoy where Lionel Chandler spoke. It had been years since last I talked with Chandler, and I was pleased to chat with him now. A month later I visited his family in the country, ate well at their table, and renewed my friendship with my two former students as we enjoyed long walks.

Later in the year, in November, I met a young writer named Herbert George Rhodes. The man went by his initials, and they could be seen on the covers of several books he had published. He said he had read most of my books and added that *New Bleak Street* reflected with high accuracy his own life at one time. I rather liked the feisty little man, a foot shorter than me, and accepted an invitation to visit him and his wife. It was the beginning of a warm and lasting friendship between the two of us. More than once Rhodes irritated me with intemperate outbursts, and yet he knew how to maintain a friendship and bring out the best in people he considered worthy of his time.

While his background was similar to mine, his personality was very different. He often claimed he was "buffeted by the philistines" even though his level of culture was about the same as theirs. Nine years younger than me, Rhodes at thirty was cheerful and happy, aggressive and optimistic, resilient and unafraid of adversity. In 1884 he had won a scholarship to the Normal School of Science in London, where he studied under Thomas Henry Huxley and acquired a scientific education. Later, because his friends admired his fertile imagination, he decided to become a writer. In the early years he lived in poverty in London lodging houses with a wife named Amy. In 1894 he published *The Time Machine* in serial form and was off to swift success. By the time he met me two years later he had a lucrative career as a writer of novels and stories in a new genre, science fiction. His income was already more than a thousand pounds a year. With persuasive logic he encouraged his friend to move in a similar direction. I wanted more money for my labor but I was unable to do as he suggested. Rhodes was writing for the market, catering to the moment, but I hoped to produce enduring works of art. My classical education was at odds with Rhodes' scientific training, but we were able to confide in one another and discuss any topic in full detail. We had an easy give-and-take friendship and liked each other.

The novel I was writing in 1896 was called *Benedict's Household*. The title was fictional clothing for my own household. I planned to include in the book many of the unhappy situations that occurred every day in my own home. I knew it was a risky business to reveal too much, and yet I felt the story had to be told. Then I remembered my sisters who would surely object with vociferous disapproval. Natalie in a fury and by way of revenge might even try to sue. So in timorous defeat I put the book aside and began something new. It might have been a powerful novel written directly from life, but near the end of summer it became another failed project on a heap of abortive work. In later years I regretted the loss of *Benedict* and my decision to go to another subject.

All the material I needed was there in front of me within my own dwelling. All I had to do was write about it. I rebuked the timid man within me for lack of courage, but to what avail? I had lost my nerve and put aside the project. Even though it might have been a moving novel eagerly read by thousands, it never saw the light of day. At one point in my life I thought I might write about all the novels I had spent hundreds of hours to create only to shove them aside as failed material. Well-received *New Bleak Street* was about authors struggling to publish finished books, but this novel would be about powerful books lost to the world for a variety of reasons. The list of reasons would be the backbone of the book, drawing all its parts together into a whole. It was an interesting idea that never became more than an idea.

CHAPTER TWENTY-NINE

Vixen-Haunted

When I became aware that 1896 would end with no book to put before readers, I went to work in earnest on a novel I was calling *The Vortex*. It soon became very difficult to write, demanding an abundance of rewriting that left me exhausted. At the same time my troubles with Natalie were escalating. Her insistent taunting, even when I tried not to listen, burned like salt in an open wound. Also I was worried about a hacking, persistent cough that wouldn't go away. I felt sick at times and despondent, but when the book was completed at the end of the year, I ranked it among the best of all my work. The protagonist saw modern life, and the endless round of social activity in London, as a whirlpool that draws hapless individuals into its maw eventually to destroy them.

The book presented relentless criticism of the rampant materialism of the time and the antics of confused, self-centered, shallow pleasure-seekers who cared only for themselves. It was also a subtle and bitter study of marriage as I thought the institution had become in the 1890's. The plot revealed more failed marriages than any book in my canon. Inevitably echoes of my own failing marriage came into the work, including a hostile wife and helpless children. To my surprise, *The Vortex* was well received by critics and the public and sold better than any of my earlier books. It pleased me to learn that the first edition of two thousand copies was sold out in a month, and a second edition was planned. That had never happened with any of my novels.

For a book of mine to go so quickly into a second edition was a rare and happy occurrence. At long last the reading public was buying my novels, reading them, and saying good things about them. Yet the circumstances in which the book was written were not good. I had chosen my second wife out of need rather than love, and once she understood the full significance of that she reacted with vengeance. She had an instinct for discovering a man's Achilles heel and pouncing upon it with fury. Her tirades disturbed me because some of the verbal abuse she spewed in my direction, though often exaggerated, rang true. I was not perfect, and I did have my faults, and to some extent I was surely the cause of her misery. But how could I blame myself entirely?

Mulling over that question kept me awake at night. I knew other causes were present to explain her behavior, but they were difficult to identify. Living with Natalie had become a painful failure as intense in its agony as living with Muriel. Our marriage brought into the world two precious little boys who could have made domestic life complete, but again I had married the wrong woman. Mistakenly I had thought my unpredictable income would prohibit anything better. The grim result was a repeat of the mental and emotional torment endured in the first marriage, a cold and crippling domestic unhappiness. That experience, visceral and daunting in its impact, shaped a cynical attitude toward marriage and a caustic contempt for a particular type of woman. Natalie's abusive behavior caused me to despise her. It led me to ponder whether force was ever justified to quell an angry wife.

Ugly events in my house spurred me to question whether marriage was ever intended to be inescapable. I thought it was time for the courts to grant an inexpensive divorce on grounds of incompatibility. That led to pungent comment in several books on the injustice of antiquated divorce laws. When separation and divorce seemed to be a plausible solution, troubled couples were made to realize with no little bitterness that the courts had placed divorce beyond their reach. In *New Bleak Street* Amy Leonhard asks: *"Isn't it a most ridiculous thing that married people who both wish to separate can't do so and be quite free again?"* She is attacking the obsolete Divorce Law of 1857, considered harsh by 1890 standards. The law granted divorce only on proven adultery after much legal wrangling at great expense. Litigants complained that it brought skeletons out of the closet even when there were no skeletons. They claimed that humiliation and loss of reputation were deliberate devices to discourage couples from dissolving a marriage.

The old divorce law was there only for the rich and powerful. The rank and file of the middle class had to endure insufferable marriages in silence or separate. Since separation seldom led to divorce, a couple not able to live together often couldn't live with anyone else. At a time when men and women of every class were asserting independence, marriage as an institution inevitably came under severe strain. In that climate antiquated divorce laws needed quick and effective revision. More than once I urged that be done. I never found out whether the movers and shakers, politicians who could bring about change, were ever influenced by anything of mine they might have read.

Also something had to be done about the servant problem. When I found that Natalie was not capable of supervising even the meekest of servants, I thought about the servant question and attempted to find solutions. I applied calm and logical thought to the problem and outlined a program that seemed quite workable. Though expressing conservative opinion on the question, I opted for flexibility and fairness. I couldn't agree with the leading character in *The Vortex* who would train only men as servants and *"send the women to the devil."* If properly trained, women could do the job. Though cynical at times and bitter, I was more thoughtful and less emotional than my fictional character. But the practical solution I eventually proposed – train young women of the middle-class to become servants – raised eyebrows in some circles.

My readers reminded me that middle-class girls were the daughters of doctors, lawyers, professors, industrial magnates, high-ranking military officers, and the clergy. Accustomed to a comfortable standard of living and graduates of the new high schools, they were thought to be made of finer fabric. Some readers saw my opinions on the servant question, as well as those on marriage and other social issues, as controversial, incendiary, and dangerous. They read me wrongly and over-reacted. Closer to the truth, I had moved away from the liberal thought of my youth to an unyielding conservative position in maturity.

2

Through the fall and winter of 1896 and into the early months of 1897 I suffered from a sore throat and persistent cough. Writing to Kurtz, I worried about my health: *"I have had a bad cough for a long time, and now in this vile weather it is getting worse. I hope to find out once and for all what is really the matter with me."* I said I would consult a doctor and move perhaps to a milder climate, leaving Natalie and the baby in Epsom and the older boy in Harrogate. In February, two months after completing *The Vortex*, I explained to her what I was planning to do. She was in the kitchen washing the supper dishes, and her anger quickly became explosive. In a rage she smashed a plate at my feet and began to scream unspeakable abuse. I was mortified by the way she twisted my announcement into something criminal.

"You are thinking about abandoning your wife and child? How could you? The law will not allow you to walk out of here, leaving us behind!"

"I didn't say anything about abandoning anybody."

"Yes, you did! Of course you did! You made it very clear you plan to abandon your wife and child! And for selfish reasons!"

"Natalie, you don't understand. I must have a milder climate to help me care for a nagging health condition."

"Your health condition! Let me tell you about your health condition! It's dirty and against the law! You're seeing another female, some dirty little whore not older than fifteen! You picked her off the street in Piccadilly, a nasty little whore! Now you want a fancy, hoity-toity place for dirty sex! Oh, I know you, all right! That's all you think about! That's all you ever think about! That's your condition!"

It was not the first time she had accused me in a jealous fury of infidelity. Ignoring her screaming baby, she cursed and shrieked and tried to strike me with clenched fists. I fended off the blows as best I could and said nothing. I had thought that motherhood would mitigate her wrath, but I was wrong. Immediately I tossed a few items into a suitcase and left to live elsewhere. She stood in the doorway screaming abuse.

Later I explained to Kurtz, my only confidant, that I had been driven vixen-haunted from home, chased away with furious insult. I placed the blame squarely on her shoulders and vowed never to return. Poor Kurtz expressed deep sympathy in his reply, and then as an afterthought he said: "*Life as you must know can be hellish. Be strong, my friend.*"

I went to Holbrook to stay with Emeritus Gifford, an old friend I had known as a boy at the Quaker school in Cheshire. Gifford, who had become a doctor, examined me and recommended a specialist. Together we went to see Dr. Philip Penn-Ashe, consulting physician at Guy's Hospital in London. I was told that the respiratory disorders suffered in Naples in 1890 were now in 1897 developing into a disease. Penn-Ashe found a weakness in the right lung and advised me to go immediately to South Devon for a milder and cleaner climate. I thought it might be tuberculosis, the disease that had killed my brother. It was later determined to be emphysema. No one seemed to know that smoking if not the cause was surely an irritant, and I continued to smoke. After the formal dinners I attended, I inhaled the blue smoke of fat and strong cigars with purest satisfaction. It was de riguer, the gentlemanly thing to do for the place and time. At home I never smoked cigars, only a pipe when I could buy good tobacco.

I spent the next few months at the little seaside town of Budleigh Salterton, discovered in 1891 when living in Exeter. For three months and three weeks I lived there, making good use of my time. My sister Maggie came to stay with me. Rhodes and his wife came for an extended visit. Their company was exactly the right medicine for me. The nagging cough became less troublesome, and I was able to breathe with less difficulty. Climbing a hill, however, or walking across the downs, as I had done with great satisfaction in the past, brought a shortness of breath. Dr. Gifford believed I wore too many clothes when walking and advised me to wear lighter clothing and walk slower. But emphysema, a progressive respiratory disease, was at the root of my condition.

At Budleigh Salterton in Devon I began to think about writing the historical novel about sixth-century Rome that in time became *Chlotilda*. My preparation was extensive and thorough and time consuming. I discussed the project with Rhodes who encouraged it, and we agreed to meet in Rome the following year. My plan was to gather material there and write the novel of the distant past soon after. In the meantime I had to worry about coughing and wheezing and went to see Dr. Penn-Ashe as soon as I returned to Epsom. When I saw the doctor in fine weather at the beginning of June, I was hoping for a good report. Instead, the physician urged me to get away from London and live *"anywhere in pure air on chalk and sand."* So just as I began to reside again with Natalie, working hard to restore a fragile harmony, I was thinking we would have to move again near the end of summer.

Elizabeth Osgood, a young woman I had met at a literary dinner in 1894, had brought us together for intense discussion. She had taken courses in the new psychology and was able to talk with us perceptively about our problems. She persuaded us to forgive one another and try to forget. Her premise was toleration, not compromise as Grant Alston had suggested two years earlier. Learn to live with your spouse in a spirit of toleration, she instructed. Accept each other's faults and live with them. And remember, she emphasized, no person on God's green earth is flawless. In time she would play an important role in my family affairs, perhaps doing more harm than good but not intentionally.

As summer began in 1897 my latest novel, *The Vortex,* had become a literary success. That alone had a healing effect and allowed me to tolerate my wife and her temper with less pain. During the summer I researched Roman history of the sixth century as preparation for the historical novel, using the libraries of London and persuading them to buy the books I needed. My classical training had already given me ample knowledge of the period, but I needed to brush up on the subject. I wanted to probe deeper into all aspects of it and take many pages of notes. Later I would draw upon my notes to fashion a story with authentic detail. Also at this time a man I had known at Thatcher College asked me to write a critical study of Dickens. I welcomed the assignment and worked on the project throughout the summer. My love of Dickens went all the way back to my boyhood. I was glad to be writing on a subject I had always liked and was being paid to do it.

In the second week of June I began another short novel, *The Commercial Traveller*. It was written rapidly in one month for the money I needed, but was published in 1898. It depicted boarding-house life with gentle good humor, but with echoes of both Muriel and Natalie. A spirited girl of the people with excellent teeth (a reminder of Muriel) holds the story together. Her strong personality displaying ferocity and fiery temper owes a debt to Natalie. As the story opens Polly Klemp is venting her temper on the hapless servant, as Natalie often did, and threatening violence: *"If it wasn't too much trouble I'd come out and smack your face, you dirty little wretch!"* Polly enjoys a good quarrel and needs at least two a day to remain pleasant. Conflict with others is the medication she needs for health and happiness. The person behind the title is a good-natured man of forty who has spent his life trying to sell things but has never been able to keep a job. At the end of the book, after narrowly escaping Polly's bear-like clutches, he marries an unassuming woman who owns and operates a shop. Though with some misgiving, he works beside his wife in the shop and they prosper.

3

August 1897 came with hot and dry weather. I made plans to go on holiday with Natalie and the children. We went first to Harrogate to pick up Walter. I was hoping we would have a wonderful time together, but the outing soon became turbulent and unpleasant. Natalie's grumbling and complaining increased in tempo while I gave my attention to the children. Then as we were eating she began to scold little Walter for nothing more than childish behavior. I spoke up in defense of the boy, but my protest only made matters worse. In a public place she vented her caustic temper on me as well, and her sour behavior spoiled any attempt to have a good time together. After describing in my diary what appeared to be a pleasant outing on a fine day in summer, I found it necessary to add: *"Of course everything spoilt by N's frenzy of ill temper. I merely note the fact, lest anyone reading this should be misled, and imagine a day of real enjoyment."* The diary entry, as I view it now, clearly shows I was conscious of posterity. Driven perhaps by wishful thinking, I believed in time my biography would be written by some enterprising soul. I wanted the biographer to set down my story exactly, avoiding the misinterpretation I had seen in other biographies.

Most of the time the misery meted out by Natalie boiled and seethed within me, but as I thought about leaving her once and for all I wanted others to know the cause. In a letter to Maggie I described my wife's misbehavior in detail and asked her to keep the letter as possible evidence in a lawsuit. I feared she might charge me with desertion and demand a large sum of money. I was thinking that with a good lawyer I might be able to divorce her even though legal proceedings would be expensive and a divorce nearly impossible. In the meantime I would keep a record detailing the frequency and ferocity of her outbursts and the trivial incidents that set them off.

One day as I was writing a letter to Miss Osgood, a small rubber ball rolled from Walter's hands into the room where I was sitting. It happened just as I was telling my friend that I had decided on doctor's orders to spend the winter in Italy.

"Where'd it go?" Natalie demanded, marching into the room.

"Where did what go?"

"You know as well as I do, the goddamn ball! The little red ball!"

"I didn't see a little red ball. Didn't see even a large one."

"You're lying!" she screeched. "You attempt to cover your lying with an unfunny joke! You're hiding the ball just to annoy me! You are lying, you foolish man! You lie just to annoy me!"

"Don't accuse me of lying in front of my son," I said, standing up and glancing at Walter who stood silently in the doorway.

"Liar, liar!" she taunted. "Dirty, dirty liar! If you don't shut up and move out of the way, I'll throw something!"

The altercation grew louder and hotter. I braced myself and made a determined effort to remain calm. I asked the boy, now more than six years old, to repeat what he had heard. As Walter began to parrot his mother's ranting, I copied the hateful words on sheets of paper. When his mother denied having said them, as I knew she would, I would have the proof for anyone to see. With a simple stratagem I had gotten the upper hand. She bristled with anger but slowly calmed.

"I pity you, Jonathan Blue, I really do. And Walter, I pity you! No boy should have a father like him! He pretends to be so high and mighty, but he's only a bore and a poor husband and father. I know it and you know it and everybody else knows it!"

"If not for me," I calmly retorted, "you'd be working sixteen hours a day in a shop or waiting tables in a low-class eatery."

"Hah! Even that would be better than this! You can't make a decent living with all that scribbling, and now you're claiming to be sick! You make me wanna puke! I'm the one that's sick!"

"Yes, I know," I wanted to say. "You really are the one who's sick."

It would have given me satisfaction, but I held my tongue. I finished the letter to Elizabeth Osgood and began to make plans then and there to put my furniture and books in storage and spend the winter of 1897 in Italy. Walter would go with Quentin back to Harrogate, and lodgings would be found in London for Natalie and Austin.

The agreeable young woman, who seemed to be soft and submissive when we met in 1890, had become in record time an overbearing termagant. In no more than two years the marriage had slipped into bickering and discomfort, and a few years after that it lay in ruins. As this second marriage spiraled downward, I began to question my personal fitness for the institution of marriage. My novels of the 1890's show marriage as an uncertain and precarious arrangement, often the result of economic factors or mere convenience, and likely productive of dark and deep misery. At times the wife is to blame, but often as not the trouble flows from a wretched husband whose sense of male dominance will not allow him to view his wife as an equal. The turn of the screw, a gradual tightening of male control, usually provokes the wife to resist or rebel. That simple human reaction tends to hasten the failure of the marriage. Also I saw the feminist movement as a troublesome cause of domestic conflict, particularly when the feminism of the wife clashes with the conventional attitudes of the husband.

Convinced that Natalie was losing all control and becoming a danger to the child, I sought the help of Elizabeth Osgood and Clara Collader. The latter had been my friend for two years and was earning a reputation as a social scientist. As early as 1895 I had said to my sister Emma: *"We see but one visitor – Miss Collader, who knows the extraordinary circumstances of the establishment and puts up with everything."* Osgood and Collader were well-meaning, compassionate women and willing to do whatever they could to mitigate the conflict. But at times I really believe their interference caused more harm than good. They were educated, self-assured, and from the upper-middle class. They were aliens from another world and Natalie fiercely resented them.

Earlier she had liked Collader, but now she thought the woman was conspiring with Osgood against her. Instead of taming her ferocity, their efforts tended to make it worse. Undaunted, they went on trying to help, and eventually Natalie agreed to place herself and her child under the supervision of Miss Osgood. Her new home was pleasant and comfortable, and the rent I paid was reasonable. Austin would be safe there and would not be abused. At all times someone would be looking after his welfare. With anguish I accepted the fact that I would never be living with Natalie and my children again. My second marriage had come to an end. The misery it brought into my life stayed with me long afterwards, rising up to hurt even when times were good.

CHAPTER THIRTY

Third Trip to Italy

I left England in September of 1897 with no plans for a prompt return. I traveled by way of Florence to Siena, where I found a room in a boarding house run by a family named Gambino. At sea I met a young American — lively, willowy, amusing and told her all about my year in America. Though my American adventure lasted only a year, I came of age there. It was a time of testing, a time that demanded hard decisions. It wasn't always a grand adventure but fruitful. I knew on returning what I would do with my life. The girl listened to my story with rapt attention and seemed to like what she heard, but when the boat docked I never saw her again. In Siena I began to savor the warmth and ambience of the country, taking pleasure in the activity of the people around me. The landlady and her sister spoke only Italian, and so I could practice using the language. At the end of the day in the quiet of my room I was able to work on the Dickens book. However, persistent coughing that had begun to pester me in Florence wouldn't go away.

I smoked as I wrote, puffing on my pipe to keep the poor tobacco lit, not aware that the tar and nicotine was inflaming the emphysema that was threatening my lungs. I longed for some honest English tobacco to tamp into the bowl with my thumb. The Italian variety was miserable stuff. My breathing grew more labored and I was losing weight. I told myself my health would improve as I began to stroll in the sunlit air of Siena. Striding briskly through the town and into the country, I thought of Italy's supreme beauty as inseparable from blood and tears. In the midst of that rare beauty I found hardscrabble lives weighted by oppression. My thoughts were on the people, their hardship and suffering through the centuries, and the pitiless blue sky looking down on it all.

Two weeks passed and I took great pleasure in the life around me. But alone in my room it seemed I had been away from home for a long time. I thought of my children, worried about them, and speculated how changed they might be when I returned. I remembered Natalie's furious temper tantrum, fleeing headlong from the malice of her tongue, and leaving behind the helpless child. Walter, the older son, was safe in Harrogate, but little Austin remained with his mother. A person who had yearned all his life for quiet domesticity, I was homesick for a hearth that had never been quiet. Also a gloomy atmosphere began to cloak the casual, happy life of the boarding house. Signor Gambino was on his deathbed. As the boarders chatted happily at table, weeping could be heard from another part of the house. During the time the man lay dying, a storm was raging with lightning and claps of thunder. It roared and died away, paused to let silence creep in, and roared again. In the interval the boarders could hear the wife crying in piercing operatic despair: *"addio, addio, amore!"* It was a drama that ended when the entire household moved into a smaller house. I was assigned a pleasant room, and there in early November I completed the book on Dickens.

The chapter on the author's female characters targeted the foolish, ridiculous, and offensive women in his novels. With bitter thoughts of Natalie stirring me to temporary misogyny, I noted: *"These remarkable creatures belong for the most part to one rank of life, that which we vaguely designate as the lower middle class. In general, their circumstances are comfortable; they are treated by their male kindred often with extraordinary consideration. Yet their characteristic is acidity of temper and boundless license of querulous or insulting talk. The real business of their lives is to make all about them as uncomfortable as they can."* I observed that women of this sort could be found in the London of my own time in almost every household, and their number was steadily increasing. The new education, touted by some as an all-inclusive panacea, had improved such women very little.

The extended liberty achieved by the feminists, I insisted, had promoted an ugly aggression and a sense of equality at odds with reality. It had exacerbated *"the evil characteristics in women vulgarly bred"* and had made them worse than ever. It had produced in great numbers *"the well-dressed shrew who proceeds on the slightest provocation from fury of language to violence of act."* I was thinking of Natalie as I penned those indelicate words. Her insults made harsher by gutter language now returned to haunt and unhinge me. She alone triggered the savage vehemence of my assessment. In that state of mind I wasn't viewing Dickens objectively. The misery of the recent past had warped my judgment.

After finishing the book on Dickens in the first week of November, I left the Gambino boarding house for Rome and Naples to begin my tour of Calabria. I would later write a book about my travels and call it *Old Calabria*. The region in those days was a backward province on the toe of the Italian boot and dangerous. The Neapolitans had warned me that brigands were in the area and sometimes attacked travelers. Though I worried about the danger, I was eager to see that part of Italy. In my imagination it was "Magna Graecia" and glorious. It held within its borders the two cultures I loved most, those of Greece and Rome. Before entering the wild place, should something happen to me, I drew up a will at the British Consulate in Naples. It was an idle precaution, I told myself, but worth the annoyance because I was traveling into the unknown. I found poverty and squalor in nineteenth-century Calabria. Time and decay had covered the grand scenes of the past, and the present was dilapidated and dirty. The manager of the inn at Cosenza, near the grave of Alaric the Conqueror, wore the shabbiest clothes I had ever seen. The place was unsanitary and smelled of rotting meat.

From Cosenza I traveled by rail to Taranto. The museum curator told me I would find little of interest there, but from my reading I remembered a strange phenomenon spanning two centuries that had occurred in the town. A large and venomous wolf spider, later called a tarantula, could be found in Taranto. Between the fifteenth and seventeenth centuries the townspeople believed the spider's bite caused a disease they called tarantism. The affliction was associated with melancholy, stupor, madness, and an uncontrollable desire to dance. Victims leaped in the air, ran about making strange noises, and spoke in unknown tongues. Dancing off the tarantula's venom was considered the only cure. The dancing was described as violent and went on for days until the dancers dropped from exhaustion. The best cure was a lively Italian folk dance that became known as the tarantella. Taranto in southern Italy was the center of this dancing disease, which spread across southern Europe. From the town's name, Taranto, came *tarantula* and *tarantella* as well as *tarantism*. I mused with a chuckle that maybe the so-called disease was a ruse to allow for dancing in the southern sunshine in defiance of strict religious rules enforced by the Catholic Church.

I spent several days exploring the area and made sketches of what I saw. I found a river mentioned by Horace, but it was only half a mile long. Sluggish, brackish, and dirty, it had nothing to recommend it. An ammunition dump occupied a place famous in classical times for its purple dye. Ragamuffins slouched in the shade of dusty trees nearby and hooted when I passed them. Another gang pestered me for handouts I didn't have. Metaponto, a town that thrived in antiquity, had nothing more than a railway station and a little eating-place that required a strong stomach. Cotrone, the ancient Greek city of Croton, was an ugly and depressing town but worth sketching. Eventually a professional illustrator would improve the sketches for a travel book.

2

Near the end of November the weather turned bad and my cough devolved into something worse. Confined to bed for five days, I had the time to write a long letter to my son Walter. I asked the boy to persuade his grandmother to read it to him and point to his father's travels on a map. *"Cotrone is a very strange little town,"* I wrote, using words the boy could understand. *"All day long herds of goats wander in the streets. No one seems to own them. No one sees them as a nuisance."* When I saw him again in England, he asked many questions about the goats. The boy was a lover of animals, and the goats' welfare concerned him.

A local doctor came to see me, thumped on my chest, and diagnosed rheumatism from exposure to the weather. I had a fever and congestion of the lungs, and he prescribed doses of quinine. It brought on vivid dreams by night and a tingling of the skin by day. When I stopped taking the drug, I was able to observe the people of the inn who took care of me. On the surface they seemed to be uncouth and ragged ruffians, but as I came to know them I discovered people with heart, kindness, and compassion. In a few days I was well enough to sit up in bed and eat. The quinine had made me hungry, and the cook came with a roasted pigeon. It was bristling with tiny bones and so greasy it slipped from my fingers. Later I traveled to Catanzaro, where several letters and the Dickens proofs were waiting for me.

In December the air of the mountain town was fresh and invigorating. I spoke in halting Italian with the townspeople and found them kind and attentive. Their children were healthy and happy, the women wore bright and beautiful costumes, and some male adult faces seemed chiseled by a sculptor. Sitting in a café and listening to the talk around me, I thought it superior to similar conversation in England. The casual talk of poor Italians, I told myself, was laced with reason and even explored abstract subjects. I wasn't aware of my bias toward England. I thought I loved my country. Yet I had felt a troubling resentment as early as my days in America. It governed my thoughts when abroad and remained with me well into maturity.

Before leaving Calabria I wanted to explore one last place, Squillace. Cassiodorus had set up two monasteries there to become the founder of the medieval scribal tradition. I went by carriage though the rain to find the vaunted town a filthy ruin. The inn was squalid and crawling with vermin. It served acidic wine with odious food. Unable to drink the wine or eat the food, I went on to Reggio to view Mount Etna. Reflecting on my travels, I concluded the modern Italians with their incompetent bureaucracy were letting their classical past fade away. The country that boasted a glorious civilization in former times was slipping into do-nothingism and all but bankrupt. The thought saddened me.

On my way from Naples to Rome, I spent a night at Monte Cassino, a monastery on a mountain founded in 529 by St. Benedict. In a thick, cold mist I went up the slopes of the mountain on a donkey with a boy for a guide. Within minutes, as I stood at the gate, the courteous prior, a wonderfully simple man, received me. I said I was gathering materials for a novel, and the prior listened with interest. Touring the monastery with my host, I absorbed its medieval atmosphere until dark. When a frugal supper was served, I sat at a large, oaken table with the monks who ate in silence. In a cold and cavernous hall each man ate lentil porridge, a slice of cold brawn, and one apple. The scanty fare wasn't enough to end my hunger, but the wine was good. I spent the night in a room with an excellent view of the valley and town below. In the morning I explored the grounds, said goodbye to the gentle prior, and took my leave. Riding the donkey down the mountain, I exulted in the rich and abundant material I was gathering. I planned to use the monastery as the setting for several chapters of *Chlotilda*, my ambitious sixth-century novel.

In Rome I gathered additional material, explored all parts of the city, spent time with English friends, and corresponded with Rhodes. At the beginning of 1898 I spoke of Natalie's ugly behavior at home, adding that I might have to return to England sooner than expected: *"Things are going on very badly. My wife has carried uproar into the house of the friend who was kind enough to take her. Insult and fury are her return for infinite kindness and goodwill. It seems impossible for her to remain there much longer."* By the time I got to Rome the life of Italy was in my bones. I had gone there to forget the ugly trouble with Natalie, but mainly to immerse myself in the ambience and warmth of the country, absorb its classical associations, and write. To my satisfaction I was able to do all that. I finished the Dickens book in Siena, corrected the proofs in Catanzaro, and researched the scenes of my historical novel. I wanted to remain in Italy until some pleasant event might bring me home in a spirit of triumph, but that was not to happen.

Disturbing news about my wife's unpredictable behavior came to me regularly. She was quarreling with the neighbors, venting her fury on Miss Osgood, and disrupting the household. She found no one to admire, and when she offered her opinion of anyone, it was to spew something profane. She recalled growing up in a poor London neighborhood and loving her life there. Then came this creature from another planet who ran off with her and imprisoned her and made her life wretched. Osgood remonstrated, saying everyone knew her husband had always treated her kindly. Natalie's response was a nasal, high-pitched laugh that grew louder and louder and grated on the ears. Living in isolation imposed by that wonderful man, she had to wear shabby clothing, endure shoddy shelter, and subsist in a lonely house on the worst food she had ever eaten. And that was treating her kindly?

She laughed and laughed, snorting with bitter contempt, her wild eyes fixed in a stare. Her benefactors reckoned her behavior irrational and unpredictable and decided she would have to live elsewhere. Elizabeth Osgood knew a working-class woman who would be willing to rent part of her house to her. Perhaps in that environment, away from educated people and close to people of her own kind, Natalie would calm down and find a semblance of contentment. But someone would have to keep a close eye on the woman for the sake of the child. That arrangement required me to dig deeper into pockets that had never been deep. I was now convinced that in one of her tantrums, even though the woman loved her child, she was fully capable of abusing him. By then I was comparing her erratic behavior to that of a lunatic and believed she was descending irrevocably into madness.

3

Natalie became unstable as the years passed and was possibly unstable with symptoms lying dormant at the time we married. But at twenty-six she was too proud and too strong to be looked after as an incompetent by such women as Osgood and Collader. They were as helpful and as kind as they could manage, but she saw them as keepers instead of friends. She believed they were in cahoots with her husband, for they often defended me when she spoke out against me. In her mind she was the victim, not me, for I had reduced her life to a shambles.

Too late I saw that a chief cause of her fury was alienation from her relatives and longtime friends. When we married she was young and lively, outgoing and gregarious, but I insisted on withdrawal, isolation, exile from her class and my own. It was a course of action doomed to bring negative results. I was stupid to think she would be happy to stay home and care for a child while I attended formal dinners in a fancy dress suit. She was expected to be content with no friends, no relatives, and no social life while I consorted with upper-class people to advance my career. Her destiny was to live her life in close quarters surrounded by people she loved. As soon as she married all that changed. I required her to live away from her world even as a woman in her prime, and she couldn't handle that. She blamed me and I blame myself.

With the help of Miss Osgood, I was negotiating a legal separation. I didn't try for a divorce because I thought the court would give Natalie custody of the two children and deny me all rights as their father, even the right to visit. So I chose separation with the stipulation that I would live apart from her but provide support. She would agree to keep her distance from me and not interfere with my life in any way. The lawyer suggested she be given a pound a week. I generously offered to double that. When the time came for her to sign legal papers, she refused. Quentin helped to get her settled in another house while negotiations continued. She told him his presence had a soothing effect, and yet one afternoon she lashed out at him with vitriolic bitterness. A moment later she meekly and plaintively apologized, saying she had seen in him the likeness of her husband as he was moving a piece of furniture. The incident convinced Quentin the woman suffered from delusions.

I left Rome in the middle of April and spent four days with Kurtz in Berlin and Potsdam. I found my old friend in good health though much older than I imagined and nervous. The man complained he was always looking for a quiet place in which to work but could never find it. I advised him to live to Italy where the noise quickly became a pleasant sound, but he had to remain close to his publisher. Kurtz was trying to make a living as a writer and had published the book on his Rugby, Tennessee experience. It was the book on which I had spent hours running down references, and in the forward Kurtz generously acknowledged my help. The militarism I saw in Berlin distressed me, and Germany was ugly compared to Italy. Germany had wealth and progress and discipline but a paucity of beauty and grace, or so it seemed to me.

After being away more than six months, and just as winter was losing its grip, I arrived back in London near midnight. I liked being in Italy and Germany seeing new places, but I was glad to be home. I wanted to be in the countryside and breathe the beauty of England in springtime. I had said to Kurtz in one of those moments of deep reflection (as we drank a second bottle of wine): *"I long to be back in England. I shall never travel again."* Kurtz found the remark surprising. He knew his friend was restless and alienated in England and felt more at home in some other country. Even though he had known me for a long time, he was not able to read his English friend at the core. If he had asked probing questions, he would have heard that I loved my country above all others in spite of the misery meted out to me there.

In the third week of April in 1898, the trees were in tiny leaf and spring was turning the countryside green. I was hoping I could find a house in the south of England soon, but more than a month went by before my personal and business affairs were back in order. I rented a room in a London hotel and quickly learned that my bank balance was less than 200 pounds. I went to the offices of an old publisher, Lathrop & Bailey, and visited a new one, Peter Robeson. My oldest friend, Dylan Crenshaw, was back in town and we had dinner together. We had not seen each other for a long time and had much to talk about. I believed I was becoming weaker from a lung condition; in Italy I had seen a spot of blood on my handkerchief. Crenshaw, robust and hearty as ever, urged me to consult a specialist. He had just returned from a voyage around the world, spending two years on a magnificent adventure.

CHAPTER THIRTY-ONE

Natalie Comes Calling

"Around the world, my friend!" he roared, lifting his wine glass with a flourish. "Around the globe! And what a trip it was! Oh, what a trip! I must do it again, soon! In Samoa, in that legendary house on a mountain, I met . . . can you guess? Robert Louis Stevenson!"

"Tell me about him," I demanded. "I've read that he was sickly all his life, struggling with tuberculosis. Died about three years ago but insisted on living his life vigorously, retaining his youth to the end. I'm told that wherever he happened to be in his travels he gathered materials for his writing, and of course I do the same."

"He filled notebooks by the dozen," said Crenshaw. "Enlivened his essays with impressions of people, places, and things. Loved the sea and wanted to sail again but was an invalid near death when I met him. Wanted to show me the sights and the native way of life but didn't have the strength. He died in 1894 shortly after my visit. Died trying to open a bottle of wine they say. Only forty-four at the time."

"That's too young to die. I'm sure he wanted to live forty more years. I'm told he had a tremendous zest for adventure. And his poor health didn't keep him down. Somehow he found the energy to move."

"He did indeed. Stevenson was an admirable man. He and I had a lot in common – world travelers, y' know, writers and sailors, Englishmen. Well, broadly speaking! I daresay a generous Englishman can embrace a Scot now and then, don't ye think?" He was laughing at his own joke.

"And I suppose a Scot might surely be capable of similar generosity," I answered in retort. "Yes! Two simpatico lovers of life."

"We could have formed a close friendship except for his health, that debilitating disease he wrestled with most of his life. But y' know, I heard he died of a stroke. All his life he worried about his tubercular condition but died of a stroke! Some real irony there."

They could indeed have formed a friendship, for Crenshaw loved ships and the sea as much as Stevenson. Later in one of his many books he would recall sailing on a square-rigged clipper and going aloft. He wrote about the experience with exhilaration and a sense of wonder but in sentences hard to digest. *"There's no such glory as the glory of the ship, and no such glory in the ship as when we lift our eyes and hearts upon her nearest reach to heaven. Would it were mine to sing the swan song of the sailing ships that soon shall be no more."* Unlike so many younger writers coming forward into their own, he never learned to write well.

The talk drifted back to my personal problems and possible solutions. Fearful that Natalie would be looking for me and ready to storm my home without notice, I asked my friend to spread the rumor that I was planning to live near my brother in Worcestershire. Crenshaw was eager to help. He was aggressive in a friendly way and moved among a variety of people. He would try to throw her off track.

In May, after spending a week in Harrogate with Walter and my family, I rented a house in Dorking. Near the end of the month I moved into the new residence with new furniture. A gentle, caring woman past middle age came to serve as my housekeeper. Shortly afterwards, with every piece of furniture in its proper place, I invited H. G. and Catherine Rhodes to visit me for dinner. They came with a bottle of good wine and good conversation. When I lived with Natalie in Epsom I felt I couldn't invite the couple to my home, explaining I had no home. Now I could have them often, for they lived within bicycling distance.

"I will teach you how to ride that new-generation machine they call a bicycle," said Rhodes, laughing. "Then you can pedal over to visit us any time you like and we can ride together!"

"It would be splendid exercise, and I would like nothing better than to spin down a country lane on a bicycle. But mind you, not on a penny-farthing with the big wheel! Trying to balance myself on two wheels of equal size is challenge enough. That big-wheel thing seems remarkably like walking a tightrope, and that I've never been able to do!"

"No big wheel, just two of equal size. It isn't difficult. You'll see. And once you learn you never forget it."

Later I discovered I had spent seventy pounds setting up the new household. So I went to work writing short stories to earn money. By the first week in June I had written three stories, which I sent off to my agent to insure a flow of income. I was now beginning to live a middle-class existence, but I would have to work incessantly to maintain even moderate comfort. The new publisher I had visited in London on returning from Italy offered me a deal that seemed better than any contract I had ever signed. Peter Robeson was willing to buy all my work for the next five years and pay me more than the going rate. I asked for a thousand pounds a year, too much for Robeson, and the deal fell through. Not once in a career of more than twenty years did I earn more than five hundred pounds, and that came in only one or two of my best years. Why would I demand a thousand pounds a year for work not yet done? The issue was complicated, one I could never explain.

At long last I was able to live with a faithful servant in a desirable place, but I worried about my security and whether Natalie in a rage would suddenly pound on my door. Nestled in the midst of foliage in a quiet neighborhood, my house was comfortable and pleasant but accessible to any person who came along. If Crenshaw had not managed to spread the rumor that I was living in Worcestershire, she could show up with a warrant for my arrest, claiming I had willfully deserted my destitute family. She had a penchant for revenge and was capable of doing without a shred of compunction whatever came into her mind.

One morning in June – the year was 1898 – the doorbell rang. It was the kind of bell one turns by hand to send a shrill signal through the house. At once I thought of Natalie. Slowly I rose from my desk and went to the door. The housekeeper had gone to the market. Instead of Natalie, furious and ready to pounce, a colporteur with a smiling face greeted me. He was a young man not yet twenty with sandy hair, pale blue eyes, thin lips under a sharp nose, and freckles.

"Good morning, sir!" he exclaimed. "I have in my hands a book you cannot do without. It is the King James Version of the Holy Bible fully annotated with splendid illustrations." He paused to size up his customer and judiciously read his reaction.

Taller than the peddler, I looked down into his thin, earnest face and smiled. "Thank you for your interest in me, young man. I do wish you well, but I'm not in the least interested in what you are selling."

"But sir," the peddler quickly replied, "this printing of the greatest book ever published is far better than any of the others. And the price is really quite reasonable."

"It's a good book," I said with an honest chuckle, "and the King James Version is the best by far. It's bursting at the seams with exciting story and good poetry. But you must know the book is mainly a collection of folk tales interpreted by religionists as divine truth. That bothers me."

"Divine truth, yes!" cried the colporteur, "but folk tales? Just a collection of folk tales? Now that's something I never heard in all my life." He tipped his hat, turned on his heel, and walked away shaking his head.

Later at a dinner of the Omar Khayyám Club, my humorous tale of this incident would entertain Grant Alston. Newly arrived on the literary scene, he was a scientist, novelist, essayist, and atheist. His readers soon learned that he had replaced religious faith with empirical reason, and many objected. He was writing books more shocking to the middle class than anything I had done. His book of 1897, *The Evolution of the Idea of God*, had brought scathing reviews from any number of people but also a huge amount of money. I had published a major novel, *The Vortex*, in the same year. The first edition of 2,000 copies was sold out in a month, but I was paid only a fraction of what Alston got for his work. I was at a loss to understand why competing authors could write controversial books and make money while I myself had never been able to do that.

2

Even though my bank account was rapidly dwindling and my income uncertain, I found it necessary to hire a woman to keep house for me. I dreaded the prospect; I had seen too many loutish servants come and go under Natalie's supervision. But in this instance fate smiled upon me. I was able to hire an intelligent and competent woman who viewed my interests as her own. She was the daughter of a farmer, had grown up in a large family in the country, and valued quiet. I quickly discovered that she was kind, patient, compassionate, understanding, and efficient. She was proud to be the housekeeper of an author, and she encouraged me to write in comfort. My bedroom, sitting room, and tiny study she made clean and orderly. When I needed a cup of tea or tobacco for my pipe, she was always on the scene to provide it.

She served me not merely for the money I paid her at the end of each week, but because she took an obvious pleasure in making my life comfortable. In a book of reminiscence that later became perhaps the one book posterity will remember, I spoke of her in superlatives: "*I find her one of the few women I have known who merit the term excellent.*" In tandem with the thinking of Thomas Carlyle, I believed my honest servant was born to serve. In that milieu, her natural element, I could tell she was happy. I surmised that were she educated and trying to do some other type of work, she would find herself quite unhappy. Living alone in Dorking, away from my sons and hostile wife, I considered myself lucky to have such a housekeeper. It was a time of anxiety and apprehension for me, and the housekeeper went out of her way to ease the stress upon me. I showed my gratitude some years later by sketching her as the best of servants. To protect her privacy, I didn't refer to her by name, nor did I give her a fictional name.

Residing comfortably in Dorking, an unruffled market town twenty-five miles south of London, I brooded over an impending crisis already affecting many people. The entire middle class was having trouble finding and keeping good domestic workers. The turbulent life with Natalie had already beaten into shape my opinions regarding the servant question. When I lived in callow poverty with Muriel, we had no servant and no problem. But my second marriage was more secure financially, and Natalie needed someone to assist her with the children. She could have managed on her own, but having another woman at her beck and call made her feel important. Though I was willing to pay a good servant decent wages, I was soon complaining that my wife was incapable of supervising domestic help.

She was either too friendly or too demanding, and she frequently lost her temper. That often caused the servant to quit without notice. Then with her usual incompetence Natalie would hire another. The next woman or girl would come into our home, chafe under abusive treatment, and leave in a huff to make way for yet another. A good servant was hard to find and for most middle-class wives even harder to keep. I thought that within a few years, unless special schools could be established to train girls for service, the entire middle class would have to do without. My prediction was precisely on target. By the turn of the century, with a few exceptions, only royalty and the very rich had loyal servants who lived on the premises.

As I thought about the servant question, I couldn't help but recall the constant bickering between mistress and servant in my own home. It interfered with my work and left me agitated and depressed. I believed the person who paid the wages should be able to deliver calm and authoritative commands and expect obedience. Natalie somehow lacked that ability. When dealing with hired help she lost her dignity and her temper. As head of the house, I could have exercised a quiet authority but remained aloof and fretted. By association I remembered an incident as far away as the southern tip of Italy that saddened me. Even there I wasn't able to escape domestic wrangling. In a hospice located in Calabria an embattled servant, old and tired before her time and mumbling in a dialect I could barely understand, complained to me of low pay and unjust treatment. I could do nothing but listen to the poor woman with a show of sympathy until she regained her composure.

The most irksome aspect of the servant question was keeping a capable servant. When Natalie failed to draw loyalty and respect from our servants, I concluded her problem was one of class. She was too close in background to the people she hired to work for her. They sensed the affinity and responded with rebellion or familiarity. My wife seemed incapable of rule, and that inevitably brought about a spirit of rebellion in the kitchen. Women of her class often revealed themselves as vulgar and silly when required to supervise another person. So it was natural for servants to lack respect and revolt against them. Through their bungling these inept women encouraged tumult and revolt.

Even though other factors were at work to undermine an institution in England that went back for centuries, I thought the main culprit was the democratic spirit of the day. Before the triumph of "glorious democracy" only those women capable of command kept servants. They knew that in every respect they were superior to their domestics, and that guided their behavior. They chose them carefully, kept them for a long time, and rarely had trouble with them. Their loyal servants took from these capable women a sense of security, a sense of belonging, and a satisfying sense of worth. However, in the 1890's the average woman of the working class hated to have another woman wielding authority over her, particularly a woman incapable of fair and firm supervision.

With the erosion of class distinction, servants both male and female were becoming indolent and insolent. The new middle class, expecting respect from employees but not receiving it, didn't know how to deal with the problem. They viewed themselves as victims of brash and aggressive young men and women who despised any woman of any class who presumed to give them orders. Only the rare woman knew how to keep her servants in line. The man of the house could have done better, but traditionally – as in my own home – husbands did not interfere. In my novels men without wives have little difficulty with domestic help. Because they are able to exert the necessary authority, their servants invariably respect them and willingly obey them. Often one finds mutual respect between master and servant. The result is a smoothly run, orderly household. In most instances in my fiction, as well as later in my life, the man living alone imparts a sense of worth to the woman who keeps his house, and she performs dependably for him.

3

During the summer of 1898 Dorking and my house were warm, sunny, and peaceful. I was eating well and gathering strength. My housekeeper prepared simple but nourishing meals, and I had lost the troublesome cough that plagued me in Italy. I tried to write a play but after desperate struggle gave it up. Natalie was looking for me and was determined to find me. In Potsdam I had revealed to Kurtz the problems I was having at home, and soon afterwards confided: *"Of course I must hide myself in constant fear of attack by that savage."* Later I lamented, *"Nothing settled yet about my wife and the little child. She does not know where I am, but is trying hard to discover and threatens to give all possible trouble."* Early in June I learned that Natalie in a fury had been harassing her neighbors and was asked to leave. Without causing a scene she walked away with the child tugging her skirts. Later, acting on the rumor Crenshaw had planted, she appeared at Quentin's house in Worcestershire. She was contrite and apologetic and wanted her husband, asserting she loved him deeply. Quentin was sympathetic but told her nothing.

Although she was now living among her own kind, Natalie was asked time and again to move away because of sudden and violent outbursts. Her fits of temper, set off by the smallest of incidents, had become so frequent they suggested serious derangement. In one house when given notice to leave, she attacked her landlady with a broom and was nearly arrested. The next day she was on the street, her child in tow, looking for another place to live. I was trying to persuade my lawyer to work out a satisfactory agreement with her, but at every turn she stubbornly resisted. Adamantly she refused to sign any papers depriving her of parental custody, and she insisted on custody of both children. She had grown up suspicious of the law and legal documents, and my lawyer couldn't persuade her to sign anything at all. So any agreement stipulating a legal separation came to a halt.

The legal maneuvering was a bother to her and causing stress. To relieve the stress she vented her caustic temper daily on anyone unfortunate enough to cross her path. By slow degrees she was becoming more violent, behavior that alarmed me. *"All work impossible,"* I complained to Crenshaw, *"owing to ceaseless reports of mad conduct in London."* Convinced that my wife was going insane, I feared for the safety of the child she insisted on keeping. In the first week of September in a letter to Kurtz, I expressed anxiety for the little boy and called the marriage criminal. Kurtz saw me as a mentor and never argued with me even when he thought I was clearly wrong. He had cautioned me to be careful, but once more his English friend was admitting he had made a terrible mistake. This second mistake in matrimony was even more calamitous than the first, for children were involved. My loyal friend wanted with all his heart to help me, but there wasn't a thing he could do.

As I was expressing dismay that Natalie would come pounding on my door at any time, she was visiting the warehouse where we had stored some furniture on leaving Epson. There she talked to employees who gave her the address of my hiding place. Without delay she went to Dorking with plans to settle the situation between us once and for all. With Austin straggling behind or tugging at her skirt, in balmy weather on a Wednesday afternoon, she came to the door of my country hideaway. Ignoring the doorbell, she knocked loudly. Her mission was a confrontation that would force me to take her back. With eyes blazing, she demanded I live up to my responsibilities as a husband and father.

"The law requires it, Jonathan Blue! You are breaking the law!"

"I can't live with you, and that *you* know. My lawyer has begged you a thousand times to sign the papers for a legal separation. He has told you, and so have I, that I'm willing to provide ample support for you and the child, but I cannot live with you ever again."

"The law requires that you look after your wife and children, and that means living with us under the same roof! Monthly payment from a distance is not looking after wife and children at all!"

The law was on her side, she insisted, but I refused to quarrel with her. To my surprise, though severely agitated and on the brink of losing all self-control, she went away mumbling to herself but not screaming or causing a scene. My heart was pounding and I felt weak in the knees but immensely relieved. Later I recalled that overwhelmed by surprise and agitation I had not even noticed my little boy. The child was there close to me, looking up at me, but I was too upset to speak a single word to him. I would have kneeled and spoken kindly to the boy. I would have tried to let him know his father loved him and wanted only the best for him. But I said not a word. It was just as well. Elizabeth Osgood had told me Austin already had an image of his father as a strange and troublesome person. For him to see me as kind and caring would have confused him extremely. Maybe so, even though I suffered feelings of guilt.

That meeting in the first week of September in 1898 was my final encounter with Natalie. I remember it as a warm and sunny day with a gentle breeze suggesting cooler weather to come. I remember after her departure my housekeeper returned from the market and fixed me a nutritious meal I dutifully ate but couldn't taste. After that day I didn't see Natalie again, nor did I see my little boy again. In later years it was said my son remembered his father and kept letters from me but knew Jonathan Blue, an author of many books, only by reputation.

CHAPTER THIRTY-TWO

When Skies Were Dark

At the beginning of 1898 I had complained to Emma that I was having terrible trouble with Natalie and was baffled by her behavior. *"N's latest statement is that she will go before a magistrate, and declare that I have deserted my family! I am really afraid she will end in the lunatic asylum."* Four years later I saw that off-hand prediction become a reality. Near the middle of February in 1902, when dark skies spilled storm clouds full of icy rain, I disclosed to Kurtz that Natalie had been arrested for ill treatment of her little boy. Qualified authorities had examined her, had concluded she was insane, and had committed her to a madhouse. *"Well, this has surprised nobody. Any number of people saw it coming."*

From the time of her commitment until the day of her death, Natalie Blue remained in close confinement. As far as I know, in all the years she was there she received not a single visitor. No person from the Blue family, including her two sons, came to visit her. Not a friend from anywhere came to ask about her, and no relatives came from London. When I published *The Philip Crowe Papers* in 1903, her name appeared on the list of people to receive author copies. After that she quickly became an unwanted person, a nobody, and all who had known her apparently forgot her. However, for the life of me I couldn't forget entirely. I'm not able to say when she died. I know only she was still alive when I was losing strength and health in another country.

At the time of her confinement I really believe she hated me, but did she ever love me? She herself found it difficult to answer that question. More than once, even at my brother's house, she claimed she loved me deeply. At other times she told anyone who would listen that she hated me with passion beyond measure. With limited experience and education, she associated learning and culture with leisure and wealth. She believed that playing the gentleman without wealth to support the role was a sham. Because as a published writer I had not gained the wealth and recognition I sought, was in fact anything but wealthy and not well known, she reasoned I was little more than a base pretender. Because I had not completed college to receive a degree, was in fact largely self-taught, my knowledge of literature and the arts was suspect to her.

To her mind, my identity as a writer with a reputation but with little material gain was all an act. It was in other words a fraudulent simulation that made me a gross hypocrite. Also if a man's economic position were no better than that of his neighbors, he had no right to snub them, as I invariably did. Moreover, if a man had friends and associates in his profession, he was obliged to introduce them to his wife, as I never did. That attitude convinced Natalie that like Alfred Yard in *New Bleak Street*, I was ashamed of my wife. That discovery eventually destroyed any love she might have had. The fictional wife, an imaginary ideal, suffered in silence. The real wife, tormented and driven by anger, did not.

I've been told if Natalie suffered from a mental disorder during our marriage, it alone could have been the cause of our bitter domestic conflict. A better explanation, however, is the theory of my old friend, Dr. Emeritus Gifford. He believed that my refusal to introduce her to my friends brought on most of the misery. Muriel, the first wife, had deeply resented the same treatment. All I needed for relative contentment was the challenge of finishing my current book and a female companion nearby. But the women who shared my bed and board were sociable creatures and needed more. They demanded more but never got it.

Natalie in particular wanted interaction with neighbors and hoped to acquire a large number of friends in her daily life. She was young and hopeful but sensitive about her background and uncomfortable among middle-class people. Her dislike of such people flamed into hatred when she came to believe they viewed her as inferior and merely tolerated her. My aristocratic temperament came into conflict with her democratic attitudes, and that added fuel to the flame. Sharing her home with a solitary intellectual who never placed her on equal footing with his relatives or friends was more than she could bear. Though clearly disturbed, perhaps the woman was not insane. If anyone could be held accountable for the misery that was consuming her it had to be me.

2

The year 1898 was filled with peaks and valleys. My domestic issues in those months were persistent and painful, but at the same time other factors were at work to make the year fruitful and pleasant. I published three short novels in that year and found my work in greater demand than ever before. I was asked to write introductions to reprints of three novels by Charles Dickens, and did it all in late summer. Publishers wanted new work from me as fast as I could produce it. Middleton & Sons said *The Commercial Traveller* sold 1,400 copies in England and 1,000 in the colonies. The book on Dickens, my attempt at literary criticism, appealed to a more limited audience but did better than expected. A collection of short stories, brought together in one slender volume, sold better than any of my longer books. Also my books were almost as well known in Paris as in London. It was a new experience for me to be in high demand and to be praised in the daily press. For twenty years I had struggled mightily to attain that goal. So in the midst of troubles causing raw emotional pain I found no small degree of intellectual satisfaction. Yet it was not enough to lift me entirely from gloom.

I had always looked forward to the changing of seasons, but now I paid little attention to birds chirping and flowers blooming. Wracked by worry and anxiety, I was not able to enjoy even the warmth of the new season. In June, however, I received a letter from a young Frenchwoman who wanted to translate *New Bleak Street*. Her name was Marie Estelle Laurent, and she lived in Paris. Her letter on light blue stationery with a feminine scent came in the third week of June, a Friday with low clouds and light rain. Unable to leave the house and fighting boredom, I made reply on the same day. For several weeks I had been struggling to write a play, but after many false starts had finished only one lame act. Conversation with a pleasant young woman who wanted to talk about my work was exactly what I needed. It would assuage my loneliness and help me get past an army of obstacles that loomed in my way.

We made plans to meet in London on July 5, but then I got to thinking the city would be hot and uncomfortable. So I asked her to visit me at the Rhodes home in Worcester Park. Rhodes and I had become fast friends – we went bicycling together – and the house with its park-like setting seemed the perfect place for a meeting. Rhodes knew that his friend needed the company of a young woman and readily agreed to the arrangement. The slim, well-dressed woman showed up the next day. As she extended her hand to me – she had beautiful hands with fingers that accented her femininity – she seemed surrounded by a fresh and flowery scent that exactly defined her. We sipped tea in the summer air with our genial hosts and chatted amicably. Withdrawing to be alone together, we walked in the garden on shaded and graveled paths and enjoyed lively conversation that went beyond small talk.

"I'm glad you had a good passage over," I began, stealing a glance at her profile. "As you know, the Channel can be unpredictable, quite rough even in summer."

"Yes, it's true. But my crossing this time was sunny and pleasant. London as usual was intimidating and crowded. It's more noisy, more confusing than Paris, and no one seems aware of anyone else."

"It can be all that," I replied. "The city is rather cold even when the mercury reads sultry. Most people agree it's not a very friendly place. I felt the same as you when I went there to live years ago."

"I got lost there," she said with a ripple of laughter. "I went round in circles and became agitated. Then something happened that disturbed me. A little child, a Gypsy beggar only five or six years old, ran up to me in Oxford Street pleading for money. I tried to ignore her, but she was so insistent! I held my own, however, and refused to give her the shilling she demanded. She pretended to cry, gave me a sorrowful look, and ran to her mother nearby. One doesn't see child beggars in Paris. I think it's against the law. But London! Oh my, so different!"

She was laughing at her own distress. Her face was smooth and radiant with that special Gallic beauty. I liked her looks and the way she talked. Her voice, throaty and even of pitch, drew my attention.

"I'm sorry you had to put up with that. Some charitable organizations are trying to rid the city of Roma beggars but haven't done much to remedy the situation so far. I hear the children work hard at begging, often earn loads of money in these lean times, and support entire families. But of course that doesn't make it right. To change the subject, I understand you want to translate *New Bleak Street*, my book about books. It's a novel published some years ago about struggling authors in London even poorer than the little beggar you met."

"With your permission of course, and I shall bring your stylish English into good and very readable French to enlarge your audience."

"For what it's worth you have my permission, but the owners of the copyright have the final word on such matters. You want to get in touch with them before you begin your project to be certain it's all legal."

"I shall do that, M'sieur Blue, if you will tell me where to find them in that vast and busy and confusing place you call London."

"The business district is better laid out than the rest of the city," I laughed, "and any cabbie will take you to their offices. I'm fairly certain they'll greet you cordially with full approval, but it's a good idea to get their written permission."

She thanked me cordially, and we began to speak of other matters. In surroundings more luxurious than I myself had ever been able to afford, we came to know each other in just a few hours. Rhodes and his wife had remained discreetly in the background and now greeted us al fresco with tasty finger food and a bowl of punch. My friends found her as I did, alluring and charming.

When the lady returned to London, I caught myself thinking about her with more than usual interest. I fell asleep as soon as my head hit the pillow but awoke an hour later in a cold sweat. Before the night was over my bed was so rumpled I had to make it up again. The next day was

Thursday, and I tried to work on the second act of my play. I sat with pen and paper in front of me but found myself twiddling the pen and staring at the blank paper. I rubbed my eyes when her image appeared before me, her face aglow with a radiant smile. It was impossible to work. My thoughts were on Marie Estelle Laurent, and I repeated to myself snatches of our conversation as we strolled along.

I could hear her voice as I remembered her words, and it was like music to my ears. She was intelligent, well educated, and self-assured. Projecting a soft femininity, she was slender, graceful, and appealing in her immaculate long skirts. I liked the way she talked and the way she moved her body with so little effort. Her conversation, her reaction to my remarks, was sensitive and sophisticated and spiced with humor. It thrilled me to hear her laugh. I left my desk, made myself a pot of tea, and went back to write a few sentences. Not a single word seemed to fit. I crushed the paper in my hands, tossed it away, and went for a walk. The weather was hot and muggy, and I returned sweaty and breathless. I was feeling a dreary agitation and thought the day would never end.

3

Marie Estelle Laurent was born at Nevers in central France and grew up in Marseille. She came from a conventional, middle-class family but acquired as she grew older some of the characteristics of the Continental new woman. Widely read and interested in art and literature, she went to literary gatherings in Paris and cultivated the friendship of intellectuals. She had a better command of English than I had of French, knew some Italian, and knew German well enough to read Kurtz's books. She had a passion for classical music and was a skilled pianist. A cultivated and bookish woman, she also enjoyed vigorous physical activity. I was surprised to learn she went hiking on rough and secluded trails thought to be too dangerous for women and had climbed mountains in Switzerland. She went on long trips, accepting the challenge of traveling alone, to places deemed unsuitable for young women. Viewing herself as a woman of the world, she traveled to foreign countries without male companionship and without a chaperone. Though women were doing new things in the 1890's, few of them were doing that.

Earlier she had been engaged to Sully Prudhomme, a French poet and essayist of considerable rank. Although he was unable to attend the ceremony because of illness, he accepted the first Nobel Prize in Literature. His collected works appeared in five volumes in 1901. At the time of their engagement he was almost thirty years her senior, and eventually they decided not to marry. When I met her, she was twenty-nine and I was forty. Friends and family knew her by her first name, but to me the name had ironic and painful association. I couldn't forget that Muriel's middle name was Marie. So in a persuasive letter I asked if I might call her by her middle name. She had always liked the meaning of the name and said I could. So from then onward Marie Estelle Laurent was known to me as Estelle. In my imagination I viewed her as a star from a distant galaxy come into my life to flood it with light.

It wasn't long before I knew she was a sensual but cerebral young woman with qualities not always positive. At the time we met she impressed me as nearly perfect. Later the bright star bringing warmth and light became a moderate new woman, democratic in outlook but also aristocratic. While her personality and mindset reflected the new attitudes, she had not discarded the best of the old. For me, tired of the woman question and all the babble it had generated, that subtle balance was refreshing. I later claimed I fell in love with her at first sight, but that was romantic balderdash. What I described as love was a feeling closer to lust. I was separated from spouse and children and living alone in obligatory celibacy. Then a beautiful woman came into my life.

When Estelle returned to London after her visit, my heart went out to her because of my loneliness and pent-up frustration. As evening was coming on I thanked my friends for their generosity and walked home to a solitary bed. In my diary I noted that a lovely Frenchwoman wanted to translate one of my novels. I said nothing of my initial response to the woman. But only four days after her visit, I was outlining a novel to be called *The Pinnacle of Life*. It would pay attention to some of the main issues of the day, but mainly it would probe the mystery of love between a man and a woman.

From the moment I looked at Estelle's handwriting, holding in my hands the letter she had sent me and sensing her femininity in the texture of the delicate paper, I felt I could love her with total abandon. In my loneliness I wanted her desperately, but doubting she could ever return my love I thought of her with caution. At the same time I was shaping the theme of my next novel, the winning of one's ideal woman after years of suffering. A fragile idealism was fanning the embers of hope. For solace I occupied myself trying to remember every moment of her visit. Sharing a bottle of Chianti with Dylan Crenshaw in a little restaurant in Soho, I spoke of her with deep feeling.

"She is more than beautiful. She has lived in my imagination all my life. Now a kind fate has allowed me to meet her in the real world. I'm confused, Crenshaw, absolutely confused and afraid."

"You're confused because she differs radically from any of the other women you've known in your life. I want you to hang on to reason, old man, and not be carried away by emotion. Enjoy her companionship, even love her if you must, but be careful. Be circumspect."

"She could never return my love, could never waste her life on one such as me. And yet I dream and seriously hope I'm wrong."

"Did it ever occur to you that perhaps she's dreaming too?"

"Yes, of course!" I chortled. "She's dreaming of translating my book and maybe another one later. Dreaming of doing business!"

"Perhaps she also feels the hunger of the human heart."

He was a good man, Crenshaw, and a good friend. He enriched my life over many years, and I was thankful for that. Later when I was living in exile with Estelle, he met her in person and described her in glowing terms: "*A very beautiful woman of high education and extreme Gallic intelligence with the most beautiful human voice for speaking that I have ever heard.*" He never knew how much I valued those words, for in praising her he was praising me. In one of his petulant moods, H. G. Rhodes had a different opinion. Writing to Crenshaw, he said: "*Your estimate of Estelle is ridiculous. She was a tiresome, weak, sentimental, middle-class Frenchwoman who wrote her letters on thin paper."* My friend found it hard to overlook Rhodes' intemperate criticism. I had tolerated similar outbursts because I truly admired the man. He wasn't a better writer than I but certainly a better man of business when dealing with publishers. Even so, he had a way of speaking his mind without restraint and apparently without caring whether his words hurt or not. He was hot of temper and wary of foreign women. He thought Estelle would ensnare a dear friend who boosted his ego. She would run away with his friend to another country. In time she did.

CHAPTER THIRTY-THREE

The Sun Breaks Through

With nervous anticipation I looked forward to Estelle's second visit. My weary heart leaped at the thought of seeing her pretty face again in fine summer weather. In the meantime I examined her impact upon me and revealed my thoughts and feelings to her. On first seeing her, I said with some reluctance, I knew at a glance that she was more than beautiful. On speaking to her I saw that she was truly interesting, womanly though strong of mind, and sweet. At a time when I thought the best of my life was over, mysteriously she came in the fullness of day to renew me with vigor and hope. When I was beaten by anxiety and worry and thought my life would soon end, she came with a promise of strength and vitality. When I thought I would die never loving a woman with unrestrained emotion, this person sent by destiny walked out of the mists of time and place into the essence of my life. Though I didn't believe in miracles, I did believe her coming was an advent close to a miracle. I freely admitted, with all the faded clichés ever invented to express the feeling, that I loved her unconditionally with every fiber of my being.

Near the end of July in 1898 she came to my home at Dorking and spent the whole day with me. My housekeeper, who knew I was expecting her, went to visit relatives. I welcomed the lady with boyish delight. I had hoped the weather would be mild and pleasant, and it was. Under blue skies and the shade of fragrant trees, we strolled down country lanes in animated conversation. All business at first, she informed me that she had reached an agreement with the copyright owners, and her translation of *New Bleak Street* would eventually be published in a French weekly magazine in serial form.

As we talked she praised the strength of my work, something I could never resist. Also she charmed me with conversation describing numerous friendships with important people in France and other countries. Her woman's voice moved me to deep feeling, and I heard it long after she left to return home. A bewitching musical instrument, it pleased the listening ear with a rhythm and sound almost symphonic. I saw in this rare person all those wonderful qualities I admired most in a woman. In my study after she left I made a list of what I liked most: *beauty, dignity, gentleness, intelligence, passion, cultivation, and eagerness to live as fully as possible.* I was delighted to learn that she played the piano. It brought back memories of my childhood when my dear father taught his children chords and played ditties to entertain us.

When she left that evening on the 8:35, I knew without a doubt that I loved her. This time, if I did any running at all, it wouldn't be away from my heart's desire but fervently toward her. The next day I wrote Estelle a tender letter – *"I hear your voice every moment"* – and requested a photograph. Not more than a week after her departure, in letters written almost every day, I passionately expressed my love. I would live for her, work for her, dedicate my life and talent to her, and make her the absolute reason for my existence. I would place myself totally in her service and do all within my power to make her happy. With eager anticipation I snatched half an hour each day to write her long letters. All my life I had been shy and reticent when asked to express my thoughts in spoken words. Now in the quiet of my study with pen in hand, I could tell the woman I loved all the secrets of my hidden heart.

My adoration of another human being was overwhelming, touching and invigorating every part of me. I had not yet received an unmistakable expression of her love for me, and that excruciating delay brought painful doubt. When she eventually made response, confessing that she returned my love in full measure, my feelings were those I had imagined for Whipple in *New Bleak Street*. At the time I was writing that book in 1890 it seemed as though I would never succeed as a novelist, and that meant I could never hope to win a beautiful woman of comparable intellect and social class. As with Whipple, the love of a charming, sympathetic, cultured woman seemed forever beyond my reach. Now in less than a decade all that had changed. A mysterious and remarkable person from another country was declaring her intense and perpetual love *for me,* and *for me* alone. She was invading my inner life, quickening my senses, and sending me beyond Cloud Nine to Seventh Heaven.

After a summer of correspondence, our letters becoming so passionate they sizzled, we looked forward to the day Estelle would return to England. On October 5, I noted in my diary that she would be coming from Paris the next day, but complications stalled her arrival until October 8. On that day, a Saturday, I met her at East Croydon, waiting forty minutes for her arrival. When the train finally rolled into the station, I was beside myself with impatience.

"I'm so glad to see you!" I cried. "I've waited so long, so long!"

She brushed my cheek with warm lips. I caught the aroma of her hair and face and could feel the touch of her hand on my shoulder. "You have a genius for loving and being loved," she said quietly, taking my hand.

Her smooth and delicate face glowed with excitement, and just looking at her gave me supreme pleasure. She was dressed suitably for early fall in a simple gown that allowed full freedom of movement.

"I feel *délice intense* on being with you again, my love. I thought I would never get here! I'm delighted we can meet again."

From the station we went to Dorking, where we spent a week of idyllic happiness together. Again my faithful housekeeper found it necessary to be away. I had feared Victorian propriety would not allow my love to spend even one night at my house, but that emotion was baseless. We threw caution to the winds, and for several days and nights thought only of each other. The larger world with its Puritan values no longer mattered. Some of my friends believed my mother was in the house as a chaperone, but she had come earlier in the summer and had departed. The two of us were alone together in our own special world.

During those days and nights we made love. Our ethereal paper love, passionate but lacking in substance, became a fusion of blood and brain and spirit. We took long walks in the country to admire the changing foliage. We talked about our future together and read to one another in the evening. Every night we made love, slept soundly, and made love again on awakening. Her perfect woman's body entranced me. I couldn't believe how beautiful nature had made her *for me*. Moreover, she was as passionate in her lovemaking as I. Her behavior created feelings of delight and wonder. When she returned to Paris, I noted in my diary: *"We have decided that our life together shall begin next spring."*

2

Two days after her departure, her vivid image inspiring my imagination and stirring my style to poetic intensity, I began to write with little hindrance *The Pinnacle of Life*. I was certain it would become the best of the novels I had crafted over two decades. As I was writing the book I sent love letters to Estelle daily. *"I dream of you every night,"* I said to her, *"I wake and long for you. All day it is you, you, you, who occupy all my thoughts."* Many of those thoughts, prompted by Estelle and the power she exerted upon me, found their way into *The Pinnacle of Life*. A good example is Irene Wentner's delicate description of a Frenchwoman she once knew: *"She was the sweetest little woman – you know that kind of Frenchwoman, don't you? Soft-voiced, tender, intelligent, using the most delightful phrases; a jewel of a woman."* Unmistakably, fictional Irene was describing Estelle as I saw her. For a moment she was speaking for me. Piers Waylock, the young idealist who falls in love with Irene, was the counterpart of me, my alter ego. After long suffering (as with me) he manages to find and adore his dream woman.

Racked by a feeling of deep-seated social inferiority, Waylock doubts Irene will ever be able to love him. The same terror held me at bay. Even when Estelle repeatedly proclaimed eternal love, I feared it might be too fragile to endure. I knew that I would have to work hard to make myself worthy of her. Fictional Waylock, in the same position, soon resolves to gain a secure place in the world before attempting to win Irene: *"Money he must have; a substantial position; a prospect of social*

296

advance." Writing to Estelle, I applied similar words to me: *"For many years I worked hard for success in literature – always regarding it as a mere stepping-stone to that much greater thing, the love of the ideal woman."* Although a malignant fate had dogged my footsteps all my life, somehow I had overcome great odds to discover that ideal person who might share with me my remaining years. The period of suffering and struggle I interpreted as a time of testing. Having demonstrated my resolve, my indefatigable determination, perhaps that jeweled crown was meant for me after all. I had lived most of my life in misery. Now perhaps I could dare hope for kinder treatment, even an interval of happiness to make me strong and whole again.

Estelle quickly became my dream woman, the ideal of a passionate heart. My perfect woman, as I now viewed this person who had come to me from another world, was no aggressive new woman. In my imagination she quickly became a gentlewoman, elegant and aristocratic. To picture her in riding habit on a prancing thoroughbred, her face aglow, her form accented, and her abundant hair tossed by the wind thrilled and delighted me. When I thought of her on a bicycle, however, the image quickly lost its charm. Teetering on a wobbly machine with thin wheels and a tiny seat, the aristocratic lady shrouded in mystery became a middle-class woman pursuing a fad. *"You are not that kind of woman,"* I said to her in one of my letters. *"I think it would be unsuitable to your dignity. Very different it would be if you rode on horseback; that I should like; oh, how splendid you would look!"* The purveyor of the new realism overnight had become a hopeless romantic. For the first time in my adult life, as I said to Kurtz, I was truly happy. *"So there! And if health does not fail me, I shall be happy for many a year."*

As summer and fall passed into gray winter, the visionary gleam faded into the light of common day. I suggested that Estelle learn to ride the bicycle for exercise. I knew she had accepted the new womanhood, and cycling was part of that identity. It was nothing like riding a stalwart, spirited horse but it was good for a woman's health. She harbored enthusiasm for outdoor activities and was eager to try cycling. It would be fun, she said, to ride the country lanes laughing and hooting as I tried to keep up with her. On the surface Estelle was one of those "advanced women" whom I had long regarded with ambivalence. But beneath the appearance, deeper than I was able to probe at that time, were qualities of the French conventional woman. In my dreams she quickly became the strong-minded lady of a lord, an aristocrat exerting a commanding presence. In reality she was a middle-class woman eager to please the ones she loved. Her quick intelligence enhanced her physical beauty and gave her the quiet dignity that beauty alone sometimes lacks. Easily it placed her in the ranks of the better new women.

3

Piers Waylock in *The Pinnacle of Life* publishes an article in a Russian journal on the new womanhood in England. Mrs. Berkovich, a strange woman who dabbles in the lives of others, is eager to discuss its ramifications. She tells Waylock that she herself could never become one of his new women because she prefers to live in the sun and air rather than in books. He replies that she is mistaken in her view of the new woman as cerebral, bookish, and sheltered: *"The new womanhood has nothing to do with any particular study. It supposes intelligence, that's all."* For years I had made this view known to all my friends. I had said exactly that to Kurtz in Germany and to Crenshaw wherever he happened to be. Quite early in my career I had said to my sister Emma that cultivation of mind and strength of intellect would go a long way toward improving the lot of women. When Estelle exhibited that cultivation of intellect I prized, she quickly became my perfect woman. I found that her Gallic education and native ability accentuated her femininity, sexuality, and spiritual aura. Also it allowed her to ignore the heavy religious burden that dogged my sisters. That alone, in my opinion, made her an accomplished woman transcendent of type.

After all the analysis both head and heart told me Estelle Laurent was simply a woman in love with a man, a Frenchwoman in love with an Englishman. Her behavior was neither conventional nor avant-garde. She did what she thought was right, guided by a personal moral code, and dismissed public opinion inclined to scorn her. I believed her coming into my life was an act wrought by destiny. I confided that I found it difficult to resist the belief that some ineffable force had sent her to me. This rare and beautiful woman had come mysteriously from an unlikely place to take possession of my life, and she had come at a crucial moment. But instead of assigning my good fortune to a loving god with the power to intervene in human lives, I gave the credit to an impersonal, abstract force: *"If ever destiny brought man and woman together, it did so in our case."* No other explanation was possible. All my adult life I had derided religion with its faith in the supernatural and its talk of miracles. Now I was skirting the beliefs of my family to describe a mysterious event that had shaken my soul.

The profound impact of our meeting I explained in the context of philosophical determinism, a concept that had already entered several of my books. One day when I was a carefree schoolboy ignorant of man's need of woman, a female child was born in a country with a different language and culture. In spite of those differences, from the moment of conception she was meant *for me.* She lived gracefully through girlhood and entered womanhood without knowing that mysterious forces were guiding her to a man in whose mind her image burned like a flame. In a distant place a struggling author was groping his way out of darkness, moving slowly but deliberately from obscurity to reputation, so that eventually the two would meet. Agents of fate prompted her to learn a language other than her own and become a translator. They sent her to meet a person who valued the love she was capable of giving as *"the supreme attainment, the pinnacle of life."* My theory of love was aglow with idealism but also tempered with determinism. *"I am a determinist,"* I said to Estelle in one of my letters. *"I know that nothing could happen but that which did, for every event is the result of causes that stream endlessly from first murmurings into eternity."*

The love story of Piers Waylock and Irene Wentner, exactly my own, reflects with fidelity this line of thought. At the heart of the story, deftly moving it forward, is the deep and abiding influence of Estelle Laurent. I acknowledged as much in a letter I wrote shortly after meeting her: *"I am constantly thinking about my book. It has undergone changes since I met you. Indeed, it is you who are shaping the book much more than I."* It was not my intention to flatter her; I was utterly and earnestly sincere. Appearing at a time when I was losing hope and direction, I believed she had given new life to my imagination and made me a better artist. I had planned the book as a love story interwoven with social and political issues, but gradually I worked the threads of the story into a philosophical fabric that came of my own experience. I drew upon Plato and the Platonists, Schopenhauer and the determinists, to give drive to my story, but the main source of inspiration was my love for a woman who had come into my life when I needed her most.

I was writing about ideal love with the same elation Balboa must have felt when he stood on a hilltop in Panama to view the wide Pacific. Love's vast complexity was a profound discovery, and when its parts fell into place to make a whole I was delighted. Thoughts new and refreshing ran through my psyche and into the book. That mysterious phenomenon we call love is the one thing that makes life worth living, the one thing in all of human life that makes any person complete. It is the one great value of our existence and the only absolute sincerity. If an illusion, it is that which crowns all other illusions. But ideal love cannot be called an illusion, for it dwells among us and is real. To miss love is to miss everything, and yet love in the higher sense is very rare. Few people are capable of it and fewer still attain it. To some it falls like rain from the heavens, but others acquire it only through patience, suffering, searching, and sacrifice. Those who receive it must be worthy of it or must struggle to become worthy. It is supreme for the very few and the very fortunate, and it brings invariably a new life and a new soul.

I believed with religious zeal that I belonged to that group of persons required by fate to make themselves recipients of transcendent love. Eagerly and without restraint I embraced heavenly love, and it changed my life completely. Released from gloom, I lived in sunshine.

CHAPTER THIRTY-FOUR

Dear Maman's Emotion

At the beginning of 1899 Estelle Laurent was living with her ailing mother in Paris and waiting for me to come to her. In England I was putting my affairs in order for what I knew would be a sea change in my life. More than ever I wanted to be free of Natalie, but she believed a publicized divorce would reflect shamefully upon her and the children. Even though she had no social life and didn't truly belong to the middle class, she feared the stigma of divorce. I had hired the best lawyer I could afford and hoped the man would persuade her to act reasonably, but her behavior was beyond reason. Stubbornly she refused to sign pertinent papers, saying with tiresome repetition that she would settle only for a legal separation. She demanded in writing a percentage of her husband's income each year and custody of the children. Support payments would increase as my income increased but would never drop below a stated figure. If those requirements were met, she would consider signing one legal document. Anything else was out of the question.

Crenshaw came down on the train from London one blustery afternoon, carrying in a small satchel a bottle of wine, a wedge of cheese, and a loaf of bread. He examined every nook and cranny of my house and pronounced it admirable. I had some butter to slather on the bread, and we washed it down with passable wine. The bread was good and the cheese delicious. While eating we discussed marriage and divorce and the laws in other countries. It was the one thing on my mind.

"Perhaps you could make inquiries about an American divorce," he said as he struggled to slice the cheese with a bread knife. "The laws there are really quite liberal."

"I've already done that," I replied. "I think I would have to go to one of the western states. The travel alone would be expensive, not to mention the time it would take. But of course the big question is whether a divorce anywhere without the woman's consent would be valid. I might go all the way to Arizona, more than 5,000 miles, to achieve nothing."

"That's a chance you would have to take, and even then an American divorce might not hold up in France. And yet whether valid or not, it could possibly offer a show of legality to let you marry. You would have to consult a solicitor there and work out the details."

"I've talked with Estelle about it, and it's her opinion that legal shenanigans could take months or even years and cost a fortune. She's impatient with legal maneuvering. She wants us to live together now and let our love tell us if it's right or wrong."

"I can understand her thinking. It's much the same as mine. Marriage is a thing of the heart, y' know, more than a piece of paper with legal gibberish. Have you told your people in Harrogate about Estelle?"

"No, I don't have the nerve. I'm sure they would never understand. But her mother knows the whole truth and gives full consent."

"Well, that's good to hear, old boy. At least you don't have a problem there. The Frenchwoman somehow escaped the Puritan canker."

"I know, and for that I'm grateful. But I'm afraid the people in London will manufacture a scandal and whisper to one another. I'm fairly well known at present and can't afford a scandal. Even divorce among some of the more conservative chatterers is seen as scandalous."

"The world's disapproval doesn't seem to bother your lady as much as it does you," said Crenshaw, shrugging his shoulders and savoring his sandwich. "Here, have some more bread and cheese. This is good!"

I was unwilling to admit even to myself that I worried about breaking the law and being caught. I had weathered that calamity once before as a callow youth. In my maturity it was unthinkable. To be arrested could destroy the reputation I had struggled so long and so hard to establish and maintain. I thought of Oscar Wilde. My case was nothing like his, of course. But should a scandal of any sort develop, I could suffer a severe loss of income or worse. Just thinking about it was painful. Then as I cracked my knuckles a subterfuge came to mind.

"Maybe by a slip of the tongue in offhand conversation you could let it be known that Natalie is dead? Say she died unexpectedly in one of her rages? That would probably ease the burden for us."

"I'll see what I can do, old boy. I wouldn't be averse to telling a white lie for you. It would be my pleasure if I thought it would help. But word of mouth in London doesn't go all that far these days."

"I shall be grateful for whatever you do. In any event I leave England in April and will follow my heart, as the romantics say."

"And my best wishes will most certainly go with you, my friend!" He raised his wine glass in salute, "I shall send you bread and cheese and a good bottle of wine as soon as you're settled!"

"Thanks, Crenshaw, but don't utter one syllable about this to anyone. You're the only person in all of London who knows this story, and I'm certain you'll keep it under wraps."

"My lips are sealed. Absolute silence and I shall do what I can."

He put on his heavy overcoat with its fur collar and made ready to walk to the station to catch the 9:48.

"It's not all that cold, y' know!" he cried out when we were in the street. "I'm hoping the weather remains jolly temperate a bit longer. I planned to go south for the winter, but I won't be striking my tent to move out in this kind of weather."

"I wouldn't mind if Old Man Winter himself went south!"

Always I complained about the weather in winter. My sisters had a running joke about it. If their brother didn't grumble about the cold in November, he would surely do so before Christmas. The winter of 1898-99 was mild. In January the thrushes and blackbirds were loudly chirping in the balmy air, and the sun was shining with the warmth of spring. But I was certain the sorry scheme of things wouldn't allow the fine weather to continue more than a few days longer.

"We pay for our pleasure with three parts pain," I said to Emma.

"Balderdash," was her reply.

"Cold and frost will come with a vengeance in April or May."

"Balderdash," she repeated.

The mild winter was kind to my health. I worried about the lung condition, but Estelle's gentle support was making me stronger. I could feel it in every bone. My uncertain health was improving.

2

After I finished *The Pinnacle of Life* I wrote prefaces for a new edition of Dickens. I produced twelve in all, but the edition was a financial failure and only six were printed for half pay. The good health of earlier months slipped away in March. For six weeks I was painfully ill. First came a severe attack of influenza that made my joints ache. Then came bouts of catarrh, lung congestion, and pleurisy. I remembered the recent death of a famous duke who had died of pneumonia following severe influenza, and that did little to improve my peace of mind. All sorts of ailments made me writhe in pain. But the eczema, which had tortured me in warmer weather, didn't bother me with its agonizing blisters. Also no signs of phthisis (pulmonary tuberculosis) came forward. Even though the illness suspended all work and left me in a weakened condition, I had no cough and nothing red on my handkerchief. By the end of March, shielded from the southwest wind, I was able to sit in the warmth of the sun outside. I was now eager to live in cool and clean mountain air with a spirited, loving, and beautiful woman.

At the end of April in 1899 I had not regained all of my strength. Even so, I was able to pack my books and personal items and some furniture to be shipped abroad. Then something very troubling happened. I had placed with great care fifty of my favorite books in a sturdy, cardboard box. In transit to the warehouse the box fell to the pavement, ripped open, and spilled the books. Gasping, and coughing, I gathered them up as fast as I could and managed to salvage most of them, but the effort and excitement left me shaken. To Rhodes I complained I would rather move into my grave than move my belongings again. I didn't know a strenuous nomadic way of life lay in store for me.

As my imagination leaped into the future, I pictured myself living with lovely Estelle in some idyllic place. We would grow old together in tender affection, domestic peace, and rare happiness. Eventually I would tell my family the whole story, and they would come to visit. The fantasy reminded me of plans to go to Worcestershire for a few days to visit Walter at Quentin's house. I would have to do that before leaving England. While the boy spent most of his time in Harrogate, he lived a few days each month in Worcestershire. The arrangement was meant to protect him from his mother who might appear at any time to harass him or try to take him away. My sisters were afraid of the woman and wanted nothing to do with her. Their dream was to lure the younger son to them and have the boys grow up together, but that never happened. Austin remained with Natalie.

I left England never to live there again the first week in May 1899. On the 11:30 boat for Dieppe I crossed the English Channel. The day was sunny and bright. The next day I was having lunch with Estelle and her mother at the Hôtel de Paris in Rouen. Situated on the banks of the Seine in northern France, Rouen was a treasure house of artistic masterpieces and known for its huge clock dating from the 1300's. It was also the city where Joan of Arc was burned at the stake by the English in 1431 and the birthplace of Gustave Flaubert. It seemed the perfect place for a loving couple to begin their great adventure. In the evening, Jonathan Blue married Estelle Laurent in a ceremony that lasted only a few minutes. My bride was radiant, smiling, dignified, and as happy as she had ever been. Her dark hair drew attention to delicate features. She wore just enough makeup to highlight the beauty of her face illuminated by a chandelier. A milky white skirt and bodice enhanced her slender figure. For an instant I saw my love in classical clothing, a flowing Greek chiton caressing every curve. I thrilled to the sight of her.

Even though Natalie Blue was alive in England, we viewed our marriage as legitimate and binding. A brief diary entry described the event: *"In the evening, our ceremony. Dear Maman's emotion, and E's sweet dignity.*" The entry made no mention of my deportment. At best the ceremony was a symbolic assertion of our love for one another. It couldn't be seen as a genuine marriage, for I was legally bound to Natalie. Because of the moral question, and not willing to upset them again with news of another marriage, I didn't inform my sisters and mother. I knew they would see the marriage as illegal and dangerous if not scandalous. Also I felt they would have difficulty accepting a foreign woman as a member of the family. A decade earlier in *Comes the Morning* I had examined the insular temper of British women regarding their counterparts in Europe and had concluded with this: "*Philip wedded his Italian maiden, brought her to England, and fought down prejudice*".

A day after the ceremony Mme. Laurent returned to Paris. Grateful to be alone, we spent our honeymoon in St. Pierre en Port on the coast of Normandy. We remained there in a nebulous, hazy, delirious dream world for several weeks. The scenery was delightful and the weather superb, but for several days we spent most of our time indoors. With eyes only for each other, we had no inclination to explore the picturesque village and its surroundings. In the small hotel we found only two other guests, garrulous Englishmen whom we politely ignored. I boasted to my friend Kurtz that Estelle and I spoke only French in their presence. In the lobby my bride came across an old piano and made marvelous, melodious music on it. She ran her slender fingers deftly over the keyboard, evoking from memory Chopin's "Minute Waltz" and Mozart's "Rondo Alla Turca." To my delight she interpreted Bach's "Prelude in C Major" with finesse and delicacy, dedicating the piece to me. Then with an impish good humor, she finished her recital with Rossini's "William Tell Overture." I laughed at that, savoring each rollicking note as medication for the soul. But imprinted on my psyche, to be recalled in times of leisure, was the intimate music we made together. When the honeymoon was over, we went to live with Estelle's aging mother in Paris.

Earlier I had explained to Kurtz that I couldn't risk living in England again. If the authorities heard that I was living with another woman as man and wife, they could probably charge me with breaking the law. In future I would return to England, especially in the spring when hunger for the country of my birth seized me, but not to live there. Temporarily settled in Paris, I thought in time I would find a comfortable house in Switzerland. Sharing cramped quarters with Estelle's mother tested my forbearance, but no other arrangement was possible. She was too old to live alone, and her attentive daughter wouldn't hear of a stranger living in the flat to look after her. Wherever we went accommodations would have to be made for three people instead of two. Ominous forces were already active to make the ideal marriage less than ideal.

3

Mme. Genevieve Laurent was a woman of strong personality. Short and squat and gray, touchy but open and honest, she spoke decisively in the presence of others. She had dominated her daughter for years, and after a man came to live with them she made no attempt to cease her domination. She made it clear to me that in her flat she alone was head of the house. Within a month I was quarreling with her over the kind of food I needed to remain healthy. For breakfast each morning I wanted bacon and eggs, sausage, fried mushrooms or hash browns, buttered toast with marmalade, and a pot of tea. But in her opinion the standard English breakfast was heavy and unhealthful. French food was so much better, even for a fastidious Englishman who had been lucky enough to marry her daughter. She felt she was doing me a service by requiring me to eat properly. The fried English breakfast was a danger to my health.

She wanted happiness in her household, happiness particularly for the daughter she loved dearly, but at the same time she was a feisty and confrontational woman. I didn't like domestic conflict of any kind, and even petty vexations brought palpitation. Not able to solve the problem, I dreaded even to think about it. I put on a show of cheerfulness, pretending all was going well even when I knew that friction from a well-defined source was making a mockery of my ideal marriage.

Through June and July we lived in Paris while I worked smoothly and with great satisfaction on *Old Calabria*. I completed the book, based on the notes of my Calabrian trip, while Estelle and I were on holiday in Switzerland. For several weeks we had moved about in the Alps, seeking a place of residence beneficial to my precarious health. I suffered from respiratory ailments and had been told by a doctor to live in the salubrious air of the mountains. Domestic peace, mountain air, and wholesome food would make me whole again. I yearned for steady good health and the strength to work long hours. I wanted to be a witty and pleasant companion to my loving wife, but I had to write in solitude and worry about making a living. No project in progress meant no income.

In the modern apartment house not far from the Bois de Boulogne, I was living in pleasant surroundings but feeling no relief from financial pressure. I had promised to lend money to my brother Quentin, had to put my son Walter through school, and was legally obligated to send Natalie two pounds a week. In good conscience I couldn't live in Mme. Laurent's apartment and eat her food without paying rent. Also it was expensive to move about in the resort areas of the Alps. In the early weeks of September we traveled through several Swiss towns. At Airolo where expenses were more reasonable than in better-known places, I spoke Italian with some of the citizens.

In late September we went back to Paris for the winter. There I worked on a novel called *The Coming Man*. The title was an ironical burlesque of a phrase the women's movement had made popular, "the coming woman." Wary of giving offense to any person inclined to buy the book, the publisher wanted a change of title and had to wait to the eleventh hour until I could think of a new one. The novel was laid aside while I worked on another project but was eventually published in 1901 as *Our Shallow Charlatan*. My new project, slowly developing while the earlier one languished, was another long novel I was calling *Among the Prophets*. Later in a fit of despair I discarded it.

Generally I had trouble coming up with good titles, but this was one of my best. It's possible the text was as good as the title, but no one will ever know. Even though in a pique I called it poor stuff, it may not have been poor stuff at all. I began the book with high hopes, believing

I could make my controversial subject exciting. It was a satire on *"the restless seeking for a new religion,"* on spiritualism and theosophy and other belief systems I viewed as false and ridiculous. I sent the book off to be typed, read through its chapters in the typewritten version, decided it didn't meet my standard of excellence, and tossed it on the growing heap of nugatory work. Later it fell into the hands of my agent and was ultimately lost. It was one of many abortive novels written tediously by hand in splotchy black ink and later destroyed.

During the winter I found time to write short stories and managed to publish most of them. It was a good time for me emotionally, but the Boer War (which began in October of 1899) distracted me and robust health eluded me. The horror stories of blood and violence in the newspapers were making me ill. To Kurtz I said: *"I fear never again in our lifetime shall we see peace and quietness. Of course the outlook of literature is very gloomy. There seems little hope for anything but books, which deal with questions of practical interest. Science is swallowing up the arts. It is rather humiliating to have to live by story-telling in a time which condemns one to mediocrity."* I had managed to survive on story telling for more than twenty years but was tired of it and wanted a new direction. Sometimes in the small hours of the night I thought of academia, the spires of Oxford rising to the blue sky, the majestic buildings serene and quiet, town and gown far from the frenetic world of time and change. I longed to lose myself in the library there.

At the end of 1899 I made reply to the letter my son Walter had sent at Christmas time, saying I was glad the boy was able to write so well. I spoke of frost and snow and the harshness of winter. I asked if he had been reading any good books: *"I don't want you to spend a great deal of time in reading, but you always ought to have a book on hand for quiet times."* Then I spoke of the war in South Africa: *"I suppose you sometimes hear people talk of the war. You must understand that war is a horrible thing, which ought to be left to savages. It is a thing to be ashamed of and not to glory in. It is wicked and dreadful for the people of one country to go and kill those of another. What we ought to be proud of is peace and kindness, not fighting and hatred. You are getting old*

enough now to understand these things, and that is why I speak of them."
I hated war as nasty, brutish, and deadly. I found it hard to believe that
civilized nations could engage in warfare. Though deeply pessimistic in
maturity, I remarked that in future people would be astonished to learn
that former generations had gone to war.

Walter read the letter and took his father's sentiments to heart, I
believe. I wanted to spend time with the boy and get to know him and
let him know I would help him all I could with whatever he wanted to
do in life. But at present getting a good education was most important,
and he would have to focus on that. Of course I would pay for his
schooling even if he should to go off to college. However, it wasn't my
fate to know my son as a young man. As the years passed I began to
feel a disturbing premonition that while both sons would grow into
manhood and contribute to the welfare of old England as good citizens,
one would die a violent death. Even though at times I saw a name barely
legible scrawled on a blackboard, I couldn't be sure which son would
suffer catastrophe. I knew only the thing could happen. It brought on
sadness so profound I could feel it in my bones, and it caused me to hate
my so-called prophetic power as much as I hated war.

CHAPTER THIRTY-FIVE

A New Century

January came with wintry weather, a new year, and a new century. The sound of 1900 was new on the tongue and strange to the ear. My sister Emma was stricken with villainous influenza, and John Ruskin died near the end of the month. Oscar Wilde, convicted on a morals charge in 1895 and released from prison in 1897, would die at forty-six at the end of November. From Paris, where Wilde spent his last days in penniless exile, I assured my sister the abominable winter would soon be over. I was certain she would grow strong again in the sunshine. Writing to Kurtz, I lamented the death of John Ruskin. I viewed Ruskin as the last of England's great men: a prophetic force in the art world, a powerful social critic, and a writer of poetic prose ranking among the very best. Oscar Wilde, on the other hand, was a poseur and showman but at times a witty dramatist and passable poet. I was saddened by Wilde's behavior. Ultimately it destroyed a talented artist.

Rudyard Kipling was little more than the instrument of a capricious and malignant fate. As such, I believed, Kipling was doing incalculable harm to the human race. Earlier I had admired his robust and muscular verse, but now I despised the man as a warmonger and worse. On a personal note I worried that vitriolic and pandemic influenza could strike Kurtz. I was glad when both of us got through February unscathed except for colds. Some of my books were being translated into French and German, and the news pleased me. Also I was happy to learn that my brother's latest book as a country chronicler had been reviewed by a leading journal. That could mean more copies sold and more money, which he desperately needed.

With the coming of spring I couldn't resist returning to England. In discussion with Estelle, I insisted I couldn't conduct business entirely by correspondence. Also I needed material for my next novel. She opposed the trip because she feared it would be a strain on my health, and she thought my attachment to family might take me away from her. During our first year of marriage she could see I suffered from homesickness. Though I tried to convince her otherwise, she believed didn't view my exile as permanent and longed to be home in England. I spent most of April with the family in Harrogate and at the homes of friends in London and Sandgate. Estelle in Paris fretted over this turn of events and was reluctant to send me a photograph I requested. I explained with braggadocio mingled with flattery that I wanted my friends to see an image of the beautiful woman I had married, not merely hear talk about her. She replied she was unable to resist giving me whatever I wanted and would send a new photo as promptly as possible.

However, there was no time for such a picture to be taken, processed, and mailed, for I had made up my mind to come home to her. After a couple of days with Rhodes at Sandgate, I went to Newhaven and crossed the Channel on May 1. Earlier I had said I would be coming back with a rich assortment of new literary material: *"My mind is full of fine new pictures. I hope to have a very fruitful summer. Happily you understand better now the conditions of my work."* On reaching Paris I was seized by an attack of rheumatism that put me in bed for three days.

The flat had been rented to strangers for the summer, and we had to be out no later than May 25. We planned to go to St. Honoré les Bains, a resort town in the mountains, where we had taken a villa until the end of October. Packing had to be done, and I did it slowly under the eye of Mme. Laurent. Rigorous and demanding, she scolded me for not working faster. Moving to another place was a task that always irked me, for I disliked manual labor. Apart from pushing a pen across paper, I went out of my way to avoid it. Moreover, the packing and moving seemed always to come in warm weather to leave me breathless and sweaty. I grumbled while I worked, but the job was done in time for the three of us to leave the residence our last day there. I was glad to be out of Paris and going to a quiet place. The International Exhibition of 1900 had brought massive crowds, uproar and congestion.

The house with its large garden in St. Honoré les Bains was all we expected. I had a little bedroom for a study and a good view. I couldn't take the long walks I loved even though the countryside seemed wonderfully like England. From the narrow lanes I could see the flowers I had known as a boy – foxgloves, buttercups, daisies, saxifrage, honeysuckle, rockrose, hollyhock, larkspur, yellow ragwort, and roses. The air was filled with fragrance and I felt it could never be lost. *"And this same flower that smiles today tomorrow will be dying,"* the poet Robert Herrick had written. Surely he was speaking nonsense. The same flower came again and again, vibrant and sweet in its season, replacing the one before it. Also the sounds delighted me, the perpetual sounds. Crickets in the underbrush rattled with a loud chirping, the same chirping Herrick heard in the seventeenth century or Chaucer in the Middle Ages. Near a quiet pond the frogs croaked in sonorous harmony. In a tree nearby a colony of rooks filled the air with mournful cries. At night the toads made a noise like a penny trumpet that could be heard a mile away. When the wind came up, a leafy tree branch brushed against the windowpane near my bed and a nightjar chirred. These were good and natural sounds, not the noise of an unnatural gathering of people. They didn't bother me at all.

What did bother was the heat. But in spite of hot weather that sometimes reduced me to writing in my underwear, I worked through the summer on *The Coming Man*. I completed the novel at the end of August but had to wait until May of 1901 for its publication. My agent was negotiating to have the book published simultaneously in both England and America. The business deal consumed time but brought me £450 for the English and American rights, much more than expected.

Even though on several pages I gave the reader an exegesis of the title, the American publisher wanted a plainer title. Under pressure I frantically tried to come up with a new one and chose *The Young Man Eloquent*. If the publishers had not required something better, it would have taken the prize as the worst of many ineffective titles. At the eleventh hour, while correcting the proofs, I hit upon *Our Shallow Charlatan*, and that became the final title. Dialogue explaining the old title I didn't delete. *"Perhaps you do represent the coming man,"* a leading female character observes with a show of fierce but controlled contempt. *"In that case, we must look anxiously for the coming woman to keep the world from collapse."* Feminists in my audience, reading passages like that, were certain I supported their cause. Their movement was flawed, I explained in a public letter, but had come at the right time.

2

I was thinking clearly and writing well as I penned *Our Shallow Charlatan*. In a pleasant and comfortable villa situated in the mountains, I worked on the novel with the same ease acquired after meeting Natalie a decade earlier. The climate agreed with me and I was in the company of a superb woman who assuaged my loneliness, fed my physical appetite, listened when I spoke, supplied ideas for me to chew on, and made my life orderly. Skillfully I designed the intricate plot and created realistic characters in conflict. Dixon Lashcroft – lean, keen, affable, ambitious, and dishonest – is the charlatan. In his late twenties and eager to move ahead in the battle of life, he assumes a superiority he doesn't have. Willing to say and do anything to improve his social and economic position, he blathers plagiarized sciolistic nonsense to wealthy and powerful Lady Organder to impress her. Though pretending to be highly educated and well informed, ultimately he is seen as dreadfully ignorant. Even so, in time she decides to support him as a candidate for Parliament.

That is the moment when he thinks fortune has turned a shining face upon him, but he soon discovers he is merely the plaything of fate. After losing the election and finding himself caught in his own web of deceit, and after his benefactor dies leaving him nothing, he marries an aging widow with a modest fortune instead of the young woman he has long admired. As the book ends he is told just after his marriage that a dishonest trustee has stolen the fortune he expected to live on without working. His pursuit of the one big break to bring him wealth and fame has come to nothing. The charlatan must work for an honest living. It is retributive justice, a theme that recurs frequently in my novels.

The plot when summarized sounds unoriginal and wooden. Readers, however, found humorous satire, informed commentary on social issues, and characters that rank among my best. While the charlatan is the main character, he is surrounded by a bevy of women ranging in age from May Turpin in her twenties to Lady Organder almost eighty. The latter is important, for without her there would be no story. She is a magnet to draw the other characters around her to plan and hope and scheme. Her mind is sharp as a razor, and she comes vividly to life as she exploits her power and position in her part of the world. Of humble birth, she doesn't go along with do-nothing aristocrats who would maintain the status quo at any cost. She believes in progress, helping the poor in a practical way, and advancing the rights of women. I can hear her speaking now to one of her conservative guests: *"I don't agree with you at all. I should like to see as many women doctors as men. Miss Lake has studied medicine, and a very good doctor she would have made."*

Using her wealth to help others, Lady Organder is the type of philanthropist I most admired. She is convinced that it's better for the poor to be fed and housed than for the wealthy to have a pretty landscape to view. In the picturesque village of Shawe, to provide employment in a time of agricultural depression, she has built a hideous paper mill belching smoke day and night. Situated on a pretty meadow beside a shimmering pond, the ugly mill is at odds with the harmony and charm of the ancient village. Yet those who work there know their jobs have saved them from grinding poverty. Though I deplored the desecration of the countryside by such projects, I was in sympathy with Lady Organder and could appreciate what she was doing.

A judgment of practicality became the yardstick by which I measured the work and worth of lady philanthropists. Spending time among the poor as visitants from another world was not enough. Dispensing pious religious tracts, simplified pamphlets on hygiene, and purple passages from great literature was of no benefit whatever. Classical music delivered by the best orchestra in all of Europe would have a lasting effect on maybe one in a thousand. It wouldn't soothe the spirit and elevate the soul, as many female philanthropists believed. Only work at jobs paying fair wages could rescue the poor. It would bring a sense of worth and allow them to live their lives with dignity free of want.

Close to Lady Organder, and performing as her secretary and companion, is a remarkable young woman named Sylvia Lake. At twenty-eight she is levelheaded and decisive with a mind of her own. Earlier she studied pharmaceuticals and became a pharmacist in a midland hospital, but her present position pays more. Wholesome, healthy, and intelligent, she rides her bicycle vigorously wherever she chooses. She is studious and finds time to read Nietzsche and other philosophers. Shortly after meeting Lashcroft, she strongly suspects he is nothing more than a charlatan. Later she reads the book from which he has stolen even the language of his ideas, and in the novel's climactic scene she annihilates him with infallible proof. She is something of a new woman but also an opportunist looking out for herself. At the end of the story she rejects a marriage proposal so as to build a career for herself. *"Does that offend your sense of what is becoming in a woman? You will see, when you think about it, that I am acting strangely like a male creature. We females with minds have a way of doing that."* I had Clara Collader in mind – her honesty, intelligence, and self-assurance – as I created Sylvia Lake.

Iris Woodlander, a conventional womanly woman, stands in contrast to Sylvia, who is seen as the coming woman. At twenty-two she married a man twice her age and now at thirty-four is a widow with a comfortable income from his investments. She is seen as a sincere woman but listens to the shoddy advice of the charlatan, who tries to turn her into an emancipated woman. In love with him, she fastens on every insincere word he mutters and tries to read dull books that will free her soul. In league with a charlatan and blinded by love, for several months she tries to be like him. Assuring her that she is every inch his equal, he calls her "a good fellow." Essentially feminine, she has no desire to be a fellow, good or otherwise, and gradually reverts to her womanly self. She wants to be his dutiful wife and eventually gets her wish. But just before they marry Lashcroft offers a different kind of advice: *"After all, you know, you're a very womanly woman. I think we shall have to give up pretending that you're not."* Then he adds indulgently, remembering a phrase he read somewhere: *"It's all very well to be womanly, but don't be womanish."* Iris is glad to hear she will no longer have to pretend. Unlike her husband who is seven years younger and just beginning to understand, she has learned that swagger and pretense bring alienation and pain.

3

September came in a blaze of color. In the mountains the weather was breezy and pleasant. I wrote to my old friend in Germany, congratulating him on the positive reception of his cycling book. It had been written for pensive people, and was being taken seriously by the medical community. The book was selling well, and on the income he received Kurtz moved to more comfortable quarters. My travel book, *Old Calabria,* had been serialized in the *Fortnightly Review,* and the managers had paid me £130. In the spring Shipman & Hill would publish the Calabrian adventure as a well-illustrated book and would also pay £130. Altogether my travel book reaped £260, which couldn't be seen as a pittance. At last Kurtz and I were making enough money to live a decent existence.

I was now writing smoothly and with quiet satisfaction *The Philip Crowe Papers.* The piece would be published with that title as a book, but would appear serially as *An Author at Leisure.* A book of mellow reminiscence and partly autobiographical, I had been thinking about it for a long time. In a letter to Kurtz I explained what I was trying to do: *"I imagine an author who has led a long and grubby life, and who at the age of fifty is blest with a legacy which gives him £300 a year. Forthwith he goes down into Somerset, establishes himself in a cottage, and passes the last five years of his life in wonderful calm and contentment. After all the years of writing fiction, the thing is doing me good."*

The weather was already chilly in the mountains, and I dreaded the coming of winter. We would spend a week at Nevers with Estelle's relatives and return to Paris near the middle of November. Then I would begin at once another novel that was growing in my head. I worried that people were forgetting my work: *"No periodical takes any particular interest in me; I am seldom spoken of nowadays. I feel I am beginning to lose even what little public I had."* I knew I would have to publish soon to place myself in the public eye again. Even though the critics would misread, misunderstand, and find fault, I would have the publicity.

In December I spoke of entering another new year, and I hoped my health would remain steady until I could finish *The Vanquished Roman*, my scholarly historical novel of the sixth century. I had begun the writing, after many delays, and had finished two pages. *"The beginning is fearfully difficult,"* I said to Kurtz, *"for I have to find a new style."* I had the plan of the story in detail on paper and thought it would make a powerful book of high authenticity. *"One thing is certain – I know my period."* Though it sounded like boasting, I really did know my subject. Few people in England had a deeper knowledge of Italian history in that century. It was an intricate political, civil, personal, and ecclesiastical mosaic.

As 1900 came to an end I was thinking about the welfare of my younger son. No electrifying news had come in the mail, and I was hoping that at long last Natalie had settled down. My lawyer, a man named Brewer, was paying her support of £104 a year. I wanted the child out of her hands, but the law was on her side. For a small fee Elizabeth Osgood had agreed to keep an eye on Natalie to see that all went well. I had taken my older son, Walter, away at the right moment, and the boy was living happily in Harrogate. I would soon have to think about his future and find a more advanced school for him. As indicated earlier, from time to time I had disturbing visions of an unkind fate involving the boy. My younger son, Austin, would in time be taken from his mother to grow strong in the country and live an ordinary life.

CHAPTER THIRTY-SIX

Health a Bête Noire

For several months, living in the mountains and breathing clean air, I had gone without my books. In Paris in the little cramped flat where there was no room for even one overnight guest I insisted on keeping a few books, but most of them had been left behind in a Dorking warehouse. Now at the beginning of 1901 they came to me in a big wooden box splintered at one corner. As Mme. Laurent looked on with dismay, wondering where the contents of the box would go, I eagerly pried it open and found my books damp and musty but undamaged. I tugged them out of the box, sniffing them and caressing the covers as I turned the pages. It was a ritual I always used to become reacquainted with each volume. Estelle understood. Her mother did not.

"We have no room for all these books!" the older woman exclaimed in the only language she knew.

"I will find room," I said quietly.

"Nous n'avons pas de place pour ces livres!" she said again, growing more agitated when required to repeat.

"Please don't worry, dear. I will shelve them in the bedroom."

Once I had promised Estelle that I would never allow my books, as the collection got bigger and bigger, to spill over into our bedroom. "There is a line to be drawn between body and mind. So anything of the mind stays out of the bedroom."

"I agree," she replied with that musical laugh of hers and a twinkle in her pretty eyes. "We must keep our two lives separate."

Now I would have to go back on that promise. In the tiny apartment there was nowhere else to keep them. I wanted to live in a house with a library, or at least a spacious study with books on every wall, but that was a dream I would never attain.

By the time I had carefully set each book in its proper place, I had caught a severe cold. I blamed it on the warehouse in Dorking. *"The dampness of the books gave me a bad cold from which I am just now recovering,"* I said in a letter. It was the dampness of England, however, and that made the cold easier to bear. I was yearning to see my friends and family there. Perhaps I could return in the spring and take Estelle with me. I had to wait until summer.

The news came in January of 1901 that Queen Victoria was dead. She had ascended the throne in 1837 and had ruled not unkindly in parlous times for more than sixty years. Much of her power as a monarch had been taken away by Parliament, but she could still make decisions to harm or to help. I believed she had always acted for the good of her people, and I hoped King Edward VII would do the same. I wanted to be in Westminster Abbey for the pomp and circumstance of the coronation but dared not travel in Siberian weather. The cough that had troubled me for months was no better. The death of the Queen – I believed the South African War had killed her – moved me to think of my own mortality: *"Strange to think that when I was born,"* I said to Clara Collader, *"Victoria had already reigned for twenty years, and that I am already beginning to feel old at the time of her death. I cough rather badly, and I'm taking cod liver oil, but I hope the end of this terrible weather will help me. Meanwhile I am advancing slowly, but I think well, with my historical novel."* I went on to say that elaborate preparations were being made for *Old Calabria*. *"It is to be illustrated with full-page pictures in colour and with engravings."* I knew the book would be costly but liked the attention given to it. Things in the business world were looking up for us.

From the end of February to the first week in June, Estelle's translation of *New Bleak Street* (the project that had brought us together) was published serially in the *Journal des Débats*, a magazine highly respected in France and read by thoughtful, educated people. I could tell she was proud of seeing her work in prestigious print, and I was happy for her. I encouraged her to take on another translation project, for she was good at it, but she said caring for her aging mother was sapping her strength and consuming most of her time.

In early spring H. G. and Catherine Rhodes paid a visit after spending several weeks in Italy. I wanted them to stay overnight but the little flat, "bleakly elegant" as Rhodes described it, was too small. Also Estelle was ailing, coming down with the flu, but trying bravely to be gracious even when sick. Years later in a book of reminiscence, Rhodes would say he had found me "in a state of profound discontent, thin and feverish and too weak to work." I supposedly complained with bitter invective that Mme. Laurent was in complete control of the household and starving me. I was tired of French food and the French way of life, according to him, and wanted to live again in England. But I had convinced myself I couldn't do that so long as Natalie remained alive. Rhodes's sense of humor drove him to exaggerate my quirks of personality. He did that with other friends, often querulous and ungenerous as he did it. Yet it seems no one complained loudly enough to lose his friendship.

He was making a lot of money as a writer, and he believed that I with experience and talent could have a similar income but for my stubbornness. I envied Rhodes and made no secret of it, but it wasn't envy with spite. I was glad my friend was doing so well and was charitable in my appraisal of the man. To Kurtz I wrote: *"Rhodes is wonderfully prosperous. He has built himself a beautiful house on the cliff at Sandgate, where he communicates with London by telephone! That kind of thing will never fall to me."* As I wrote those words I remembered Myra Medlock back in Boston. She was the first person to mention that incredible device to me. Through time and space I could hear her saying, *"Do you know about the telephone? It's a wonderful invention."*

2

As the spring of 1901 came with wind and rain and slow warmth, Dr. Gifford in England began to ask about my health. I replied I seemed to be in fair health but was losing weight. I went on to inform Gifford I was thinking of coming to England to put on a few pounds. More than once I had complained to Dylan Crenshaw about not getting the kind of food I felt I needed to maintain my weight and remain healthy. Crenshaw, as well as other friends, eventually came to believe that my descent into fragile and uncertain health was caused by undernourishment. Estelle's mother, on the other hand, believed the way to stay healthy was to stay away from fatty foods and eat three scanty meals each day. She ignored my pleas for substantial breakfasts, calling them greasy and gross.

In a letter to Crenshaw I revealed my longing for English food: *"I am thinking night and day of an English potato, of a slice of English meat, of tarts and puddings, and teacakes. I look forward to ravening on these things!"* Dr. Gifford also got a letter showing a decisive yearning for native food: *"I wish I could look in on you. I would roar with joy at an honest bit of English roast beef. Could you post a slice in a letter? – with gravy?"* I hoped I was entertaining my friend with outrageous humor, but Gifford said to his wife on receiving the letter: *"Why this is written by a starving man!"* Later he agreed with Rhodes that *"French starvation is causing Blue to go to pieces."* That opinion, simplistic and exaggerated, missed the truth. I simply had a craving for traditional English food.

At the end of April, I suffered an attack of influenza and was examined by a French doctor. The physician discovered serious respiratory problems – severe emphysema, chronic bronchitis, and a dark spot on the right lung. He advised me to return to St. Honoré les Bains as soon as possible, or go to some other mountain retreat sheltered from winds. I should go for rest, proper diet, clean air, and moderate exercise. But instead of following the physician's orders to solve the pulmonary problem in a place conducive to health, I yielded once again to the lure of the old island in springtime. I went home to England with Estelle.

We spent a couple of days in London while I conducted business. From there we went to Sandgate to visit Rhodes and Catherine in their new home. It was a fine house with every modern convenience and a splendid view. There I ate with gusto the hearty English meals denied me in France, began to put on weight immediately, and was persuaded to stay longer. In a single week I gained several pounds. Thin and gaunt when I arrived, my color and healthy look returned. That convinced my friends that for months I had not been eating enough for good health. They persuaded me to see a London doctor, who supported the French doctor and spoke of wavering health. After several days in the Rhodes home, Estelle went back to Paris to look after her ailing mother.

I was left alone in England and made plans to stay longer. At the urging of friends, and without consulting my wife, I decided to become a patient in a sanatorium. I hoped to find a cure for my condition and forget I was ever ill. I wanted to tell my protective and solicitous spouse all about it but couldn't be certain how she would take it. When she finally received the news from Rhodes, she fumed over an important decision made without her consent and sent him scolding letters. Flabbergasted by their assertive tone, Rhodes soon refused to make reply. Undaunted, Estelle posted letters to Catherine Rhodes and poured out her stricken heart to a sympathetic listener.

She had heard from them that I would be in England for most of the summer. Her first agonized thought was that I would stay there and not return to her, and that brought panic and devastation. She found it hard to believe her husband could recover his health without her. No French doctor would ever take away an ailing husband from his supportive wife and put him in the care of strangers. From the age of fourteen she had cared for her invalid mother, and that made her specially qualified to look after her husband. But if the English friends and relatives teamed up against her, she would find herself helpless and desolate. She had no wish to oppose so many people and probably the invalid himself. *"If he is now convinced that France will be his death, as he was three years ago that England would be, he will probably choose to live there rather than with me."* She added that if I made that choice, it would kill her.

Estelle claimed my health was breaking even before she met me, and so in no sense would she bear the burden of thinking it started with her. As soon as she met me in Dorking I complained of ailments that puzzled her. I looked strong and healthy but assured her that I suffered from phthisis, emphysema, eczema, no appetite, a steady loss of weight, and sleepless nights. Some nights, she soon learned, I paced the floor shrieking with such intensity I frightened my housekeeper. I confided it had to do with my nerves after the frightful life I had lived, and I felt the climate was doing me harm. So without delay she consented to become my wife and restore my health. Absolutely without stinting she gave her all to me, and her dear mother was sympathetic. *"I am quiet on this point,"* she asserted in summary. *"I know France has not been fatal to him."*

3

Rhodes suggested she find a housekeeper/companion for her mother and come immediately to England. She replied she couldn't imagine leaving her mother for even a week. The woman was near the end of her days and could die at any moment. Her heart was quite worn out and it was a miracle she was still alive. A fortnight ago, on returning from England, she had thought her beloved mother was dead or dying of neglect. *"Do you see in what a painful position I find myself? But that is not all – far from it. Jonathan regards living again in England a very dangerous situation and so do I. The woman to whom he is legally bound is looking for him, is surely in pursuit of him and will find him. I am fascinated by all I've heard about 'that terrible woman,' but I'm afraid of her. Any meeting with her would surely send chills of fright up and down my spine."*

Estelle couldn't bear the thought of conflict with violent Natalie. I had told her that in her rages the woman was incredibly strong and often vented her temper on women. Hearing that made her quake in fear. A tongue-lashing would annihilate her. No violence would be necessary. She would die of humiliation. And what about my family in Harrogate? Would they not help me through my illness? Would I be more pleased in their company than hers? *"I know what a power they have over him. I cannot forget that last April, after I had done my utmost to protect him, he fled away like a madman to see them, turning away from my supplications and tears."* She would not be able to meet them if she came to England, for they knew nothing of her existence. They would hold her in scornful contempt and that would break her heart. But if my health should take a turn for the worse, she would fly to me without a thought for anything or anyone. *"What can I be for him now? What can I do? Nothing."*

Rhodes replied that he doubted my family was more important to me than her, but she took small comfort in that. She assured him that after living with me night and day for more than two years she knew me better than Rhodes could ever hope to know me, and she did not exaggerate the power my family wielded over me. She said I once explained that I didn't inform them of my marriage because I wanted to spare their feelings. *"Do you think I was not deeply hurt by that?"* Another time I said I had to live not for her but for my children. *"Do you think I did not understand and yet was deeply hurt?"* In time she removed those painful remarks from her mind, she added, but now in solitude and misery they had come back to haunt and tear.

She confessed that for some time she had known her husband was plainly unstable. She had detected that quality in his character even before marriage but tried to persuade herself it was the result of past events in an unhappy life. Happiness, she thought, would erase it, but it was in his blood and incurable. She could see my supposed instability in constant changes of mood and the desire for change itself. In situations when I could not have change, I would become restive and discontented and the bad seed would assert itself. I would become intolerable, hating my present condition, even in the presence of one who loved him more than life itself. *"Of course that makes life very difficult."* She insisted that my dissatisfaction with household matters was a mere façade. My discontent sprang from dissatisfaction with the world itself. Though she had tried to have me forget the miseries of the past and make me happy, my temperament was so rooted in gloom that happiness, real and true happiness, would forever elude me.

Though exaggerated and not entirely accurate, her analysis of my condition had within it a lot of truth. But she was wrong to suppose I cared more for my family than for her. My letters to her, silly with terms of endearment, are proof that I loved her with tenderness equal to her love for me. However, wrenched from the one she loved most in the world, Estelle's misery and jealousy quickly distorted the truth. She felt I had been lured home to my native land and had abandoned her. Though England had not been kind to me, she could understand my feelings. She couldn't understand, however, the role my friends were playing as they persuaded me to live away from her. They had told me that if I returned to her I would soon die. If I did not return, she would die.

In her despair she wrote many letters, not just to Rhodes and his wife but also to me. And of course I was quick to reply to every letter, always assuring her of my undying love and my desire to return home as soon as my health permitted. She was thinking home for me was England, but I myself knew with conviction that living with her was my home wherever we happened to be. I had complained about my life with her and her mother in Paris, but I expected my grumbling to be taken in stride. The habit of complaining was deeply engrained in my nature, and there was little I could do about it. I had begun to complain of loneliness at the school in Cheshire, even though my brothers were in the same school. The habit ran through many painful years afterwards, particularly when I found myself increasingly at odds with the world. Now that I knew I was causing her pain I would never complain again. I assured her in letter after letter that I would be a model husband, cheerful in adversity even if it killed me.

CHAPTER THIRTY-SEVEN

Summer of Separation

Natalie had shown indifference to my complaining, and so had my family in Harrogate. Highly strung Estelle, on the other hand, detected the aberration early, worried about it, and magnified it. She learned of the false starts and shattering losses I had suffered, and she correctly attributed my gloomy outlook to corrosive misery. I had lost my father and brother by untimely death, had lost a chance for distinction in the academic world because of one stupid act, and now after twenty years of struggle appeared to be losing a secure place as a respected author. The effect of all this was a deep dissatisfaction with the world around me. It brought complaining, or whining as Rhodes put it, which I hoped he would see as nothing more than self-expression. My friends later in life soon discovered I was fastidious, of worried mind, and finicky. Rhodes in one of his typical outbursts, triggered by an abundance of whining in one of my letters, called me a social coward. That hurt.

I readily admit I was often lacking in verve and nerve but was no coward. To label me such was irresponsible. H. G. Rhodes was a visionary with a talent for friendship but also a blowhard with an abrasive personality. Friends saw me as a sensitive man of intellect and talent but also a whiner. I found fault with everything, including the weather. I soon discovered that when not overdone, the faultfinding had therapeutic value. The grumbling, vented always in private, brought perverse satisfaction and strength to endure. Estelle had tolerated the querulous temper of her mother for many years and was willing calmly to accept this quirk of my nature. She knew my life had not been easy, and her first thought was to bring calm and comfort into it.

Mine was a troublesome character flaw. Yet to my credit I was always polite and considerate toward her, though less to her mother. In my letters at this time, even though I stressed the importance of remaining in England to gain weight, I was careful not to say anything that would alarm her. I spoke of the generous, warm-hearted concern I was finding in the luxurious new home Rhodes now owned at Sandgate: *"The kindness here is incredible. Cream comes every day from Devonshire. Tremendous eating! In one week I have gained nearly 3 kilos in weight!"* Dr. Gifford had said that everything depended upon putting flesh on a frame that was almost skeletal. Also he advised me to see Dr. Philip Penn-Ashe, the specialist in lung diseases I had consulted in 1897.

I knew Estelle was distressed over the separation from her, and I tried to calm her by saying one summer apart could mean many bright summers together later on. Dr. Penn-Ashe advised me to go to a sanatorium. I was unwilling to go, but yielded when my friends urged as a final argument: *"What good will it be to Mrs. Blue to have your company this summer and in the winter become a widow?"* It was argument I couldn't oppose. At whatever the cost, I hoped to regain my health and vigor and live for many years. In anguish and doubt and tearful because an unkind fate had separated me from the woman I dearly loved, I agreed to go to Dr. Kate Parker's newly opened sanatorium in Suffolk.

I went there near the end of June and stayed six weeks, taking the open-air and over-feeding treatment in vogue at that time. I thought my right lung was threatened by tuberculosis, but none of the doctors who examined me found any evidence of that. Estelle remained distressed, and I worried as much about her health as my own. I asked my friends to write to her and impress upon her that nothing on earth could keep me away from her longer than a month or two. Some of them thought I might not return to France, but that never entered my mind. To be with my wife for only a month and die was better than living many years without her. My friends were not able to read the depth of my passion for Estelle, and she herself was unsure of it. But I knew without a doubt that I would never be able to live without her. She was the absolute pulse of my life, my only reason for living.

In less than an hour after arriving at the sanatorium, I was sternly and quickly put to bed. I was exhausted and wanted to sleep but found it difficult to rest because a woman nearby was coughing day and night. I had heard that Estelle and her mother had moved to Autun in central France and were waiting for me there. That set up a longing for her that seemed unendurable. I wrote to say I was under the care of a highly skilled doctor and would join them as soon as I could. *"Dr. Parker makes a good impression,"* I said to Rhodes in a letter. *"She has been invited, I hear, to read a paper at the forthcoming international congress on tuberculosis – a distinction which must mean something. She seems to think that a few weeks will see me as well as I can ever be."* Then I added: *"The most interesting person here is a Miss Archer, a vigorous type who will serve me one of these days."* That person was Evelyn Archer, thirty-four years old and a lecturer in classics at Cambridge. Her condition was serious but not fatal. It had not deprived her of energetic talk.

From peaceful and pleasant Autun, Estelle wrote to Catherine Rhodes to thank her and her husband for their kindness toward me. They had taken me into their home, had insisted that I rest as much as possible, and had fed me prodigiously for two weeks. In Autun in July it was hot and sunny, but a dependable breeze came over wooded mountains to cool the village. Estelle and her mother found the summer weather in the clean and quiet mountains delightful, but worried about where they would go when winter came. I had said I would not live in Paris again. That upset both women and was causing unrest and tension. Writing to me, my wife spoke of household matters and her servant: *"a very honest girl but with no memory whatever."* She admitted that her mother had *"executive power"* in the household. For her to say that so long after our marriage really bothered me.

Also she thought I wanted her to live in solitude and discard her friends. It was the same complaint Natalie had made more than once, behavior that eventually damaged the second marriage beyond repair. But Estelle had been introduced to my friends, as Natalie was not, and they found her charming. Now miserably unhappy and unsure that her beloved husband would soon recover and return to her, she had a little complaining herself to do. She wrote that I often protested she was extravagant in handling expenses but thought nothing of spending money on the Harrogate people and *"that woman"* somewhere in England. Also she couldn't believe that after being away for two months I planned to visit Harrogate when released instead of coming directly home to her. *"I thought I was dreaming! A man advised not to fatigue himself intends to rush in this extreme heat, wet with perspiration, to a smoky town and run the risk of losing all the good acquired."* Only one thing relieved her distress: her husband would finally tell his family about her.

2

Much to her surprise I didn't go to Harrogate. In the second week of August in 1901, I traveled directly to Autun. Writing to Kurtz, I said my health, though vastly better, was too shaky to risk going in the heat of summer to visit my family. I had instructions to guard my condition carefully. In future, I said to Kurtz, I would sleep with my windows open and end the conflict with Mme. Laurent over the nourishment I needed to remain strong. I would find a way to eat good and rich food that would keep the flesh on my bones and a bounce in my step. My metabolism would use the calories to make me strong. I didn't have to worry about becoming fat. My emotional health at this time was also better. I had taken a long respite from work and was eager to get back to it with exciting plans to write several novels on contemporary issues and finish the historical novel. A new generation of novelists was on the scene in 1901 and taking the art form in a new direction. I knew all about them and encouraged their efforts. My own work by comparison was beginning to look old-fashioned. I would have to rethink my position and dress my work in new clothes.

In Autun the three of us lived in a fair degree of happiness until October. My friends heard I liked the place and found it charming, but in my diary I called it damp and doing me more harm than good. Leaving Autun, we were the guests of friends who owned a country house overlooking the Loire. It was the longest river in France, and I wanted to explore parts of it, but winter was coming on fast. We stayed there until the end of November, but went briefly to Paris for a medical checkup and to pick up winter clothing. When the doctor suggested a warmer climate, the three of us by now restless nomads, moved southward to a town called Arcachon.

I wasn't tubercular, as I had feared. But the examination did show a gradual hardening on the surface of the lungs, and the emphysema was becoming worse. At Arcachon I spent my days resting in the open air in a place inhabited mainly by invalids. All my life I had loved to roam country lanes, amble along riverbanks, stroll through city streets, and meander through dangerous slums. Now I discovered it was a task for me to trudge a mile without losing breath and strength. Also in that place I did little work, complaining to my friends (with humor I hoped) that any work was all but impossible on a chaise longue.

Half reclining in the open air and shielded from the wind by tall pine trees, I made slow progress on an abridged edition of Forster's *Life of Dickens*. Shipman & Hill had invited me to prepare a new biography of Dickens by thoroughly revising John Forster's masterful biography. I named a fee of £500, explaining I would keep as much of Forster as I could but insert my own observations. It would be a demanding task, I added, and would tax my strength. The firm countered with an offer of £150 for an abridgement, claiming people were not reading the book any more because of its length. I didn't like chipping away at a solid book to make it shorter. The procedure smelled of philistinism, but I needed the money. So dutifully I reduced the three-volume Forster to less than a quarter of its original length. Because of the many changes I made, my version was more than a scissors-and-paste job. I worked on the assignment through November and December. Near the end of the year I learned that *An Author at Leisure* had been accepted for serial publication. Payment would be £150. As a book titled *The Philip Crowe Papers* I would get an additional £50.

When Christmas came I weighed 169 pounds and believed my health was slowly returning to normal. I was eating better and feeling better. I was able to take walks in the cold of winter and return with only a little shortness of breath. My color had flowed back into neck and face, and I could breathe better at night. Even though I continued to suffer from the lung condition, my mood was moderately jaunty. Estelle, however, had become the *garde-malade* of both husband and mother and was showing signs of losing strength. Although she would have it no other way, caring for two invalids placed her under great strain. Our ideal marriage was now being challenged by the hard knocks of life in the real world. As my health declined, however, the unconditional love of that remarkable woman somehow grew stronger.

3

The month of January in 1902 saw the completion of the Dickens project, but the days were dreary and the month seemed interminable. The weather was damp and cold, and patches of snow covered the ground. The wind in spite of the sheltering pines whipped around our building, rattling the windows and making the old house groan. Even though I longed to feel the bracing effect of exercise, walking in such weather wasn't a pleasant activity. I remained inside, sedentary, restless, and fragile. On the whole, the climate was tolerable but nothing like South Devon where I had wintered three years. Although mountainous Arcachon was closer to the heavens, it didn't have as much sunshine. My health would improve faster in Devonshire. *"And this encourages me with the prospect that some day my exile may come to an end."* I was tired of living among strangers in a country I could never love. I wanted to return to England. Estelle suspected as much, and yet I said not a word to her about it. Divulging my cast of mind would have made her miserably unhappy, and that I didn't want at any cost.

For most of my life I had complained about all things English, but now I wanted to return with my charming wife and live happily ever after in a comfortable house somewhere in the country. However, an obstacle of no small size stood in my way: *"Were it not for Estelle's mother, I should go and settle in Devonshire or Cornwall. But we cannot take the woman out of her own country."* I would have to wait until she died before I could think of returning to England. My dream was to live quietly and without worry in country peace as Philip Crowe had lived, though not alone. Crowe, my own invention, was an author who had retired at the age of fifty on a legacy of £300 a year. He lived in a pleasant little cottage in Somerset and passed the last five years of his life in calm and contentment. In those surroundings he was tolerant and patient, mellowed and philosophical, and finally at peace with the world. Crowe was an alter ego and part of a dream, but my vision of a quiet retirement with supportive Estelle was fast becoming a tortured dream.

As the winter dragged on with temperatures day after day below freezing, I grew restless and discontented. Kurtz wrote to say his recently published novel had brought him no recognition whatever and very little money. Though not surprised, I felt genuine pain when I read his bleak confession of failure: *"I gave away a dozen copies. Of those, one was not acknowledged at all. Four were acknowledged without comment. Three men told me they had no time to read the book. Two ladies said only they liked it. The remaining two, one of them yourself, spoke kindly and with interest."* The letter with its air of hopelessness spurred me to sadness and anger. My old friend had worn himself out struggling for years against great odds to achieve nothing. I grieved for him.

In February came news that made me feel somewhat better. Miss Osgood, the woman who had tried to help me when my second marriage was crumbling into ruin, wrote to inform me that Natalie had been arrested for mistreatment of her little boy, found insane, and committed to an asylum. The woman had become more disturbed than ever, had in fact slipped into certifiable lunacy. Those close to her had seen it coming. Now in custody she would no longer be a threat to the child or anyone else. Austin would grow up on a farm in Cornwall near a good school. I had heard the horror stories of baby farming, how wretched people abused helpless children put in their charge, and I was fearful. I was willing to pay half a guinea a week, or whatever was necessary, to erase any risk of my child being beaten or starved.

When told the boy was healthy and happy and under the supervision of a woman who lived nearby, I felt immense relief. *"I cannot tell you how greatly I am relieved,"* I said to Kurtz. *"Indeed, I believe this event is already having a good effect upon my health."* For years I had fretted about Austin, believing the boy would have no future and blaming myself. Now came the news that he would be safe in a good place among good people. *"My mind, on that score, is enormously relieved. I always felt myself guilty of a crime in abandoning the poor little fellow. He will now have his chance to grow up in healthy and decent circumstances."*

At Arcachon I thought of writing a story involving the boy but wrote instead a satirical short story called "Miss Fletcher's Pastime." It was about a self-confident high-school teacher engaged in endless activity beyond her daily work. I modeled her after Evelyn Archer, the extraordinary woman I had met at the sanatorium in Suffolk. Archer was a liberally educated new woman, witty and talkative, intelligent and gregarious. A teacher, but no ordinary teacher, she was a lecturer in the classics at Cambridge when I met her, and near the beginning of her career. In almost every detail, except for satiric exaggeration, the fictional character reflects the real woman. The highest-ranking teacher in all of my work, Miss Fletcher is vastly energetic, strong of will, and purposive. Even though she works long hours and seldom gets to bed before midnight, she faces the challenge of each day with enthusiasm and vigor.

About twenty-eight and dressed in tailor-made clothes, she walks faster than anyone in Millwater but never seems hurried. The townspeople know the woman as a university graduate with a prestigious degree and admire her strong-minded competence. She is a friend of important people and has earned a reputation for being bold and clever. Instead of casting her glance demurely downward in the presence of men, she looks them full in the face and minces no words. Her passion, or pastime, is to motivate the unmotivated. That requires her to dabble constructively in the lives of others. Readers liked the humorous vein of satire running through the story but found Miss Fletcher abrasive. I, on the other hand, applauded her strength and energy and found her amusing. She brought back pleasant memories of Miss Archer.

In letters to my relatives in England I spoke of my writing projects and the daily burden of life but said nothing of Estelle. That bothered me for I wanted to tell them all about her. I wanted to stand on the rooftops and shout to the world that I had married the most beautiful woman in all the universe, but in no way could I bring myself to do it. My appetite, I was happy to report, was keen. My cough had all but disappeared, and I could walk a couple of miles without fatigue. However, the emphysema was a nagging problem and left me breathless when I tried to walk uphill. Arcachon had many hills but couldn't be called a beautiful place even in springtime. I found it depressing and planned to exchange it for the seaside town of Saint Jean de Luz at the foot of the Pyrenees close to Spain. I really wanted to return to England to see my family and friends again, but thought it would be folly even if I could afford it. *"Of course I don't like this long absence from the good old island, but I must look after my health. Wind and cold I must avoid."* I liked America and I liked Italy better than Germany or France, but England in spite of the harsh treatment meted out to me in my youth was home.

CHAPTER THIRTY-EIGHT

Saint Jean de Luz

Towards the end of April in 1902, after much indecision and hesitation that left me out of temper, we departed Arcachon to rent a furnished chalet at Saint Jean de Luz. All three of us liked the place and wanted to live there but had to consider the cost. So instead of moving into the expensive villa, we rented three rooms in a house inhabited by a quiet family. I was growing stronger now, twice as strong as six months earlier, and we hoped to settle in one place for as long as possible. Our plan was to live in Saint Jean de Luz, enjoying the seclusion and favorable climate, for at least a year and perhaps longer. The picturesque little town, where many of the people spoke Basque, was nestled between sea and mountains and indescribably beautiful. I walked about without fatigue to explore the place. When I wasn't able to sleep that first night in new surroundings, I listened with rapt attention to the sharp, clear, urgent notes of a nightingale. I imagined the bird was sending a message to me and hoped I was interpreting its subtleties correctly. *"A nightingale sings all night behind the house,"* I confided to my diary with an air of wonder. I was certain it was a good omen.

May came with sunny days but with a cold north wind and heavy rain in late afternoon and night. I believed my health was improving as I put on more weight, but I complained bitterly of passing the days in idleness. Never in my life, even as a boy, had I been so idle. Lounging and resting day after day and doing nothing productive was agony for a man who placed high value on work. Though writing was tiresome, I was able to read as widely as ever but had no access to books.

"I wish I could be reading today in the same old way," I said over breakfast. "I hunger for good, substantial books. I can't get them here even by mail. Books make books, you know, and I can't write with full competence without them."

"Perhaps one of these days, dear Jon," Estelle replied soothingly, "you'll be living near a good library. I promise you I will make it happen. Just hold on a bit longer."

"Thank you, sweetheart! It's the only way I can avoid this miserable folly of barren hours. How will you do it?"

"You'll see! But it isn't fair, love, to call your life barren."

"I didn't mean it that way. I was speaking of idleness, forced idleness gnawing at me, biting me in spite of a craving for work. I do wish to live near a library with thousands of books."

"It may happen sooner than you expect, but you know we can't live at present in a big city. The air wouldn't be good for you, and you would lose the good health you've worked so hard to regain."

"I know. It's impossible for me. So many things impossible."

"Be patient, love, and don't speak that way. Speaking so negatively is defeatist, and you know it. Things will get better for us."

From the time I left London to live in the country I had sorely missed the British Museum. I had spent so many pleasant hours there, reading with a purpose and writing constructively. I remembered the days of poverty when I went there not merely to read and work at my writing, but to keep warm. Over the sinks in the men's room was a sign reading PLEASE, NO MORNING ABLUTIONS. I chuckled at that. The library had become a haven for unwashed denizens who drifted in from the cold for its warmth and to clean up. In that faraway time, though my small inheritance made me feel I was better off than they, I was one of them and the library a place of refuge. It was a gentle, undemanding home for those who had no home, and we knew it. My poverty was harsh in those days, but I was young and strong and hopeful. Now I dreamed of living near the great library once more and using it to read and study and even to rest with its odor of old books in my nostrils. It was painful to think I would never see that august creation of Englishmen ever again.

2

Near the end of May the three of us went back to Paris to rent a cheaper flat to be occupied as a temporary residence. Mme. Laurent's flat was rented when we were out of the city, and the lodgers couldn't be disturbed. The search was difficult and time-consuming, but eventually we found a suitable place and moved our furniture and books into it. The weather was hot and wearisome and the task strenuous, but I bore the toil better than expected. Now that summer had come I felt stronger and more hopeful, even though my lung condition was much the same. We spent the month of June in Paris and returned to Saint Jean de Luz at the beginning of July. A week later I got to work on *Will Fareburton*, my new novel, but found I lacked the energy to write more than a few hundred words each day. I remembered earlier times when I had worked eight to ten hours a day to write several thousand words. After lunch, to coddle my lung condition, I got into the habit of going to the seashore to lie down on the beach and breathe as deeply as I could. Later I believed the damp and salty air brought on bronchitis, and so I began to walk inland away from the sea. To test my mental capacity, I went through a Spanish grammar in a single afternoon and in the evening read one page of *Don Quixote*. Three weeks later I had read sixteen chapters of that masterpiece and had achieved a lifelong ambition, reading Cervantes in the original. I was now able to read the original literature of seven languages, a remarkable achievement if I do say so.

In the fine weather of summer Estelle and I went on moderate walking tours to explore our surroundings. A cooling breeze came from the sea and the skies were often cloudy. That made the heat of summer endurable. I was getting some exercise and eating well. In this new and beautiful place I found an abundance of edible fish and excellent dairy products. I went on reading *El Ingenioso Hidalgo Don Quijote de la Mancha* in the original Spanish and dipped into many of the fifty books I had brought from Paris. I wanted to read through the *Iliad* again and return to my Roman novel of the sixth century, but I knew I had to finish my current project to pay the bills. I plugged away steadily on

338

Fareburton, writing a page a day before noon, and bringing Saint Jean de Luz into the novel. We had a good servant and all went well even though I worried about the girl spending many hours in a damp underground kitchen. An ailing servant could spell trouble for the entire household. Yet Estelle and her mother were in better health than for a long time, and I was feeling a steady progress toward good health. I had not found the emotional tranquility I was seeking, for the money question continued to nag me, but the summer was pleasant for the three of us, and we were guardedly happy.

The remainder of 1902 saw not the gradual improvement in health I so earnestly hoped for, but a steady decline. An overwhelming fatigue descended upon me, and try as I might I couldn't regain vigor with rest. I ceased to make entries in my diary, that record of my emotional life that I had kept for fifteen years. A workbook as well as a diary, it confided my thoughts and feelings to myself and to a future reader who might take an interest in Jonathan Blue. I continued to work on *Will Fareburton,* but only for two hours each morning. Estelle and I met attractive people in Saint Jean de Luz, English and French, and went into Spain with them. The most interesting person for me was an Oxford don with a Dickensian name, Butler Flaghorn. He was a learned man and taught one term each year at Oxford. The rest of the year he spent at his home in the little village. Living there alone, he boasted a fine library that he invited me to use as my own. He had written a history of Spanish literature and was viewed as an authority on the subject. He was also a student of oriental languages and literature. Six years younger than me but in poor health, he was well enough to pursue his studies. Because I was mainly self-educated, I stood in awe of university dons, and here was a don who wanted to be my friend. I admired the man and hoped to study Arabic with him, but time was running out for both of us.

In a letter to Clara Collader, penned in black ink with an unsteady hand on Christmas Eve, I observed that 1902 had gone by entirely too fast. I added that the year was passed in ailing idleness with not much at all accomplished. Since mid-summer I had been pottering at a novel but had managed to write only half of it. Hearing from my publisher that

The Philip Crowe Papers would be published as a volume in January left me thinking about the book and its reception. *"On the whole I suspect it is the best thing I have done, or am likely to do, the thing most likely to last."* It was the only one of all my books that could be called an unqualified success. The same shallow reviewers who pronounced *The Pinnacle of Life* a failure were enthusiastic in their praise of *Philip Crowe.* The book quickly became a topic of conversation in London. It was read and discussed with admiration by the men and women of the English colony in Saint Jean de Luz, and I quickly became their local celebrity. I met with a group to read selections from the book, and afterwards a few women eagerly asked for my autograph. For a few days I felt important!

It was a temporary yielding to vanity, but to be admired by others pleased me more than I was willing to admit. More than fifty strangers wrote to me praising the book. That cheered me even though I sent no replies. A clergyman in England wanted to know if Crowe's superlative housekeeper was available to take another position. If so, he wanted to hire the woman at a good wage. He enclosed a stamped, self-addressed envelope for my reply. His letter brought amusement to our household. Mme. Laurent insisted I write to the parson and set the man straight. Estelle laughed and laughed and so did I. Then I remembered that a decade earlier a plagiaristic parson had paid me the honor of using some of my stuff as his own, and I had quarreled with the man in the newspapers. Despite the jolly urging to "do the right thing and tell the man the book is fiction," I didn't respond to the inquiring parson.

Though I was heartened by the favorable reception of *The Philip Crowe Papers*, it brought only recognition and little money. People who passed the book on to their friends would have found it hard to believe that a book read by so many had brought its author only £200. To the end of my life I complained bitterly that my books earned me scarcely enough to live on. Hack writers, *"the petty scribblers of the day,"* were being well paid for trash to entertain the masses. Books of thought and substance were not selling. Cerebral and with satire not easily understood by all readers, my books lacked a large and eager audience.

Early in 1903 Dylan Crenshaw came to visit. As usual, he came with a bottle of wine, a loaf of French bread, a wedge of cheese, and some fruit. It was not like him to visit his old friend without a present, or to show up without notice. So he wired that he was coming, and we were expecting him. He met Estelle for the first time and found her charming. With blustery expansiveness and embroidery, he accepted my comely wife with unconditional approval. *"She was a very beautiful woman,"* he said in praise of her, *"tall and slender, of a pale but clear complexion, melancholy but lovely eyes, and a voice that was absolute music."* Crenshaw had not been so willing to accept Natalie, but now his open admiration of Estelle was a gift I treasured.

During his weeklong stay in the little hotel nearby, we talked of the old days going all the way back to our college years in Manchester. We remembered our hopes and dreams in those halcyon days of earnest and callow youth. Crenshaw had plainly stated he would become an adventurer and author. I had only hinted at what I proposed to do with my life, even though all my friends thought I would remain in the academic world and become a scholar. Then I fell into a villainous love affair that murdered my youthful dreams. Crenshaw lost his sense of purpose and wandered without a compass for years. In time both of us found a center of gravity to anchor our existence and became men of letters looking to a bright future. However, competition was fierce. Anyone who could write a sentence and put it into a paragraph was scribbling for money-hungry publishers. Neither of us got the recognition or recompense we deserved. We lived in grim poverty as we began our careers but remained energetic and hopeful in uncertain times. Both of us in maturity reached a comfortable position in life with some recognition but without the fame and fortune we had sought. It was bittersweet reminiscence, salty and pungent, but funny at times and satisfying.

Our friendship had remained stable and strong over many years, and that brought satisfaction to us both. Crenshaw had become a restless wanderer, traveling through countless countries around the globe and supporting himself by writing about his adventures. I had remained in England to author more than twenty books and had carefully cultivated a reputation. By the turn of the century some influential critics were placing me among the best of the novelists writing during its last two decades, and I was better known than my friend. Now I was hoping to prove my ability as a scholar-artist with *Chlotilda*, the historical novel in progress. Crenshaw, born in 1857 (the same year as I), was in robust good health and strong as ever. Even though most of his many books fell stillborn from the press and rapidly went out of print, in angry and rugged persistence he wrote one after another year after year.

Later he observed that when he visited his friend in France, he saw disturbing changes in me. I was no longer the trim, fit, and healthy person he had known most of his life. In fact I appeared fragile and feeble, moving with a gait that made me seem much older. I was thinner than I had ever been in the past and unhappy with the skimpy food I was eating. I confided it could never be compared to hearty English fare. My home was sparely furnished and didn't have even one over-stuffed chair to sprawl in beside the fire. I hinted I wanted to return to England with a loving wife and live quietly in the countryside. But the uncertain health of Mme. Laurent – her daughter believed she could die any day – stood in the way of that aspiration.

He thought his old friend was burdened by too much worry. I worried about Mme. Laurent, my servant's well being in a damp kitchen, my wife's fragile health, and my own. I seemed to be guarding my condition so carefully that even in mild weather I hesitated to leave the house. Once a great walker, I now found walking a burden. Crenshaw didn't know that his longtime friend was suffering from sciatica, a chronic neuralgic pain in the hip, back, and thigh. It was only one of my ailments but a disorder that made me almost lame and no longer capable of walking briskly. The sciatica lasted for a painful three months, faded away for a month or so, and came back again for another three months.

In February Günter Kurtz sent a long letter in which he praised *The Philip Crowe Papers* and discussed the book in detail. It seemed to him that his old friend, reflected in the calm and contented Crowe (a bookish and solitary man), had mellowed and was now at peace. To set the record straight, I quickly made reply: *"Made my peace with the world, you think? Why only in a literary sense. The troubles about me and before me are very grave, and any day I might find the world very much my enemy. My need of money grows rather serious, for though we live very economically indeed, I earn so little, so little! Last year my income was not quite £300."* Even though I was losing "combative force," I assured my friend that in maturity I continued to be at odds with the world. I went on to say that Crenshaw had made no peace in his latter years either and was writing inflammatory books just for money.

I often thought of my homeland but doubted I would see England or London ever again. A decade earlier I had written *To Live in Exile* and found on reading the proofs that it was more autobiographical in some chapters than I had known. As I wrote I had abundant material from my own experience to draw upon, for I had lived in figurative exile during most of my life. Now I found myself living in literal exile in a little town I described as beautiful, but a place that could never be compared to London in a country that could never be compared to England. It was at most a sleepy, remote village on tawny, hardscrabble soil, almost in Spain and overlooking the southern-most portion of the Bay of Biscay. Mme. Laurent, suffering from cardiac trouble, had left her beloved and sophisticated Paris to live with her daughter and a moody foreigner in rude and crude Basque country bereft of French civilization. My precarious health had made her an exile too. I was sorry for that and tried to tell her how sorry I was. She made no reply, only nodded her head in acquiescence. Later I learned the woman was willing to endure hardship and exile because her daughter, whom she loved more than life itself, loved the man behind it all.

CHAPTER THIRTY-NINE

Fatigue and Resignation

Towards the end of March when I was writing one page a day instead of my usual ten, I completed *Will Fareburton*. The novel's protagonist loses thousands in a bad investment, becomes a grocer, and sinks to a lower rung on the social and economic ladder. As he struggles to make a living, he is forced to compete with a rival grocer. The man is competent but has a drunken wife with a corrosive temper (Muriel and Natalie once more). She treats his customers shabbily, causes them to go elsewhere, and ruins the business. Honest and compassionate Fareburton is saddened by his competitor's failure. His bandy-legged clerk, raised in the savagery of the commercial arena, has a different reaction.

"It's well he went under!" he crows in triumph. "He didn't have it in him! He deserved what he got, brought it on himself!"

In a brown study and brooding on the matter, Fareburton sadly concludes that his neighborhood of festering slums is a place of internecine warfare. It is a man-made jungle where for economic survival one must kill or be killed. *"He stood appalled at the ferocity of the struggle in this vast field of battle."* Near the end of the novel after long and painful struggle, Fareburton regains his former position and marries sensible Bertha Cross. All her life she has lived with her mother in genteel poverty, clinging to middle-class values while trying to keep up appearances. *"They lived, as no end of respectable families do, a life of penury and seclusion, sometimes going without a meal that they might have decent clothing to wear."* I called the novel *"a light, fanciful book"* in spite of strident social criticism and echoes of my years of struggle in London.

The landlady Mrs. Wick is one such echo. She is similar to my own landladies when I lived in one poverty-bitten lodging house after another. Fareburton goes to such a place hoping to rent a clean, well-ventilated room at reasonable cost and becomes an object of scrutiny. *"The landlady seemed to regard him with peculiar suspicion. Before even admitting him to the house, she questioned him closely as to his business, his present place of abode, and so on. He was all but turning away when at last she drew aside and cautiously invited him to enter. Further acquaintance with Mrs. Wick led him to understand that the cold misgiving in her eye, the sour rigidity of her lips, and her generally repellent manner were characteristics of a more or less hard life amid London's crowd."* Mrs. Wick in my last novel and Mrs. Blatherwick in the first are birds of a feather very similar in appearance and even in name.

Motivated by a grasping and greedy self-interest, Blatherwick fastens upon the denizens of her neighborhood like an evil bird of prey. She drinks heavily, screams angry abuse in a gin-thickened voice, wields a club expertly, favors low prostitutes, brawls with other harridans, and uses the language of the gutter with no regard for society's rules. *"She was slatternly in the extreme, and had the look about the eyes which distinguishes persons who have but lately slept off a debauch. He noticed that her hands trembled, and that her voice was rather hoarse."* The hoarseness, shared by most of my early landladies, was a sign of the alcoholism that afflicted them. And of course they had a tendency to shout and scream rather than talk. Even as a boy I thought women should be soft of voice and gentle of manner, but my London landladies were often the opposite. Wick in the last novel is more presentable than Blatherwick of the first but is also scabrous and dishonest. She preys upon her tenants in paltry ways, spies on their private lives, and gossips.

Another echo is the lady philanthropist painted by a deluded artist named Maynard Mayfield. Years before I wrote this last novel, I had recorded in my commonplace book an incident involving *"two smug middle-class females in conversation with a ragged old woman on the pavement.*" Racked with age and disease and nearly blind, she was expressing her weariness and her longing to die. In response to this cry for help, one of the smiling, silly, smugly aggressive women chirped, *"Oh, that's very nice!"* I stored the scene in memory and dredged it up to satirize ineffectual philanthropists among the poor. But to drive home my point I turned to an idealized painting by Mayfield of a *"tall, graceful, prettily clad young woman, obviously a visitant from other spheres."* She is shown in the act of comforting the poor in a dirty and narrow street. One hand displays a book. The other comforts a gaunt and hungry child whose face is illuminated with innocent adoration.

Close by slouches a thin, unhealthy, edentulous, crestfallen woman with a sickly infant at her breast. With an awestruck gaze, she plainly adores this representative of health, wealth, and charity. Behind them stands an unemployed costermonger dressed in rags. A dark expression of wonder is stamped on his weathered face. Every detail of the picture is complete except for the gorgeous, glowing face of the visitant. It remains a blur of color with its features only slightly defined. The artist as yet has not been able to capture the purity and radiance the face of this angel of mercy must clearly show.

If the man had the courage to speak truthfully, observes Fareburton who speaks for me, he would drop the romantic claptrap and paint realistically. He would show not only a rough disgust in the costermonger, but impatience bordering on mockery in the child's face. He would emphasize curiosity blended with contempt in the mother's face and a look of cold superiority in the visitant's. He would paint the woman *"as sharp-nosed and thin-lipped with a universe of self-conceit in the eye."* Both art and life, Fareburton insists, could benefit from a realistic portrayal of the scene. Forget the ideal and the romantic and show life as it is, not as it ought to be. Only then will people begin to notice the artist's work. Fareburton's cynical, satirical, and humorous appraisal of the practitioners of personal philanthropy in the 1880's is my own. In the interval between my first and last novel my views on philanthropy underwent a sea change. Between overly sweet and nauseous Meredith

Albright of the first novel and gruffly pragmatic Will Fareburton of the last is a thunderous gulf as wide as an ocean.

2

An understandable echo in this last novel is my remembrance of Natalie and how she constantly disturbed my household as she quarreled with the servant. I wasn't able to purge myself of that part of our domestic conflict, and so it came uninvited into this story written late in my career. The widow Mrs. Cross, who lives with her daughter Bertha, is depicted as a mean-minded servant abuser. *"Poor as she was, she contrived to hire a domestic servant. To say she kept one would come near to a verbal impropriety, seeing that no servant ever remained in the house for more than a few months. The space of half a year would see a succession of some half dozen female servants. Underpaid and underfed, these persons (they varied in age from fourteen to forty) were of course incompetent, careless, rebellious, and Mrs. Cross found the sole genuine pleasure of her life in the war she waged with them."* Mrs. Cross is bitter remembrance of Natalie exaggerated for satirical effect.

Sensible and even-tempered Bertha is appalled by her mother's behavior but has no power to interfere. Day after day the battle between mistress and servant clatters on. The constant bickering brings meaning to the woman's shabby existence. *"Having no reasonable way of spending her hours, she was thus supplied with occupation. Being of acrid temper, she was thus supplied with a subject upon whom she could fearlessly exercise it. Being remarkably mean of disposition, she saw in the paring-down of her servant's rations to a working minimum, at once profit and sport."* The woman isn't a replica of my second wife, only a model in satirical mood. Qualities that define her character are exaggerated with humor to make her grotesque and meaner than Natalie.

I was tired when I wrote *Fareburton*, and it shows. Reading its chapters before mailing, I was amazed to find it repeated much of what I had already said in previous books. I sent the manuscript to my literary agent Pinehurst, asking him to place the book with a journal or magazine to run in serial form. He replied he would do that if he could, but it would take time. I waited for the slow wheels of business to turn, but nothing happened. For several months I waited, believing my agent would surely place the work eventually. When no suitable publisher came forward, I wrote to Pinehurst to say my long-delayed historical novel, would soon be ready for publication. I was certain the volume would impress publishers as a monumental work, and I wanted Pinehurst to sell it to the house willing to pay the most. They would compete for it, and the agent would choose the highest bidder as in an auction. I would finish *Chlotilda* in a few weeks, and it might appear in print before *Will Fareburton*. However, time was growing short for me. Neither book did I manage to see as a published work.

As the spring of 1903 came with tremulous hesitation to the mountains, I returned once again to my Roman novel and worked on it as vigorously as I could. I had been writing it for a long time, and in the meantime other writers had published novels perilously close to the same period. I worried about that but told myself I had a deeper and wider knowledge of the sixth century in Italy than anyone presently writing. My book would eclipse their work in all respects and show the reading public a side of me they had never seen before. I had been calling the book *The Vanquished Roman* but later named it *Chlotilda* after its Gothic heroine. To Kurtz I confided that even though I was troubled with doubt and the writing laborious, it gave me great pleasure to finish a chapter and move on to the next. I feared I was growing old too fast and might not finish the book, but with renewed determination I made slow and steady progress toward the end.

I would have made even better progress had it not come time to move again. In June we folded our tent and went to live in the neighboring town of Saint Jean Pied de Port. I hoped to benefit from the change of air and regain the strength that Saint Jean de Luz, for reasons I couldn't understand, had denied me. *"Sciatica worse than ever,"* I said in one of my many letters to Kurtz, *"I earnestly hope my health may improve, for I am getting weak to a dangerous degree."* The sciatica interfered with my sleep, and I feared that without sleep my body would never mend. Earlier

I had said I was eating a dozen raw eggs every day, stirring them into glasses of raw milk, and feeling the benefit. But I seemed to be losing spiritual strength as well as physical strength. Other than the pain that plagued me, I couldn't be certain of the cause.

Was the devastation brought on by something psychological? Had I convinced myself that I was now old and would die before my time like my father and brother? Did I see with a sense of loss that my lovely, vibrant, ineffable Estelle was also growing old and tired under constant stress? Did I finally realize she was no longer my splendid, heavenly dream woman? Under great strain as she feared her beloved husband was dying, she feared her mother was dying too. At the same time she was suffering from neuralgia. Even though her face and neck were in pain and her nights sleepless, she was unsparing in the care she gave me and never complained. Also, burdened by her mother's condition, she gave the elderly woman round-the-clock care as well.

3

I was now beginning to believe that my destiny had betrayed me. Earlier I thought a kind fate had blessed me, but now it seemed to be turning sourly against me. My analytical mind was burdened by numerous questions that also troubled Estelle. Had our nomadic existence in search of a favorable climate become too much for me to bear both physically and emotionally? Was I finding myself unable to tolerate her invalid mother? Did the exile in France and the loss of my sons and family in Harrogate prey relentlessly upon me? And what about the inadequate income? Was that good reason to look back in bitterness over the years and question the value of my struggle? Pinehurst had grumbled that I was always in need of money and required him to sell a book in such a hurry that he had little chance to negotiate terms. Perhaps my frame of mind was hindering the return of good health. Whatever the cause, my physical well being began to spiral downward.

In July of 1903, a month of sunny days, I reported to Kurtz that I was working steadily on the historical novel and was certain the completed work would depict Italy's sixth century with an accuracy readers would admire and talk about. I complained, however, of insomnia and feared that my fragile health could break at any time. *"My sciatica is slightly better – oh, the torments of the last half year! But I am afraid it is insomnia that will kill me. I do not know what it is to sleep for more than 2 or 3 hours in a night."* Except for the heat I couldn't detect the causes of the insomnia. Estelle said too much worry kept me awake, but I worried less in 1903 than in former times.

A month later I was telling my mother to make her feel better that my sciatica had faded and I could work without fatigue. My letter contained not a word about not sleeping well. I said I was able to take limited walks near the town to enjoy the mountain scenery and the tranquility of the Pyrenees. Though not as grand as the Alps, the panoramic view lifted my spirits and dazzled the eye. The pristine air was pure and tonic and I breathed it deeply, but unlike the Romantic poets who loved mountains, and poets I deeply admired, I wasn't able to imbibe strength from elemental nature. I had to find it somehow deep within my own will, and to do that was becoming harder and harder. I loved my wife and I loved the mountains, but something I couldn't put my finger on was telling me I should be in England on native ground. Crenshaw had told me Robert Louis Stevenson, dying in Samoa, had no desire whatever to see Scotland once more. That made the yearning that pestered me even more mysterious. I suppose it was family I really wanted to be with again. I wanted to hear the amiable talk and laughter of my sisters and mother in Harrogate and that of my brother in Worcestershire. Most of all I missed my sons. I needed them and they needed me.

CHAPTER FORTY

Jonathan Blue's Final Hours

In October of 1903, even though the task was proving almost too much for him, Jonathan Blue discovered with satisfaction that he was more than half done with *Chlotilda*. By early November he had completed two thirds of the book, but as winter came his health declined. He was forced by physical weakness to put the manuscript aside but continued to work on it whenever he could. *"I might be finished,"* he said in a letter to his sister Emma, *"before the end of January."* He planned to remain in Saint Jean Pied de Port through the winter, finish the book, and go perhaps to Geneva in the spring. He would not live to see the New Year. Just before Christmas, with five chapters of his last and most difficult project yet to be completed, he fell desperately ill. Blue held on through Christmas but steadily grew worse. He became semiconscious and delirious, thrashing on his bed in a deep sweat. He threw off the covers and called hoarsely for his wife. Though sick and weak herself, she was there absolutely in loving attendance during his final hours.

Fevered Estelle, trying desperately to help her husband, lapsed into a state of painful shock. In telegrams and terse little notes she informed Blue's friends in England and Germany that he was dying. Dylan Crenshaw was himself seriously ill at the time but managed to go to his club to find a telegram from Rhodes: "HAVE RECEIVED WIRE FROM ESTELLE BLUE. SAYS JONATHAN DYING, COME IN GREATEST HASTE. I CANNOT GO, CAN YOU?" Crenshaw wired Rhodes, saying although he was seriously ill he would make the trip in the dead of winter if Rhodes could not. He also sent a telegram to Estelle, saying he was sick but would come if she wanted him there. He got no reply but did receive a wire from Rhodes who was on his way. Rhodes had left England on Christmas Eve, and hoped to be at his friend's bedside within a few hours. As Blue's oldest friend, Crenshaw felt it was his duty to go also. He left London by the last train, crossed the Channel to Paris in a steamer, got a little rest on the way, and immediately set out for the Pyrenees and Saint Jean Pied de Port. He got there dreadfully sick and exhausted to find his longtime friend dead. Grief made him sicker. Jonathan Blue had died on December 28 after turning forty-six in November.

On Sunday, December 27, Estelle in utmost agony scribbled a hasty note to Kurtz: *"I have a terrible piece of news to tell you. My dearest Jon is dying des suites of a bronchio-pneumonia from which he suffers since already 3 weeks. Every hope of saving him must be abandoned and his end is now awaited at every moment. He is delirious since 7 days and speaks about his Chlotilda, which he leaves unachieved with the last 5 chapters missing! This idea adds to the dreadful sorrow I have. You will share it I know."* Before mailing her message she added a poignant postscript: *"Monday. Died today this afternoon."* On that day H. G. Rhodes returned to Paris and to England just as Crenshaw was arriving. There was talk of bringing Blue's body back home for burial, but Estelle would have none of that. She argued that she would not be able to visit his grave in England, and that would augment her grief beyond endurance. She had loved him with greater intensity than anyone else in the world, including his family in England, and she wanted his remains to be with her in France. Crenshaw and Rhodes, in sympathy with her grief, assented but were puzzled. They asked what could have brought on the death of their friend so rapidly at the relatively young age of forty-six.

2

For three weeks and more Estelle was consumed by worry about her husband's health. Her anxiety settled upon him, and he began to worry also. Nothing but his health was of interest any more to either one of them. Intellect had surrendered to feeling and physical pain and the fear that he would soon die. The work and study of a lifetime faded into insignificance now. Any accomplishment that might immortalize his name was of no consequence. The London literary scene and the world itself no longer mattered. All he had done as he reviewed his life was to work and struggle and worry about the future. Now the past was of no importance and neither was the future. Only the moment stood supreme. Only as defined by his health, his rapidly declining health, did the present have meaning. He was casting aside the last of his illusions, coming to know that one cannot measure life by happiness, nor death by longing. In moments of despair, even in his youth, he had longed for relief in death, but during those horrific three weeks that seemed to go on forever he wanted to live. Only one thing really and truly mattered, and that was living with the woman he dearly loved. He wanted life in spite of the constant pain that kept him awake at night. It was better to feel pain than feel nothing. He was not an old man dying of old age, he wanted to live. His eyelids were heavy, but somehow he managed to open his eyes to see another man near his bed.

The Reverend Josiah Cobble was a seedy-looking person with pale hair and a white face. He was getting on in years and had the look of one who lived too little in the open air. His torso appeared to be too heavy for his thin legs, and he walked with a shuffling gait. He had served as the chaplain in the English community at Saint Jean de Luz for a number of years and but for a starchy predilection was generally well liked. He viewed himself as a pastor in the old sense of the word, as one who looked after his flock. When he heard that Jonathan Blue, the novelist, was sick and perhaps dying, he offered his services by sending a polite inquiry to Estelle. Shaken by overpowering grief, the woman was not able to think clearly. She asked her mother whether the chaplain should come as a friend or as a clergyman.

Mme. Laurent knew that Jonathan was impatient with the representatives of organized religion. However, as she thought about it, she concluded he might find comfort talking to a fellow Englishman who understood the nuances of his language. Certainly the chaplain could do no harm. The two had met earlier and seemed to like each other, and so at the eleventh hour after much indecision Cobble was shown into the sickroom. He sat beside the bed and talked quietly with Blue. He wanted to be alone with the dying man and do all he could to save him from the fires of hell. Estelle had asked the good parson to visit her husband as a friend, but he couldn't resist performing his duties as a clergyman.

Later Cobble reported that during the last hours of his life Jonathan Blue made it quite clear that he wanted to die in England. He wanted to see a doctor there and be restored to health, but if that were not possible he wanted to die on English soil and be buried there.

"I am dying, Mr. Cobble," said Blue, speaking softly with heavy hesitation. "I want you to do something for me. Mr. H. G. Rhodes, author of *The Time Machine*, is coming here. I want you to persuade him to bring me home to England to see an English doctor. I won't be too sick to travel, but I'm running out of time. Please tell him to make haste."

"You can see an English doctor, my friend, without going all the way to England," the parson announced.

"Where? Who?" the sick man asked, surprised. "Is it possible?"

"Dr. Murray residing in Biarritz is a good friend of mine. During the fourteen years I've known him he has saved my life more than once. He is a very competent physician and will do all in his power to help you."

"Go at once, please, and telegraph him. I shall be grateful."

Biarritz was a famous resort on the Bay of Biscay not more than twenty-five kilometers to the north. Dr. Murray arrived on the same train as Rhodes. He went immediately to the sickroom, looked in on Blue, and reported the man was beyond additional medical help. Jonathan Blue was dying and would probably breathe his last before dawn. However, Blue lingered far into Monday morning. In her confusion and grief Estelle thought he died in the afternoon. The exact time of death was unimportant, he was dead. Jonathan Blue died on December 28, 1903. He had wanted to go home again, home to rest and read and no longer live as an exile, but his final resting place was Saint Jean de Luz in France. A number of English people, including Dylan Crenshaw but none of his family, gathered for the ceremony.

A decade later Crenshaw would publish an ersatz biography, a roman à clef, of the novelist who became his friend when they were young and mischievous. The thinly disguised story of Blue's life and career, and the role he played as dependable good friend in the author's life, was not the best of Crenshaw's books but oddly the most durable. Some in the literary world scorned him for writing the tell-all book. He defended himself by saying Blue believed any publicity was good publicity, and anyone who could read (except for the paid critics who couldn't) would see the work as an honest tribute. It was opinion spoken with the same audacity that had drawn Jonathan to Crenshaw in their youth. Estelle may have read Crenshaw's book, but whatever opinion she might have had was lost in the mists of time. The book was the first biography of the novelist, though disguised as fiction and not entirely accurate. It was written by a loyal and well-meaning friend, caused little damage, and proved valuable to later biographers.

Jonathan Blue was buried in the midst of wild flowers at the top of a modest cemetery in Saint Jean de Luz. If you go to that alien ground and examine the plain and simple tombstone to read the inscription, you will be reminded of a life that was bravely lived though not entirely well. As you walk away from the cemetery, you will view the broad expanse of the Bay of Biscay and look into Spain.

3

Before Jonathan slipped into unconsciousness he and the Reverend Cobble talked quietly for more than an hour. Driven by righteousness and a sense of duty, the parson wanted to speak of religion and the saving of souls. As a clergyman, he placed his fingers on the dying man's forehead, pronounced a benediction, and murmured a blessing.

"My friend," he said to Blue, leaning in close and placing his palm on the dying man's cheek, "you are going home."

"God's will be done," said the novelist in firm reply.

Those words were later called a deliberate fabrication, and friends of Blue disputed them. Even the family in Harrogate, while wanting deeply to believe, found the parson's pronouncement hard to accept. Estelle knew that for most of his adult life her husband had been a reluctant atheist. During their four years together he softened somewhat into agnosticism but never expressed to her any belief in a biblical heaven or hell or almighty god. He had said to her more than once that we make for ourselves on earth our own heaven or hell, and death ends it all. A sudden, deathbed conversion was therefore not believable in spite of Cobble's reputation as a truthful god-fearing man.

For Blue it was a time to look back on his life and sort through his thoughts and feelings, not to speak earnestly about religious belief with a chaplain. So he lay there thinking, drifting in calm and reflective waters, as Cobble was talking. His thoughts embraced his sons who would grow up without him, and he hoped their lives would be longer and better. He thought of his brother Will who had died too soon, cheated by chance or by some arcane power that lurks in darkness. He thought of Muriel who lived and died in misery, surrendering to an unknown force that destroyed her when young. He was thinking of his father and about his untimely death also. Thomas Blue had been a kind and loving man, a vigorous man who put his family before himself, but his life was cut short. He remembered the man's last words, a familiar line from Tennyson: *"Break, break, break on thy cold grey stones, O Sea!"* Later, looking at his father's books, Jonathan had finished the line: *"And I would that my tongue could utter the thoughts that arise in me."*

The private thoughts that flowed like torrential rain into the corners of his mind Blue did not utter. In an instant he spanned the years of endless labor. The grueling toil he viewed as so important throughout his life now seemed unimportant. At one time he could name all the books he had written in chronological order. Now to recall and repeat even one title, as he approached the end, was a requirement demanding labor and of no importance. Only the beginning was important, the salad days of youth and the bright hope. Where were they now, those wonderful days of promise? Where had they gone and so fast? What had happened to the hope that sustained him when times were brutal? Pain and disease had taken its place all too soon, but why? What good had come of the struggle? What did it all mean? Perhaps in the glare of reason his moment in time had no meaning whatever.

On a planet spinning in space life had begun. On that same planet in all its infinite forms life would end. The meaning of life could be found only in the living of life, and that he had done. It mattered not how long he had lived nor how well. He had come into the world to produce, and that he had done. He had made a substantial contribution to a society he often castigated, and he believed the gift would endure. He had done his work grumbling at times and with little grace, but he had worked. His labor had produced fruit, something vital that might enrich others in a later time. He had done what he set out to do. He had married, had children, and worked hard. He had contributed something of value to nimble minds. Could any person ask for more? He was not seeking salvation in this moment of crisis, only a modicum of satisfaction.

The idealism of his youth and the resurgent idealism he felt after meeting Estelle now seemed of little value. The idealist had wanted more than life could possibly offer. The realist clamored for life as he found it but lost it too soon. Vaguely he felt there was something better than the realism he had lovingly placed in his novels. Had he found this better thing in the grand historical novel he was leaving unfinished? In this last hour the fog was lifting and he was beginning to see things clearly. He was on the brink of a startling discovery. He was looking at something of great significance, but in the glare of sunlight on fog he couldn't see exactly what it was. The nightingale that sang all night in back of his house, delivering a message with urgent intensity, seemed to know more than he knew. Perhaps the bird had something to tell him, but the message had come as a cipher in an unknown tongue. Was there a meaning somewhere that he had missed? In the darkness that was closing in upon him he could see only flashes of truth.

He thought of head and heart, of reason and intuition. He couldn't be positive that reason was of much help in the conduct of life. It seemed to him that life was a meandering river, living and flowing through frost and sun without awareness of what it touched. So in a world of mechanical cause and effect what was the good of reason?

Perhaps feeling was all that mattered. He remembered the violence of his emotions with Muriel, the warmth of his loins with Natalie, and the pounding of his heart with Estelle. With all three he was driven by the life force, a pawn with no mind of its own, a puppet dancing on strings. When he surrendered to passion he had felt phenomenal vigor. His mind had worked with burning clarity. Yet in maturity he had found that self-control, self-respect, and transcendent love could be as invigorating, as any surrender to passion. It was the lesson Estelle had taught him. In the last four years of his life he had loved that delicate and deserving woman as no man had loved, and for that he was grateful. She had loved him too, and he gained strength from knowing her love was unconditional.

Now these recollections, so airy in their lack of substance, taxed his strength. Yet relaxed he was, more relaxed than he had ever been, not weary and worrisome but completely relaxed and without pain. In the distance a soothing male voice from a shadowy figure no longer in focus was talking, consoling, cajoling. But the sound of his words mingled with the murmuring of a stream, and they bubbled along as leaves in the stream. He thought of the rivers he had loved in his youth. Quiet rivers and tumultuous rivers, all with energy and beauty. Somewhere in the room he heard a voice mumbling something about living and life and dying and death, and he made no effort to understand.

Of one thing, however, he could be certain: living was painful, dying was not. He no longer feared that passage into the night; it merely completed the process that began when he was born. It was all a pattern just like the pattern on the ceiling that would soon give way to another pattern. The flowing rivers he had walked beside in wonder told him that everything in a temporal world was in flux and would pass. His time had come, his moment had moved on, and someone else would fill the next moment. Any pattern he had made was now yielding to another. He opened his eyes and looked at the ceiling and his lips began to move. As the parson spoke of God and everlasting life, Jonathan Blue was appealing instinctively to gods older than the god of Israel, older than any of those in the cradle of civilization. In the fever of his last moments he mumbled a prayer to them all: *"Let there be peace in the valley for my star and me."* Sitting beside him and holding his hand – she had entered the room moments before the end – Estelle in unspoken grief nodded and smiled tenderly at the blank face.

Author's Note: *Estelle lived until the summer of 1954. She was injured in a street accident in Paris and died shortly afterwards. Though she outlived her husband by more than half a century, she did not marry again. Jonathan Blue's second wife, Natalie, died at 45 in 1917 of "organic brain disease" in asylum. It was a phrase doctors used for disturbed people when no real cause of death could be determined. During all the years of her confinement she wore her wedding ring but never revealed the identity of her husband. Her death certificate described her as "wife of .... Blue, occupation unknown." Walter, Jonathan's older son, grew up to go off to war as a soldier. He was killed in World War I. The younger son, Austin, also went to war but survived, emerging with the rank of Captain. He married, had three children, later became headmaster of a rural school in Switzerland. Born in 1896, he died at 79 in 1975. Blue's younger brother, Quentin, born in 1860, died at 77 in 1937. The mother and sisters lived to the end of their lives in their small English town. They wept when they heard Blue was dead but never asked precisely where he was buried.*

KEY TO THE NOVELS OF GEORGE GISSING

James Haydock	George Gissing
Workers at Sunrise	Workers in the Dawn (1880)
The Outsiders	The Unclassed (1884)
Emily Claremont	Isabel Clarendon (1886)
The Populace	Demos (1886)
Elaine of Lambeth	Thyrza (1887)
Comes the Morning	A Life's Morning (1888)
The World Below	The Nether World (1889)
The Liberated	The Emancipated (1890)
New Bleak Street	New Grub Street (1891)
Wilfred Windset	Denzil Quarrier (1892)
To Live in Exile	Born in Exile (1892)
Redundant Women	The Odd Women (1893)
Jubilee Year	In the Year of Jubilee (1894)
Eve's Ambition	Eve's Ransom (1895)
Slumbering Embers	Sleeping Fires (1895)
Guest in the House	The Paying Guest (1895)
The Vortex	The Whirlpool (1897)
Commercial Traveller	The Town Traveller (1898)
The Pinnacle of Life	The Crown of Life (1899)
Our Shallow Charlatan	Our Friend the Charlatan (1901)
Old Calabria	By the Ionian Sea (1901)
The Philip Crowe Papers	The Private Papers of Henry Ryecroft (1903)
Chlotilda	Veranilda (1904) posthumous
Will Fareburton	Will Warburton (1905) posthumous

Printed in the United States
By Bookmasters

Printed in the United States
By Bookmasters